PRAISE

Nora Roberts Land
"Ava's story is witty and charming."
—Barbara Freethy #1 *NYT* bestselling author

Selected by *USA Today* as one of the Best Books of the
year alongside Nora Roberts' *Dark Witch* and
Julia Quinn's *Sum of all Kisses*.

"If you like Nora Roberts type books, this is a must-read."
—Readers' Favorite

Country Heaven
"If ever there was a contemporary romance that rated a 10
on a scale of 1 to 5 for me, this one is it!"
—The Romance Reviews

"*Country Heaven* made me laugh and cry...I could not
stop flipping the pages. I can't wait to read the next book
in this series." —Fresh Fiction

Country Heaven Cookbook
"Delicious, simple recipes... Comfort food, at its best."
—Fire Up The Oven Blog

The Bridge to a Better Life
Selected by *USA Today* as one of the Best Books of the
Summer.

"Miles offers a story of grief, healing and rediscovered
love." —USA Today

"I've read Susan Mallery and Debbie Macomber...but
never have I been so moved by the books Ava Miles
writes." —Booktalk with Eileen Reviews

The Gate to Everything
"The constant love...bring a sensual, dynamic tension to
this appealing story." —Publisher's Weekly

MORE PRAISE FOR AVA

The Chocolate Garden
"On par with Nicholas Sparks' love stories."
—Jennifer's Corner Blog

"A must-read...a bit of fairy magic...a shelf full of happiness." —Fab Fantasy Fiction

The Promise of Rainbows
"This is a story about grace, faith and the power of both..."
—The Book Nympho

French Roast
"Ms. Miles draws from her experience as an apprentice chef...and it shows...I loved {the} authenticity of the food references, and the recipes...looked divine." —BlogCritics

The Holiday Serenade
"This story is all romance, steam, and humor with a touch of the holiday spirit..." —The Book Nympho

The Town Square
"Ms. Miles' words melted into each page until the world receded around me..." —Tome Tender

The Park of Sunset Dreams
"Ava has done it again. I love the whole community of Dare Valley..." —Travel Through The Pages Blog

The Goddess Guides Series
"Miles' series is an **exquisite exploration** of internal discomfort and courage, allowing you to reclaim your divine soul and fully express your womanhood."
—Dr. Shawne Duperon, Project Forgive Founder, Nobel Peace Prize Nominee

"The Goddess Guides are a **world changer**. Well done, Ava." —International Bestseller Kate Perry aka Kathia Zolfaghari, Artist & Activist

Also by Ava Miles

Fiction

The Merriams Series

Wild Irish Rose

Love Among Lavender

Valley of Stars

The Love Letter Series

Letters Across An Open Sea

Along Waters of Sunshine and Shadow

The Dare Valley Series

Nora Roberts Land

French Roast

The Grand Opening

The Holiday Serenade

The Town Square

The Park of Sunset Dreams

The Perfect Ingredient

The Bridge to a Better Life

The Calendar of New Beginnings

Home Sweet Love

The Moonlight Serenade

The Sky of Endless Blue

Daring Brides

The Dare River Series

Country Heaven

Country Heaven Song Book

Country Heaven Cookbook

The Chocolate Garden
The Chocolate Garden:
A Magical Tale (Children's Book)
Fireflies and Magnolias
The Promise of Rainbows
The Fountain of Infinite Wishes
The Patchwork Quilt of Happiness

Dare Valley Meets Paris Billionaire Mini-Series
The Billionaire's Gamble
The Billionaire's Courtship
The Billionaire's Secret
The Billionaire's Return

The Goddess Guides to Being a Woman
Goddesses Decide
Goddesses Deserve The G's
Goddesses Love Cock
Goddesses Cry and Say Motherfucker
Goddesses Don't Do Drama
Goddesses Are Sexy
Goddesses Eat
Goddesses Are Happy
Goddesses Face Fear

Other Non-Fiction
The Happiness Corner: Reflections So Far
Home Baked Happiness

Valley of Stars

THE MERRIAMS

AVA MILES

To my kind and brilliant editor, Angela Polidoro, who's been with me since my first book and shares my love of the savannah, food, Paris, and so much more—thank you for being one of the best divine partners ever.

And to my divine entourage, who helps me open myself up to so much more.

Old boyfriends, lovers, and crushes are some-
times like bad pennies—
they come back when you least expect them.
Usually a woman simply needs to toss them
aside.
They're more trouble than they're worth.

But that rare old coin...
stamped perhaps with tragic yet treasured
history, deserves closer inspection.
With some simple buffing, it might shine right
up.
And be worth every bit of effort and then
some.

That's what some people call a lucky coin.

The kind you take with you everywhere.

The kind you tuck close to your heart.

Clara Merriam Hale

Intermediate Matchmaker Extraordinaire

CHAPTER 1

MICHAELA MERRIAM FROZE IN THE DOORWAY OF HER brother's office. Connor was called the Big Bad Wolf behind his back, both in the family and in the office, but he wasn't living up to his reputation today. The traitor was sitting with Boyd McClellan, her former boyfriend, best friend, and fellow adventurer. The lack of visible bruises or flesh wounds told her all she needed to know. This "meeting" she'd been summoned to was a ruse of the worst variety.

Her brother had sold her out.

Boyd wasn't even situated in the hot seat, in front of her brother's massive rosewood desk. No, they were sitting on his cozy Italian leather couch with an effing silver coffee service on the shiny black marble table in front of them like they were long-lost friends.

Sure, she'd never been close to her eldest brother, but this was ridiculous. Both men lowered their cups at the same time when they noticed her in the doorway. She felt her breath catch as Boyd's chocolate brown eyes met her gaze. Damn him for still making her pulse skip and her heart flutter. His hot muscular body hadn't gone saggy with depression over losing her, and he hadn't changed his hair—it was still that same shaggy brown mass that defied the precision of scissors and tempted a woman's fingertips.

She shouldn't be feeling any of *this* after breaking up with him six months ago. He'd betrayed her and her family business, and her brother damn well knew it.

"What the hell?" she all but shouted across the room.

Boyd cocked his brow—an outright challenge—and her fire surged from the bonfire variety to an outright forest fire.

"Michaela, come join us," Connor commanded, rising from the couch and crossing to her.

She gave him her best glare, perfected from years of dealing with five occasionally pushy older brothers. Of course, Boyd was pushy too, which had been both comfortable and perfect for her at one time. "Not just yet. I'm trying to decide who to punch first."

Connor's mouth twisted, so at least he felt some remorse. Boyd only kicked his long legs out, crossing them at the ankles. She noted he was wearing an elegant navy suit, no tie. Dear God, the sky had fallen. He never dressed corporate.

And man, did the sight make her mouth water...

Damn him.

"You didn't answer any of my messages, Mickey," Boyd said to her, his voice as smooth as a rock skipping across water.

No, she hadn't, although his last message had tantalized her like a cup of water to a thirsty man in the Sahara: *I think I found the Valley of Stars.* That valley—the supposed location of a rare healing flower of mythical proportions—was her unicorn, her Holy Grail. She knew all the stories about it. Her most trusted guides in East Africa swore it existed, but they'd told her the location was a closely guarded secret, protected by a local tribe for generations, something she believed to her bones. The flower was also Boyd's Holy Grail, but they weren't partners anymore. They couldn't be. Didn't matter that he was the best she'd ever had—in bed and out of it.

"It's Michaela to you, Boyd."

"This meeting must seem highly irregular," her brother interrupted, taking her arm, "what with your history, but it seems we have business with Boyd here."

Michaela yanked her arm away, not caring if it was unprofessional. This whole setup was unprofessional. "You've got to be kidding me, Con. Six months ago, you chewed me out in this very office because I didn't get Boyd to sign our usual nondisclosure agreement before he started working at Merriam Enterprises. Heck, you even demoted me from the job you'd promised me, saying it was fitting for the, and I quote, 'lovesick snafu.'"

Her brother stared at her with his creepy bi-color eyes, courtesy of Heterochromia Iridis. "Michaela, this is *business*, and right now, I'm more concerned that you once again let your personal feelings for Boyd keep you from hearing out his business proposition."

"Is that what he's calling it these days?" she sneered, careful not to look at Boyd because under all that fire raging inside her, there was an avalanche of tears threatening to break loose.

"Worse, when I pulled your travel records since the breakup and read your reports on who our competitors were on the superfoods you were hunting, I noted Boyd's company wasn't one of them. I got to thinking that wasn't a coincidence."

Her heart sank. Yes, she'd purposefully chosen objectives that weren't also being pursued by Boyd, not wanting their paths to cross. How could she explain to the Big Bad Wolf that she'd needed time to toughen up after their breakup? Her brother wasn't the sort to be moved by such things. The motivations he cared about were professional, not personal. "I got the appropriate approvals from Iggie."

"*Dr. Ignatius Vajra*, Director of Merriam Enterprises' Plant Sciences division—"

"Under the Merriam Pharmaceuticals umbrella... Blah, blah, blah."

"You also stopped pursuing a superfood you and Boyd had been working on before he left," Connor said, all boss now.

"That's my fault," Boyd interrupted. "Michaela and I submitted a grant on an Indonesian tree berry, and we flipped for the full rights after the breakup. I won."

He was covering for her. She'd flipped for it and texted him to inform him of his victory. It had pissed her off to pass up that hunt, but they couldn't pursue the grant together, working for competing companies. Of course, she could have lied about the outcome of the coin toss, but one of them needed to care about fairness.

"You did what? Michaela, there are departmental approvals—"

"Which I got," she said, crossing her arms. "Connor, I don't need to be reminded how things work around here."

She was the youngest Merriam, but she'd poured her heart and soul into Merriam Enterprises, just like everyone else. Which meant Connor and her next eldest brother, Quinn, Big Bad Wolf one and two, were her bosses. Sure, she'd followed Connor around when she was a kid, pretending her satchel was an attaché and filling his ear with her plans for traveling the world, but they'd all grown up since then. Sometimes it felt like they'd grown apart.

Or maybe she was just the odd woman out. Trevor and J.T. were twins and had that weird bond even scientists couldn't explain, and although Michaela was probably closest with Caitlyn, her only sister, most of the time Caitlyn and Flynn paired off to talk fashion and the like. Connor and Quinn were cut from the same cloth—cloth for an expensive business suit, no doubt.

There was no denying Michaela was the baby of the family, the outlier. The girl who not only liked bugs but caught and studied them. Who boiled down plant compounds and made slides for her microscope. But she'd found her niche in the family business, and she was proud of the contributions she'd made. The *profitable* contributions.

This wasn't how you treated someone on your team, and her brother should damn well know that.

"Connor, you called me up here for a meeting and submarined me with all this crap about Boyd's *business* proposition. If you're upset with—"

"You're damn right I'm upset with you," her brother shot back. "You've been searching for the Valley of Stars for years. Boyd says he told you about this in his message. Why didn't you call him back?"

She'd left her phone at the office for a week after receiving his last message to ensure she wouldn't give in. "Because we broke up, Connor." Business ran in her brother's blood, but she hadn't expected him to be this clueless.

"From what Boyd's told me, this could be a huge find for us! Can't you see why I might be questioning your business sense?"

Her brother believed the Valley of Stars and its mythical flower existed? Boyd wasn't messing around. She'd thought he might be trying to tempt her into having a post-breakup conversation, but surely he wouldn't have brought things so far if he didn't have the goods. Only...why would he want to share such a huge find with her?

"This is all my fault," Boyd said, finally standing up but staying across the room from her, wise man. "I could have done a better job of reaching out. Michaela, can we please set aside our past issues for the moment? Like Connor said, the Valley of Stars is one of the rarest finds of the century perhaps."

"You don't need to tell me how rare it is, Boyd. You know how much I want this find. But you can't blame me for being suspicious either. When you first reached out, I just couldn't see why you'd share such a hallowed find with your competitor. If you hadn't left Merriam for Hendricks Pharmaceuticals—"

"You're misremembering things, Michaela—"

"You're playing some game here, and I can't believe you, Connor, are playing into it," she said, crossing her arms in front of her.

"Enough!" Connor pointed to the couch. "Sit down, Michaela, and don't say another word until you hear us out."

She bit her lip, wanting to bark *you're not the boss of me*, but technically he was, damn him.

"Michaela, would I ever put Merriam Enterprises in jeopardy?" her brother asked.

"Aren't you questioning my motives? I would never hurt our company either."

He let out an aggrieved breath. "Come sit. Please."

Connor rarely said words like please and thank you.

"Fine." She stalked to the couch as the men took their seats again. "But I'm walking out of here if I hear any bullshit. And I will not apologize for my language. Boyd isn't a regular walk-in."

Boyd's feet were in the way, so she kicked them, noticing he'd even slapped on her favorite cologne. The animal! "Were you raised in a barn?" She sat on the exact opposite side of the couch, leaving Connor to sit between them.

"You know where I was raised," Boyd said blandly. "We didn't have etiquette classes on the local street corner. Too many drug deals."

"Civility would be a good start, you two," Connor said, clearing his throat and pouring her a cup of coffee. "Let's begin again."

Boyd leaned forward and plucked two sugar cubes out of the bowl before she could. That he remembered the way she took her coffee pissed her off even more. All the little details from their time together were still lodged inside her brain, everything from how he liked to sing Shania Twain in the shower using the shampoo bottle as his microphone to how his face was creased from sleeping with his hand tucked against his cheek. If she could redo her dissertation, she'd look for a plant that erased painful memories and didn't have side effects.

"I hope you washed your hands," she said, flicking him a glance as he plopped the cubes into her coffee. She would *not* thank him for the sugar.

"When we were on one of our treks, I'd go days without washing my hands."

His mouth formed a smirk, and she knew what he was thinking. *You didn't mind my hands then. They were all over you whenever we had the chance.*

"I'm a simple man," Boyd continued, picking up his coffee.

Bullshit, she thought. He was as complex as a DNA strand and crazy smart, and she used to think he was fun and sweet and super sexy.

"Let's move on," Connor said, crossing his ankle over his knee. "Boyd, perhaps you should begin by outlining why you came to Merriam with *a joint venture* for this find."

A joint venture? But temptation was starting to get the better of her, if her vital signs were any indication. Connor wouldn't have arranged this little tête-à-tête otherwise. Her big brother wasn't the type to tilt at windmills or pour money into legends.

"I left Hendricks last month after realizing they weren't a good fit for me." Boyd shrugged as if to say it was no big deal. Like he hadn't left to work for a competitor.

She gripped her cup so she wouldn't punch him in the face.

"I've started my own company, something you know I've talked about doing, Michaela."

Part of her was impressed he'd managed that feat years ahead of his personal timetable. He'd dreamed of pursuing his own vision for the future of superfoods and plant science, separate from the big pharmaceutical companies, which weren't always interested in promoting natural alternatives.

"When I got a solid lead on the Valley of Stars, I knew my time at Hendricks was over. They might have compelled me to keep the location secret or taken over the site and destroyed the find."

Hendricks was cozy with several health insurance companies, and she'd heard nasty rumors about how they'd handled other miracle cures from nature. Boyd had heard the rumors too, of course. That he had chosen to work with them anyway had made his betrayal all the more painful. Merriam Enterprises might not be perfect, but they did adhere to strict ethical protocols.

"I don't have the capital or resources to go after something this big on my own yet, and I don't want to wait a few years until I do."

That made sense to her so far. "Continue..."

"As you wish, Dr. Merriam," he said with a smirk. "I'm also not sure I want my company to specialize in large-scale manufacturing and distribution, something Merriam Enterprises has down pat as an established Fortune 500 company. My niche has always been finding medicinal plants, working with local people on fair trade and access, and testing it according to modern standards. Given our past relationship and my regard for the way you do business, I came to you."

Was he telling the truth? She searched his eyes. At one time, she'd thought they were so connected they could practically read each other's thoughts. But she hadn't known he would choose Hendricks, hadn't even guessed it was in play. She didn't trust him anymore. Worse, she didn't trust herself to read him. Her instincts were broken when it came to Dr. Boyd McClellan, and somehow that hurt worse than anything.

"The terms of the joint venture Boyd laid out are acceptable to me," Connor said. "We've shaken on it with the plan to formalize our agreement in writing when you return with the find."

Her brother wasn't putting this down on paper? What the hell? He was usually such a stickler for doing things by the book, and Boyd had burned them before.

"If you're only interested in giving us manufacturing and distribution, Boyd, why do you want me on the ground?" she asked.

"You and I have always wanted to find this flower. I couldn't imagine not having you and your expertise on the trip." He looked her in the eye as he said it, and she fought the urge to look away. He did respect her as a colleague, but he wasn't giving her a full answer, and they both damn well knew it.

"The only addendum to the understanding Boyd and I have concerns your welfare on the trip," her brother said.

"My welfare?" Her cup rattled as she set it down. "I can handle myself, Con."

"I know that," Connor said, "but I told Boyd everyone in the family would feel better if you were accompanied by a family member."

"Who'd feel better?"

Connor's brow winged up. "Contrary to what you might think, I do care about your welfare, Michaela. Boyd says the travel won't be too strenuous. I was thinking Uncle Arthur and Aunt Clara might be a good choice, along with Hargreaves, of course."

Her mouth twitched, thinking of Aunt Clara's butler accompanying them. Funny image aside, it wasn't a bad idea. They were game for anything and would be good buffers. In fact, Aunt Clara had mentioned wanting to come along on one of her treks. She'd thought it would be fun. But Boyd agreeing? Insanity. "You are aware my aunt and uncle and their butler, Hargreaves, are all eighty."

Boyd stared her down. "I am."

"And you agreed?" she asked.

"I told Boyd I was uncomfortable asking Dr. Vajra to act as a chaperone and emotional mediator," her brother said.

"Iggie as chaperone," she said, shuddering. "That's ridiculous."

"That chaperone comment will look funny in a minute," Boyd said, clearing his throat.

She shot him a glance as he and her brother shared a look she didn't understand.

"Given your history," Connor said, "Uncle Arthur and Aunt Clara can ensure things remain *professional*. We may also want to document the story too, and no one would be better suited for the job than Arthur Hale."

Their honorary uncle, Arthur Hale, was a famous journalist who'd founded the newspaper known as the Voice of the West. The fact that he'd recently retired would only make an article, or series of articles, from him that much more valuable. Still, she suspected her brother's primary concern was that Boyd might make a move on her. Or worse, that she'd try and jump his bones. He wasn't wrong. She'd taken one look at him and gone all achy in the belly. His familiar scent hadn't helped. "Your faith in me is inspiring, Con."

"I also trust that if there is more of the emotional interplay between the two of you that I saw earlier—"

"I don't know what you're talking about," she said, trying to keep a straight face.

Boyd snorted. "Really? You know, my mom might suspect foul play if I end up dying on this trip."

This time she snorted. "Your mom *loves* me. When we broke up, she called me to say how upset she was. She cried on the phone, you moron."

He flinched, his naturally leonine skin color leaching to white. "She didn't say—"

"This interplay is exactly what I mean," Connor said. "Besides Uncle Arthur and Aunt Clara, Dr. Vajra will also be representing Merriam Enterprises."

Now Boyd's comment made sense. She lurched to her feet as Boyd held out his hands and said, "Told ya."

He and Iggie had never gotten along. "No way. Connor, I don't need him to babysit me." Or boss her around, something he excelled at doing. Iggie was a Grade-A scientist, no doubt about it, but he was as obnoxious as he was qualified.

Unfortunately for everyone who worked beneath him, he was also a renowned kiss-ass to the people who "mattered."

"Besides being impractical," she continued, "there's a reason Merriam sends entry-level employees into the field." She had her doctorate, sure, but she wasn't afraid of sleeping under the stars. Iggie would want hotel rooms or luxury tents.

Connor smoothly rose, buttoning his gray suit jacket like he had all the time in the world. "This is an important find, and Dr. Vajra will be an asset. He's a noted researcher and the head of our Plant Sciences division. Plus, if you got hurt on this trip, Merriam Enterprises would have no one representing it. I can't take that chance."

"But he doesn't have the right field skills." She cast a glance at Boyd. "I shudder to think how he'd react to peeing outside."

"Crude, Michaela," her brother said. "I imagine everyone will rise to the occasion."

"Boyd, please, tell my brother how ill-suited Iggie is for this trip." *How you two are like oil and water.*

Boyd finally stood. "Your brother insisted on this point, Michaela. We'll make it work."

"Make it work?" Boyd didn't compromise. It was one of the things she'd always liked about him.

"It's what your brother wants to make this happen." His voice sounded pained, but it didn't waver.

"What aren't you telling me?"

He shoved his hands into his pants pockets and jingled change.

As a tell, it was obvious. He was hiding something. She blinked, then narrowed her eyes.

Connor gestured to Boyd. "He had some conditions of his own."

Hence his quick agreement to Connor's ridiculous terms. "Of course he did," she said, her voice laced with frustration. "Let me guess. He won't tell you where the valley is."

Her ex-boyfriend's mouth tipped up. "I figure we all bring some trust issues to the table, so it's allowed. I'll fill you in incrementally as we proceed."

"You're spoon-feeding me the itinerary? You've got to be kidding!"

"Tell her the other condition," Connor said, smoothing his tie.

"I can't guarantee we'll be able to extract the find," Boyd said.

She rocked back on her heels. "Why not? If we find it, it's—"

"A piece of cake?"

There he went, finishing her sentences again.

"Before we go any further, we should call Aunt Clara and Uncle Arthur and talk about them accompanying you two," Connor interrupted, moving toward his desk and picking up the phone. "Martha, will you get Arthur and Clara Merriam Hale on the line, please?"

He punched a button on the console and set the receiver down on the desk, motioning Michaela closer.

It rang twice before Uncle Arthur answered and barked, "Hale residence."

"Uncle Arthur, this is Connor and Michaela. How are you this fine day?"

"About as fine as I was yesterday, sonny," he spat back. "Why in the world are you calling? I didn't know the Big Bad Wolf made personal calls during the day. Now Michaela is another story. How are you, honey?"

"Pretty good," she said, smiling. "Can you get Aunt Clara on the line?"

"That sounds ominous," he said. "She's doing her pretzel-thing this morning to increase her stamina and live longer. I'll see if she can untangle herself."

"Pretzel-thing?" Connor whispered.

Colorful speech was their uncle's staple. She laughed. "Yoga."

"Ah," he said, shaking his head.

"You've got us both here now," her uncle said. "What's got you two calling on a workday?"

"Business," Connor said. "I have a proposition for you. Do you remember that jerk who betrayed Michaela and broke her heart?"

Boyd shot her brother a look that could have stopped a gangster in his tracks.

"Is he still bothering her?" Aunt Clara asked. "I could bean him with a frying pan for hurting our girl."

Boyd was studying his toes now, Michaela noticed. Good. Best he understand how things were going to be with her and her aunt and uncle, if they came.

"Well, it seems Boyd has found this rare flower that's known for being a cure-all, and for business reasons, I've agreed that Merriam Enterprises will partner with him.'"

"Must be a big find for you to partner with someone like that," her aunt said.

"I'm right here in the room," Boyd whispered.

"Shhh," Michaela said, whacking him with a hand.

"Anyway, I'm loath to send her with this jerk alone," Connor said, giving Boyd a pointed look, "so I'd like to know if you'd be willing to go to Africa with them and chaperone. Maybe break up a few emotional moments. We'd also love to have you write some articles about the experience, Uncle Arthur, if you're so inclined. The travel shouldn't be too strenuous. Mostly Land Rover and boat."

"Speak for your own bones," Uncle Arthur spat out. "I

haven't been in a Defender 90 since my safari in 1978, and my backside still twinges every now and then when I see a picture of a lion."

"Oh, stop dramatizing, you old poop," Aunt Clara said. "I've always wanted to go on safari. Michaela, honey, we've talked about going on one of your trips. This sounds like a capital idea."

"Does it?" Uncle Arthur drawled. "I'll need some background if you expect any articles to come of this. I don't do that for just anyone now that I'm retired, you know."

"No, you still only read a dozen newspapers every day and drive me crazy," her aunt said, making him harrumph. "Michaela, do tell your uncle what he needs to know."

She gave her smile plenty of teeth as she glanced at Boyd. "Well, we'll be seeking a fabled healing flower in a place called the Valley of Stars. Until now, no one has found it because it's been a carefully guarded secret." She gestured to Boyd. "Care to add anything?"

"Who are you talking to, dear?" her aunt said.

"Me," Boyd replied. "I'm the jerk you all have been talking about."

"Oh, goodness!" Aunt Clara breathed out. "Well, hello there."

Uncle Arthur barked out a laugh. "I hope you have a thick skin. You'll need it."

"If not, I'll ask to borrow a rhino's," Boyd said. "Good to meet you both. Delighted to have you on board. So, picking up where Michaela left off, the valley hasn't been located because it's been closely guarded by a tribe for centuries. From what I've discovered, a few other people may have found it, but no one's been allowed to bring out the flower."

"Why are they allowing someone to bring it out now?" Uncle Arthur asked. "Clara, where is my pad and pencil? I need to write this down."

"Will you please try and be a retired journalist, dear?" Aunt Clara asked.

"Black ink runs through these veins, my love," he said.

"The tribe is looking for an ethical partner to share the flower find with the world. The tribe realizes the find won't stay hidden much longer. Locals are leaving their tribal areas for opportunities in the cities. Heck, even the Maasai have cell phones now to communicate with the children they're sending away to school."

"Urbanization's long reach," her uncle mused.

"You found someone from the tribe who told you all this?" Michaela asked. If he was this confident, he had more than a lead—he had an in.

He shrugged again. She bit her lip to keep from yelling at him. He'd never held out on her before.

"Do you know when the valley was first mentioned in a text or book?" Uncle Arthur asked. "I'd like to do some reading."

Boyd gestured for her to take this one. "The first mention was in a travel journal by a British naturalist in 1878. He'd come upon the location while documenting birds in the area. He fell sick, and the tribe supposedly found him and healed him with the star-shaped flower. After he left, he told two friends about his miraculous recovery. They went out to search for the location."

"Sounds like a page out of Allan Quatermain in *King Solomon's Mines*," Uncle Arthur said. "That *would* make one hell of a story."

Michaela's excitement was building too. This was starting to feel like more than a trick or ruse. They might actually be on the cusp of making history.

"My goodness," her aunt said breathily. "Do they know what became of the two friends?"

"The story goes that one never returned, and the other was said to have gotten sick and died," Boyd said. "The tribe didn't heal the man since he'd come out of greed."

Connor frowned. "Greed, huh? Boyd, you left out that part."

"There are lots of stories out there," Boyd said, pulling on his jacket like it was uncomfortable. "Right, Mickey?"

So he wanted her to have his back, huh? He'd make it up to her later. "Exactly. Connor, this really is the chance of a lifetime."

Boyd nodded. "Bottom line. We're the tribe's best bet for going global."

"And two companies working together looks less greedy," Michaela said, back in the flow of reading his thoughts and anticipating his next sentence. "It shows collaboration. They'll know we're capable of being team players and working with them rather than taking the flower for ourselves."

"Yes," Boyd said with a glance at her brother. "Plus, in our business, Michaela and I are what some call true believers."

Yes, they were, and it was one of the reasons she'd fallen in love with him.

"But we aren't the only true believers," Boyd added, pointing to his watch. "I'd like to get going as soon as possible."

"We'll be ready as soon as you need us, won't we, Arthur?" her aunt said. "And Michaela, don't worry about Boyd there. I swear to you on Grandpa Emmits' grave that I won't let him do anything to upset you. I'll bring my new sewing scissors in case he tries something. They're extra sharp."

Boyd made a show of crossing his hands over his privates, a move that normally would have made her laugh. Instead, she made a point of not staring at said privates. She had a feeling she was still tempted in that department.

"Hargreaves will be on watch too, dear," her aunt said in that emphatic way of hers.

"As will I," her uncle said. "So when do we leave?"

Connor shifted his gaze to Boyd. "Our private jet will pick the three of you up in...say three days? Will that be enough time to prepare for the trip?"

"Are you asking us or Michaela?" Uncle Arthur asked.

"No, three days won't be enough," Boyd said, shaking his head. "These nice people will need vaccinations and malaria medicine, right, Mickey? Oops, sorry. Michaela?"

"Yes," she said, tapping her foot in excitement. "Care to narrow it down enough to tell us what country we're traveling to? It has a bearing on the shots and such, you know."

He smirked again. "Kenya with a little jaunt to Tanzania perhaps. Maybe even Uganda."

Three sizeable countries situated around Lake Victoria. How nice. "Clear as mud," she said, flicking her hand at him as if to swat a gnat.

He laughed and gestured right back.

"Shots!" Uncle Arthur said. "Maybe we should rethink this. My backside is too bony for needles these days."

"You'll be fine," her aunt assured him.

"I'll arrange for an infectious disease doctor to visit you in Dare Valley tomorrow," Connor said. "I hope I don't regret this."

"Wonderful!" Aunt Clara said. "In that case, how soon can we travel?"

Michaela got enough checkups before her treks to know the answer. "Two weeks is best."

Late October would be the perfect time for a trek across the savannah. It was one of the driest times of the year, and temperatures would be in the high seventies to low eighties during the day, dipping to low sixties or high fifties at night. The wildebeest would be starting to migrate. Breathtaking. Nature was the best office in the world to her mind.

"That works for me," Boyd said. "Since I can't make the shots work faster."

"Finally, you agree you aren't a miracle worker." The smile she gave him was all teeth.

"No, guess not," he said, his tone suddenly serious. "I lost you, after all, didn't I?"

Is that how he felt? There was nothing she could say to that.

Boyd looked away, picked up his coffee, and drained it. "I assume you'll inform Iggie of the details, Connor."

"Yes, of course," her brother said.

"One final condition before I go. Have Flynn undo whatever he's done to my satellite cable TV. Since we broke up, the only show it plays is *Dora the Explorer*. Twenty-four seven. It was funny for a day, but not six months. Even Marvin's bored of it."

Marvin being his Tokay gecko. She wanted to ask about the little guy, but instead she said, "Flynn did that?"

"You didn't know?" he asked. "The cable people were worried about the hack, but I assured them it was targeted at me once I deduced the culprit."

Connor was already laughing, and Michaela bit her lip to keep from joining him. Flynn *would* see it as a brotherly show of revenge to force Boyd to endure endless reruns of her favorite TV show from childhood.

"That's a good one," Arthur said, guffawing. "I'll be sure to remember not to piss off Flynn."

"Then I believe that covers it," Boyd said. "I'll see you soon, Mr. and Mrs. Hale. Connor. Michaela."

He walked out of the office after saluting her. *Saluting* her.

"Since he's gone, is there anything else we should know?" Aunt Clara asked.

Connor turned his head to look at her, his smile

fading. "Yes, Aunt. Michaela is still in love with that jerk."

Her heart burned in her chest as silence permeated the room.

Her brother was right.

CHAPTER 2

BOYD DIDN'T LIKE BEING SUMMONED TO THE MERRIAM compound in chi-chi Napa Valley, but he didn't feel like he could refuse—not when Shawn Merriam himself had texted to request his appearance hours after his meeting at Merriam Enterprises.

At least the unexpected invitation gave him an excuse to text her. He suspected she was done ignoring him. She'd be pissed that he'd boxed her into this trip, but now that they were technically colleagues again, she was too professional to ice him out.

Your DAD wants to talk to me at six tonight at the house. If you don't hear from me again, you might see if he buried me facedown in the vineyard. If you want to make sure I survive, you might want to show up at 6:15 to intervene. Also, I didn't want to go to Connor. I wanted to go to you. We should talk.

She didn't reply for nearly an hour, which must have killed her. One, she always answered promptly unless she was out of the country. Two, she'd want to know why her father had summoned him. And three, she'd want to kick him in the proverbial balls for his comment about Connor. He should probably wear an athletic cup tonight.

Gosh. Where to start? You're a jerk. I can't believe you

went to Con. My DAD? Did you eat some bad mushrooms in the lab? I hope Dad buries you. I'll happily dance on your grave.

That made him laugh.

In a red dress? You're a knockout in red. Are you coming to save me from the parental unit? Your mother might be up to bat after your dad finishes.

Assumpta Merriam was a wonderful woman—until crossed—and he imagined Michaela had spun a good story putting their breakup squarely on his shoulders.

My mother wouldn't expend the effort to dig you a grave. She'd simply pour lighter fluid on your worthless carcass and set you on fire. Or...leave you for the vultures.

Michaela was magnificent.

Being apart from her was the worst punishment he'd ever endured—even worse than his dad leaving when he was ten. Thank God she was the same plain-speaking, sometimes scary woman he loved like crazy. He'd been a goner ever since the day he walked into the lab to see her rip open the fang-like maw of a Venus flytrap to rescue three tree frogs. The poor little devils had escaped their terrarium only to be lured in by one of the world's creepiest plants. Her mind had fascinated him as much as her physical directness in the beginning, which he'd come to learn was from being the youngest sister in a family of equally direct and physical men, especially her brother, Trevor.

He arrived a few minutes early at her parents' house. For an October evening, the temperature was still in the upper eighties. The vines would appreciate the heat. The two-story Spanish-style home was decorated with clay planters resplendent with bougainvillea and jasmine, and the fig trees under the awning were flush with green and purple fruit. He remembered plucking a fig once and feeding it to Michaela. Another time, he'd tucked a purple bougainvillea flower behind her ear.

He wanted those times back, dammit.

He knocked on the massive double doors, resisting the urge to tug on the navy jacket he'd thrown over his T-shirt and jeans.

"Thanks for coming, Boyd," Shawn said the moment he opened the door.

Boyd extended his hand, and the man took it. "I didn't think it wise to refuse," he said honestly.

Shawn gave a wry smile. "You could have, of course, but you're right. It would have made a statement. Asking you here is part of me turning over a new leaf as a father."

Boyd had to wonder what he meant by that, but he expected Shawn would tell him in good time.

"Come in. We'll have a drink and talk about this upcoming trip. If Connor agreed, you must have made one hell of a pitch."

Word traveled fast in the Merriam family. Boyd entered the rich, open space. He'd always loved this house, as much for its bold textures and colors as the sweeping vistas. Michaela had grown up here, and on some level, she didn't understand this wasn't the norm for most people. Even though she didn't come off as a rich girl, her family's fortune had always provided certain comforts and an unassailable safety net. They'd made their mark—just like growing up in a bad neighborhood in Oakland had shaped him. Michaela had never understood why being financially independent mattered to him, or why he might not want to cash a Merriam paycheck for the rest of his life. To him, he might as well have printed "kept man" on his business card alongside his formal title. Iggie and other employees had only made it worse by calling him MBT when she wasn't around: Michaela's Boy Toy. In his old neighborhood, he would have handled such an insult with a good punch to the face. But the business world had different rules. After attempting to turn the tide, he'd ultimately given in to the inevitable. The only way he would be taken seriously as a scientist was to work somewhere else.

"Wine or something stronger?" Shawn asked, leading him into the living room and crossing to the Art Deco bar caddy in front of the floor-to-ceiling windows.

"After today?" He knew honesty was the only way to play it. "Whiskey."

"Perfect." Shawn uncapped a thirty-year-old bottle of single malt and poured a healthy measure into two Waterford crystal tumblers.

Boyd took one of the tumblers from him and lifted it. "To the most wonderful woman in the world, your daughter."

Shawn's mouth curled into a smile before he drank from his own glass. "I thought your move today indicated a new press for my daughter's affections."

He followed the man through the open French doors to the farm table under the portico. As they sat across from each other, Boyd couldn't help but think of the other times he'd sat at this very table. They'd shared family dinners here, Boyd holding Michaela's hand under the table, but the only thing that felt the same was the bougainvillea in bright reds and pinks wrapped around the large timbers overhead, shading them from the rays of sunshine illuminating the lush green lawn.

"I need to know, Shawn... Did you keep your word to me?"

The older man took his measure for a moment, his brow furrowed. "I won't let myself be insulted," he said at last, "but I must admit I'm puzzled why you asked me to keep it quiet. Wouldn't it have helped your case if Michaela knew you'd asked me for her hand in marriage right before she broke things off?"

Boyd snorted. "No, I knew it wouldn't help. When I took that job with Hendricks... She wouldn't listen to reason. She thought I'd betrayed her and your company." And she might very well have kicked him in the balls for thinking he needed to ask her father. He'd only done it as a courtesy.

"Not my company anymore," Shawn said. "I'm trying to focus on being a better father. Seems I'll have the chance to help Michaela after what I heard today."

Boyd almost choked on his ice. "How soon did Michaela call Assumpta?"

"The moment she left Connor's office," Shawn said, kicking back in his chair. "She blew hot, like she does. Then she said something that gave me and Assumpta pause. That's why you're here, Boyd."

He took a drink to steady himself. "Just lay it out, Shawn."

"She said she was scared to go." Shawn sipped his whiskey, making a show of acting casual. "You know Michaela isn't afraid of anything."

The words reached into his chest and gripped his already aching heart. No, Mickey didn't quail at much, but there was one thing she did fear. "Truthfully, Shawn, Mickey and I are both afraid of our feelings for each other. It's why we circled each other like two wary cats for so long before we even started dating. And it's why she went off her rocker when I took that job—sorry, but she did—and why I nursed some seriously injured feelings and hurt pride for four months before I came up with a plan to win her back."

Shawn set his drink down and put his elbows on the table, leaning forward slightly as if they were in a huddle. "So, this trip is what I thought."

"Shawn, I'm carrying around an engagement ring in my pocket this very minute." He'd used his signing bonus from Hendricks to buy the ring. Michaela was the largest ball of fire he'd ever come across, and he'd wanted a stone to represent her power and passion. Still, the stone looked too small to his eyes. If all went well, he'd be able to afford something better once they found the Valley of Stars. And he could finally buy his mother a house in a safer neighborhood.

"I don't need to tell you that you have your hands full, Boyd. You know that. But I'm willing to give you a boon."

A boon? From Shawn Merriam, the ultimate Big Bad Wolf? Retirement really must change a person. And people said miracles didn't happen anymore. "I'd be grateful."

"My sister, Clara, is coming along—at my son's wise discretion."

He fought a rude noise. Connor could have insisted that they bring a team of trapeze artists, and Boyd would have agreed. Nothing was going to stop him from finding the Valley of Stars and winning Michaela back. But three senior citizens... Even if the uncle wrote another Pulitzer Prize-winning story about the experience, Boyd still wasn't sure bringing them was a good idea. Don't even get him started on Iggie.

"I'm going to tell Clara I believe you have good intentions toward Michaela. My sister has a certain tendency toward matchmaking, although I'll encourage her to be discreet, of course. If Michaela thinks for one moment—"

"We'll all rue the day," he said, laughing.

"Shawn," Boyd heard Assumpta call from the French doors.

They both looked over, and she raised a hand, both a greeting and a warning. Boyd made sure to smile over the quiver in his belly.

"Michaela just drove up. You'll want to wrap up your talk. Boyd, I hope you won't think it rude that I don't invite you to supper. Until I'm sure of your intentions with my daughter, I'm afraid you aren't safe around me with a paring knife."

His smile felt a little more genuine, despite the threat. God help him, it was the kind of thing Michaela would say.

Shawn's shoulders shook from repressed laughter as his wife pivoted, walking out of sight. "God, I love that woman. I swear, the moment I saw her, I was done. My tongue seemed to swell in my mouth. I couldn't put together two words. Her dad fortunately liked me, which is why he'd invited me over for supper in the first place. Noah never admitted it, but I think he hoped we'd like each other. He often said one of the happiest days of his life was our wedding day." Shawn stood and clapped Boyd on the back. "I hope I can say that about you and Michaela someday. Have a good trip."

He watched as the man walked back into the house. Animated sounds came from the family room. Michaela was having a moment. Boyd took another sip of his whiskey, bracing himself for their first private encounter since the breakup. He needed to be at the top of his game. But there was no preparing for the angry volcanic goddess who stormed out of the French doors, her hair trailing around her like the parabolic storm about to erupt. All the spit dried up in his mouth, and he was consumed with the crazy urge to take her into his arms and kiss her.

"You're alive!"

He downed his whiskey and stood up, reaching for control. "Yes. But I took the precaution of wearing a cup, just in case. Wanna see?"

She thundered across the flagstones to him. To his surprise, she came close enough to touch him, and then she trailed her fingers down the lapel of his jacket. "Oh, you know me so well. I never could resist you, Boyd."

The words were music to his ears, but something about the way she said it told him he was in for it—so he wasn't completely surprised when she rapped him on said cup. The thwack reverberated through his balls. "Ouch!"

"Of course I don't want to see. I've been trying to forget everything about you since we broke up."

"Ah... How sweet! You really know how to put a guy in his place."

She chuckled darkly. "I was kind of hoping you were joking about the cup, but I love knowing you felt you had to wear one to visit me and my family. Better get used to wearing it."

He couldn't imagine the discomfort of wearing it long-term on their trip.

"Your dad seems to be finished with me," he said, taking her in. She'd changed from her business threads into a dour brown cotton maxi dress he knew she'd selected to disguise the curves he'd always loved. Like it mattered. She could wear a trash bag and he'd still want to make love to her. Hear her sigh as he pressed deep. Cry out as he made her come.

God, it had been so long.

"I wish *I* were finished with you," she said, her green eyes narrowing. "Boyd, you're up to something, and I don't like it."

"Come on," he said, taking her arm. It was the first time he'd touched her since that horrible day, and even though it was a simple touch, he savored the familiar feel of her skin beneath his fingertips. She clearly did as well because he heard her gasp before she glared at him. "Your mother threatened me with a paring knife. I don't want to hang around here after that, but we still need to talk."

"You have some explaining to do," she said, yanking out of his hold. She stalked into and through the house. Neither of her parents emerged as she made a beeline for the front door, Boyd trailing behind her. "Dammit, Boyd! I told you we were done."

"Seems we aren't," he said as they walked through the front door. "Come on. I brought my bike. I'll take you to our favorite spot."

"We don't have a 'favorite spot' anymore," she informed him, standing tall in the waning sunlight in the circular driveway punctuated by an honest-to-God fountain. Growing up, he'd been lucky if he could get the water to drain down his family's rusted-out pipes.

"You can't erase the past, Michaela."

"Maybe not, but I had a burning ceremony with Caitlyn," she said, her gaze steady. "I *burned* the past."

Leave it to her to think a mere fire could erase what was between them. "Bullshit," he said. "You can't burn away what we had. But let's leave that aside for now. Don't you want to know more about how I found the Valley of Stars?"

"Sure, dangle the carrot." She swatted the air dismissively. "I'm taking my car."

Probably for the best, he thought. It would be torture to feel her pressed against him on the bike. "Fine."

He stalked off to his used Honda bike. He couldn't wait to buy a Triumph. It was another item on his bucket list, but he'd only get to it after he took care of the women in his life.

After putting on his helmet, he swung his leg over the bike, turned on the engine, and punched the gas. Zooming past Michaela's red Toyota 4Runner, he heard her honk at him—something she'd always done when they were going somewhere together like this, him on his bike, her in her car. The slap of hot wind ruffled his clothes, and he welcomed the feel of it as he leaned into the curves. Being calm and focused for this first post-breakup talk with Michaela was critical. He had important groundwork to lay.

The bike was faster than a car, and he'd already stalked to the edge of the cliffs at the overlook by the time she pulled in and parked. Filling his chest with a deep, cleansing breath, he turned to face her. The force of her presence was still a shock, like surfboarding in high tide and knowing the big one was going to take you under. Her long brown hair was limned with gold from the waning sunlight, and her strong yet curvy body was still visible under the loose dress as she strode toward him in that determined, efficient walk of hers. Some women sauntered. Michaela Merriam ate up the ground under her feet, in complete command of everything around her.

"This had better be good," she said, fisting her hands at her sides.

He couldn't help but grin. "First, let me just say...you

still look like a goddess. Maybe Pele, the Hawaiian fire goddess, because you're so pissed at me."

"That kind of comment is off-limits." She kicked a rock at him. "Now, how did you discover the location of the Valley of Stars? Because if this is a ruse—"

"You think I'd make a deal with the Big Bad Wolf if I didn't have the goods? Come on, Mickey! I'm not suicidal. Connor would end me."

"So would I," she said. His heart flipped in his chest as she came toward him, stopping next to him at the edge of the overlook. "Talk."

He sat on the guardrail and extended his feet. "Do you remember Joseph, our guide in Tanzania?"

"Of course! He was wonderful. Professional. Kind. Honest."

Three qualities hard to come by in a guide, Boyd had discovered. "That trip was a near perfect success. Easy in and easy out. We found the berry we wanted. Got along with the locals."

"I remember, Boyd. I was there. Quit stalling."

He gave her a look before continuing, "Joseph's cousins are part of the Maasai tribe who guard the flower, and he visited them after our trip. Mentioned you and I might be the people they've been looking for. The tribe has a medicine man and woman, a husband and wife team."

She cocked her head. "That's unusual."

Didn't he know it? The Maasai were known for being patriarchal, even when it came to roles in herbal medicine, which were often bestowed to women in other traditional tribes. "Seems they've both had visions of a couple being the answer to their prayers. The woman has a huge heart and likes to help people. Sounds like you."

"I can't wait to hear about the man," she said dryly.

"He wants to share his knowledge with the world

and speaks elegantly. Dare I say it's an apt description of me? Plus, one of the pair has a special affinity for snakes, it seems."

"Well, that part describes you, anyway," she said, tapping her hand against her leg. "It's weak, Boyd... I mean, you know I'm a sucker for all things mystical and you can go either way depending, but—"

"Joseph got to thinking we might be the couple the medicine man and woman had seen. Remember how I told him about being a snake charmer after we came upon that rock python—"

"That snake was thirteen feet long!" She held out her hands to punctuate the comment. "Even I freaked. Thank God Marvin was back at your tent sleeping. How is he, by the way?"

"He was depressed after our breakup, but he's coming out of it. I told him you're coming with us on our next trip." When a country's Customs laws allowed it or Boyd had an expediter, he brought his Tokay gecko along on scouting trips. Marvin always sounded the alarm if something attempted to enter his tent. "Anyway, the medicine man and woman want to meet us."

"Asking for us specifically is a good sign," she said, nodding. "When did Joseph call you?"

"Six weeks ago. I reached out to you, but you ignored me. I told him you were away on a trip, which was technically true."

"Keeping tabs on me, Boyd?" she asked.

"More like hoping to run into you on the road," he admitted, picking up a rock and throwing it across the makeshift parking lot. "I figured you were purposefully avoiding me. Today, your brother confirmed it."

She shrugged. "Big deal. I had my own mark to make after I got demoted because of you. But let's not get sidetracked. So you met with Joseph..."

"Like I said earlier, he's willing to take us to the tribe,"

Boyd said, fighting the urge to reach out and finger the brown cotton of her dress billowing in the breeze. "The rest is up to us. According to Joseph, we'll have to convince them we're worthy of the find."

Her brows slammed together. "*Worthy?* That sounds ominous."

He'd thought so too at first. "Don't get ahead of yourself. Joseph has already vouched for us. They wouldn't have given us a meeting otherwise. Except...we might need to pretend we're a couple on this trip. Share a tent. Be affectionate. From the way Joseph described the vision, that seemed important."

He had to try.

She sliced her hand through the air. "In your dreams. A couple doesn't have to mean a romantic couple. A couple could be business partners, which we seem to be at this point. Trust me when I say, I hope our association is both brief and painless."

This time he did touch her dress when the wind blew it against his leg. She was so beautiful. Had he told her enough? "I'm all for the painless part. The last six months have been brutal."

"Stop saying things like that," she said, her tone seething.

He stood up, prepared to take on the tiger. "You think you're the only one who got hurt? This wouldn't have happened if you'd listened to me about the Hendricks job instead of going off the rails thinking I'd betrayed you and your family. Give me some freaking credit, Doc."

She shoved him in the chest, but he was prepared for it. "You took the job without even telling me about it!"

Before she could blink, he had her hand in a martial arts grip pressed against his heart. He didn't care if she felt it pounding. "That's because you got mad and shut down when I talked about looking outside Merriam

Enterprises for a job after the fellowship. Jesus, why couldn't you see that I wanted to be my own man?"

"And that's supposed to make me feel all soft and mushy inside?" Her green eyes glowed like emeralds. "You basically said working with me and my family's company is emasculating to you, you jackass! How could you think I'd be okay with that?"

He thought of the jeers about being Michaela's Boy Toy. Yeah, they'd found their mark, but what man wanted to admit that to his woman, least of all one as powerful as Michaela? "Mickey, this was about me becoming financially independent. You know how important that is to me."

He almost cursed when he saw the sheen of tears in her eyes. She cried so rarely, it felt like the end of the world whenever it happened. "Money! Always money. It was the only thing that stood between us, and it's exactly what split us up in the end. When are you going to understand that I don't care about that?"

This argument was as familiar as the laundry soap he smelled on her clothes. Well, he knew his lines just as well as he knew hers. "Well, I do, dammit! I don't come from what you do. I need to be my own man. If you truly loved me, you'd understand. The Hendricks job gave me a signing bonus, a great salary, and respect. My credentials and my work stood on its own."

"You're an idiot!" She stormed over to her car. "It wasn't like that."

"Bullshit!" He stormed after her. "But everything is different now. We'll find that flower in the Valley of Stars, and then we'll share it with the world. Together. You'll do it from Merriam Enterprises, like you've always wanted, and I'll make a name for my company. Don't you see? I've thought it all through. This joint venture is the perfect situation."

She shook her head. "No, Boyd."

Needing to look into her eyes as he said this next bit, he

reached out and tipped her chin up. "Mickey, I'm going to win you back. This trip is a full-court press."

"You're wasting your time, Boyd."

He gazed into her eyes, taking in the uncertainty. The anger, still so hot. And something else—the passion they'd always shared. "If that's the case, you won't mind me testing your theory."

His mouth lowered, slow enough that she could back away. When she didn't, he felt a rush of triumph, quickly chased out by ecstasy and agony, in equal measures, at the first touch of her lips. He traced the curve of her lush lower lip with his tongue. Heard her breath harshen in time with his. Yes, it was still there, the passion, the want, but this God-awful longing was new. She still wanted him, but she didn't want to. And he still wanted her but was terrified she'd crush him again.

Sensing her uncertainty, he closed his eyes and let himself fall into the kiss. She gave an answering sigh, and he knew she'd done the same. Savoring the moment, he opened his mouth, giving her access should she want to take it. She did. He groaned and pulled her close. Then closer. Thought about laying her back against the car and simply ravishing her.

When she raised her hands to push him away, he stepped back without hesitation. "I've missed you," he said simply.

"I've missed you too," she whispered, "but that doesn't change anything. I'll see you in two weeks." She was already pulling away.

"That's what I wanted to tell you," he said, following her to her car. "I'm going ahead to set up everything with Joseph. I'll meet you in Nairobi. I didn't expect the delay with your family."

"Connor's a tough negotiator."

He watched as she climbed into the driver's seat and put on her seat belt. "Do you really want them to come?" he asked through the open window.

"Yes," she said. "It will be nice to have Uncle Arthur's take on things in addition to them chaperoning. Better get used to the fact that you're not getting any."

He snorted. "Honey, you forget the original purpose of chaperones."

She turned on her car. "What's that?"

"They're supposed to keep two people who desperately want each other apart until they're married. I figure that's where we've always been heading."

"You're crazy!"

She shook her head at him as she sped out of the parking lot.

He walked back to the cliff and pulled her engagement ring out of his pocket. Clenching it in his hand, he inhaled the fresh air, assuring himself the kiss and her soft sighs were an indication that it was possible to win her back.

Because he couldn't embark on this trip without hope.

CHAPTER 3

ARTHUR HALE WAS A LOT OF THINGS, BUT HE SURE AS HELL wasn't a moron.

His wife seemed to disagree, however. That was the only explanation for why she was holding out a pith helmet to him as they prepared to board the Merriam corporate jet. "Good God, woman, this isn't *Gunga Din*. We're going on safari, not conquering Africa for the British Empire."

Arthur caught their usually inscrutable butler smiling. Clara thrust the hat against his chest. *Oof.*

"It's a *safari* helmet, Arthur. You'll need it to protect that hard noggin of yours from the sun. It's going to be warm, and I don't want you overheating. You get so grouchy."

He snorted, taking the helmet, knowing the wise thing to do would be to quietly put it aside later or outright lose it when she wasn't looking. He'd enjoyed watching Cary Grant and Douglas Fairbanks Jr. in the production of Kipling's classic—who cared if *Gunga Din* was in India and not Africa?—but he wasn't about to dress like them. "Who are you dressing as? That Karen Blixen woman Meryl Streep played in *Out of Africa*?"

She shared an ominous glance with Hargreaves. "While we were waiting for our final medical clearance after our vaccinations, Hargreaves and I have been researching."

"What exactly? I'm the one who should be researching, but I can't find any mention of this flower online. Clara, we don't know a goddamned thing about this trip. We don't even know where we're going. Do you have any idea how big Kenya and Tanzania and Uganda are?"

Hargreaves cleared his throat. "Kenya is about thirty thousand square miles wide while—"

"Oh, Good Lord, Hargreaves, if I wanted trivia, I would have brought along Trivial Pursuit." Privately, he thought the butler would have been a hell of a fact checker for his newspaper, but he wasn't about to say so. "You know, dear, this is our third international trip since we've been married."

"I'd like to think of it as our fourth honeymoon, my love," she said, batting those big blue eyes of hers.

"Have I told you today how happy I am that we reunited after all these years?"

She leaned up and kissed him on the cheek. Hargreaves looked away like usual, and since he wasn't watching, Arthur took the opportunity to caress her backside. She still had one hell of a backside.

"Have I told you how I feel like I'm coming more alive every day?" she asked, taking his arm as they ascended the stairs of the plane. "I never imagined being nearly eighty and feeling like I'm finally starting my life. This is why we're living to one hundred, Arthur. I won't hear any different from you."

"To be with you, my dear, and in good health, I'd live to two hundred," he said, casting a wink over his shoulder at Hargreaves, who'd started wrangling bags out of their trunk. He always insisted on carrying their bags, even if someone younger offered to do it for him. "Think your butler could make it that long?"

"He's doing yoga now too, Arthur, and teaching me tai chi. You should join us. They're renowned health boosters."

He snorted, then waved his hand when he saw his niece

appear at the top of the airplane steps. "Michaela, come save me from your aunt. She's threatening me with more of her New Age ideas."

Michaela laughed, putting away her phone. "Nothing wrong with that. Sorry, I was talking to Flynn. Didn't hear you arrive."

"How is your brother?" Arthur asked. "Did he fix Boyd's cable? I laughed myself silly for days thinking about that. Downright diabolical of him."

The girl's mouth was twitching. "Yes, it was. To think, he'd kept it a secret this whole time."

"Hate to break your bubble, kid," Arthur said, stopping when they stepped on board the plane. "Your brother, J.T., spilled the beans that he and Trevor knew."

"It's the twin thing. If one knows, it's guaranteed the other does." Michaela pointed to his hand. "Ah...Uncle Arthur, why do you have a pith helmet? No one wears those anymore."

"Finally, someone with sense." He cut Clara a glance. "Talk to your aunt. She thinks Hollywood is a good place for information on how one conducts him or herself in the field. Of course, most of the characters who wore pith helmets in those movies ended up dead."

"*Arthur*. Hello, dear," Clara said, kissing Michaela's cheeks. "Don't mind him. He's too crusty for his own good. Really, the number of times he's complained about getting a few shots in his backside."

Arthur rubbed his posterior for Michaela's benefit. "I've barely been able to sit down. And we haven't even started rough riding in a Land Rover yet."

"Enough," Clara said. "Hargreaves has our luggage. We weren't sure how long we'd be gone, so we packed enough for four weeks."

Four weeks? "You didn't tell me that, Clara. I could have told you it was too much."

"Darling, we raided your drawers. I don't know how

you didn't notice. Besides, Hargreaves and I have packed what we need."

"We'll see what Boyd has planned, Aunt," Michaela said, trying not to laugh.

He leaned in and kissed her cheek. "Don't try and tell her, Michaela. She's an expert. You know, if it weren't for the chance to flex my journalistic muscles again, I'm not sure I would have agreed to this trip. *Chaperones.* I'm supposed to be the Matchmaker Jedi, not a mere chaperone." A nickname he thought he'd earned after helping Caitlyn Merriam, Michaela's sister, find happiness with her suitor and now-fiancé.

"You can't give yourself a nickname, Arthur." Clara plopped into one of the white leather seats. "Someone else has to do that for you. And there's nothing 'mere' about being a chaperone for two people clearly as combustible as Michaela and Boyd."

"Oh brother," Michaela said.

Arthur couldn't help but smile. Oh, he did love to get Clara's goat. "She's just put out that she's in the intermediate matchmaking class," he told their niece as he sat next to his wife.

"You never know what might happen," she said mysteriously. She'd talked to her brother, Shawn, last week, and ever since, she'd been making cryptic comments about Boyd, and how there were two sides to every story. Like he didn't know that as a journalist. Flynn had said something similar, but Arthur planned to make up his own mind. Always had, always would.

Michaela took the seat across from them. "Aunt, trust me when I say, your only task here is chaperoning."

And yet she hadn't denied Connor's assertion that she still loved the man. He'd bet the farm she had the hots for him too. Clara was right about the combustible part, not that he'd tell her yet. He couldn't give her too many points this early in the trip.

Yet he took her hand, and she squeezed his fingers, communicating she thought Michaela doth protest too much. Well, whatever Clara's goal, Arthur had his own: he'd do whatever it took to keep Michaela from getting hurt by Boyd McClellan, and in the meantime, he'd look out for his own lady. All the better if he wrote a kick-ass story along the way. As for donning his Matchmaking Jedi outfit, which certainly didn't include a pith helmet?

Well, they'd have to see...

**

When they landed at Nairobi's international airport, Michaela was happy to see Joseph waiting for them in the shade of one of the hangars.

Oddly, she was deflated Boyd wasn't anywhere in sight. Her tummy had started doing excited somersaults as the plane landed, her traitorous mind conjuring up memories from previous trips and fantasies about what might happen on this one.

"Joseph!"

She waved and he strode forward, smiling, dressed in a cream long-sleeved shirt and brown trousers. At forty-five, the only wrinkles he had were laugh lines around his mouth and eyes, he liked to say, with a touch of gray in his black hair for the wisdom he'd acquired.

"Dr. Michaela," he said, shaking her hand, the customary greeting. Although she'd told him multiple times to call her Michaela, he considered it improper. She counted it as a victory that he'd shifted from Dr. Merriam to Dr. Michaela.

"Hello, my friend," she said warmly. "It's wonderful to see you."

"You as well. I hope you had a pleasant flight."

"We did," she said, turning to the others who were making their way down the stairs. When they were fully deplaned, she gestured to the party. "Joseph, please meet my uncle, Arthur Hale." And so began the round of hand-shaking. "My aunt, Clara Merriam Hale. Their friend, Clifton Hargreaves."

Hargreaves extended his hand and said, "I'm their butler. Please call me Hargreaves."

Joseph nodded. "Dr. Boyd told me you would be joining our party."

"And this is Dr. Ignatius Vajra," she said, trying not to frown at the way the man was already lifting his straight nose in the air, something he did to establish his authority. Some of the people at work giggled about it, but she found it too obnoxious to laugh about. The next words—"my boss"—were even harder to spit out. She wanted to kill Connor for insisting Iggie come along.

"A pleasure, Dr. Vajra," Joseph said in his ever-cheerful way, extending his hand.

"Indeed," Iggie said, ignoring it, making Michaela want to smack him. "God, it's hot here, isn't it? I don't know how any of you stand it." He pulled out a battery-operated fan from his starched khaki safari togs—clearly, he'd shopped at the same store as Aunt Clara.

"It's the hot season, so we acclimate," Joseph said companionably, God bless him. "You will as well. The bush will be a bit cooler. Nairobi swelters with all the cars. Traffic was terrible, but the minivan is waiting."

"Is Boyd with the minivan?" she asked finally, not wanting to sound too eager.

"He's meeting us at Wilson Airport," Joseph said. "Had some last-minute details to see to for our trip." Turning to Iggie, he added, "Can I take your case for you, Dr. Vajra?"

Iggie clutched it close after hefting his laptop case higher on his shoulder, peering at Joseph suspiciously. "No, I plan to keep my possessions with me at all times."

If he weren't her boss, she'd have sent him right back on the plane. He'd delayed their departure in Denver by arriving late from a phone call with the office. To make matters worse, he'd promptly asked Hargreaves to hang up his jacket. Uncle Arthur had set him straight on Hargreaves' role, tapping Iggie on the shoulder and pointing to Clara, saying, "Hargreaves is her butler, not yours, good man."

Michaela had almost kissed him. If Iggie continued to act so superior and entitled, they weren't likely to get very far. Their success depended on the goodwill of the tribe entrusted with the flower's protection. Iggie hadn't gotten the memo, it seemed, and since he was her boss, it wasn't like she could point it out. She was hoping Boyd would do it, and she planned on doing some silent cheering when he did.

"I'm so happy you're here to take us to Wilson then, Joseph," Michaela said. "We'll meet you after we go through Customs."

"Boyd has already expedited your party, Dr. Michaela," Joseph said. "Come with me. The official is waiting to process your party."

It wasn't an uncommon arrangement for business trips, and she was grateful Boyd had thought to take care of it. They followed Joseph into one of the Customs offices, painted a strange shade of mauve that would have been more fitting for a bathroom. The official asked for all of their passports and started stamping them. She noted he hadn't asked for their yellow card vaccination records. When he got to Iggie, he thumbed through every page of his passport, his mouth dropping into a scowl.

"Your visa doesn't seem to be in order, Mr. Vajra," the official said. "I'll need you to stay here. The rest of you can go."

"It's *Dr*. Vajra and that's ridiculous."

Joseph made a shooing motion with his hands and started to usher her aunt and uncle and Hargreaves out of the room.

"His visa should be in order," Michaela said, hanging back. "We got ours at the same time."

"Ma'am, he's traveling under a different passport than you are," the official said, giving her a hard glance. "You're an American, and your papers are in order. Please, join the rest of your party."

Iggie was starting to sweat at his temples. "But there are a ton of Indians in Kenya. The British brought us over to manage this country."

His historical recitation was both insensitive and challenging, not something that would gain him favor with the Customs officer. "It will be fine, Iggie. Don't worry."

"You should go, ma'am," the official said, taking Iggie's arm. "This could take a few days to work out."

"A few days?" she and Iggie said at the same time.

"*Ma'am.*" The man stood at full military attention. "Please leave now."

She nodded. "Of course. Iggie, just answer their questions." *Try to be nice, for the love of God.*

"I shouldn't have to answer anyone's questions," he said with a huff. "My visa is in order."

She reached for patience. "Fill out whatever new forms they require. We'll wait for you." She didn't have to ask if he had his cell phone, which was always on him, even in staff meetings. Although he likely didn't carry it when he went to see Connor. Her brother wouldn't stand for it, for one, and Iggie respected those above him. Just not those he considered below him—Michaela included—although since she was a Merriam, he was a bit more circumspect with her.

Perhaps that had something to do with Boyd's dislike of Iggie. While she couldn't believe most of her colleagues would have been ugly to him, she'd believe it of Iggie.

A hard glance from the Customs official prompted her to cut off the moment of self-reflection—so not the time—and head to the door. There was nothing more she could do.

Joseph rushed over to her as she emerged from the office. "We should go, Dr. Michaela, and see about our luggage. I can come back for Iggie once he's finished. He has his cell phone, yes?"

"He does," she said, casting a glance at her aunt and uncle and Hargreaves. They were all tired, even after sleeping on the plane. And the jet lag...

The time difference was nine hours for them, ten for her. Sure, they'd overnighted in London, but today's flight had been almost nine hours. They'd left London at six in the morning, eight Nairobi time, since Boyd had texted her that he wanted to leave for the Maasai Mara today and not stay over in Nairobi.

It's only a forty-minute flight, he'd texted. *Sure,* she'd replied, *tell that to my older companions. They aren't used to traveling two days straight.* But Boyd hadn't relented, saying his timetable had already been set back by two weeks. She'd talked to Uncle Arthur and Aunt Clara, and they'd insisted they were game. Hargreaves went along with whatever they decided. Well, with Iggie being held by Customs, they were going to be delayed a bit longer.

After signaling to her relatives that she'd only be a few minutes longer, she pulled out her cell phone and called Boyd.

"Hey, Mickey! Here at last. Welcome. Are you coming my way? I'm scorching on the landing strip, but the plane is ready to go."

"Hello to you too. Look, Iggie is caught in Customs. Some visa thing. We can't leave today. The official said it might take a few days. Do you want to book a hotel or shall I?" She had a few she preferred from past trips.

"No, come to Wilson. If Iggie is being held that long, we can't wait around for him. Remember how I got delayed in Malaysia for three days because I happened to be on the same plane as those missionaries, and the officials refused to believe I wasn't with them?"

He'd had her go ahead, and he'd caught up with her. "What do you propose then?"

"I can hire someone I know in Nairobi to help Iggie find us once they let him out. You know I'm right."

Although she couldn't deny he had a point, Iggie was a Merriam employee. She couldn't just abandon him out of convenience. "I feel I should do something more. He's not used to this kind of problem, Boyd. Not like us."

"So call your headquarters and get your people started on trying to get him out earlier. Of course, that could backfire. You know how some officials don't like it when outsiders try to interfere with their Customs decisions. But we can't wait. You know that."

She did. "I still feel—"

"Think about your family members," he said, cutting her off. "The longer you dawdle, the more tired they're going to be. Mickey, I have super nice accommodations waiting for everyone. Aren't you ready for a hot shower and a bed?"

Even though the family jet was hardly uncomfortable, it was essentially the same as any plane—a long metal tube. She craved the simple convenience of water and shut-eye after a long journey. "Fine. We're coming your way."

"I'm breathless with anticipation," he said and then disconnected the call.

Time to call Connor directly. He'd want to hear this news from her. By her count, he'd be well into his morning even though it was barely seven o'clock in California.

"Hello, Michaela. I didn't think you'd check in this soon, as resistant as you were to the idea. Is there some problem?"

Resistant? You bet. She loved being off the grid on her trips. "Yes. Iggie has gotten detained in Customs on a visa issue. The official said it might be a few days, so I thought our people could work on having him released earlier. Unless they feel that might piss people off and delay things more."

"A visa issue, huh?"

"Well, he's Indian and it's Kenya," she said in frustration. "Who knows the reason? After dealing with Customs all over the world, I've stopped trying to find any rhyme or reason for this sort of thing."

"Are you delaying the trip for Iggie?"

"Boyd doesn't want us to, and I tend to agree. He says he'll hire someone in Nairobi to help Iggie catch up to us."

"I see," Connor said, humming on the line. "I think it's wise to go ahead, but this hiccup has my gut twitching. You don't think anyone got wind of Boyd's find, do you?"

She thought it through. "It seems improbable. I mean, why delay Iggie and not me or Boyd? We're more essential to the operation."

"Have you ever had trouble in Kenya before?" Connor asked.

"Sure," she said, feeling her jet-lagged brain catching up with her body. "It's like everywhere else we go. Depends on who we come across, if they have a power trip, if they don't like outsiders, or if they're corrupt."

"This official didn't ask for a bribe?"

"No, but it's not always about bribes, Connor."

"No, it's not," he agreed. "All right, I'll get someone on it if that's prudent. Given the situation, I'd like you to call in daily for updates."

Not her preferred way of doing things, but she knew he was right. "I was going to have my phone on for Iggie obviously, but you're going to hate the phone bill. I might have to use the satellite phone in places to check in, certainly upriver, I expect, if we need to keep communicating that long. Texts are the best if they come through, so you should use that as our primary method of contact."

"I don't care about the cost, Michaela," Connor said. "I only want to make sure Iggie gets out and you and the rest of the party are safe."

That brought a smile to her face. "I love you too, and we'll be fine."

"I'm going to reach out to some people," he said. "Leave your phone on."

"Keeping it charged is a bigger problem on the road, but I can do that in the Rover," she said.

"I shudder to think of the plumbing you'll be facing on the road."

She laughed. "Any time you want to accompany me..."

"I prefer Michelin restaurants and indoor toilets that flush, thank you."

"Oddly, the plumbing issue has never bothered me."

"How are we even related?" he asked dryly.

"I wonder that sometimes too."

"Ha. Ha," Connor said. "Be careful, Mickey."

"Always. Bye, Con."

When he ended the call, she crossed to her drooping party. "All right, let's go. Customs is keeping Iggie. Something about his visa. I just called Connor and he's getting people on it. We're going to continue on with Boyd, and Iggie will meet us in the field."

"Iggie's visa, huh? Are you sure they didn't detain him for being an asshole?" Uncle Arthur was rubbing Aunt Clara's back as he said it.

"The former probably," she replied, motioning to Joseph to lead them out.

"It's the way he holds himself and talks to people," her aunt said. "Like he's above everyone. Imagine him thinking Hargreaves was here to serve him. And Joseph, I was mortified when he didn't shake your hand."

Joseph simply shrugged. "It's not the first time someone has refused."

She clucked her tongue. "It's abominable. I don't like him, Michaela. Honestly, I wish Customs would keep him for the entire trip."

She did too, but it wouldn't be professional of her to say so. "Well, if you have anything else to say about him, now's the time."

Her uncle snorted. "He'd better be good at what he does. I wouldn't hire someone who comports himself like that, and if it comes to it, I'll tell Connor."

Although she doubted any of this would get back to Iggie, she resisted the urge to cheer. "Fine, no one likes Iggie, but Connor wants him here, so he's here. I'm sure everyone is tired, so let's get going. We have another plane to catch."

Everyone groaned.

After loading into the minivan, they set off for the local airport. Everyone's spirits lifted at the sight of giraffes ambling along in the game park they passed on the way. There was something so arresting about the sight of the larger-than-life animals against the backdrop of a modern city. When they arrived at Wilson, Boyd was waiting for them on the tarmac. He had on loose tan pants and a white cotton shirt, his go-to on trips like this, and he looked good enough to eat. With no pith helmet in sight. Oh, she was punchy.

She was horrified to realize she was happy to see him.

He walked forward in his long-legged stride and stretched out his arms. "Welcome to the land of milk and honey."

"That's the Promised Land, you idiot," she said, just to be contrary, as he walked toward her. The glint in his big brown eyes told her he was happy to see her too. Maybe too happy. Surely, there was no need for him to get so close. What was he doing?

When he grabbed ahold of her by the upper arms and kissed her flush on the lips, she knew. Bold was his signature, one of his most attractive qualities. When they'd started going out, she'd loved his directness and had responded in kind. Both of them were physical people, and they'd always understood each other on that level. But this was more than that...

He was reminding her of their potent connection, something she couldn't allow. Their impromptu kiss at the overlook had been a mistake, a weak moment that she regretted.

She'd also replayed it in her mind too many times to count.

"Dammit, boy, you stop that right now!" Uncle Arthur came over and swatted Boyd on the shoulder. "Step away from my niece. I'm much too damn tired to be a chaperone right now."

Boyd laughed. "The next time I kiss her, please say something like 'Unhand her, you miscreant.' I'd love that."

"You have a good vocabulary," her uncle said, crossing his arms—a gesture undercut by his obvious attempt not to laugh, "for a bounder."

"I think we're going to get along just fine," Boyd said. Turning to Clara, he said, "Mrs. Hale, how are you this fine afternoon?"

"I'm eager for the next leg of our journey, young man," she said, standing up taller.

Boyd gave Michaela's arm a quick squeeze—she hadn't pulled away despite her best intentions. "Mickey, can you get everyone settled on the plane? The in-flight entertainment is all primed and ready."

"It is?" Her aunt's pace seemed to pick up as they walked to the plane.

"Along with the pretzels and seltzer water, no less," her uncle said with a laugh. "Clara, it's a *safari* plane."

"A six-seater Cessna 210," Hargreaves said.

Arthur harrumphed. "Good eye for a butler, but I still think we'll be lucky if the seat belts work."

"They do," Boyd called. "I checked. No pretzels, Arthur, but there's a cooler full of bottled water. I know how thirsty traveling makes Mickey here."

His downright sexy wink made her stomach flip again in happiness.

"Hargreaves, will you help Joseph with the luggage so we can get going?" Clara asked.

Boyd crossed to Joseph and the two shook hands. "I'll help Joseph with the luggage, Hargreaves."

"It's my job, sir," Hargreaves said, his voice carrying across the tarmac. "Please settle yourself on the aircraft. Joseph and I will see to everything."

Boyd went around the van and popped open the back, grimacing like she'd expected. Her aunt had brought an appalling amount of luggage. Hargreaves only had a black carry-on, God love him. She fought the urge to smile at Boyd's expression.

"Hargreaves, this is all the luggage you're getting right now." He handed him the carry-on. "I have enough respect for my elders—like Joseph here—to be offended if you insist on hauling more. You've been traveling for two days, man. Give a little in this moment. We'll have you dig the Defender 90 out of the mud if we get stuck, don't worry."

Hargreaves cast him a look through narrowed eyes before taking the bag. "You and I will come to terms, sir, sooner or later."

"But let's make it later," Boyd said. "Mrs. Hale? Are these all yours?"

"Yes, Boyd," her aunt called gaily. "I hope I can call you Boyd."

"Beats jerk." He pulled a face. "Mickey and I going to help you repack for our trip up-country if that's okay with you. She should have told you to pack lighter."

"You might have mentioned it, young man," Clara said with a piercing look. "I trust you and Michaela to pack what's best, but I won't abide you touching any of my underthings, Boyd."

"I wouldn't presume," he called as they walked up the steps to the plane and disappeared. "Why didn't you give your aunt some guidelines?"

She went over and socked him. "Since I didn't know

much about our trip, I didn't make any suggestions. Besides, you're already the bad guy, so I figured I'd let you really fall into that role. I like being the good niece."

"You set me up, Doc?" he asked under his breath, leaning close enough for her to catch his scent—man, sweat, and a tinge of musky aftershave. "You know that kind of game turns me on."

"I couldn't resist a little fun after what you pulled." Her belly grew tight, and she fought the urge to lean into his hard body. She loved it when he smelled like this, so primal. His scent had always been its own foreplay. She made herself lean back, hoping to break the tension. "I'll send the extra stuff back to the corporate jet. It's leaving tomorrow."

"I've missed you, Mickey. I can't stop thinking about that kiss at the overlook."

"We can't do things like that," she said, her knees trembling at the mere suggestion. "That kiss—"

"Made me want to strip you naked and take you then and there," he said, tracing a line of sweat dripping down her neck. "Tell me the truth, did you think about it too?"

Lying wouldn't do anyone a service. "My body might not be over you, Boyd, but my heart sure as hell is."

He stopped short. "Huh. I hadn't thought of that. Your body and heart aren't in accord, huh? What about your mind?"

"My mind sees you as a business partner. Nothing more." Oh, she was such a liar.

"Hmm. I'll have to think on that." He brought his finger to his lips and licked it slowly. "You still taste the same in the heat. Salty. Lush."

She gulped. Fought a whimper.

He lowered his hand slowly, but his dark eyes were as hot as the tarmac. "You should probably get on board before we give everyone a show. You aunt and uncle might need you to introduce them to—"

A loud shriek tore through the air, followed by her uncle's unmistakable shout. That jolted her out of her reverie.

"They've met Marvin," Boyd said, laughing. "You'd better go rescue him."

"Oh, poor *Marvin*." She hoped his tail didn't fall off at the stress. "Why didn't you say anything?"

"My brain went soft when you stepped out of that minivan. Even after traveling for two days, you're still the most beautiful woman in the world."

He'd always said that. Didn't matter if they were drenched from tropical rains or she had mud on her face. To him, she was the *complete enchilada*, he'd teased. No one else had ever made her feel so desirable. So important.

"Marvin will be happy to see you, Mickey."

Another loud shout had her running to the plane, taking the stairs two at a time, only to come upon Hargreaves standing in the narrow aisle holding Marvin behind the neck in a perfect reptile hold. What the—

"Hargreaves saves the day," Arthur was saying, rubbing his brow. "Where did you learn that?"

Marvin gave a loud croak, his orange-spotted turquoise body twisting in the hold. "Madam had a boa constrictor for a short time, and I took a class on handling reptiles. I'm quite proficient."

"You had a boa, Clara?" Arthur asked, wiping his brow with a handkerchief.

"I bought it hoping it would keep Reinhold out of my bedroom." Her aunt leaned her head against the window she sat beside, tragedy lacing her tone. "Who knew I would come to love it so? My plan didn't work though. Reinhold had people take my poor Peanut away."

Michaela walked toward Hargreaves in the short aisle. Part of her wished her aunt's first husband were still alive so she could kick him to death. Instead, she said, "You named a boa *Peanut*? I love you, Aunt. Here, Marvin, don't be scared."

He croaked seeing her, his light blue eyes blinking up at her.

"You poor baby, being awakened out of sleep by all these people. Boyd should have introduced you properly. He's a bad man, isn't he? Oh, I've missed you."

"You know this beast, Michaela?" her uncle asked, sucking in a breath.

"Oh, he's no beast." Clara leaned forward from the middle row she and Arthur had chosen. "Look at his coloring. He's splendid."

"Yes, he's Boyd's. And I'm glad you see the beauty of him, Aunt Clara. He's a very special Tokay gecko." Her ability to gain the gecko's trust had shocked Boyd, and he often said it was the reason he'd decided to live with her. Love him, love his reptile, he'd said on their second date. His tone had made it sound like a joke, but she'd known better than to believe that. And so she'd enacted a patient campaign to make Marvin love her. Losing him in their breakup had been hard on her. She'd missed his loud croaking and surprisingly playful spirit.

"A Tokay," her aunt said. "Amazing. You'll have to tell me more about him."

"Sure thing, but first, Hargreaves, I'm going to open my hands. If you'd put Marvin down in my palms, release him, and step back quickly, he won't bite you."

Hargreaves gave her an inscrutable look. "Am I to understand this reptile will be accompanying us, miss?"

"How do you like my little fella?" Boyd asked, appearing in the doorway of the plane. "He's good to have along in the field. He chases off unwanted animals that wander into camp at night. One time, Marvin terrorized a male baboon who'd torn open my tent. Remember, Mickey? You got up to pee and found them squared off in mortal combat."

She'd almost screamed, but she'd caught herself. Baboons were notorious for being both ill-tempered and unpredictable. "It was a Hallmark-card moment for sure. Okay, Hargreaves. Drop the lizard."

Hargreaves did as she'd instructed. "I'm delighted this fellow will be joining our party, miss, as I'm sure everyone else is. I only hope you don't expect me to converse with it. I'm not versed in reptile."

"Just talk to him like he's a friend, Hargreaves," Michaela said, stroking the top of his head, eliciting a croak.

"I didn't know scientists spoke to their reptiles," Hargreaves said.

Michaela shrugged. "I talk to every reptile I work with. Maybe I'm weird."

"If she is, I am too," Boyd said in solidarity.

"We lose one reptile in Customs only to pick up another," her uncle said dryly. "What's next?"

"Did I hear you call Iggie a lizard, Mr. Hale?" Boyd asked in delight, coming up behind her. "A poisonous one for sure."

She felt his body heat and knew he was using the opportunity to touch her hair, likely on the pretext of calming Marvin, who was peering up at him.

"First, it's plain old Arthur, and yes, I called Iggie a lizard, although 'asshole' seems more apt. Now, any more surprises, young man?" her uncle asked, giving Clara's arm a comforting pat even though he seemed the most upset of the group.

"None I can think of except that we're sleeping in tents tonight," Boyd said. "Michaela, let's resume with the repack. We'll be airborne in a jiffy, everyone."

"Tents?" she asked. "You said, and I quote, 'super nice accommodations.'" She didn't mind personally, but she'd hoped for one night in a safari lodge to help her family acclimate.

"They're *nice* tents," Boyd said. "Of course, if anyone wants to stay here in Nairobi at the InterContinental Hotel, I won't say a word to Connor."

He was hoping they would bow out. She gave him the

stink eye to let him know she saw through his devious plan. Now who was playing games? He only laughed and ruffled her hair.

"Like we'd turn around now," her aunt said in her best haughty tone. "Young man, see to my repacking before I poke you with my knitting needles for suggesting we'd abandon our niece."

"We're along for the entire ride, Boyd," her uncle said, no-nonsense to the bone. "Stop insulting us and trying to make us beg off. Trust me, we're much tougher than you imagine."

"You'd have to be," Boyd said, caressing her nape. "This one is so stubborn I call her Rocks For Brains sometimes, but I love her. Come on, Mickey. Let's handle this luggage situation and get going."

"I have this horrible feeling I'm going to want to kill him before we finish this trip," her aunt said after Boyd left, buckling herself in as everyone took their seats. "Is that how you felt, dear, when you were dating?"

"Some days." She stowed Marvin against her chest and followed Boyd out of the plane to see about her aunt's luggage.

And then there were the other days, she thought, when she hadn't wanted to kill him at all.

She'd wanted to stay with him forever.

CHAPTER 4

MICHAELA'S FAMILY—BOYD WAS INCLUDING HARG-reaves for efficiency—was tougher than he'd expect-ed. At eighty and newly retired, Arthur clearly hadn't lost any of his grit. His wife was still something of a mystery. He knew from Michaela, who'd told him the story before they broke up, that Clara had been estranged from the family for decades over a business matter. Seeing Clara back in the fold gave him more hope.

But he still planned to lose Michaela's chaperones—without offending them, of course.

Hence their camp. Although there were plenty of high-end tented safari camps in the Maasai Mara, this wasn't one of them. Theirs was a simple setup in the literal mid-dle of nowhere. Only her relatives hadn't seemed peeved. They'd practically cooed over the sweeping vista of golden grasses swaying on the savannah and a trio of giraffe run-ning to the west as the golden sun descended in the tur-quoise sky. Okay, Boyd had to admit the scene took his breath away too.

After all the gasps and awe, Clara had led Arthur over to the tent that had been assigned to them, her posture that of a French aristocrat on the way to meet Madam Guillo-tine, and swept the canvas aside as if bracing for the worst.

She'd disappeared inside, and he'd cocked his ear for any muttering as her husband joined her, closing the flaps tightly. Hargreaves seemed to be inspecting the small mess tent and their makeshift dining area.

Michaela strode up to him and poked him with her finger. "You're purposely trying to get them to turn tail and run."

"Ouch." He grabbed her hand and brought it to his chest, hoping she wouldn't kick him next. "When was the last time you got a manicure?"

"Don't try and distract me. You'd better be nice to them. They're my family. Now let go of my hand."

Nice? A nice man wouldn't have bribed that Customs official to detain Iggie for a few days. If he'd learned one thing about his former supervisor, it was that the man had a knack for offending everyone he came across. Which was exactly what they didn't need. He'd figured a few days of Customs hell might humble Iggie. Or perhaps convince him to take the first flight back to California.

He still didn't buy Connor's motivations for including Iggie on the trip. His gut told him the Merriam brother known as the Big Bad Wolf was up to something. Maybe Boyd was a little paranoid, but he'd learned to trust his gut.

"We can *talk* about it in my tent," he said, looking her square in the eyes.

"You mean these accommodations?" She swept her free hand toward one of the tents. "They're too basic to be called tents."

Yeah, he was keeping them basic. No swanky safari lodges for this crew. Upriver and at the Valley of Stars, they'd have to turn real basic. If the city slickers couldn't hack it, it was best for everyone if they figured it out sooner rather than later.

"You know perfectly well this is a decent campsite," Boyd said, stroking the sensitive backs of her knuckles, causing her to gasp. She hadn't pulled her hand back, and so he was continuing their dance. "I rented beds for Pete's sake, Mickey, instead of just going with bedrolls by the fire. We also have a cook named Jaali, and Simon's here to help set up and be our park guide. If it were just you and me, you know we wouldn't have anyone else along besides Joseph. We—"

"After close inspection," Hargreaves suddenly called out, approaching them, "I believe this setup is acceptable."

Michaela tugged on her hand, and Boyd frowned as he relented and let it go. Damn butler seemed to be in the chaperone camp as well. "I'm glad it meets your standards, Hargreaves."

The man's inscrutable face didn't alter one bit at his sarcasm. "I have met Masters Jaali and Simon, and they are both professional and proficient in their work. The bush kitchen is quite innovative, I must say. Shall I assume we're having the chickens in the icebox for dinner? I can help with the preparations, sir."

Dear God, what was he going to do with this man? Michaela bit her lush bottom lip, struggling not to laugh. "Hargreaves, please call me Boyd, and should our cook and other helpers need anything, I'll be sure to ask you. For now, why don't you go to your tent and get cleaned up? I had them warm water for showers for everyone. Each of us gets two minutes given our water rations."

"Since the shower is basically the size of a flower pot," Michaela said, "two minutes is optimistic."

"I did say basic, Michaela. Actually, Hargreaves, my mother used to serve in a capacity not unlike yours. Why don't you treat this as a vacation? She always said her work was never done too, a quality I admire, but surely everyone needs a break."

Michaela cleared her throat. "Boyd's mother is a maid at a luxury hotel in downtown San Francisco, Hargreaves."

"Has been for over twenty years now, working herself to the bone," Boyd said. "I'm hoping this find will change all that. She deserves retirement like everyone else and a nicer house in a safer neighborhood."

Michaela gave him a sharp glance before turning back to Hargreaves. "Of course, a butler's duties are very different than a maid's, I expect, but I'm no expert."

The man's face didn't slip an inch, his formal but welcoming smile still in place. "I'm sure Mrs. McClellan is an admirable woman, but yes, miss, my role as Mr. and Mrs. Hale's butler is very clear. I serve them in their every need. This trip will be no different."

He didn't begrudge the man his duty, but seriously, he was going to have to put his foot down. It struck him that he could take a different tack. "Hargreaves, I appreciate your stance, but these men I've hired to help us… They need the money to feed their families. You take that away, I won't have any use for them. Also, it's an insult in their culture, and not one I'll abide."

There, that was a more compelling argument, and it had the benefit of being somewhat true.

Michaela put her hand on his back, a gentle warning.

Although her touch pleased him—it *always* pleased him—he wasn't going to heed her this time. "Also, when was the last time you roasted anything on a spit over a campfire? Or cooked with local ingredients like banana leaves or matoke and dhania?"

"Matoke are plantains and dhania is fresh coriander," the man informed him. "It has been some time since I've cooked fresh fish in banana leaves, but the dish is quite satisfying as I recall."

A snort came from Michaela, and he had to give her points for not laughing outright. This man was a marvel. "Fine, you know your ingredients. All I'm saying—obviously poorly—is that this isn't your usual show, and it might be better for you to take a back seat. Help Clara and Arthur in whatever ways they require but leave the rest of the arrangements to us. Okay?"

"Your view of butlers is quite limited, isn't it, sir?" Hargreaves asked, cocking one perfect eyebrow in his direction.

"Growing up where I did didn't afford me a view, Hargreaves," he said, his smile tight.

"Oh, stop," Michaela said, pinching his back before dropping her hand. "Hargreaves, you always seem to find a way to help people without making a big deal out of it. I trust you'll do the same here. Boyd isn't used to working nicely with others, which is why the concept is so foreign to him."

"Hey now—"

"Boyd also likes to be in charge," she continued, waving her hand in the air. "Let him think this camp is his purview. You and I know better."

"Yes, miss," Hargreaves said, his mouth tipping up more on the right side.

So the man was amused. Terrific.

"I'll see to my ablutions before dinner then, if you'll excuse me." Hargreaves bowed and then turned around and headed to his tent.

Michaela poked Boyd in the chest the moment he disappeared. He didn't mind. If he could get her to keep poking at him, he could get her to listen to him and reconcile.

"You should have told him it upsets you to see people working so hard in hospitality, especially at his age, because of your mother."

Bull's-eye. "Leave my mother out of this." She was still cleaning up after rich people, and he was counting the days until he had enough money to pluck her out of that life. He just hoped she wasn't too prideful to accept what he wanted for her.

"Fine," she said after a moment, her face falling. "We won't talk about your mother issues. Just stop pissing people off."

He sucked in a long breath. "Who am I rankling? I'm a likable guy."

Her snort carried across the camp, making Joseph and their two helpers look over. "Now, tell me where we're going?" she insisted. "I'm tired of all the secrecy about our itinerary."

"I love this game of cat and mouse, if only because it's rankling you so. You're so hot when you're rankled," he said.

"Is a knee to the balls enough rankling?" she asked.

He laughed and leaned into her a little. She cleared her throat, a move he knew covered a whimper. "That wouldn't be nice."

"You don't think?" She reached up to touch him, trailing her hand up his chest and into his hair. That slow, hot touch had him caging her hips with his hands. Was she going to kiss him? Could it really be that easy?

Then she yanked on the ends hard.

"Ouch!"

"You deserve it for rankling me. I'm taking my brief shower since the water is warm. I'll see you at dinner."

He stepped in front of her before she could leave. "Wanna conserve water?"

"You never give up, do you?" She laughed but trailed her hands across his chest again. "I think I'll pass."

The way her fingers trailed across his muscles said otherwise. "What about sharing a tent? We've never been apart on a trek before. I'll be lonesome without you."

She cast a lingering look at his crotch before lifting her eyes to his. "I was wrong to kiss you at the overlook. Now it's all we can think about. But we're both adults, and giving in to it would be madness."

"At least you admit it." That was progress he could work with.

"I'm off to clean up."

"Come on, Mickey," he called after her. "You know it's only a matter of time."

She gave him a rude gesture before disappearing inside her tent. All in all, things were going pretty well. Iggie was out of the way, and Michaela was touching him back and talking about wanting him. He signaled Joseph over.

"Any word from your cousin?" he asked softly.

"Sironka will be at the meeting point the day after tomorrow," the man replied just as softly. "He will lead us to the boats on Tuesday as planned. Of course, something could delay him, but it's unlikely. Even if he wasn't *moran*, he's protected by strong medicine."

Boyd knew enough of the Maasai language to know Joseph meant warrior. "Always good to send the baddest guy from the village protected by the gods."

Joseph laughed. "His mother named him Sironka on purpose. She had a vision of him being a strong warrior but not one who sought out fights. It means 'the pure one.'"

More talk of visions. The modern world often felt divested of magic and a sense of wonder, but both things still thrived in certain places, and Boyd mostly loved it. He knew Michaela did too. Unless, of course, it turned too dark. Legends could end up hurting people too.

Regardless, he doubted he could use the visions to persuade Michaela to embark on the trip without waiting for Iggie. She'd need some solid convincing. The more miles he put between them and the head scientist, the better. Once they got into the restricted area and dense forest, Iggie wouldn't be able to follow without a guide.

"Joseph, I'm going to sing in the shower and change before dinner. Everything set for tonight?"

The man smiled. "Yes. Simon even gathered wildflowers for a bouquet for Michaela like you asked. Said he ran into a lion who looked him over before moving on. He joked that maybe the lion had a fight with one of his lionesses and needs flowers to get back in her good graces."

Boyd had run the risk of telling Joseph about his "temporary" fight with Michaela, but time was ticking on his plan. Would the medicine man and woman reject them if they showed up and they weren't back together? He didn't want to go there.

"Let's keep those flowers for tomorrow morning. I bought a bouquet in Nairobi for her." Flowers were easier to come by in the city market, and these had looked to be a combination of local blooms and ones flown in from South Africa, whose flower season was in its final throes.

"Dr. Michaela is not as mad as I expected her to be after your description," Joseph said. "Still, she isn't sharing your tent."

"Hopefully a temporary situation, Joseph," he said, waving a hand at himself. "Who can resist all this? She'll be like the tick bird to my rhino. See you at dinner."

He sang some Shania Twain in case Michaela heard him. His spirited renditions had always made her laugh. The shower was over before the song, though, so he continued to sing as he changed into black cotton pants and a loose gray shirt. Slapping cologne on his cheeks after shaving, he almost laughed at himself. When had he ever shaved or brought cologne on a trek?

But Mickey liked smooth skin sometimes, and the smell of cologne mixed with sweat. He'd brought it to remind her of the old days when she used to rub herself all over him so their scents would be combined. He checked on Marvin. The gecko was sleeping in his makeshift traveling terrarium, which basically consisted of a soft-sided pet carrier with mesh panels stuffed with a couple of local plants he'd procured upon arrival. Marvin would be all over the tent and the campsite after nightfall doing his happy little gecko thing. Fighting a prickle of nerves, Boyd picked up the bouquet of flowers and headed next door to Michaela's tent.

He called out "Mickey?" before opening her tent flap and ducking inside.

Her aunt sat on the twin bed, making him draw up short.

She was knitting what looked like a navy sweater, the mere sight of which made his skin want to itch in this heat. Apparently, her chaperoning duties had begun.

"Planning to catch Michaela in the shower, were you?" she asked, her needles moving the yarn with brisk efficiency.

"I'd hoped you were joking about your knitting needles on the plane," he said, chuckling. "And no, I was only bringing Michaela some flowers like a gentleman. See?"

"Gentleman, indeed." Clara lowered her knitting and held out her hand. "I'll give them to her after she's cleaned up."

The way she was running interference prompted him to be cheeky. "Ready to turn around yet? The bathrooms must have come as a bit of a shock."

"You mean the gallon bucket with the rudimentary board on top with the hole in it?"

"I had the men make that for you and Arthur due to your...ah, advanced years," Boyd said, biting his cheek. "Hargreaves has the same."

"My thighs are in better shape than Arthur's, so thank you for that," she said with a snort. "I won't even contemplate Hargreaves'. As for the shower...the flower pot with the bottle of warmed water was ingenious, if you ask me."

She was as confounding as her butler. Then again, she was Michaela's aunt—he shouldn't have underestimated her.

"We won't turn around, Boyd," she went on, "so stop trying to make us bolt. You called my niece Rocks for Brains, if I recall, and I can be just as stubborn. Arthur as well. If for some reason you concoct anything additional to test our goodwill, I won't do things like, say...give Michaela these flowers."

As an argument, it was a compelling one, and the way she wielded those knitting needles made him suspect he'd find himself up close and personal with the pointy ends if he offended her niece. "Truce then."

"Good plan, young man. You may go."

He glanced at the scarlet cloth draping the doorway to the makeshift bathroom. Michaela could hear everything they were saying, for pity's sake. "Mickey, I know you're listening. Come see the flowers I found for you. They're some of your favorites: Cape daisies, Cape Heath, and even Star of Bethlehem."

"That's nice, Boyd, but my aunt will give me to them like she said. I'm still dressing."

He wanted to scoff and ask her what, exactly, she was dressing for. They both knew simpler was better in the field.

"Enough stalling," her aunt said. "The flowers, Boyd." She waved her still-extended hand.

Growling, he handed her the bouquet. "I'm trying to win her back," he said in an undertone, "and you're not helping."

Clara's mouth tipped up. "It's because I believe in second chances that I'm not ordering you to take these flowers with you when you leave. Now go."

He did as she'd asked, but he looked back when he reached the front of the tent. "Second chances, huh? I'll hold you to that, Clara."

"As you should, my boy." She lifted the flowers and studied them. "All nice choices, I might add."

He took one last glance in the direction of the scarlet cloth concealing Michaela from view. "Of course they are. I know what she likes."

"Are you planning a lantern-lit dinner next, Boyd?" Michaela called as he was lifting the tent flap. "It won't work. I'm not dazzled by romantic gestures."

"Liar."

Her face peeked out from behind the cloth, her hair pinned up, baby curls trailing in a sexy array down her neck. "I am not."

He leaned against the tent flap, careful not to use his

full weight. "I remember you telling me once on a trek that you'd never known kerosene lanterns could be so romantic. And you love bouquets of flowers. Any kind."

"I don't remember the part about the lanterns," she shot back, disappearing behind the cloth again. "Only the smell."

Boyd couldn't help but grin. She was so full of it. "As for dining under the stars...I've asked the Universe to dish up a shower of falling stars. How many nights have we pulled out a bedroll and watched the stars in each other's arms?" He left out the part about them making love slowly and steadily under the night sky since her aunt was listening.

"You'd better be ready to tell me more about where we're headed," Michaela snapped. "I won't be kept in the dark any longer."

He hadn't expected any different. "If you show me a little leg, I'll tell you right now. Just lift the drape." He was mostly joking.

A brush came sailing out of the back of the tent, nearly nailing him in the chest. Clara laughed.

He reached down to pick it up, laughing. "Temper, temper. You used to love giving me a safari striptease."

"*Boyd!*"

Since her aunt was laughing, he didn't see the harm. "Shall I put on the Victrola?"

"You brought a Victrola?" Clara asked with a gasp.

He bit the inside of his cheek to keep from laughing. "No, I just use a small battery-operated portable system."

Clara set the flowers aside and stood, drilling him with the kind of glance a cross teacher would deliver to a disagreeable pupil. "Let me clue you in on something, son. Never joke with a lady about music. Or romance, for that matter."

"Exactly!" Michaela called out. "Get out of here, Boyd. Before I throw something else at you."

He clutched his hands to his heart. "Is it any wonder I

still love you, Mickey? The way you speak to me—"

Something volleyed through the air before smacking the side of the tent and falling to the ground. A lotion bottle? "You never had decent aim, Mickey, but there are so many other things I love about you."

"Get out!"

"I'm getting," he said, chuckling, lifting the flap and ducking out.

When she was this riled up, there was usually more than a kiss ahead in his future.

He couldn't wait.

CHAPTER 5

MICHAELA HAD ALWAYS LIKED DINING UNDER THE STARS. Boyd knew it, of course, and wily man that he was, he'd used that knowledge to make their dinner look like a date. The soft lantern light *was* breathtaking, accenting the wildflowers in the makeshift crock in the middle of their picnic-style table. Hypnotic chords of Brahms trailed through the camp from his sound system, strategically placed nearby.

Then there was the view. He'd picked a spot with an unlimited view of the plains, and with the twilight hours upon them, one could make out the dark silhouette of wild game like antelope and giraffe on the horizon.

He'd designed this evening to remind her of their good times—all the way down to the Indian food their cook had prepared—and so far, it was working.

That sexy smile. Those big, dark eyes. She soaked them in, even though she knew she shouldn't, waiting for his big hand to brush her leg under the table. He'd positioned her to sit next to him, of course. Maybe she'd stab him with a fork if he made a move, or, and she knew this was bad, she might let his touch linger.

No one had ever touched her like Boyd.

"I can't say I ever had a hankering to sleep in a makeshift

tent in my retirement, but this campsite is pretty good despite the 'bathroom' situation," Arthur said. "If you'd have told me I would be eating Indian food on an African safari, though, I wouldn't have come. Not even for a juicy story. Traveling usually affords me the opportunity to escape Hargreaves' Monday Indian buffet."

Clara leaned her head on Arthur's shoulder and laughed. "Oh, you're such a fuddy-duddy about Indian food. If you'd done any research, you'd have known Indian food is quite common in Kenya. Hargreaves here is right at home. Aren't you, dear?"

"Yes, Madam," he said, forking up a spoonful of the delicious curry.

The butler sat on Clara's other side, his posture as perfect as if they were in a finishing school rather than the great outdoors. Hargreaves usually never ate with the Hales, but as Boyd had pointed out to him when he'd offered to eat in his tent, doing so could attract mice, which would in turn attract snakes as well as other animals. Hargreaves hadn't been able to quibble with that one, especially since Joseph had also joined them. Simon and Jaali had deferred, and no one had pushed them. They hovered by the campfire, talking quietly.

"Jaali has everything in hand," Hargreaves said. "This curry is excellent, and the view spectacular." His awe was unmistakable as he gazed off in the distance.

"Michaela *loves* Indian food," Boyd said, snaking out a hand to touch her arm. "That's why I hired Jaali from Nairobi. The restaurant he'd been working at had just closed. He's going to make Saag Paneer with butter chicken tomorrow."

Normally this news would have made her groan in delight, and Aunt Clara did make a happy sound in the back of her throat, but Michaela knew his game. "That's nice, Boyd, but we're here for work, not food." Even if his thoughtfulness was sweet.

"Indian food for the whole trip?" Uncle Arthur croaked like Marvin did when he spotted something displeasing. "I'll go to bed with indigestion after two nights of spicy food in a row."

"Spice does not cause indigestion, sir," Hargreaves said, wiping his mouth properly with a napkin.

Michaela considered the table setting again. Usually they used paper products sparingly on a trek, and Boyd darn well knew it, but everyone had been given a napkin. Then there was the china. For God's sake. Her uncle had joked about Aunt Clara taking her cues from *Out of Africa*. Maybe Boyd had done the same.

"Don't tell me about my stomach, Hargreaves," her uncle barked, making Joseph laugh before he could muffle it with his hand. "I've lived with it longer than you have, and it's—"

"Enough about your stomach," Aunt Clara said, patting his back. "Open your mind. Take in the vista. Arthur, even at twilight, have you ever seen a sky this magnificent? I didn't know it was possible to see so many stars before darkness fell, and they feel so close. It's like I could reach up and sweep them into my hand. And the music and the lanterns! I'm telling all of our newly engaged friends that safari is an ideal honeymoon."

"If you want to eat curry the whole trip and get eaten by a wild animal," Uncle Arthur shot back.

Boyd's hand grazed Michaela's thigh—finally!—and she waited a moment to cut him a look. Her flesh tingled at the contact. She poked him in the side to tell him she understood why he'd chosen this moment and did *not* approve. She and Boyd had often joked about being wild animals when it came to each other, the instinct to mate so strong between them. It had been like a compulsion, making them both remark that it was nature's way of telling them they were each other's mate for life. Now that reminder only seemed scary.

He couldn't be her mate.

Could he?

"Still," Uncle Arthur said, kissing Aunt Clara's cheek, "if I have to die of either a lion wound or indigestion from Indian food, I'm glad I'm with you, my dear."

"You're such a romantic," she said dryly. "Boyd, I hope Arthur doesn't hurt Jaali's feelings with his testiness."

"He'll be fine, Clara," Boyd assured her, tearing a piece of naan in two and handing half to Michaela.

She caught Joseph's smile when she took it. He'd been watching them tonight. Was he wondering about their breakup? The way they were now was a stark contrast to how inseparable they'd been on their last trip with Joseph. They'd been in complete sync and unable to keep their hands off each other. Oh, she shouldn't be thinking about that. Her thighs were tingling again.

"Boyd wants me well-fed and watered, Joseph," she told him as an explanation, shaking the bread in her hand. "Finding the flower is important to both of us."

"He's feeding his woman like a man does, Dr. Michaela," Joseph said, picking up his glass half-filled with wine. "I seem to remember him doing it on our last trip."

When he gave her a knowing look, she stuffed the bread into her mouth.

"I'm not his woman—"

"Tomorrow, we're going to be driving for quite a long time," Boyd interrupted, giving her a warning look. "We'll camp again tomorrow night, and then a boat will take us to the next leg of our destination."

When it came to sharing their itinerary, he was still as vague as mud. That had to stop. She'd have to find a way to coax the information out of him. *Maybe you should play his game*, a devilish little voice whispered in her head. *Give him a kiss if he gives you the first leg of your destination.*

Except she wasn't sure she could stop at a single kiss.

She wasn't sure she'd be able to stop at all. Her thighs weren't tingling now; they were burning.

"Iggie needs to be released tomorrow morning," she said, taking a hard line. "Once we get on the boat, it will be harder for him to intercept us."

"You're probably right," Boyd said, giving her a playful wink. "But I'm hoping he's tied up with bureaucracy a little longer. He's a pain in the butt."

"Hear, hear," her uncle added, lifting his wine glass.

"He has been since my first day at Merriam Enterprises," Boyd continued, "when he treated me like I was a kept man. Excuse me a moment, everyone. I'm going to check on dessert."

A kept man? He had to be kidding! He'd never told her that detail.

"My dear," her aunt said, leaning forward in the soft light, "I must confess, Boyd's growing on me. His boldness does have a certain appeal, and he cared enough about your likes to hire someone to cook your favorite cuisine. Are you sure you knew the whole story when you broke things off with him?"

"Broke things off?" Joseph sat up straighter. "What is this? I thought you'd only had a fight."

"We've severed our personal relationship completely, Joseph," she said, noting the shock on his face. Maybe she shouldn't have been so blunt, especially given what Boyd had told her about the seers' visions, but she didn't want to lie to him. And she didn't want to let herself pretend the "fight" wasn't permanent. "This trip is all business. If you'll excuse me a moment, I need to see about this whole dessert thing."

She strode off in the direction Boyd had gone to the mess tent. He was conversing with Jaali, who'd left the fire and was arranging mango slices dotted with ground cardamom on a white china platter. "Can we speak for a moment, Boyd?"

He turned, smiled, and bowed formally. "Of course, Michaela. Jaali, this looks wonderful. I'm so happy you agreed to come with us."

"Thank you," the man said, also with a short bow and smile. Hargreaves' manners were invading the camp, it seemed.

"The curry was delicious," she told the cook, offering a smile in turn. "It's a delight to have such incredible food on this journey. Thank you."

"You're welcome, Dr. Michaela," he said, again with a small bow.

When she and Boyd walked away, she eyed the best place for their talk. She didn't want to share their private business with anyone else. Boyd must have sensed what she was doing because he took her arm and led her past their circular encampment toward one of the Rovers. The light from the camp still illuminated his face, and she was glad for it. It afforded her the opportunity to see the wariness creep into his eyes.

"What the hell is going on, Boyd?" A breeze washed over her, making her wrap her shawl tighter around her shoulders. "Dessert? Curry? China! What is wrong with you? We never trek like this, and you know it."

"Since you love food, I made additional arrangements. What was I supposed to do? Cook for your entire family? I also hoped these kind of details would make you feel special. Appreciated even."

She rocked back on her heels. "What?"

"I worried a lack of appreciation was one of the reasons you walked away from me. That I didn't do enough to show you how much you mean to me. Not only romantic gestures like flowers and date nights, but sharing in the mundane, practical details of life like grocery shopping, dusting, or making the bed. Living with someone isn't only hearts and flowers. I understand that better now."

She'd wanted to hire a cleaning lady, and he'd outright

refused. He hated the thought of hiring someone to clean for them like his mother cleaned for the people at the hotel. She'd tried to point out that the service economy employed people, but he'd shut down. Of course, it could have been the money issue. He'd always insisted on paying half of the rent, utilities, and groceries when he'd moved into her place. That had been a thorny issue in some ways. She had a trust fund, after all, and while she was hardly a spendthrift, she had greater means than he did. Which meant she'd had to relinquish certain comforts to ensure he felt he was doing his part.

Still, he was talking crazy. She hadn't left him because of anything so mundane. Stuff like that didn't matter at the end of the day. "What do you mean? Details like who did the last grocery run had nothing to do with why we split, and you know it."

He looked off, casting half of his face in shadow. "I'm not so sure anymore. After I got over my injured pride and anger, and then the hurt, I finally could step back and analyze things less emotionally. I figured you wouldn't have been so quick to think the worst of me if I hadn't given you cause to doubt my love for you. This trip is as much about fixing whatever I broke so I can have you back as it is about finding the flower, Mickey."

He turned to look at her, his eyes narrowing on her face. His musky scent washed over her, and she reached out and touched his cheek, feeling the pull between them.

"Are you wearing a bra?" he asked.

"Where'd that come from?" She stepped back from him.

"I can always tell when you're wearing one *or not wearing one*, and it's been driving me nuts all night. You never wear a bra on our treks. You've always said you feel freer because most women in the countries we visit aren't so confined. Are you wearing one because of me?"

"Yes!" She poked him in the chest. "I didn't want to inspire more of your lust-driven fantasies."

He laughed. "Seriously? Mickey, all I've been able to think about is what bra you are wearing. Is it the white one with the baby blue bow? I love that one. Or the black one—"

"Stop this! We're totally getting off track."

"Blame it on my lust-driven fantasies." He grinned at her. "Better yet. Can I see it?"

"No! Focus. Talk to me about that comment you made at dinner, about feeling like a kept man."

"I'd rather talk about your bra." He tilted his head. "Are you wearing matching panties?"

"Boyd! Iggie didn't treat you like a kept man. That's your own messed-up perspective. You always believed people thought less of you as a man because I had a bigger bank account. That's bullshit."

He shook his head. "All right, I've forgotten about your undies. Bullshit? Mickey, this is why we always fought about money. You don't see what's going on around you. *Of course* Iggie treated me like that. So did other Merriam employees."

She stalked away, not wanting to hear that. These were her people. "I knew you had problems, but it was a compatibility issue. Iggie isn't easy for anyone to get along with."

He followed her. "True, but most of your Merriam colleagues thought I was getting special favors because of my relationship with you."

"You got that fellowship at Merriam on your own merit. My God, if what you're saying is true, then they must have said the same things about me."

"You're a Merriam, but you were there because you're damn good."

"So I can be there on merit, but not you?"

"I didn't expect it when I took the position." This time he stalked away, the star-filled sky a mesmerizing backdrop behind him. "Out in the field and at school, no one questioned my merit, but at Merriam, it happened all the time. I was Michaela Merriam's boyfriend, not a published summa cum laude Ph.D."

"That's crap!"

"No, it's the truth. I didn't tell you because you're right. Having my colleagues call me MBT, Michaela's Boy Toy, at work was emasculating. I thought I could handle it. Turn it around. I'd been bullied before, but I finally realized it wasn't possible. Not when the head boss led the charge. That's why I went after another job."

"You should have told me all this. I would have helped you."

"Helped me? Look emasculating up in the dictionary, Doc. What would you have done? Say, 'please don't call my boyfriend MBT or be mean to him.' It would have made it worse for both of us."

That they'd called him that and she hadn't known... "But we were in a relationship."

"Yep, but some battles you have to fight alone. I finally bowed out. Hendricks saw my merit, which is why I took their offer. By the way, it was a damn good one. I don't understand why you'd think I'd betrayed you and your family by doing what was professionally best for me."

"*Because you promised me we were a pair.*" She strode to him and pushed at his chest. "Partners, you said. We went on research trips and treks together. We did everything together." *We loved each other.*

"In school," he said, "and even at Merriam when I could be a help and not a hindrance to you. We'll have that chance again now that I have my own company. We'll be equal partners."

"You're not hearing me," she said and started to move away in defeat.

He caught her hand. "Don't walk away. This is too important. I'm listening, Mickey. Finish what you need to say."

His touch sent a jolt of heat up her arm so she snatched her hand back. "I had time to step back and analyze things too. Boyd, you let your pride get in the way of our relationship. That's what broke us up. I can't be with someone who sees my wealth and corporate opportunities as a liability. I'm sorry they treated you like that at work. But, I am a Merriam. I can't change that, nor would I, and big whoop. I'm just a person like anyone else. Why can't you accept that loving you made me want to share things with you? You wanted a job at one of the best companies in our industry, and I had the means to introduce you to the opportunity. But you got the fellowship yourself. You earned it. If our situations were reversed, wouldn't you have done the same for me?"

He let out a harsh sigh. "Everyone expects a man to provide for his woman. I needed to at least stand on my own two feet. Maybe it shouldn't have bothered me, what people said, but it did, and I didn't feel like I could do my best there. More, I needed to prove myself as a man."

She threw out her hands. "This is horseshit. Do you think you're the only one who's ever felt that way? I trek around in parts of the world few would visit. No makeup. Showering infrequently if at all. Wearing sweaty, day-old clothes most of the time. I know when a lion is hunting me and how to remove a python from my tent."

"All things I love about you, I might add."

"A lot of people would think that doesn't make me much of a girl. Like being a girl is all about makeup and clothes and playing it safe. Dammit! My entire life I've felt weird for being me even though I know my family loves me anyway."

He drilled his finger in her direction. "You know it was like that for me too. If I hadn't gotten my scholarships and stipends, I wouldn't have made it to college. Most of the people in my neighborhood didn't."

"I know all this, and I admire you so much for it, Boyd, but—"

"Let me finish."

His harsh command had her throat closing up. She stood quietly in the darkness as he ran a hand through his hair. They were both shaking from the emotion bandying back and forth between them like a couple's game of mahjong. Part of her wanted to cross to him and lay her head against his chest. She hadn't known about the remarks people had made to him at Merriam Enterprises. The last thing she'd wanted was for him to feel bad about himself. Like he was lesser than.

"Michaela, my whole life has been about me becoming my own man so I could provide for myself and my family. Because you said you loved me, I thought you'd support that need in me. Like I support and love you for knowing how to remove a python or big hairy tarantula from our tent. Do you understand what I'm saying?"

"Not sure if everyone understands it, but the entire camp certainly heard you," a craggy voice said a few yards off.

Michaela spun around as her uncle and aunt stepped into view.

Arthur gave them both a gimlet stare. "Forget about chaperones. This is where I assert my role as cornerman in a fight. I think that's enough rounds for tonight, you two. Why don't you both go to your tents and cool off? From the sound of it, we have a lot of traveling tomorrow."

"I agree with Arthur," her aunt said, her voice strained. "You two aren't going to solve this tonight. Let's all get to bed. It's been a long day."

Boyd came forward, fists clenched. "But we were finally getting somewhere."

Her throat closed up. Were they? To her, it had felt like they were fighting over old territory. Saddened, she headed over to where her aunt and uncle were standing. "They're right. We've been going nonstop, and tomorrow doesn't sound like a picnic."

Boyd extended his hands to her, and she fought the

urge to take them. He finally lowered them, and she could see his jaw working.

"But you will think on what I said, right?"

Something inside of her throbbed as she watched him stand alone in the darkness. He seemed so far away from her, and she feared the distance between them wasn't the sort that could be crossed. "I'll think on it, Boyd."

"Okay, and I'll think on what you said too," he said slowly. "But I don't want to rob anyone of dessert and coffee. I'll turn in early. Good night."

He wandered off, and she slowly headed back to the dining table only to find it absent of Hargreaves and Joseph, who must have excused themselves. Oh, what must Joseph think of her now? Her aunt rubbed her back and kissed her cheek. "We left some dessert for you."

"Thank you." There was no way she could force it down now. "Let's all go to bed."

She watched as the light peeking out from Boyd's tent went out. As she headed to her own tent, she could hear him talking to Marvin, but she couldn't make out the words. His friendship with Marvin had always made her smile, but tonight it made Boyd seem even more alone. More unapproachable.

Simon and Jaali were huddled at the campfire and didn't look around when she bid them good night. Of course they'd heard everything too. Well, she wouldn't let any more awkwardness creep into their tiny group.

"Good night, Aunt Clara. Uncle Arthur."

"Good night, dear," her aunt said as her uncle blew her a kiss, a rare and yet moving gesture. She wanted to catch that kiss and hold it close.

Even when the lights in the camp went off, she remained awake in her dark tent, listening to Marvin's cute little croaks. Her heart wouldn't stop aching. *They treated me like a kept man*, he'd said during their fight, his usually strong voice shot through with emotion. He'd never told her that before.

Somehow knowing he'd felt that way broke her heart into even more pieces.

Chapter 6

Sunrise's bold, jewel-toned streaks seemed to echo the light radiating from Clara's heart as she surveyed the savannah.

The cup of strong black tea in her hand was steaming in the cool morning, and her limbs felt invigorated by the quick yoga routine she'd done while Arthur slumbered in their makeshift bed of two twin beds shoved together. She hadn't minded the hardness of the thin mattress or the wild calls in the night that she had yet to recognize except for Marvin's distinctive croaks.

She was on a grand adventure.

At nearly eighty, she'd thought her life was over. Willed it to be so at times. Then Arthur and the Merriam children had surged into her life like a tidal wave, ushering her out of the mausoleum of her existence and the house in New York City where she'd confined herself for decades. Before, she'd been like the lone baobab tree off in the distance. Now, she looked forward to each new day and the promise it held. Today was no exception.

"My dear," she heard her beloved Arthur say, coming up behind her. "I missed you when I woke."

She kissed him on the mouth and handed him her tea to share, admiring the small herds of zebra and wildebeest dotting the horizon. "I couldn't miss my first sunrise on the savannah. I figure we'll find time for a quickie later if we're lucky."

"A quickie, huh?" He looked around before giving her bottom a warm caress. "Never knew people our age could have those until I met you."

"It's a wonderful surprise, isn't it?" She laughed and held up her arms to the blue and orange sky. "Oh, Arthur, I'm so happy. I mean, look at this view. Oh! Is that a... Goodness, it's a lioness and her cubs. We should..."

"Stand still, I imagine," Arthur said, putting himself in front of her. "Granted, they're twenty yards away, but still. I don't have much skin on my bones, but if they decide to make a meal of me, you'd probably have enough time to get away."

The mama lion had blood on her furry mouth, and so did her four babies. Oh, they were cute little fur balls, even with the evidence of their morning feeding. They continued their morning walk across the plain, glancing at the camp with nothing more than passing interest. "We're both too bony, it seems. Now that you're awake, let's go over our game plan."

Something metal rattled, and she looked over to see Simon join Jaali in the mess tent. The waking camp had summoned Hargreaves, who exited his tent with his usual efficiency. He lifted his hand in greeting and crossed to the mess tent, likely seeing about their breakfast.

"Michaela and Boyd aren't awake yet?" Arthur asked.

"They haven't been seen yet, no. I expect they both slept poorly after their discussion last night."

Arthur handed back her cup of tea. "They have some pretty big issues to sort through. Money is cited as one of the top reasons for divorces and breakups in our fair country. Did you know that?"

She patted his arm. "I read *Cosmo*, Arthur. Of course I know that. I feel bad for Boyd, honestly, not just our niece.

Listening to him talk about needing to make his own way independent of the Merriam fortune and contacts reminded me of some of my conversations with you when you first came to New York as a young man."

Arthur sighed loudly. "I understand where he's coming from. Even though your grandfather helped me get that job at *The New York Times*, I wanted to be seen as the best damn journalist out there. In the beginning, it felt like an uphill battle since Emmits had put in a good word for me. Some thought I was his inside man on the paper, someone who'd write stories on his behalf. Wall Street is full of those kinds of deals. I had to prove myself from sunup to sundown and then some."

He'd been full of piss and vinegar then. Still was. "Even after proving yourself, you left New York to make your own mark with your newspaper, something everyone thought folly at the time."

"Except for your grandfather," Arthur said, smiling fondly. "He always believed in me. When he offered me start-up money for the paper, I insisted it would be a loan. I didn't want charity."

"Boyd seems cut from the same cloth," Clara said, "which speaks of good character...but also stubbornness. Michaela isn't wrong either. Money isn't as important as love."

Arthur put his arm around her shoulders. "And yet, to love a woman like she deserves, a man needs to feel like he's his own man. I don't know that I can adequately explain our species."

"I've read *Men Are from Mars, Woman Are from Venus* too, dear. I only wish..."

"Don't dredge up the past," Arthur said. "They're not us, Clara."

Although they hadn't dated when they were young, they'd taken a shine to each other. Their paths had diverged for much the same reason Boyd and Michaela had parted.

Her niece's relationship was different, of course, and Clara had reminded herself of that while doing yoga. "I'll do my best. You were right to call their discussion to a halt. They needed a time-out to reflect. Sometimes you stop hearing what the other person is saying when things get heated."

"They'll either work it out, or they won't," Arthur said, his practical side making her grimace. "However it goes, we'll be here for her."

"Doesn't mean we can't help," Clara said, turning as Hargreaves approached with a tray filled with fruit and bread and another pot of tea and a cup for Arthur. "Thank you, Hargreaves. We'll take our breakfast in our tent since Boyd and Michaela are still asleep."

"Is that wise, Clara?" Arthur asked. "Boyd said it attracted wild animals."

"We're breaking camp *after* breakfast, dear. Nothing to worry about."

"As you say, Madam," Hargreaves said. "One thing to consider before I arrange your breakfast. Joseph expressed surprise that Boyd was still slumbering. He'd mentioned wanting to start early."

"I imagine his talk with Michaela last night has something to do with his late start. We'll retire to our tent in a minute, Hargreaves."

"Retire, eh?" Arthur asked, nodding in that direction after her faithful butler was out of sight. "Are you planning something, Clara?"

"Yes, dear." She caressed his craggy cheek. "I plan to have *you* after breakfast. But first, let me finish what I was saying."

"Like I could stop you."

She punched him lightly. "I think you should talk to Boyd when the moment presents itself. Let him know that you understand his situation."

He barked out a laugh. "Is that so? Want to write down my main talking points too? Good God, Clara, I've been dispensing relationship advice for decades. I've got this. You, my dear, might also want to talk to Boyd. I figure I'll do the same with Michaela. Might be good for her to hear another man's perspective. Speaking of, would you like to hear my perspective on how your ass looks in those tailored pants?"

He never failed to notice her body, God love him. "Am I inspiring some of your primal man to emerge, my dear?"

She caught the glint in his pale blue eyes before he took her hand and tugged her toward their tent. "Always."

Hadn't she said she was lucky? Since Hargreaves had already departed, she launched herself at Arthur the moment the tent closed. Breakfast could wait.

She'd wallowed away too many years to lose more time.

***

Wasn't it Boyd's bad fortune to wake up with Marvin and not Michaela?

Opening his eyes and seeing his lizard resting on his bare chest wasn't a first. Sometimes the little fella used him as a heating pad, and because he liked to cuddle. Although most people didn't realize it, some reptiles were affectionate, and Marvin certainly fit the bill.

Marvin gave a soft croak, what Michaela used to call his lizard purr, and Boyd traced the orange spots along his turquoise spine. "Good morning to you too. Did you have a good night? I heard you croaking. Chase away any snakes or baboons?"

Marvin croaked again as Boyd rolled over, making the lizard skedaddle. Grabbing his watch, he eyed the display. "What the hell, Marvin—"

It was after seven. How in the hell had he slept so late? Oh, wait. He'd spent hours tossing and turning, thinking about his fight with Michaela.

"Our Mickey is the most aggravating woman in the world. Croak if you agree, Marvin."

The gecko remained silent.

"She's also so beautiful it breaks my heart."

Marvin croaked.

"*Now* you agree," he said, patting him on the head. "Of course, you have terrific taste in women. But seriously, Marvin, we're going to have to work a lot harder to get our Mickey back. I need you in tip-top shape."

Marvin croaked again.

"Okay, I know you'll do your part. She's the only girl I've ever dated who fell for you. The moment she met you, she reached into your terrarium to touch your head, and that's when I knew she was a keeper for life."

He thought about the engagement ring he carried in his pocket. Would he have the chance to show it to her? Would they ever get past the bitterness that had settled between them?

"Come on, Marvin," Boyd called, picking him up. "Back in your mobile home. We've got to get a move on."

He heard some muffled laughter in the next tent, followed by a low groan. Sex sounds?

That had to be Arthur and Clara. Well, hell... He supposed he should be happy for them. Who didn't want to have a thriving sex life into their twilight years?

He got washed and dressed. Dabbing on Michaela's favorite cologne felt more heartbreaking than hopeful, but he wasn't a quitter. He wouldn't let himself get mired in negativity. Striding out of his tent, he stopped short.

Michaela sat at the dining table in the center of camp, the morning light picking up the golden highlights in her brown hair as she sipped a cup of tea. She was still the most beautiful woman he'd ever seen, and he imagined that would be true until the day he died. He walked toward her, noting how his mouth curved into a smile as though it was his body's natural response to seeing her.

It probably was.

"Good morning," he said, sitting across from her at the table.

She raised a wary brow. "Mornin'. Looks like we both slept in. My aunt and uncle seem to have gone back to bed. Joseph took Hargreaves out for a brief nature walk with Simon."

"Your aunt and uncle have the right idea. If things were different between us, we'd be back in our tent too. Or we wouldn't have left it."

She set her teacup down hard. "Don't, Boyd. I'm in no mood."

He held up his hands. "All right. I won't talk about wanting you if you'll promise me something."

Her level gaze would have made most men turn tail and run. "What?"

"When you're ready, we finish the conversation we had last night. I want to better understand why you felt we needed to break up, and I want to share why I think we should get back together." There. That was fair and calm, wasn't it?

"I don't see the point, but there was something you said that I might want to hear more about."

She rose from her chair, giving him an eyeful of her beautiful curves.

"Best have your breakfast," she said, gesturing to the table. "We can start packing up the camp when everyone returns, minus my aunt and uncle's tent if they haven't reappeared."

His mouth quirked up. "Good idea. I don't think anyone wants their tent to come down while they're—"

"Napping?" She chuckled. "That's what they call it. Oh, by the way, there's still no word from Iggie. Connor texted me that our people are working on his release."

"Good thing Iggie wasn't around last night," Boyd decided to say. "I wouldn't want him overhearing our personal matters. In fact, it's one of the reasons why I'm glad he's not with us. I don't want your reputation to suffer."

She cocked her hip. "Mine, huh? Not yours?"

He stood as Jaali approached with a plate of food. "Yes, your reputation. It means something to me because I love you. Iggie made up his mind about me a long time ago."

"I won't argue with you," she said, smiling at Jaali as he set the plate down and left promptly to give them privacy. "I had enough of that last night. Any word on our destination today?"

He pointed east and tried not to let his lips twitch. "We're going that way."

Fire sparked in her eyes, but he thought he could see the tiniest hint of amusement behind it. "I told my aunt I only wanted to kill you *sometimes* when we were together. This is one of them. East, he says! Ugh!"

He laughed as she stalked off, her backside swaying in her loose pants.

Joseph smiled as he returned to camp and took a seat across from him. Wonderful. Time for another kick in the butt.

"You and Michaela seem to have very different versions of your current predicament, my friend," he said in a lowered voice. He folded his arms calmly on the table, but his dark brown eyes were ever watchful.

"She still loves me, Joseph," he told the man in a tone that wouldn't carry across the camp as he picked up a banana and peeled it. "And I love her."

"But you do not live together anymore," Joseph said. "That is a concern. My cousins saw a *couple* in their visions, Dr. Boyd. This could change our travel plans."

He took a few bites of the banana to give himself a moment to consider his response. "Do you know the exact timing of the visions, Joseph? Maybe they were seeing the past—or the future. Michaela will be mine again, my friend. Trust me when I tell you that."

"I do trust you, Dr. Boyd. I only hope you are not wrong because I fear my cousins will not show you two the Valley of Stars and give you the healing flower unless you have pledged your love for life."

Shit.

"We will see what my cousin, Sironka, says when he finds us at the meeting spot tomorrow. I fear he may not take us, given this new situation. He will be very unhappy."

Boyd took a hasty gulp of his tea, barely noticing when it seared the roof of his mouth. That would be a problem. Sironka was the guide who was to take them through the restricted territory to his family's village. Joseph alone couldn't do it. No one entered the valley without a guide from the village. According to Joseph, it had been so since the passing of Kenya's Witchcraft Act in 1925, which had outlawed traditional medicine and its practitioners. The people in the Valley of Stars had offered protection to traditional healers and such, an act that had required them to close their doors to anyone who might report them.

"Don't count me out yet, Joseph," he muttered, looking at Michaela.

The woman in question glanced over her shoulder in the act of pulling out the front stakes of her tent, as if sensing his silent regard. Their eyes held, and he watched as a line of sweat trailed down her neck. Although he'd been too worked up at the time to properly register it, she'd surprised him with her talk of being an untraditional girl. Of not fitting into her family. She'd never told him that before, and he'd neither seen nor heard anything in her family to give him that impression.

Joseph smiled warmly. "If I were a betting man, I'd say your chances are fifty-fifty right now, Dr. Boyd."

He pushed back from the table and grabbed a slice of fresh-baked bread. "By tomorrow, my chances will have improved, Joseph. Just wait."

"I certainly hope so," Joseph said, patting him on the back as Boyd passed.

"Find me a baby elephant or giraffe today, my friend,

and this will all turn around." Not that he was fool enough to get too close, but Michaela turned into a total ball of mush around baby wild animals. "Or a black leopard." A rare find, and more valuable for it.

"Simon and I will tune into the safari guides' radio stations. Although I didn't know we'd be sightseeing on the way to the meeting spot."

"A small concession in the game of love, my friend. Let's get going."

He walked over to where Michaela was working, but she pulled out the last stake before he could get to it. She'd always insisted on doing everything herself, something he admired in the field. Except she'd always done it at home too. Sometimes it had rankled, how she wouldn't let him do things for her. He used to think she was taking away his chances to be the guy in the relationship. Now, he had to wonder if he'd gotten it wrong. She'd felt like an outsider when she was young, but instead of repressing her identity, she'd embraced it. Maybe being independent was as important to her as it was to him.

Mickey smiled at him, a victorious smile, but he just tucked her hair behind her ear and walked back to his own tent.

CHAPTER 7

MICHAELA HAD TRAVELED TO NATURE'S MOST CAPTIVATing hotspots, but these wild grasslands had always pulled at her heartstrings in a special way. They had three Land Rovers to carry their things, and Michaela's group was in the middle, with Simon and Joseph in the lead and Jaali coming in last. Boyd had taken the wheel, of course, and since it was a given her aunt and uncle and Hargreaves would ride together, she'd taken shotgun. She'd decided to ignore him as best she could and let the magic around her seep into her soul. Her party seemed to have fallen under the spell of the savannah too, what with the gasps of delight coming from the back.

The grasses—varieties like Rhodes, red oats, lemon, and star—were scorched in places from the higher temperatures and lack of rain. The occasional baobab tree studded the landscape, their massive, squat cylindrical trunks topped off with dense tapering branches. The trees many Africans believed God had planted upside down were actually the largest succulent on the planet, collecting water in the rainy season into its mostly hollow tube-like trunk to sustain itself when the rains didn't come. Beyond that, its leaves boasted strong nutritional components for humans: vitamin C, sugars, potassium tartrate, and calcium. She'd eaten a delicious soup from the baobab's leaves and drunk a coffee substitute from their seeds, which were roasted over an open fire.

Everywhere she looked, she saw nature's wisdom, her greatest passion. Boyd shared that passion, and usually they exchanged remarks about the landscape and its treasures when they passed through the wilderness.

But he was unusually quiet and tense this morning. Heck, he was practically white-knuckling the steering wheel. His tension was rubbing off on her, so she fixed her gaze on the herds of zebra, gazelle, and topi, wildebeest, and Impala antelope grazing ahead.

As they rode toward the herd, keeping a respectful distance, Boyd broke the silence by pointing and saying loudly, "There's a cheetah stalking on the edge to the right, looking for a meal."

Damn but he'd always had the eyes of a hawk. She caught the spotted animal stalking through the grass, every muscle intent on its prey.

"I see it!" her aunt cried from the back of the Land Rover as the cheetah broke into a sprint and raced in on its chosen prey, causing the antelope on the edges of the group to veer away and take off running. "Goodness, it moves fast."

The cheetah seemed to be leaping off the ground with each stride, so majestic in its power. "Sixty-five to seventy miles an hour," Michaela called over her shoulder. "The topi are crazy fast too—"

"Fifty miles an hour," Boyd said, turning and grinning at her before dialing himself back.

In moments like these, she could feel that familiar click between them: thinking the same thought, finishing sentences, sharing the same joys. It only made it harder when the distance between them felt like a crevasse.

"Let's watch the kill close up," Boyd said, steering them in the direction of the chase as the rest of the Rovers followed.

When Boyd hit one of the larger ruts in the grassland, her uncle exclaimed with a loud *ouch* while her aunt gave a gusty laugh.

"Faster, Boyd!" Aunt Clara called out.

Michaela looked back, delighted to see her aunt practically hanging out of the open cab of the Defender. Hargreaves sat in the middle, binoculars clutched in his hands. Arthur was holding onto the metal frame for dear life, but his eyes were glued to the scene.

She was surprised at the amount of sightseeing they'd done in the three hours they'd been driving. Despite their talk, this wasn't a safari—they were here on a mission. But she wanted her aunt and uncle to have fun, and Boyd seemed determined to make that happen. He'd even turned them in the direction of a black leopard, one of her favorite animals. Of course, he knew that, and their eyes had met and held before she'd looked away. His face had fallen after they'd finally given up their search. She'd resisted the urge to thank him anyway.

"By God, she's got him," Hargreaves shouted out loud, his British accent somehow starker for the uncharacteristic shouting. She'd never heard him raise his voice before.

Sure enough, the cheetah closed the remaining distance and pounced on the antelope's posterior, bringing it down. The cat's sheer speed caused it to soar through the air for a moment after it took its prey down, and it had to slow and correct its course to return to the wounded animal.

"Incredible!" Her aunt gripped the cab's frame. "I should feel horrible for that poor animal, but there's something majestic about the chase and catch, isn't there?"

"Indeed, Madam," Hargreaves answered, leaning her way and lifting his binoculars. "But this is—"

"The circle of life," Arthur said, snorting. "Hargreaves, I expected something more original from you."

"Sir, would you like me to describe Darwin's treatise on survival of the fittest? Would that be more original?"

The butler lowered his binoculars and passed them to Aunt Clara, who quickly lifted them to her eyes.

Another snort came from Uncle Arthur before he turned back to the scene. "Clara, are you bloodthirsty enough to want to watch it eat the poor beast? Woman, I didn't realize something like this would excite you so. But it is pretty cool, I must say."

She didn't lower her binoculars. "Cool, indeed. It's incredible. Moving. Sad. Captivating."

"That's the savannah for you," Boyd called out. "It's a ringside seat to the way nature works out here. There's nothing like it anywhere else."

"No, there isn't," Michaela said, turning as naturally toward him as a plant to the sun. Their eyes met and held again. Earlier, when she'd looked up to see him watching her unpack her tent, a tremor had gone through her entire body. And when he'd come over to pull out the last stake for her, something she hadn't needed him to do...she'd thought he'd be pissed when she did it herself. Or that he'd feel emasculated by it, a charged topic in their recent discussions. Instead, he'd just touched her hair and then walked away, and nothing else he could have done would have confused her more. She'd felt like he was trying to tell her something, but perhaps that was only her confusion talking.

"Anyone want to get closer?" Boyd called after returning his gaze to their makeshift road.

"No, I'm good," Aunt Clara said. "Oh, I can't wait to see what's next."

"You won't have long to wait, Clara," Boyd said. "I called in an abundance of good sights today, and I know the Universe won't let me down."

That sounded both nice and suspect. "Like what?" Michaela asked.

"How does a baby elephant sound?" he shouted so everyone in the back could hear. "Anyone want to see that?"

Michaela blinked, her suspicions confirmed. Damn, he knew she went all soft when she saw one of those little guys. "You jerk," she hissed.

His response was a fiery, determined glare.

"Stupendous, sir!" Hargreaves shouted back, making everyone look at him. He blushed a bright red. "Excuse me. I seem to have gotten carried away."

"Get carried away, Hargreaves," her aunt said, handing his binoculars back. "If you can't get moved by all this, something is wrong with you. Also, I like your safari outfit. I wasn't sure if I should say anything."

He had on tailored tan cotton slacks and a tan shirt to match, as well as an oilcloth hat in the Outback style. Although Michaela was no fashionista, she thought it quite dashing on him.

"I thought he'd modeled his outfit after Dr. Jones in *Raiders of the Lost Ark*," her uncle said, his lips twitching.

"We certainly couldn't say that about your khakis and straw hat, now, could we, sir?" Hargreaves replied, his mouth lifting in a snarky smile, although surely Hargreaves would never use such a word.

Thank God they were here as buffers. She didn't know what she and Boyd would be doing otherwise. Maybe fighting... Maybe...

No, she wouldn't go there right now.

"Clara picked this outfit out with your help, you numb-skull," Uncle Arthur said, making Michaela laugh. "I'm never letting that happen again."

"Sorry, Uncle, I think you look quite...handsome." She cleared her throat to muffle her laughter, although she wasn't the only one chuckling.

"Right! Make fun of the old man. Heck, Boyd, you might as well let me out. That cheetah can have me after she finishes with the antelope."

"Oh, you old poop," Aunt Clara said. "Hargreaves is only teasing you because you teased him."

"Exactly, Madam."

Her aunt and Hargreaves exchanged a bemused glance, while Uncle Arthur's glare made it clear he knew they were having some fun at his expense.

"Female serval cat at one o'clock," Boyd called, distracting everyone.

It struck her again that he was really playing up the guide bit. If the two of them had been traveling alone, he would have stuck to their destination, only diverting if they saw something special. Or if their desire became so powerful they needed to stop for a quickie in the back of the open cab before continuing their journey. Her insides tightened at the thought of sex. God, she missed it. She hadn't found anyone after their breakup who'd interested her or charged her engines enough for her to go there. No one else had given her the kind of earth-shattering pleasure she'd experienced with Boyd, and better yet, they'd always talked and laughed together. Before, during, and after. That was something she doubted she'd ever experience with another man. Seeing his strong, large hands on the wheel, she had to admit she was more than tempted. Wasn't it smart of her to admit it to herself? Her inside temperature was starting to boil, and she gave in to the urge to fan herself. The hot air in the open cab was sufficient cover.

"Warm?" he asked, reaching behind his seat.

She looked back and watched him pop open the Grizzly cooler, one that kept ice intact up to ten days. When he turned back to her, he held out a piece of ice. His brown eyes darkened as she took it, and she could sense the memories between them. In times past, he'd have run the ice cube down her cleavage and then up her neck—a deliciously cool caress. Water would pool in places he'd talk about touching later, and she'd lean back in her seat, fantasizing about their love play while he drove.

She put the ice in her mouth and looked away, crunching it. Making love with him would be such a bad idea.

Or was it? Maybe they could have sex, and it could just be sex.

Oh, it was tempting, but she knew in her heart it wouldn't work. Not for either of them. She kicked the dashboard.

"Thank you for the ice," she said.

"You're welcome, Doc." He flashed her a cheeky smile. "Let's find you a baby elephant, shall we?"

He picked up the radio to convey the message to Joseph.

"Are you seriously diverting our travel to find me a baby elephant?" she asked him, holding on to the dash when they hit a bigger than normal rut.

Her uncle grunted, but her aunt emitted a delighted squeak like a little child might.

"Yes, I am," he answered, reaching out quickly to caress her hand. "I know they make you happy, Mickey."

"I don't need or want you to make me happy," she said, clutching her seat belt instead. "Dammit, Boyd!"

"Too bad, Mickey, because that's how it's going to be. We're making good time, don't worry."

"You still haven't told me where we're going, which really pisses me off." Better to get angry than lusty. She spied the horizon. They were heading northeast through the savannah, if her internal compass was correct, and while she had some ideas about their ultimate destination, one could never be certain with Boyd.

"All in due time, Doc. Sit back and enjoy the ride until I find you a baby elephant. Then you can get all mushy."

She crossed her arms and shifted her gaze back to the golden, swaying grasslands, catching sight of an ostrich running at top speed, its tall, spindly legs almost humorous given its portly, brown-breasted body. They came across a lion sunning itself, and Boyd made everyone laugh—even her—by singing "Can you feel the love tonight," prompting Aunt Clara to join in.

An hour later, Joseph contacted Boyd over the radio to report an elephant sighting. Part of her wanted to tell him to keep driving, but she couldn't bring herself to do it, and Boyd followed Joseph's Rover to the east. When they caught sight of the herd grazing in the distance with a single acacia tree for company, its branches spanning out like a giant umbrella, she scanned the herd eagerly, searching for a baby elephant. She finally spotted the little fella with his trunk wrapped around his mama's tail. Although it annoyed her that Boyd knew her so well, her heart melted a little, like the Sahara sun had softened the red hots her uncle always kept in his pocket.

"Do you see the baby?" she called out over her shoulder. "It's the sixth elephant over from the left. He's hiding a little behind his mama's hind legs."

"We'll see how close the bull will let us come," Boyd called back. "If they puff out their ears, we'll need to retreat."

The herd was already watching them approach, and Joseph wisely slowed down the closer they came. The bull walked forward, putting the rest of the herd behind him. Their cavalcade came to a stop, and everyone let their cars idle.

"Be real quiet now," Boyd said. "Give him time to see we aren't a threat."

If the elephant charged, Boyd would back up straight away, but they'd done this before, any number of times, and no bull had ever charged them.

"I don't know if you're aware, but elephants are matriarchal. The oldest female, in the center of the herd, is the leader," Michaela said in a lowered voice. "Most of the elephants are her daughters and their offspring."

"Not the bull, eh?" her uncle whispered, turned in his seat to watch the show. "I didn't know that."

"An evolved species, then," her aunt said. "The baby is adorable. I understand why you go all mushy at the sight of them, Michaela. My heart seems to have split wide open."

Its floppy gray ears were adorable, and the crook of its dark mouth looked like a permanent grin. The baby's intelligent black eyes met hers, and the air seemed to whoosh out of her lungs. Oh, elephants were special and then some. They'd fascinated her ever since she'd seen her first one at the zoo when she was four years old. That fascination had only grown when she'd learned about the fact that they had graveyards and grieved their fallen. Only two other animals grieved at such a level: magpies and chimpanzees.

Her uncle chuckled softly. "That strip of fur on top of his head makes him look like Mr. T."

"Oh, Arthur, how unromantic," her aunt said.

"Remember those two calves we watched play in the mud in the river, Mickey?" Boyd asked. "That slide they made with a tree branch was ingenious."

The baby leaned his head against his mother's leg again. "They were coated in mud by the end. One of their moms came over and sprayed them with water to wash them off. It was like she was saying, all right, playtime is over. Let's clean you boys up."

The baby moved under the mama's belly, nuzzling.

"Did you know a baby elephant can drink up to twenty pints of milk a day?" Michaela asked in an undertone.

"That's three gallons," Hargreaves said, his voice laced with awe. "Gracious."

"They breastfeed for about two years," Boyd chimed in. "Those lucky devils."

"You're disgusting, like usual," Michaela told him.

"I'm a man who likes boobs and is also a scientist," Boyd countered. "Judge me not."

Arthur chuckled. "I'm a leg man myself, but lately I'm finding I like boobs and—"

"Enough," her aunt said. "You're ruining my reverie."

Her uncle and Boyd chuckled for a moment, then everyone fell silent.

One of the elephants nudged another, and they started playing. A third elephant joined in, and Michaela knew they were in for a show. A few of the others continued to graze, but one by one, they joined in the fun. Nudging each other. Trumpeting. Twining trunks and swinging them. Michaela started laughing when the baby gave up nursing and trotted over, looking to play as well. One of the older elephants quickly engaged the baby by nudging it in the rump, which made it topple to the ground. It immediately rose to its feet, giving a loud squeak, and trotted back looking for more fun.

They watched the herd for over twenty minutes, but finally Michaela knew she needed to urge Boyd to move on. When she looked over to speak to him, she discovered he was watching her. The soft light of love filled his gaze, something she recognized from their time together.

"Happy?" he whispered for only her ears.

Her throat clogged up like an old well. "Yes, but we should get going."

"I suppose," he said, reaching out and touching one of the wild, wind-blown curls by her ear. "I've always loved seeing you like this. Thank you for letting me... Never mind. All right, everyone." His voice was louder. "We're going to get going. Take one last look."

Her aunt had said she didn't want to take too many pictures because she didn't want to view this trip from behind a camera. But she pulled out her digital camera quickly and shot a few pictures. Michaela watched as Hargreaves did the same.

"You look happy, niece," her uncle said, giving her a wink. "I guess Boyd gets a red hot today. Here, sonny."

Boyd reached a hand into the back seat and groaned when the melting candy plopped into his hand. "Thank you, Arthur. I will always treasure this moment."

Uncle Arthur laughed. "Good to know. Let's make tracks, folks. My old bones can't take much more traveling."

"You're fine," Aunt Clara said, stowing her camera under her seat. "Thank you, Boyd. I know we haven't come for sightseeing, but I'll never forget this moment."

"Hear, hear," Hargreaves said.

Boyd put the car in gear, and as he started to back up, the baby elephant lifted its head and started to trot toward them. Michaela covered Boyd's hand on the stick shift. He stilled completely. "Stop. I think he's—"

"Coming this way," her aunt breathed out, extending her hand to him.

"Clara, put your hand back in," her uncle said.

"Shh," Michaela said, her gaze tracking to both the bull and the mother, who hadn't moved a muscle but stood watching. "This is unusual. Let's see what happens."

Ears flopping, the baby continued trotting toward them with its big feet, its trunk leading the way. Its eyes seemed to hold a playful glint.

"It isn't scared," Hargreaves whispered. "My God."

"Be quiet everyone," Boyd said. "We don't want to spook any of them. Clara, make sure your hands are in the vehicle."

When it reached them, the baby stopped right beside the Land Rover, its trunk reaching for Aunt Clara. Michaela turned slowly to watch as it caressed her aunt's face, tickling her playfully under the neck, making her laugh.

"Laughter is okay, Aunt," she told her, watching in complete awe.

The elephant tipped her hat up, causing it to fall into her lap. "Oh, you precious thing," Aunt Clara said. "Why, you're a sweetheart."

The baby caressed her aunt's cheek and then stepped back. Those brilliant, sensitive eyes were trained on her aunt, or so it seemed, but it turned its head to look directly at Michaela. Her breath stopped and chills raced over her body. The intelligence in those dark eyes was palpable, and she felt like it was looking into her very soul. The moment seemed to stretch on for eternity, but before she could even gasp, the baby elephant turned around and lumbered back to the herd, racing across the grasslands as fast as its little legs could carry it.

Michaela slumped in her seat. "That was…"

"One of the most incredible experiences of my life," her aunt breathed out. "When it looked at me, I felt like it knew me somehow. I can't explain it."

"I broke out into gooseflesh all over," Hargreaves said, his hand over his chest.

"Too much information," her uncle muttered.

"Oh, do give us a moment to marvel, Arthur," her aunt said, grabbing the back of Michaela's seat. "Did you feel it, Michaela? The knowing in its eyes?"

"Yes," she said simply. She knew exactly what Aunt Clara meant. The wisdom in the calf's eyes had shocked her.

"Well, that was a first," Boyd said. "Whew! Clara, you must be a good luck charm when it comes to elephants."

"What a wonderful thought," she said, grinning. "Oh, I'm so happy I came. Thank you."

"Don't thank us yet since we have a ways to go, but you're right. That's a memory to treasure. In all my time in the field, I've never seen anything like it. Right, Mickey?"

When she turned to gaze at him, she realized her hand still covered his on the stick shift. It was like they were holding hands. She lifted it off quickly and pressed it to her stomach. "There was something…"

She looked away, searching for the baby elephant. The herd was moving on, and the baby had resumed its position behind its mama, its trunk wrapped around her tail. "We should go."

"Leaving shouldn't make you sad," Boyd said, making her look back at him. "Do you want me to follow the herd for a while?"

He'd do it if she asked—she knew that with all her

being, and her heart shuddered at the knowledge. "No, let's head to...wherever we're going tonight."

As they left the herd behind, Michaela fought the urge to cry. Boyd had always been attentive to increasing her happiness, and early on, it was one of the reasons she'd thought they might be forever.

Her body already longed for him, and now her heart had joined the chorus. She feared her mind would come next, and then she'd have to face the decision she'd most feared before coming on this trip.

Would she, could she take him back? And how much of a mistake would it be this time?

CHAPTER 8

BOYD HADN'T EXPECTED MICHAELA'S FAMILY TO TAKE TO safari so, and after today, he knew it was less likely they'd stay behind. The insanely intense moment with the baby elephant only seemed to make them more eager to stay the course.

Arthur had even helped Simon set up the Hales' tent, saying it was never too late for an old dog like him to learn new tricks. Of course, Simon had protested about him being an elder and all, which had only made the man harrumph. That man could harrumph like no one Boyd had ever met. One had to admire him. Clara was clearly made of the same mettle, and Hargreaves and Jaali were laughing softly in the mess tent making the dinner. *Together.* Under any other circumstance, Boyd would have been grateful for the harmony of the camp.

He only hoped they could withstand the next leg of the journey. Since he didn't exactly know what that would look like, his stomach felt a little queasy at the thought of bringing them along.

At least Iggie was probably out of the picture. Michaela had checked in with her brother again, and apparently Connor had made no headway in getting him cleared through Customs. At this point, Boyd imagined the delay had as much to do with Iggie's temperament as it did the bribe. Once Sironka arrived to take them to the village, it would be hard, maybe even impossible, for an inexperienced traveler to follow them.

Michaela didn't seem to mind much, thankfully. She was in her tent, singing to herself as she washed up from the day. A good omen, since she always sang when she was happy. He withdrew the flowers from one of the coolers and arranged them in a vase on the table in preparation for dinner. Wood was crackling in the fire Simon had made. The distant sounds of a gnu grunting and the hair-raising call of a hyena punctuated the soft rush of the wind over the grasses.

"Flowers again, Boyd?" Michaela asked, coming out of her tent in a black cardigan sweater and white harem pants, a practical choice given the protection they provided from mosquitos and other insects capable of flying or crawling up pant legs. Boyd tucked his pants into boots for that very reason.

His gaze traveled to her breasts. No bra tonight. He wondered if that meant anything, but he wasn't fool enough to ask. Rather, he plucked a yellow Cape daisy from the vase and handed it to her. Truly, he wanted to tuck it behind her ear and kiss her, but she would probably kick his shins for that. "Beautiful flowers for a beautiful woman."

She took the flower. "Thank you, Boyd. Not just for this, but for earlier. I know you went out of our way to show us those elephants."

"Not much, and it was worth it," he said, loving the way she was watching him. The wariness had vanished, at least temporarily, from her green cat eyes. He felt like he'd climbed Kilimanjaro and checked it off his bucket list. Had the baby elephant turned the tide?

"As Time Goes By" started to play, and Michaela's eyes narrowed.

Dammit, he wished Joseph hadn't chosen that exact

moment to turn on the music. He'd probably thought he was helping. Sure enough, when Boyd looked over his shoulder, the man was grinning at them. Boyd waved a hand in his direction and turned back to Michaela.

"You aren't seriously going to play the entire *Sleepless in Seattle* soundtrack for dinner, are you?" She tucked the daisy behind her ear, her mouth twitching. "That's desperate, even for you."

He held out his hand to her. "You're right. I am desperate. Desperate to have you back. Will you dance with me, Mickey?"

"If she doesn't," a rough-as-sandpaper voice said behind them, "will you resort to asking me or Clara?"

Michaela laughed, turning away from him and hastening over to her aunt and uncle, who'd emerged from their tent glowing.

Another *nap*? God, they'd found the fountain of youth. He wondered if they knew they were beating the statistics on human sexuality. Professors would vie to study these two and write about them in an academic journal.

"I'll dance with you, Uncle," Michaela said, grabbing his hand and ruining Boyd's plan.

"At least it's a tune I recognize," her uncle said. "Good ol' Jimmy Durante. He knew how to croon back in the day."

Clara crossed to Boyd and extended an elegant hand to him. "I guess that leaves you and me, Boyd. Unless you can't handle a woman like me?"

Arthur barked out a laugh. "*I* can barely handle you, my dear."

"You handled me fine just before we left our tent, dear," she said with a pointed look at her husband before turning back to Boyd. "I'd like to say it's all this fresh air and the wild animals, but truthfully, Boyd, we're always like this. Thank God."

"I was just thinking you two are a wonder," he said, pulling her in close and leading her into a turn.

She danced with as much gusto as she did everything else in life, and they quickly found a rhythm.

"You dance very well, Boyd," Clara said, pulling his eyes away from Michaela resting her head on her uncle's shoulder. They looked sweet together.

"Thank you, Clara, as do you. That's no surprise though. I've found most people in your generation are exceptional dancers. I learned a long time ago that if I wanted to dance at a wedding, I'd do better to ask the older women on the guest list. A friend's great aunt taught me the waltz when I was nineteen after the bride and groom cut the cake. I caught the old-school dance bug then and there."

"I'll ignore the 'older woman' comment since it's been such an incredible day."

He raised their arms as the song ended, and before she could protest, he dipped her.

She clutched his forearms but didn't panic. "The first time I dipped Michaela, she freaked out and took us both down. I don't know who laughed harder."

"Did you dance growing up?" Clara asked him as the first strains of "A Kiss To Build A Dream On" spread through the camp.

He caught Simon swaying as he broke more twigs for the fire. Joseph was staring off into the horizon, likely watching for Sironka. The lanterns cast a soft glow now that sunset was giving way to darker shades of blue and inky black. Looking around, at Simon and Arthur and Michaela, listening to the laughter floating on the wind from the mess tent, he realized everyone seemed happy. The harmony was as tangible as the gentle wind blowing across the savannah. The change was refreshing, and he decided to enjoy the journey, not only Michaela's presence and the thought of their ultimate prize.

"I grew up around a lot of break dancing and hip-hop," Boyd said. "I suppose I've always liked music and dancing for what it told me about people and their culture. It's something I love to learn about when I'm traveling. Perhaps we can have Jaali play us something later. He likes singing Benga, a popular music from the late 1940s to 60s."

"What's it sound like?" Clara asked.

"Benga is pretty cool, actually. It incorporates traditional dance rhythms from the local tribes with traditional stringed instruments like the nyatiti, a type of lyre, and the orutu, their version of a fiddle."

"I can't wait to hear it," she said, and he believed her.

When he'd first met her, he hadn't quite known what to make of her. She was elegant and privileged, certainly, but she had some strange quirks—the eighty-year-old butler and her easy way with Marvin.

After today, he was sure she had the heart of an adventurer, something she likely hadn't had much opportunity to indulge in given she'd been born at a time when few paths were open to women save nursing, secretarial work, and being a wife and mother. It sounded like the wife part hadn't gone particularly well the first time around, from what she'd said about buying a boa constrictor to keep her husband out. That comment had surprised him so much, he'd hesitated before announcing his presence on the plane.

"You know," he decided to add, "we have something in common, Clara. Besides your lovely niece."

"We do?" She swayed in time with him, her long hair trailing around her shoulders in the breeze.

"I used to keep snakes when I was a kid."

"The nonpoisonous kind, I imagine."

"Yeah, although I always wondered about raising the poisonous kind." He paused, thinking for a moment, then added, "We didn't live in a great neighborhood. Someone broke into our house one day while my mom was at work and I was at school, and the next day my class went on a field trip to Redwood Regional Park. A kid came across a Pacific Gopher snake. Not the least bit dangerous and yet everyone lost their..."

"Shit? I'm familiar with crass phrases, Boyd. Continue."

Again, she surprised him. He nodded. "Indeed. I caught that snake and brought it to my teacher, begging to do a school project on it. She agreed. When I was studying it on the front stoop of my house the next day, I noticed the people passing by seemed totally creeped out."

"I imagine seeing a young boy holding a snake might do that," she said.

"Exactly! I figured a snake might be as good as a dog for protecting our house, so I caught a few more for our backyard and house over the next month. My prize was a California king snake. It had white stripes on a black body and topped out at four feet. Everyone was scared of him."

He led her into a turn, which she executed flawlessly. "Why didn't you get a dog?"

He couldn't bring himself to meet her gaze when she turned to face him again. Usually, people were so weirded out by the story, they didn't ask follow-up questions, or they did, and the questions were all about the snakes themselves. No one had ever asked him this. "We couldn't afford the dog food. I found a stray when I was eight, but my mom got upset about the money it would cost to feed him, so she brought him to a shelter." He'd cried like a baby after she'd taken the dog away.

Clara put her hand on his arm. "That must have been very hard on you and your mother."

He'd never imagined it being rough on his mother. She'd worked so hard to keep everything going, he couldn't imagine she'd allow sentiment over a stray dog to drag her down.

"What did you name your king snake?" she asked.

"Conan," he said, "after Conan the Barbarian. I figured he'd have a snake like that."

"A good name," she said. "Although I've never seen the movie. Arthur! Come here and dance with me. Jaali is about to bring dinner out."

"As you wish, my love," Arthur called.

She took Boyd's arm and hauled him over to the other dancers. With as much subtlety as a stampede, she nudged Michaela into Boyd's arms. "Niece, dance with Boyd. I'm growing to like him more and more." She stepped into Arthur's embrace, pressing her cheek to his.

Michaela stood gaping at him, her body warm and soft in all the right places. At five ten, she was tall for a woman, and he'd always loved how perfectly she fit against him. "Stardust" was playing, and he put his hand on her back and held out his other hand. "Shall we?"

She put some space between them before taking his hand. "Appropriate physical contact only."

He snorted. "What in the hell is *that*, exactly?"

"Well, my mom tells a story about one of her school dances... A nun, Sister Margaret Richard, I think, came up to her best friend and her date and thrust a ruler between their pelvises after dragging them apart, saying, 'Come now, you two miscreants—leave room for the Holy Spirit.'"

"You're kidding me!"

"Could I make that up?" she countered as he led her into a turn as the song came to an end. She resisted for a moment, and he had to urge her into the circle with his other hand.

The next song started, and he felt his lips twitch. "Any objection to dancing to 'Makin' Whoopie'?"

"It's not like the song inspires lustful thoughts," she said as she matched his slow and easy rhythm.

Maybe not. But being close to her *did* inspire lustful thoughts. "In other times, we would have bumped and grinded to this one pretty good," he said in an undertone.

"Those days are behind us, Boyd," she said softly.

"Sadly." Dare he hope there was a strain of regret in her voice? He tipped her chin up so their gazes met. "Michaela, I'll do anything to get you back. Missing you every day was... I never want to be without you again. When I woke up this morning, knowing I was going to see you, I felt... hopeful. You're my baby elephant."

Her gaze flew to his, and he saw the war between longing and fear in her eyes.

He dropped her hands, sensing she needed a moment. Sometimes it was best to step away and let things simmer.

"Thanks for the dance, Mickey." He put his hand over his heart. "Maybe you'll consider a walk with me after we eat. I'd like to share more about our trip upriver. Jaali! Are you ready with dinner?"

He strode off to the mess tent, contented by the shocked look he'd seen on her face.

Right now he'd bet she'd join him on that walk.

CHAPTER 9

DINNER COULDN'T END SOON ENOUGH.

No one was in a bad mood, per se, but there was an unsettled feeling in the air. Her uncle kept squirming in his chair, his backside clearly bruised after a day of rough riding; her aunt seemed lost in thought, whether from fatigue or something else; Hargreaves mentioned the murder mystery he was reading was a real nail-biter; Joseph seemed to be scanning the horizon even though darkness had fallen; and in the soft lantern light, Boyd looked like a lion hungry for his prey.

Her.

She was doing her best not to stare back. When he got primal like this, it was hard to ignore the answering flutters in her belly, and even harder not to think of all the places they could have sex—in her tent, against the Rover, pretty much anywhere. She'd gone braless tonight because her breasts felt too sensitive to encase. He'd noticed, of course, and the force of his heated gaze had tightened her nipples.

Ugh! She was supposed to be Dr. Michaela on this trip, not Mickey. She should be pushing him to tell her more about the game plan.

Except she couldn't stop thinking about the way he'd

said she was his baby elephant or his invitation for a walk after dinner.

A walk with him sounded exciting.

And dangerous.

Finally, Jaali brought out the fruit for dessert. Although it was passion fruit, of all things, and Michaela's mind kept conjuring images of Boyd feeding it to her, drizzling juice over her lips and licking them clean. Oh, my God, she was boiling inside and fanning herself would only make it obvious.

He seemed to know it too by that wicked little quirk of his mouth. She had the urge to stick her tongue out to be contrary, but he'd find that arousing probably. He had a weird sense of humor.

"Well, I'm off to bed," Joseph said, rising from his seat. "I'll bid everyone good night."

The entire table murmured, "Good night," and moments later, Hargreaves stood. "Madam, do you require anything else?"

Aunt Clara shook herself. "No, please be excused, Hargreaves. Enjoy your book."

"Thank you, Madam. Good night to everyone."

Again, the rest of the group, Michaela included, bid him good night. Her uncle pushed a hand to the table to steady himself as he rose from the chair. His muffled groan made her frown. "Can I walk you to your tent, Uncle?"

"Gads, no," he said, slashing his hand through the air, "leave a man a little dignity. Clara, love, you've been somewhere else all night. Let's get you off to bed."

"I've been thinking about the baby elephant and the incredible story Boyd told me earlier," her aunt said, coming to her feet and putting her arm around her husband. "I didn't have the chance to ask you, Boyd. Do you still have Conan and the others?"

Michaela couldn't help but stare at Boyd, shocked by her aunt's allusion to Conan. Boyd rarely shared that story with people he'd just met. "Afraid not, Clara. Marvin's my only pet these days."

He glanced at her and gave a slight shake of the head, as if warning her not to give the real reason for why he no longer had the snakes. Some thieves had broken into their house one day and shot all the guard snakes so they could take the TV.

"Well, Marvin seems a good soul," Clara said. "I'd like to make friends with him before we depart and head our separate ways. I've never held a gecko before. I'll have to learn more about them."

Michaela admired her aunt's adventurous spirit. She never balked from a new experience. "Tokay geckos aren't the easiest to befriend, Aunt."

"Didn't a baby elephant come up to me today?" Gesturing to Boyd, she added, "How did you come by Marvin?"

"I found him in Indonesia. A truck full of reptiles had been smashed into a tree and abandoned. Poachers on the run, I'm guessing. He was the only survivor. I heard something croaking softly, sounding half-dead, and I looked in the back and found Marvin. He wasn't more than a baby. I couldn't leave him there, so I took him along and hoped he'd live."

"Once Boyd got the proper approvals, he kept Marvin with him nonstop for the next week and took care of him," she said, thinking of his determination to see the animal make it. "The vet later said Marvin wouldn't be alive if not for Boyd."

Boyd rolled his eyes. "I did what anyone would. It took a while for Marvin to trust me after that trauma, but I won him over."

You always do, she thought.

"But sure, I'd be happy to introduce you two again, Clara. Only, if he doesn't take to you at first, it's not personal."

"I did well enough with Peanut before his unceremonious removal," Aunt Clara said. "We should be fine. Tell Jaali that dinner was delicious. I need to get Arthur to our tent while he can still walk."

"I'm good enough to walk," her uncle blustered. "Only stiff as hell. Usually that's not something a man complains about. Right, Boyd?"

"Depends on the location of the stiffness," Boyd said. He laughed, and Aunt Clara and Uncle Arthur both did the same. Michaela didn't join them. "Good night, you two."

"Good night," Michaela said, rising and kissing them both on the cheek.

Her aunt and uncle moved slowly to the tent, and Michaela winced. "I forgot about the body's reaction to a full day of rough riding."

His lips twitched, and she threw her paper napkin at him.

"I didn't mean that. Jeez, Boyd." Of course, her traitorous brain reminded her of what it was like to ride *him*, his muscular chest under her hands. She broke into an all-over sweat.

His shoulders were shaking as he rose. "Let's give Jaali room to clean up. He won't start unless everyone is gone." He met and held her gaze. "So, Mickey, are we to have a walk tonight?"

So he wasn't going to pressure her to be alone with him. Somehow that made it harder to resist. And she did want to know more about their trip.

She glanced at the sea of black surrounding their camp. "Will it be safe?" Even with the half moon and the blaze of stars in the sky, everything was cast in darkness. But darkness didn't affect all species equally. Lions, leopards, porcupines, civet cats, white-tailed mongoose, aardvarks, and cape hares would all be able to see just fine.

"We're not walking too far out of the camp," Boyd said.

"You know I'd never put you in jeopardy. We'll bring Marvin."

"All right, but I want details, Boyd."

"As you wish." He grinned, and then he was striding off, so quickly she wondered if he was worried she'd change her mind. She waved at Jaali, who lingered in the open flap of the mess tent, and he lifted his hand in response.

"Dinner was wonderful, Jaali. Everyone wanted me to tell you so. Your butter chicken made me so happy."

"Thank you, Dr. Michaela. Your uncle seems less pleased with Indian food, something Mr. Hargreaves told me not to worry about. But I plan to make matoke with beef to please him." He gave a short bow before heading to the table. "I will clean up now and then find my bed."

Michaela studied Boyd as he reappeared with Marvin resting on his chest. "He'll probably want to transfer to you. Just giving you a heads-up since he moves—"

Marvin scurried down Boyd's arm toward Michaela. She extended her arm, letting Marvin begin his climb to his favorite position, nestled between her breasts. "If you make one rude comment—"

"My lips are zipped," Boyd said, grabbing a lantern off the table. "Thanks for dinner, Jaali. We'll see you in the morning."

"You watch out for the lion out there, Dr. Boyd. I heard him calling earlier. He's hungry."

Her stomach flipped a little. Usually lions avoided firelight, but they'd be on the periphery of camp. "Do you think we should still go?"

"Marvin will sound if the cat is close. Even from his relaxed position."

"If Marvin weren't so comfortable, I'd sock you for that." The gecko gave a soft croak. And nestled closer. "Still, let's not take the chance."

"Fine. My tent or yours?"

Had that been his plan all along? No, he couldn't order up a lion, nor would he.

"I have maps in my room," he added, gesturing to his tent. "I imagine I could scare up a cup of tea for you too. You like a cup before bed. Always said it helped you sleep."

They were wasting time. "Your tent then, but if you try anything..."

He held up his hands. "I know, I know. Come on, Mickey. I promise *I* won't initiate anything..."

She didn't miss his meaning, but it didn't stop her from following him into the tent. She could control herself, right? He was so close behind her, she could feel his body heat. Not a good start.

The flap closed, and he set the lantern on the floor by his bed. Like usual, his mosquito netting looked like a tornado had hit it. Boyd thrashed around a bit when he slept, and his big body often got tangled in the netting.

To banish herself of that image, she said, "A twin? How is it you haven't fallen onto the floor with the way you thrash around?" Plus, he was six four, but she wasn't going to mention that. He'd turn his "size" into something suggestive, and they didn't need any more sexual tension rising between them. It was bad enough she was in his tent after dark. What were Jaali and the others going to think? Oh, she should have stayed at the table with him, but then Jaali would have had to wait longer.

"Maybe we should go back out—"

"It's a bit tight, but I don't..." Boyd paused, stopping short of the double entendre, then said, "Before I tell you about the next leg of our trip, I'm going to ask you to do your best to let me finish and not overreact."

She snapped to attention, and Marvin croaked. "Sorry, buddy. What did you do, Boyd?"

"Sit down and I'll tell you, Doc."

"You first."

He sat, a small smile playing on his lips—oh, he knew

her game—and she pushed the netting aside and sat a few feet away from him.

The lantern light in the tent was a little too like mood lighting to serve her purposes. "Don't you have another lantern in here?"

He rose and lit it. "Better? Do you want to put on a nighttime puppet show like in old times? Remember how we used to joke about the things people had to do for entertainment before TV?"

"I remember," she said, cutting him off. "Time to confess, Boyd. Marvin, if he doesn't tell the truth, I'm throwing him to the lion outside." She glanced up in victory. "See, he croaked, which means he agrees with me."

Boyd laughed. "First up, I didn't like concealing things from you, but when Connor proposed his terms and included Iggie in the mix, I didn't like it. Then he added your relatives—who are nice people, I'm discovering—but I didn't know them or see why we needed a journalist to write a story. I felt like this whole trip and everything I wanted out of it was slipping through my fingers."

Marvin scampered off her chest and onto the floor when she turned on the bed to face Boyd. "I wouldn't have chosen Iggie, but Connor wanted it—"

"I don't trust him, Mickey," Boyd said harshly, making Marvin croak. "See, neither does my gecko. And I don't buy your brother's reasons for wanting him on this trip. Redundancy, my ass. He's never insisted on sending someone from headquarters with you on one of your other treks."

She'd thought of that too. Even after she'd been demoted, Connor had always let her go alone. "You do work for another company now."

He pounded his chest hard enough that it probably hurt, making Marvin croak again. "*My company*, Mickey. No threat to you and yours. I promise you."

"You're upsetting Marvin."

"He's agreeing with me."

Yes, he probably was. "Go on. What else? I know there's more."

"I don't know the exact location of the Valley of Stars." This time she croaked, "What?"

He held up a hand to forestall her reaction.

"You drop a bomb like that, and you expect me not to react?"

He cleared his throat, and Marvin scampered over and scurried up Boyd's body until he came to rest on his shoulder. "One of Joseph's cousins from the village is coming to meet us."

"You know I want to punch you, right? Only Marvin's presence is preventing it. When? Wait! Joseph was watching for someone at dinner, wasn't he?"

Boyd nodded. "He didn't make it tonight, so likely tomorrow. You know how it goes. He's coming on foot. Amazing, right?"

"Don't try and distract me. Boyd, what in the hell *do* you know?"

"Their village is here in Kenya, between the Loita Hills and the Sekenani Valley. Restricted territory."

"Marvin, I can't stand it anymore, so chill a sec." She gave in and punched Boyd lightly on his free shoulder. "I expected it was restricted. After all, the flower has been hidden for a hundred-plus years, but why can't Joseph take us? I thought he was our guide."

"He's our 'in,' so to speak," Boyd said, reaching for her hand, making Marvin scamper to his lap. "Look—"

"What else? You might as well spill everything. I could kill you right now."

"I know, but you won't. Ah...how about this? Sironka— that's Joseph's cousin—might refuse to uphold his end of the deal because we're no longer a couple."

She let out a string of curse words.

He playfully covered Marvin's head. "Not in front of the gecko."

She patted Marvin when he croaked. "I am so not amused. Are you kidding? Their medicine people are that particular about their visions?"

He shrugged. "Joseph seems to think so, but I want to be clear. That's not why I've been trying to woo you. I want you back—all the way."

The way he said it, softly and yet with determination, made her heart flutter.

Remember that he broke your heart. He rejected you as a partner the moment he took that job.

"It's going to take more than wildflowers and baby elephants," she said, standing up. "Dammit, Boyd. Do you have any idea how this makes me feel?"

He set Marvin aside and rose, towering over her in the short enclosure of the tent. His scent seemed to reach out and wrap around her, and her belly tightened in response. "I didn't want it to be like this either," he said. "I wanted you to fall in love with me again. Or maybe have sex with me first and then fall for me. The last thing I wanted was for us to be restricted by someone else's timeline."

She couldn't speak for a moment. His dark brown eyes were gazing warmly at her in the soft light, his desire and love for her palpable.

"And yet here we are. So what are you saying? Am I supposed to just grit my teeth and have sex with you for the sake of science?" She shoved him in the chest.

He put his hand on her shoulder. "God, no, I don't want you to grit your teeth and do this for science."

But they did need that flower, and if they had to look like a couple, maybe they should practice being one again. She *could* use it as an excuse to do what she wanted. The idea seemed to fill her entire body. Her core tightened, and suddenly, body, heart, and mind all clicked like a giant lock on a door.

She grabbed him by the shirt and yanked him close, rising on her tiptoes and pressing her mouth to his.

He stilled in shock for a moment before fisting his arms around her and opening his mouth. Yeah, she didn't want a gentle 'welcome back' kiss either. She wanted tongue and heat and teeth.

His all-too-familiar hands gripped her hips, bringing their bodies flush together. He was big and hard, and she was oh so wet, and nothing else seemed to matter. Maybe she'd been overthinking this, and nothing else *did* matter. She grabbed his head and ravaged his mouth, making him moan.

She'd missed his mouth, those full lips, that aggressive thrust of his tongue. *Yes, yes, yes.* His big hands slid inside her harem pants and cupped her bare bottom, palming her cheeks. She lurched against him, and he rubbed himself against her, making her moan.

"God, Boyd," she muttered between kisses.

He dipped at the knees to press them together in the most delicious way possible, and she could feel her sex-starved body revving for climax. It had always been like this with him—wild, crazy, hot. She opened her legs, and he put his knee against her, the pressure so intense she cried out. God, she was coming and she didn't want to hold back.

"Do it," he whispered harshly, releasing her mouth. "Let go."

Another strong, urgent press against her soft sensitive skin, and she was crying out, putting her mouth to his chest to muffle the sound. *Oh, yes, God yes*, she thought as the pulsing continued and his hands continued to wreak havoc with her body.

Suddenly, his warmth was gone, and he was depositing her on the bed. She reached for his pants. "I've still got the patch, by the way, so let's get these off you."

He stopped her, the look in his eyes almost anguished. "I can't... This can't... Shit, I won't let the medicine people's vision be the reason we make love again."

"What?" She shook her head, trying to clear sex from her mind.

"If you ever thought I used you—or this—to get what I wanted, it would kill me. Kill us." He moved her away from him and picked up Marvin like he was a shield. "I want you back too much for that. Unless you're ready to take me back for good, I think we should say good night."

She licked her dry lips, hoping to keep the taste of him close to her. "You're calling this off? Because of that? Are you trying to be noble?"

"I want you to understand how much you mean to me." He put Marvin down again and laid his hand over his heart. "Tell me the truth, were you letting things take this course because I gave you an excuse?"

She thought about throwing her shoe at him. "You make me sound cheap."

He ran a finger over her cheek before letting his hand drop to his side. "Never. But I won't let you think I am either. I'll handle Joseph's cousin tomorrow. You should get to your tent."

He was right, she supposed. Sex had been way too special and important to both of them.

But...

Sighing, she got up and left the tent, giving him one last look over her shoulder.

His muffled curses followed her into an uncertain darkness.

***

Arthur exited the makeshift bathroom, if it could be called that, to discover his incorrigible wife talking on her phone in bed.

"Land sakes, Clara," he growled. "What are you doing, woman? We're supposed to have left communication behind."

"She couldn't bear to be deprived of my insanely good

looks for the entire trip, Uncle," he heard their nephew Flynn say. "Skype seems to work intermittently, although I've boosted our signal."

Techie Boy Wonder knew his fair share of tricks, but right now Arthur was more concerned with his aching backside. Angling closer to the bed he shared with Clara, he peered at the screen. Flynn's sandy brown hair could use a cut, in his opinion. "Clara has my insanely good looks, Flynn," he quipped. "What's she need yours for?"

"Good to see you too, Uncle. Aunt Clara says you saw a baby elephant today. Are you feeling all warm and fuzzy on the inside?"

"Heck no. My backside is black and blue from bouncing around in that metal contraption all day."

Flynn didn't bother to muffle his laughter. "Sounds wonderful. I should join you."

"Gads, no," Arthur barked. "We've got enough people on this loony-bin errand. And we're having Indian food every night—in Africa!"

"Yes, yes, the sky is falling," Clara said, giving him one of the pointed looks she reserved for when he bitched about Indian food. The woman just didn't understand him sometimes.

"Aunt, to answer your question—"

"Before your uncle so rudely interrupted us..."

Another look from her, prompting him to shrug.

"I liked Boyd a lot," Flynn said. "He's trying to win her back, isn't he?"

"It's as obvious as the nose on your face," Arthur said as he lowered himself onto the mattress with a groan. "Right now, I'd say he's closing in after the baby elephant excursion."

"Michaela is motivated by baby elephants the way some women are motivated by diamonds."

"I couldn't agree more," Clara said with a determined nod. "Your father called me before I left saying he wanted me to know he would have done everything he could to help Boyd win back Michaela if he were traveling with us."

"Dad said that? Whoa! Hold the phone. He must have his reasons."

"That's what I thought," Clara said. "All right, dear. I need to go. Only wanted to make sure you were doing all right in Vienna. Arthur, Flynn's staying there this week."

Living up to his reputation as an international playboy. "With a beautiful model, I imagine."

"You bet. Ingrid is smart and beautiful and conversant in six languages, one of which I'm eager to communicate in."

"Get a room, Flynn. Arthur and Clara signing out."

"Tell Michaela hi—"

The screen went blank as Arthur disconnected the call.

"Did you really just end my call, Arthur?" Clara asked, folding her arms across her lovely chest. Yes, he still noticed those things.

"I did. It's time for bed. I'm bone-tired and my ass is hurting like I busted a bronco."

She got up and started rummaging around in the bag on the collapsible side table. "Here's some liniment," she said, handing it to him. "Rub. I'm going to call my brother. There's something more here. I know it."

He took the tube of liniment and sniffed it. "Peppermint? You want me to smell like a candy cane? Maybe you want to lick me?"

She laughed. "Why discriminate? You smell like cinnamon from your red hots. Sometimes, Arthur, I wonder—"

When she cut herself off like that, mid-thought, it was a sure sign she was annoyed with him. She brought up her brother's profile, and Arthur pulled his pants down. Rub peppermint into his backside... She'd rue the day.

Too bad he was desperate enough to try it.

"Arthur, please remove your bum from my camera angle," she said, grandly sitting on their bed again.

He harrumphed. But he kept rubbing, groaning at the pain. God help him tomorrow morning when he woke up. The next day was always worse.

Skype rang, and Shawn picked up the video call. "Clara, dear! What a surprise. How's it going?"

"Wonderful," she said, beaming at her younger brother. Since they'd reconciled, she radiated pure sunlight whenever she spoke to him. "Shawn, I wonder...is there any particular reason you're so supportive of Boyd winning Michaela back? I'm coming to like the boy quite a bit on my own, but with a bit more information, I feel I could be a more useful matchmaker."

Poor Michaela had only wanted *chaperones*, but anyone with eyes could see the girl was conflicted. Part of her wanted Boyd, but she also wanted to kick him in the shins.

He'd bet anything Michaela and Boyd were going on that walk he'd asked about earlier. The young man had some moves; he'd give him that. The pre-dinner dancing had been a good call.

"I can't tell you everything because I gave my word to Boyd," Shawn said. "What I can say is that his intentions toward her were and are honorable. I would welcome him into our family. Is that helpful?"

Arthur sure as hell would say so.

"Yes," Clara said, caressing her lips, lost in thought. "Give Assumpta our best."

"The same to Arthur and my daughter, of course," Shawn said. "Bye, Clara."

"Bye, dear." When she clicked off, Clara threw her phone aside. "Honorable intentions, he said. He must mean marriage. Right, Arthur?"

His backside was starting to burn from the liniment, but he decided not to mention it. He'd met his quota of ornery comments for the night. "Sounds like it to these old ears. As the Matchmaker Jedi—"

"It really doesn't count when you name yourself, dear." She started to undress in the tent.

He paused in the act of rubbing his posterior. "Care to help me now that you're done with your calls?"

"Hargreaves is versed in Swedish massage. I could see if he's still awake and ask him to give you a good rubdown."

She was still irritated about his nickname. Sure, he had given it to himself, but he deserved it. "I'd let Hargreaves rub me down when pigs fly... As I was about to say, to my way of thinking, we should let Michaela and Boyd work it out on their own. We referee when needed. Let them bend our ears when asked. Otherwise, we stay out of it."

Her scoff was audible.

He continued, "I don't think Boyd needs help in the matchmaking department. The music before dinner was a stroke of genius, and that baby elephant find was even better. God knows what else they'll get up to tonight, but I sure as hell am not going to listen. I plan to stick my earplugs in and tune everything out."

"Did you bring an extra pair? I seem to need them. Pronto."

Okay, he was pontificating. "By the by, what's going on with Hargreaves? His enthusiasm knows no bounds these days."

"We don't speak of such things, but I would imagine he's a little like me. After spending all those years cooped up in that Manhattan mausoleum, his soul craved a grand adventure."

Clifton Hargreaves was still a mystery to him, and Arthur didn't expect this one to ever be fully solved. But he'd come to like the man all the same, notwithstanding his Indian food. "No one can blame a man for that. Certainly not at our age."

"Speak for yourself," Clara said, stretching out her legs and rubbing lotion over them.

Arthur pulled up his pants and capped the liniment.

She deserved to be romanced properly, which meant he wasn't going to lunge at her with his pants around his ankles. "Allow me, dear."

When she thrust her legs in his direction on the bed, he wasn't thinking of the loud lion's roar in the distance or the infernal *gekk-gekk* call of Marvin the gecko.

No, Arthur was thinking he was luckiest son of a bitch in the world for having such a sexy wife. "Have I told you how much I love you today, dear?"

If a lion got him, he had no regrets.

Chapter 10

FRESH-BAKED BREAD WITH FIG JAM USUALLY ROCKED Boyd's world in the bush.

But as he sat with Joseph, scanning the horizon for Sironka, he could barely choke it down. Their voyage to the valley might end today. He'd stewed about it all night, unable to sleep after Michaela left his tent. Not even Marvin's companionship had comforted him. Still, he didn't regret his decision. Preserving the path to Michaela's heart was more important than finding the Valley of Stars.

"You are troubled this morning, my friend," Joseph remarked, drinking the near-black tea. "We will see what Sironka decides when he comes. You know the old proverb: a flea can trouble a lion more than a lion can trouble a flea."

"Was that in *The Lion King*, Joseph?"

"Dr. Boyd, that saying is as old as these lands," Joseph said, laughing.

He laughed with his friend, but all his joints felt like taut rubber bands. Michaela still hadn't emerged from her tent. Clara and Arthur came out of their tent, and he waved them over to the table. "Hey, Arthur! Have you heard the one about the lion and the flea? Joseph, tell him."

Clara sat next to him as Joseph and Arthur conversed

on the other side of the table, and she surprised him by putting a gentle hand on his arm. "I wanted to tell you that you're doing a good job with Michaela. Keep it up. She's like most of us Merriam women. Won over more by actions than words."

He was sure his brows must have risen in surprise. "Thank you, Clara, but today might be the end of our trek, and I doubt a baby elephant and some dancing under the stars changed her mind."

What he couldn't say, not to her aunt, was that last night hadn't been enough either. Although he'd already re-played the moment of her climax dozens of times.

"The end, eh?" she asked, smiling at Jaali, who brought over a tray of jam and butter for Clara. "I don't know what you mean by that, but I for one intend to be positive today."

Boyd needed to get in that mindset, and he figured a good-spirited jab might help him get there. "Arthur, you smell like a candy cane today. Let's hope the animals don't think you smell like dessert."

The man whacked the table. "Damnation! I told Clara that liniment stunk to high heaven."

"And yet your posterior feels better," she said, slicing a piece of bread and adding butter and jam as Hargreaves came forward with a tray of tea for her and Arthur. "Thank you, Hargreaves. Did you discover the murderer in your book?"

"It was the butler, Madam," he deadpanned.

Arthur chortled. "That's a good one, Hargreaves. We'll have to watch out for you from now on. Of course, if you make any Indian food once we return home, you might have to worry about me doing *you* in. I will need a respite from that cuisine."

"Oh, put some bread in your mouth, Arthur," Clara said, sipping her tea.

"Jaali is making a special native dish in your honor to-night," Hargreaves said.

Arthur ripped a piece of his bread off and dabbed it in Clara's jam. "What is it?"

"I doubt you know it, sir," Hargreaves said, still standing beside the table in a formal posture. Boyd wondered if he had an identity separate from being a butler. It seemed to fit him like a second skin. Boyd's mother was like that. She had trouble sitting down at the table with them. It had always bothered him.

"Tell him anyway, Hargreaves," Clara said.

"Matoke with beef. I've been assured it's delicious. Of course, it depends on how today goes."

"Speaking of," Joseph said, rising. "I think I'll take another walk about."

Boyd nodded.

"My journalistic nose says something is up," Arthur said, thrusting a bony finger his way. "Clue me in, Boyd."

"A warrior is coming today who will decide if we are to continue our trip to the village," Hargreaves said. "If you'll excuse me, I think I'll watch with Joseph."

Boyd's shock from the revelation that Jaali, who wasn't much of a talker, had shared all of that with Hargreaves was equal to Arthur's reaction. "What in the Sam Hill does that mean?"

"Since Boyd and I aren't officially a couple anymore, we may not be allowed to continue," Michaela said.

Boyd turned, not having heard her exit her tent. She'd braided her hair, something she did when she was thinking. Given the intricacy of the braid, she must have done a lot of thinking. Did she regret their brief encounter? Had it triggered more longing or resoluteness?

"You'd better explain, Boyd," Clara said, tapping the table. "Otherwise, Arthur will continue to bark, and while I'm used to it, Michaela looks tired and would likely enjoy a peaceful breakfast. Come, niece. Sit beside me."

Her position at the table made it impossible for Boyd to see her.

"Dr. Boyd!" Simon called from the edge of their small camp. "Joseph's cousin is coming."

He lurched out of his seat. The others followed suit. Scanning the horizon, he found the lone silhouette of a man in the traditional red clothing of the Maasai.

Joseph was standing with Hargreaves and Simon, a grin on his face, and he patted Boyd on the back when he reached the trio. "I told you Sironka would find us."

"Incredible," Hargreaves mused.

"But how?" Clara asked.

"We're in the middle of nowhere," Arthur added.

"Ask him when he comes," Joseph said. "Your eyesight would delight a cheetah, Simon. Well done."

"Thank you, Mr. Joseph," the man said. "Shall we break camp, Dr. Boyd?"

He caught Michaela watching him. Her mouth was tight. She wanted this find as badly as he did, but they both knew the score. The matter was out of their hands. "Not just yet, Simon. Joseph, shall we ride out and pick him up?"

"No, he likes to walk for days without end," Joseph said, chuckling. "Of course we can give him a ride. He is a warrior, not an imbecile. What warrior would not want to travel faster? The old ways of the Maasai are coming to an end, I'm afraid. Modernity."

Boyd nodded. Globalization was changing tradition-al ways of life everywhere. "Mickey, do you want to come greet Joseph's cousin?"

Their eyes met, and he nearly hugged her to counteract the sorrow in her normally vibrant green eyes. She didn't expect Sironka to take them to the village, he realized. Well, he was going to do as Clara advised and stay positive. Like he'd told Joseph, perhaps the vision had been of the past. Or, hopefully, of the future. As far as he knew, there were no hard and fast rules for this sort of thing.

"I'd love to come," she said, her voice as lackluster as gray clouds.

"We'll stay," Clara said, taking Arthur's arm. "Be the welcome party. Oh, I'm so excited. I've never met a warrior before. Do you think he'll agree to take a picture with me? I very much want to frame it and put it in my sitting room. Arthur has loads of photos with politicians and the like in his office. I'm starting one of my adventures."

"A capital idea, Madam," Hargreaves said. "Joseph, is there anything special Jaali and I could prepare for your cousin?"

Boyd wanted to commend him for his courtesy. It was exactly the sort of thing he should have thought to do.

"A cool glass of milk would be welcome," Joseph said. "Do you want to drive, Dr. Boyd?"

"I'd be happy to," he said. "Grab a piece of bread, Mickey. I don't want your blood sugar crashing from not eating."

"I'm fine," she ground out.

So she was going to be stubborn. "You don't want his first impression of you to be your growling stomach. I'd like him to know I feed my woman."

She stalked off to the table and grabbed his half-eaten bread, stuffing it into her mouth. He repressed the urge to roll his eyes.

"Anything else we can do, Boyd?" Clara asked, her eyes on the horizon. "How far do you think he walked?"

"Four or five days," Joseph said, passing Boyd the keys to the Rover. "He also came down the river. His village is located in dense forest, a fair distance from here."

"Why didn't we make it easier on the man and travel closer?" Arthur asked.

Joseph answered, "The land is restricted beyond that horizon. Only those with special permission from the chief may pass, and only then if they are accompanied by a warrior in the tribe."

"I see," Clara breathed out. "You should get going. Save the man in this heat."

The temperature wasn't yet eighty, but it was a warm morning. "Everyone ready?" he prompted.

They piled into the Rover, Michaela riding shotgun. Heading toward Sironka, Boyd felt torn between excitement and nerves. If Joseph's cousin refused to bring them any farther, he was going to be devastated. To get this close to the Valley of Stars...

The golden grasses swayed in the breeze as they raced ahead. A Ruppell's vulture soared overhead, its impressive eight-foot wingspan casting their car in shadow briefly. Beyond it, a tawny eagle flew across the savannah, landing out of sight, likely sighting prey. Boyd soaked it all in. If this was to be his last day in the Mara for a while, he was going to savor it. Michaela didn't seem to be of the same mindset. Her fists were clenched tightly in her lap, her gaze directed forward.

Boyd slowed the Rover as they came closer to Sironka, and the tall, lean man stopped to wait for them. His hair was clipped short to his head, and he was wearing the Maasai's famous beads around his neck. He lifted a hand in greeting as Boyd drew to a halt. Joseph exited the cab and crossed to his cousin, shaking his hand and speaking in the Maasai's rapid-fire Maa language.

Boyd called out a simple greeting in Maa, exiting the cab, and Michaela did the same. Sironka turned and smiled. "I am happy to find you here, my friends. The journey to reach you was a good one."

"You speak English?" Michaela asked. The next instant, her cheeks went pink, and she added, "I'm sorry. I'm only surprised. I understood you and your people live in a more remote area, and I assumed..."

The tall man rested his spear on the ground. "My sister learned English in her schooling in Kenya and returned to the village two years ago to teach a few members of our tribe. I was honored to be among them. My mother had a vision it must be so. She is a *laibon*—a healer—like my father."

"I'm Dr. Boyd McClellan." Boyd extended his hand to the man, who took it.

"It is good to meet you," he said with a brief bow.

"This is Dr. Michaela Merriam," Boyd said, completing the introductions. They'd agreed it was prudent to follow cultural rules of etiquette, and in certain parts of the world, it was the norm for men to introduce women. "She has traveled all over the world to find rare plants to share them with people everywhere, but out of all the places she's visited, this land is one of her favorites. As you might imagine, it is also one of mine."

"I am pleased to hear that," Sironka said. "Of course, the grasslands are very different than my home. Shall we meet the rest in your party? I counted five more people in your camp besides you."

Boyd wasn't surprised the man had such keen eyesight or that he'd paid such attention to detail. Out here, a person's survival could depend on it. "We have a repast waiting for you. Please." He gestured to the Rover.

"Come sit in the back with me, Sironka, so we can speak of your family while Dr. Boyd drives us." Joseph glanced at Boyd as he said it, as if silently ensuring him that he would make a case for the trip to continue.

They all climbed back into the car, Michaela next to Boyd, and as he started the engine, she covered his hand on the gear shift. He stilled in putting the car into first. Gazing into her eyes, he made the attempt at a smile. Yeah, she was wondering if this was the end of the line too. She squeezed his hand and released him, so he slipped the car into first and headed back to the camp.

Clara and Arthur came forward with their arms linked, looking like a unified front.

"This is Dr. Michaela's family, Sironka," Boyd said. "Mr. Arthur Hale, a world-renowned journalist, and his wife, Mrs. Clara Merriam Hale, an incredible artist of handicrafts."

"What a lovely introduction, Boyd," Clara said as she took Sironka's hand and then moved out of the way so her husband could shake the warrior's hand as well.

"You are a weaver of cloth, Mrs. Hale," Sironka said, bowing briefly, the gesture a little grander than the one he'd made for Boyd and Michaela out of respect for their position as elders. "The women in my village would be honored to see your handicrafts."

"I would be honored to show them," Clara said, motioning for Hargreaves to step forward. "I like to keep my husband warm. Our home is in the mountains and it can be very cold."

"It is good to keep your man warm," Sironka said.

"I am a lucky man, indeed," Arthur added. "We are very happy you have traveled so far to meet us."

"The honor is mine," Sironka said. "It is not often elders such as yourselves come to visit us, especially from so far away. Everyone in my village is eager to meet you."

That sounded encouraging, Boyd thought. He'd feared the addition of Michaela's family would put them off when he'd informed Joseph of the change, but the warm welcome made sense. Elders were revered here.

"Sironka, this is my dear friend and the man who makes everything run smoothly for me," Clara said. "Mr. Clifton Hargreaves."

"I'm honored to meet you, sir," Hargreaves said with a slight bow.

Sironka extended his hand to the butler, who shook it. "You are British, I hear, from your accent. It is a pleasure to meet you, Mr. Hargreaves. We should all be lucky to have someone make everything run smoothly."

Boyd waved Jaali and Simon forward and finished the introductions. He noted that Sironka shook hands with both of them. So far, he'd greeted everyone with the same degree of regard—commendable behavior, as far as Boyd was concerned. While he respected that every culture had its own rules, it nonetheless bothered him when someone refused to shake hands with a woman or someone they deemed inferior to them. This tribe clearly didn't operate that way. They were remarkable for having a female healer, for the secrecy that clothed their village, and for their inclusivity. He was excited to learn more about them.

If they made it.

"Please, come and sit. We have some refreshments."

Everyone came to the table except Hargreaves, Simon, and Jaali, and Boyd let that be. Jaali brought over a glass of milk, a plate of fruit, and more fig and mango jam for the warrior, who took the slice of bread Joseph had cut and started slathering it with butter and jam. Boyd took in more details as Sironka ate. His red robes had a pattern of horizontal white and blue lines, and a dagger was tucked into the carved leather sheath on his waist. His spear rested against the table's edge as he drank the entire glass of milk.

"A good cow," he said, "but not as good as the ones I own, I think." He laughed, and Joseph clapped him on the back and joined him.

"I expect no one in the village has cows as good as yours, Sironka," Joseph said as Jaali appeared with a pitcher of milk. "How was your journey?"

"Pleasant." He held out his glass for more milk. "There were many good signs. How has your journey been? Mr. and Mrs. Hale, is this the first time you've been to our lands?"

"I came many years ago," Arthur said. "It is a pleasure to be back."

This was the world-traveled journalist talking, not the grumpy retiree who bitched about peppermint liniment. He rather liked both sides of the man, he had to admit.

"This is my first visit, Sironka," Clara said, "but I've already decided it won't be my last. I expect some of Arthur's grandchildren might return with me after I tell them about this place. It truly is beautiful."

"Wait until you see our land, Mrs. Hale," Sironka said. "Is everyone prepared to leave today?"

Boyd felt Michaela take his hand under the table and clench it. Was she holding her breath like he was? Had Joseph been able to talk Sironka around? Or maybe the whole them-being-a-couple thing wasn't as important to the visions as Joseph had thought. Boyd certainly wasn't going to ask for clarification.

"We are, good man," Arthur said with an emphatic nod, "although if you would like a few more hours to rest before we leave, my backside will thank you."

"Oh Arthur! I don't think Sironka traveled all this way to hear *that*." Clara swatted him as Sironka laughed loudly.

"My grandfather would say the same, I expect, if he had to endure a trip in that Land Rover for days," Sironka said. "You are a brave man, Mr. Hale. Mrs. Hale, that goes for you and Hargreaves too."

"It's nice to have someone appreciate our age, Sironka," Clara said with a smile, "but like I tell everybody, I feel decades younger than I am—and I plan to live until I'm a hundred."

"I expect you will do so," Sironka said. "The gods favor you both. Come, I will help break down the camp. Then we can depart."

Michaela tightened her grip on Boyd's hand. He looked over at Joseph, who smiled and shrugged when their eyes met.

Sironka rose and picked up his spear. "Mrs. Hale, would you mind making me a handicraft on our journey? It would be a great honor for me to wear it."

The warrior lent her a hand, and she rose to her feet. "I'd love to. I read the Maasai wear red because they believe the lions fear the color. It just so happens I brought some red yarn with me. Come, tell me what you'd fancy. I'll show you what I'm making Arthur. I love your robe, by the way. Can I hold your spear?"

Arthur was shaking his head as Clara and Sironka walked off to her tent. "Well, that was easy. Seems we're a go for the rest of the trip. We might have a good story brewing, after all. What in the world were you two so worried about?"

Boyd was wondering the same.

"I'd better watch that Sironka with my woman," Arthur said with a wink. "She's so beautiful, men just can't help themselves." He rose and hobbled off after them.

Once the others were out of hearing, Boyd turned to Joseph. "Anything else to add, my friend?"

Joseph stood, chuckling. "I'll only say the gods clearly favor this journey. I'll make myself ready."

When he left, Michaela squeezed Boyd's hand. She hadn't once let it go. "Oh. Boyd! We're going, we're going, we're going!"

"Seems we are, Mickey. See, I told you we had nothing to worry about."

Her gaze fell to his lips before rising to meet his eyes. She wanted to kiss him, and God knew, he wanted to kiss her as much as he wanted to go to the Valley of Stars.

"I'm going to kiss you right now," he said, lowering his head. "If you don't want—"

She cut him off by pressing her lips to his. His heart exploded with hope, and he closed his eyes, wanting to savor the moment. Maybe this meant the visions had been of them in the future.

"I promised you we'd find the Valley of Stars together," he whispered against her lips. He'd promised it on their second date over a year and a half ago. Did she remember?

"Yes, you did."

When she edged away, he opened his eyes. She was smiling in that secret way of hers.

Pride flooded him at the realization that *he* had made her smile like that this time, not a baby elephant.

He wanted to shout to the heavens. Instead, he kissed her on the lips again. "There's something I'd like to show you."

It was time. If he wanted her to open her heart to him again, he needed to be honest.

He reached into his pocket for his wallet. He opened it and drew out her engagement ring.

Her gasp carried across the camp.

"I'm not proposing right now, but I needed to show this to you. I was planning on asking you to marry me when I came home from Hendricks with my job offer. I'd even asked your dad."

She reeled back. "What?"

He cleared his throat to cover the hurt he still felt from that memory. "Things didn't go like I'd expected that day, but I've been carrying your ring around in my pocket every day since. I told myself I'd fix things...that I'd propose someday, and you'd say yes. I made good on my promise about the Valley of Stars, and here's another promise. If you'll let me, I'll love you for the rest of my life. And I'll buy you a bigger and better ring when I can afford it."

"Don't talk like that! It's beautiful." Tears—an alarming sign—were filling her eyes, and she reached for the ring, only to snatch her hand back. "Why didn't you tell me all this before?"

"Because your reaction to me getting my dream job hurt my pride," he said harshly. "It didn't feel like a good time to ask you to marry me. And maybe I was afraid you'd toss the ring in my face. You were mad enough."

"Oh, Boyd, I don't know what to say," she said, her voice cracking. "Last night...I was wrong to use the trip as an excuse to do what I wanted."

The emotion in her voice gave him the courage to lean forward. She closed the distance, and their mouths met again. Softly. Oh so sweetly. Longing rushed up in him, and he had to put a lid on the corresponding hurt.

"I'm glad you still want me, Mickey, but I meant what I said. I want you back all the way." He kissed her again, long and lingering, not caring that they were in the middle of the camp. "Think about that as we travel to the village. I'll await your answer."

He pocketed her ring and left the table.

Right now, he felt like luck was on his side. Maybe Joseph was right and the gods favored them. He didn't much care about the why of it.

He only wanted his Michaela back beside him.

CHAPTER 11

MICHAELA DIDN'T CARE THAT OTHERS WERE TAKING DOWN their tents in the camp and packing up. She was in the middle of a major emotional crisis.

Boyd had wanted to marry her, exactly what she'd wanted for their future together, and he'd even bought her a ring. A beautiful ruby. How could he talk about buying her something bigger and better? She'd wanted to sock him for saying that. Money again! Her family had never wanted for it, no, but her parents had taught them all that a bigger price tag didn't make one thing inherently better than another.

Oh, she needed to talk to her sister.

Eyeing her phone lying next to her on her bed, she broke her cardinal rule and called Caitlyn. Wasn't it a miracle they had cell coverage anyway? Hopefully, the fact that her sister's lavender farm in Provence was in a similar time zone would prompt another miracle: she'd answer.

When she did, Michaela closed her eyes and gave thanks to the Universe above.

"Mickey! What are you doing calling? Are you okay?"

"Oh, Caitlyn! I had to call you. I need advice. Help. I don't know. Boyd just told me he'd planned on proposing before I broke things off."

"Propose? No way!"

"He even asked Dad! I can't believe Dad didn't say anything." Probably because he'd known she was so upset. Her mom would have cautioned him against interfering. But still...

"He asked *Dad*? That's gutsy. Wow! I wouldn't have thought Boyd would go so traditional."

"Me either." And yet, he did traditional things like pull her chair out for her, help her with her jacket, or carry the groceries. She'd balked at that sometimes—something that had made him angry, she remembered. "I'm going crazy here. I mean, we're leaving for the Valley of Stars in a few minutes—"

"That's great, Mickey. It's been your dream."

"And then Boyd takes out this ring—"

"He has it with him? Wowza! Keep going."

"He wants me back the whole way. I mean, he even... Oh, crap, this is a little embarrassing. I might have been open to having sex with him again. Nothing long-term in my head. But he wouldn't go for it. He said he didn't want that."

"My head is spinning. That's a lot to take in."

"I know, and I don't have long to talk. We need to leave."

"Okay, let's dial it back. I'm going to take a page out of Ibrahim's playbook here since he helped me sort through my own issues."

They'd dubbed Caitlyn's master perfume maker the Perfume Jedi, a nickname he'd earned for asking questions about a person's truest desires and motivations. "Is he close by?"

"No, he's with Beau talking about the men's cologne. Mickey, here's question number one: what do *you* want?"

She remembered the way Boyd had looked at her as he held the ring out, his eyes full of vulnerability and sadness. She'd crushed him, and it struck her that it must have taken a massive amount of courage for him to approach her again. Heck, he'd given her the Valley of Stars. But that wasn't the question Caitlyn had asked her. "Oh, I don't know. I need to think about it."

"Good thing you'll have plenty of time in the savannah to do just that," Caitlyn said. "Now for question number two."

"Okay, but then I have to go," she said, standing and pacing in the narrow space.

"What is it about being with Boyd that scares you most? Oh, and what is it about being with him that makes you feel something no one else can give you? I remember you telling me that's how you felt right before you asked him to move in with you."

She had concluded rather scientifically that she'd never exhibited the kind of feelings or responses with anyone like she had with Boyd. "I remember. We had a mushroom pizza and way too much wine at my place."

"You thought he was the One then. What changed? And has something else changed now that you know he wants to marry you?"

Had it? Did the M-word carry that kind of power? She gulped. Yeah, it kinda did, or this wouldn't have thrown her. "God! Spending all that time with Ibrahim has made you way too intense. So many questions, Caitlyn."

"But you're good with questions, Mickey. It's why you're a scientist. Why don't you break this problem down with one of your charts?"

"I *am* logical," she said, but then she sank back onto the narrow bed. "But loving Boyd isn't logical. That's always been the problem."

"Your love for plants isn't logical either, but somehow you've made it work," Caitlyn said, and Michaela could hear the smile in her voice.

"That's something to think on. Okay, I have to run. Have I told you how grateful I am for you?"

"I don't know that I was much help, but I'm always here for you. I love you, Mickey. Now go have fun finding your dream. And tell Aunt Clara, Uncle Arthur, and Hargreaves we miss them."

"I will. My love to Beau and the Perfume Jedi. Thanks, Caitlyn. You're the best."

"I feel like it these days. Bye, Mickey."

"Bye!"

She stood, phone in hand, and took several deep breaths. Her respiration needed to slow to combat her anxiety; it was a medical fact. Perhaps Caitlyn had been right about the chart, only there was one issue.

She hated to think of Boyd as a problem.

Now more than ever.

"Mickey!" Boyd called. "We need to break down your tent. Are you finished doing...whatever you're doing?"

God, she hoped he hadn't heard her on the phone. She'd tried to talk in her inside voice, but her emotions had gotten away from her.

It struck her that Connor was the person she should have called, the person she needed to call. She wouldn't think about the time on his end.

"Just a minute," she called out to Boyd. "I need to call Connor."

She heard him shuffle off as she dialed her brother's number.

"Michaela," he answered immediately. He sounded exhausted, and she felt a prickle of guilt.

"I'm sorry if I woke you."

"I wasn't asleep yet. Sleep and I haven't been seeing eye to eye for a while now."

She wanted to ask if he'd been struggling with the problem since their cousin Corey's death, but Connor didn't like to talk about that. He and Corey had been inseparable, and she knew her brother felt personally responsible for the accident that had claimed Corey's life on a Merriam offshore oil rig. The accident hadn't been anyone's fault, but try telling Connor that. "I'm worried about you."

"Don't be," he said, his voice turning hard. "I don't have any news on Iggie. Customs is being extremely disagreeable. One of their top officials asked my emissary to make an over-the-top bribe, and I'm loath to give it to the bastard."

"Understandable. Let me update you on my end. An emissary of the village that presides over the Valley of Stars arrived this morning. He plans to take us thcre. Today. I don't see waiting for Iggie."

Plus, she didn't want to do anything to change Sironka's mind. She didn't know if Joseph's descriptions about the couple from the visions had been wrong or irrelevant in the end. She sure as hell wasn't going to ask Sironka about it. Then she wondered: could Boyd have made up the story about the visions, hoping to get her back? He'd said he would do anything.

Except she knew him better than to think that. No, he wouldn't play games when it came to the Valley of Stars.

Connor was silent on the line before saying, "Tell me about the emissary."

Since she didn't know much, it didn't take long.

"Okay, I don't see the purpose of waiting either, but I don't like this additional person, Michaela. Boyd should have mentioned it. It makes me wonder what else he's been withholding."

Michaela didn't think it was a good time to share that Boyd was traveling with her engagement ring in his wallet. *His wallet!* Was he insane? What if a pickpocket had lifted it in Nairobi? Oh, her mind was running away with her.

"Look, your insistence on including Iggie made Boyd a little worried about you too," she decided to share. "But everything is good now. Honestly, I think Iggie being away in Nairobi—"

"He's not away, Michaela. He's being held by Customs officials. As for—"

"All I'm saying is that Iggie isn't the sort to inspire teamwork, Connor. He spent less than twenty-four hours with Uncle Arthur, Aunt Clara, and Hargreaves, yet he managed to rub them the wrong way."

"I don't care," he said harshly. "I wanted him there as an extra set of eyes and ears, especially since you seem to wear rose-colored glasses where Boyd is concerned."

"That's not fair! I'm acting in Merriam Enterprises' best interest, and I don't appreciate you saying otherwise. Fieldwork requires a certain set of skills, Connor, and Iggie doesn't have them."

"We're not going to agree on this. Call me from the village on the sat phone with an update. Do you have any idea where it is from your current location? I've got your camp pulled up on my screen right now."

Had Flynn rigged that up for him? "I'm not sure. It's in between the Loita Hills and the Sekenani Valley."

"Like that means anything to me," he said with a sigh. "All right, just be careful, okay? I don't like the idea of your guide being some Maasai warrior. I imagine he's taking you to a place with even more warriors."

"Maasai warriors are some of the best warriors remaining in the world, Con," she said, purposefully misunderstanding his worry. She doubted Connor would feel better hearing Aunt Clara was going to make Sironka a scarf or something, although it was completely charming.

"If that were true, they wouldn't have lost to the British."

He was being rude—she'd blame it on his fatigue. "I don't want to get into a debate over history, Connor. I need to go. We're packing up camp. Aunt Clara and Uncle Arthur are doing great, by the way. Elders are much admired by the Maasai."

"I'm delighted to hear it. The thought of you traveling with two eighty-year-olds, an equally old butler, a Maasai warrior, and your ex-boyfriend will make me fall asleep like a baby."

Sometimes she wanted to sock him. "Goodbye, Connor."

"Remember to call me with an update, and take care of yourself. I mean it. This new element makes me nervous. I've never given any thought to the kind of danger you might be in on these trips. I'm seriously re-thinking your scope of work. Goodbye."

He hung up on her, and she stared at the phone. Rethinking her scope of work? What in Hades was he talking about? Then it clicked. Corey had died on the job, and now he had danger on the brain.

"I'm coming out," she yelled, exiting her tent. Sure enough, everyone else had packed up. Aunt Clara was sitting in the back seat of one of the Rovers, showing her knitting to Sironka, who sat next to her. Uncle Arthur was in the front passenger seat with Joseph in the driver's position.

Boyd gave Michaela a pointed look. "Have a nice call?"

"Connor says nothing's changed on the Iggie front. He's still detained."

"May I pack up your tent, Dr. Michaela?" Simon asked.

Nodding, she took a step toward him, intending to help. Boyd caught her arm. "Let him. How did Connor take the news?"

She didn't plan on filling him in on the entire conversation. Some of it would only get his back up. "He wasn't thrilled, but he gave us the green light to move on. I'm going to call him from the village."

"Great! Anything to make Connor feel better. Did you tell him about us?"

She made a rude sound. "And what exactly would I tell him?"

His mouth tipped up. "That I'm going to protect the woman I intend to marry. He needn't worry."

She socked him. "Stop saying things like that. I'm in a quandary. How could you spring something like that on me? We're supposed to be out here working, Boyd."

"We are. And contrary to what you thought when we broke up, I do want to work with you. All the way."

His words unsettled her even more because she knew he meant it to his bones.

"You're driving with me today. Hargreaves is driving with Simon and Jaali."

"But I don't want to drive alone with you," she said, hating the plaintive tone in her voice. "I want to go with Sironka so I can ask him about the valley."

"He's the one who suggested going with your aunt and uncle and Joseph," Boyd said. "Seems he's very taken with your family. Arthur is hoping to pepper him with questions, I imagine. Did you tell your aunt to bring red yarn or was that another incredible sign from the gods that everything was going to go well?"

A shadow fell over them, and she looked up to see an eagle fly overhead.

"Dr. Boyd! Dr. Michaela." Joseph pointed to the sky. "That's a black-chested snake eagle. A very rare sighting. He lives in my cousin's forest. It's another sign."

"Boyd!" Aunt Clara called. "Sironka says that eagle eats lizards. Be sure Marvin is stored in his carrier. We'd hate to have him snatched up for lunch. You'll have to show Sironka your gecko later. I've been telling him all about the snakes you had when you were a kid."

Boyd seemed remarkably untroubled by that, given he was usually so reticent to share the story. He merely waved a hand at the Rover. "She's a natural ambassador. I won't have to tell Sironka anything by the time we make camp tonight. Now, I think we've had enough signs for one morning. Let's go before the sky darkens or the sun eclipses."

He was mostly kidding, she knew. She watched as Simon finished packing up her tent. She wouldn't feel bad for not helping. "You've gotta respect the signs."

"Oh, I respect them. Joseph," he called out, "if you

see an animal that means there's to be a wedding, let me know." He gave her a cheeky wink.

A wedding! She opened her mouth to give him a pithy response, but her mind went blank. Oh, no. Was it a bad sign if her brain was failing her?

"Let's go, Mickey." He pointed her in the direction of their Rover. "The Valley of Stars awaits."

***

It was official. Clara Merriam Hale was living her best life.

The golden savannah was fading behind her as they drove into the greener hills of a valley whose name she couldn't quite pronounce, and here she was sitting next to a well-muscled warrior who'd asked her to knit something for him. Thank goodness she'd brought the red yarn. Selecting which yarn to bring had been the most impossible part of packing for this trip, but something had guided her to choose the red. Now, her work was going to adorn a bona fide warrior. Pinch her.

She patted Arthur on the shoulder so he'd know she was feeling a bit smug.

He turned slowly in the seat, alerting her to his discomfort. She patted him again in sympathy. Who'd known the hills would be even bumpier than the savannah?

"How long until we reach your village?" she asked Sironka, who was looking out across the land. The regal line of his jaw was compelling, as was the strong bridge of his nose. Would it be rude to ask if he'd ever killed a lion? She knew from her reading it was a rite of passage for a Maasai warrior. When she thought about it, she wasn't sure she wanted to know. She'd feel bad for the lion, even though she understood their tribe felt they were honoring the lion with the hunt.

"As long as it takes," Sironka replied.

She heard Arthur bark out a laugh.

"Arthur always says that," she explained. "Apparently, he must have some Maasai blood I didn't know about."

"We would be honored to have Mr. Hale in our tribe," Sironka said. Although she'd made numerous requests for him to use their first names, he continued to refer to them formally. "He is rather like an old lion. Still hungry even after roaming the land all these years."

This time she laughed. "It's like you know him, Sironka. Now, what else can you tell us about your village?"

"Everyone is looking forward to your visit," Sironka said. "We have been waiting a long time, but now the time is right. There will be a great celebration when you arrive."

She wondered what constituted a long time. "That sounds wonderful, Sironka. Tell me about your mother and father. They are both medicine people?"

"Healers, you say in English. *Laibon*."

She repeated the word, and he nodded.

"My father is also the *oloiboni*," he said, folding his hands in his lap. "The spiritual leader, although this sometimes amuses my mother. She's as much *oloiboni* as my father, but the Maasai are patriarchal. My tribe less so than most."

Arthur turned around in his seat, his journalistic keenness evident in his blue eyes. "In what way, Sironka?"

His dark, angular face was striking in profile as he gestured across the lands they were crossing. "Our tribe broke away from the clan of the hyena before the British came to Kenya. The chief's son went out to kill his first lion like that one over there."

Clara followed the line of his finger to the grassy ridge a far distance off, and when she squinted, she could make out the lion sunning itself. Goodness, Sironka had remarkable eyesight. "They are beautiful, aren't they?"

He nodded. "Unfortunately for the chief, his son returned saying he'd found a wounded lion in a field of flowers and used the flower to restore the lion to health. He hadn't seen the honor in killing a wounded beast."

Clara was enthralled. "What happened when the lion was restored to health?"

Sironka smiled. "The story goes that the lion looked the man in the eyes. It's said in that moment, he knew he was meant to be a healer and not a warrior. His father threw him and all his wives out of the clan, only his mother wouldn't stand for it. The chief told her she could go as well. She practiced healing, although she had never been allowed to become a *laibon*, and when she accompanied her son, it's said he gave her the station to honor her sacrifice. From then on, men and women could be *laibon* in the new tribe the chief's son started if they had the gift for healing."

"How incredible," Clara said, hanging onto the cab as they hit another bump. "But women still can't be warriors?"

Sironka laughed loudly. "My father says women are the greatest warriors. They give birth. That battle is enough to ask of them."

Clara had never faced that particular battle, and the new regret she'd been feeling rose within her. Arthur said it was a pointless regret, especially given the number of young people in their lives, but he didn't understand. She now felt like she'd missed one of the most important aspects of being a woman.

"Your father is a wise man, indeed," Arthur said. "I couldn't have said it better. What about these visions I heard Boyd mention? Something about a couple?"

Joseph looked over his shoulder suddenly, and Clara almost called out that he should keep his eyes on the road given all the deep craters. But she wasn't a backseat driver.

She swatted Arthur on the shoulder instead. What was he doing? Trying to get a psychic prediction on whether Boyd and Michaela would end up together? As far as she was concerned, they didn't need one. The way they'd kissed in the middle of camp earlier certainly suggested a reunion was in the works.

"The couple that was to come," Sironka said. "My mother and father both had visions of them."

"We'd be delighted to hear about such visions, Sironka." Clara gave him a winning smile. "In our country, such things aren't as common, so you'll forgive my husband's interest. He's a journalist, and as such, loves to ask questions. With your permission, he might even write an article about our journey and such."

"Clara, I can tell him what I'm about," Arthur said with a growl.

"See, he even growls like a lion," Clara said, patting Sironka on the arm. She hoped that was okay. It wasn't every day one got to converse with a Maasai warrior. Oh, she couldn't wait to fill Hargreaves in when they arrived at their destination.

"I give up trying to get a word in edgewise," Arthur said. "Hey, Sironka, do you separate the men and women at this celebration we're having? I'll be able to talk without interruption then."

"We do not as an official rule," Sironka said with a laugh, "but men and women often congregate in groups. I imagine Mrs. Hale here will find many friends, as will you, Mr. Hale."

"And do you take more than one wife in your tribe as well, Sironka?" Arthur turned his head to look at her, a cheesy grin on his face.

"Like you could handle another wife," she said dryly.

"That's what my tribe says about taking more than one wife," Sironka said with a chuckle. "Not every man can handle it."

"Can you?" Clara asked Sironka. "Maybe I'll stay with Sironka here, Arthur, since you're so upset about my loquaciousness."

"You two sound like my parents," the warrior said. "They too have known each other for many seasons."

Seasons. Clara thought of all the seasons she'd gone without Arthur. It had been like living in perpetual winter. "I suppose there's only one man I want, after all."

Arthur extended his hand to her behind his seat, and she took it.

"You two make a beautiful couple," Sironka said, his smile bright. "It is an honor to be with you."

She supposed they weren't too bad.

CHAPTER 12

SIX WELL-MUSCLED WARRIORS HAD BEEN WAITING FOR THEM at the edge of the river in front of three hand-carved boats. Good news, they had two warriors in each boat to row them to their destination. Boyd hated rowing, and while Michaela could do it in a pinch, it wasn't her forte. Bad news, the boats weren't going to hold much of their supplies.

The other warriors didn't speak English, but Clara and Arthur were talking with them via Sironka. To Boyd's amusement, the tall, fit warrior was showing his friends the red yarn Clara was going to use to knit him something. Hargreaves stood amongst the group, inquiring about some of the warrior's spears and other jewelry, with Joseph translating. Boyd gestured to Michaela to step aside so they could huddle.

"How is your family going to feel about leaving behind more of their possessions?" he asked her. "Certainly, we won't be able to bring our full stock of food. You and I are used to eating on the trail, but your relatives might not be up to Maasai cuisine."

She dragged her hand across her forehead. Yeah, he was sweating too. The farther they climbed into the hills, the steamier it had become, the vegetation changing radically different everywhere they turned, from lush green to dry and back again. He'd caught sight of several plants he recognized: *juniperus* trees used for hut construction and fencing, *crassulaceae* for aches and pains, and *acokanthera schimperi* to make the poison the warriors sometimes dip their arrows in. Still, he wished they could take more time to study the plant life. Maybe on the way back.

"My aunt seems to be bosom buddies with Sironka," Michaela said, "so she'll be game. It's Uncle Arthur I'm concerned about. After driving four hours over those ruts, he's walking stiffer. Now we're climbing into boats for a few hours, according to Sironka. I'm a spring chicken in comparison, and even I'm a little achy."

He put his arm around her shoulders and rubbed. "You're doing great, but I'll rub your butt if it would help."

"Tempting, but I'll pass for now."

"I'd say you don't know what you're missing, but you do." He gave her a wicked grin. "And you're not wearing a bra today, which is driving me nuts. Come on."

She shook her head in annoyance. "If I wear one, it drives you nuts. If I don't, you're still obsessed. Boyd, focus! Hargreaves seems to be managing well. He pumped Sironka's warrior friends' hands with extra enthusiasm, I thought."

"Hargreaves is game like your aunt," Boyd said. "But I'm still concerned about leaving behind the equipment. Does your family really understand the kind of hut they'll be sleeping in tonight?"

"Perhaps we should ask Hargreaves," Michaela said. "Jaali seems content to stay behind with Simon. Sironka promised no one would bother our cars or supplies." To ensure it was so, one of his warrior friends was staying behind as well, a tall, brawny one named Kasaine. Boyd knew he would also help protect Simon and Jaali.

"He also says we'll only be gone a few days," Boyd said. "That suggests the valley is close."

"You're assuming a few days means the same thing we think it means," Michaela said.

"Right. Hargreaves! Can you come here for a moment? Joseph, you too!"

Both men excused themselves and came over.

"Hargreaves," Boyd said, "I wondered if you had thoughts about Arthur and Clara's fitness for the next leg of the journey. We won't be able to bring our tents or food, being guests of the tribe, which will mean sleeping in mud huts and eating Maasai cuisine."

Hargreaves thought on that for a moment, then said, "Madam is especially eager to visit the village, and Mr. Hale seems to be keen from what I can tell. If you'd like, I would be happy to ask them personally. Sironka told Madam that while he'd be honored to have us stay with their tribe forever, he expected it would be for three or four days at most."

Boyd glanced at Michaela, raising his brow. Clara seemed to have all the relevant information.

"He understands we all have things to get back to," Hargreaves said.

"Yes, please ask them," Boyd said.

"Joseph, what kind of food can we expect at the village?" Hargreaves asked, his tan shirt still looking shockingly crisp. Maybe butlers didn't sweat.

Joseph wiped his brow. "Meat from cattle. Milk. Honey. Corn. Cabbage. Potatoes. Sironka joked in the Rover with Mrs. Hale that he and his tribe didn't expect them to drink the ceremonial cow's blood mixed with milk after she asked about tonight's ceremony."

He caught Michaela trying to disguise her wince. Yeah, both of them would have tried it if asked, but he was relieved. "Pertinent information, Joseph. Thank you."

"I suspect Madam and Mr. Hale might already be aware of what they can expect, Dr. McClellan, but I will confirm it. Excuse me a moment."

They watched as he made his way back to the group and politely drew Arthur and Clara away. They listened intently to him, and then Clara waved dismissively in their direction. Arthur was shaking his head as Clara led him back to Sironka and the warriors.

"Your aunt makes a lot of hand gestures like you do, Mickey," Boyd said, laughing. "Do you Merriams have Italians in your family tree?"

"I don't know actually." But she seemed tickled by the realization that she and Clara had something in common.

Hargreaves crossed the grassy knoll to join them. "Madam says they're on board."

"Wonderful," Boyd said, somehow not surprised. "Michaela, do you want to help me throw the essentials into a couple of bags?"

"I will handle Madam and Mr. Hale's packing," Hargreaves said.

He fought a curse. "Hargreaves, I don't mean to be rude, but how do you know what they'll need? Have you ever been to a remote village?"

The man looked down his nose at him. "It's my job to know, Dr. McClellan. If you'll excuse me, I will make the proper inquiries and see to my duties. Joseph, I will need you for translating."

Joseph's mouth was twitching. "If you'll excuse me."

Moments later, Hargreaves was conferring with a warrior, Joseph by his side.

"Never let it be said anyone can catch Hargreaves flat-footed," Boyd said, shaking his head. He couldn't help but respect the man for it.

"I can't wait to tell my siblings how unflappable he is," Michaela said. "He's been on point for some pretty impressive things, but this... Did you know he plays the flamenco guitar? He gave Caitlyn's fiancé lessons."

"I'll remember that if I need to serenade a crocodile,"

Boyd said. "Speaking of, did you see the monsters lurking on the far side of the river?"

"Yes," she said with a shiver. "Where there are crocs, there'll be hippos. The thought of going through a crowd of hippos in one of those boats makes my gut churn. The dead-eyed crocodile is bad enough." She reached out to touch him. "Something about this feels...wrong. I might need some distracting as we travel upriver."

He covered her hand, his heart soaring in his chest. Although he knew what she meant—it felt like they'd been too lucky so far—his mind was stuck on the fact that she'd finally reached out to him. "I promise to regale you with my good humor the whole way. Don't worry, Mickey. We have two warriors in each boat. We'll be fine. Come on."

They did their best to repack only the necessities. An hour later, they bid Simon and Jaali goodbye and settled into the boats—Michaela with Boyd, Hargreaves with Joseph, and Arthur and Clara with Sironka.

As they pushed off, Boyd steeled himself for an uncomfortable few hours. He'd traveled in life-threatening waters before. At least they weren't on the Amazon. That river was no picnic, the brown river water disguising any number of dangers like the electric eels or piranhas. And yet, Michaela was right. He had a bad feeling about this.

But it was the only way they'd get to the Valley of Stars.

Maybe that was part of the reason no one else had gotten to the valley. When he'd counted at least twenty hippos, and an equal number of crocs, he decided to stop tallying them. They were in dangerous waters. Literally.

"You good, Marvin?" he asked. His buddy's travel terrarium was zipped closed and tucked between his legs. Tokays were nocturnal, so he'd likely be asleep, but that had never stopped Boyd from talking to him.

Boyd had positioned Michaela in front of him, and when he noticed a little tremor in her shoulders, he reached out and rubbed them. "How about you, babe?"

"Getting into a Zen place," she said in an uneasy voice. "I could use a joke."

So could he. "How about this one? A biologist, a pale-ontologist, and a herpetologist all walk into a bar..."

The fact that she didn't groan told him just how un-settled she was as the boat began gliding through the wa-ter. It struck him that the boats looked like a line of ducks, but he doubted Michaela would be amused if he compared them to sitting ducks just now, so he continued his litany of corny one-liners, most of which didn't make Michaela laugh, as he watched the warriors' paddles cut through the water. It felt like his mouth was operating separately from his body, which was on high alert.

When a crocodile emerged from some greenery on the opposite shore and slithered into the water, Michaela's shoulders tensed. He raised his hands to rub them, and she jumped and let out a yawp.

"Easy there, babe. I was only trying to help relax you."

"I won't relax until we're off this river," she said, her muscles like boulders.

Still, he continued to rub them, if only for the pleasure of touching her. "You know I'd never let anything happen to you."

She turned slowly, careful not to rock the boat. "You always say that, and while it's sweet, we both know some-thing out of your control could happen." As if she'd just issued a dare, something big bumped the boat, and she gasped and grabbed his hand.

"Easy," he breathed out, his stomach clenching. "You know what I missed about you while we were apart?" The jokes weren't working. Maybe this situation called for a healthy dose of truth.

"What?"

"The little freckles under the knuckles on your fingers. I think that might make me super weird, but I don't care. I love them."

"You *are* weird, Boyd," she said, her voice breathless. "But I like that about you."

"I like that you're weird too," he said, hearing the bump again under their feet. His gut seized up. "The warrior at the helm seems pretty calm, doesn't he? I mean, if there's a hippo or croc under us, he'd look more tense, right?"

"Shut up, Boyd," she said, shaking her hair back when a fly buzzed close to her. "Uncle Arthur just took Aunt Clara's hand."

"I'll take your hand," he said, reaching out to her. "I'd find it comforting, if you need a reason."

"I know you hate this part of the trip as much as I do," she whispered. "How long did he say it would take? A couple hours, right? How long has it been?"

"I never wear a watch, remember?" Boyd said, wishing he could laugh. "Sironka has a surprisingly good sense of humor. I didn't know warriors laughed that much."

Marvin croaked then, and the warrior at the helm turned sharply in his seat. He motioned with his free hand at the gecko's travel carrier. "Easy, buddy," Boyd said, patting the nylon.

"He always gets agitated when he feels a threat," Michaela said. "Based on the look our guide just gave you, he doesn't seem too pleased to have him on board."

"I wasn't about to leave him behind; no one handles him like me. Or you."

"He's a sweetheart," Michaela said. "Just has trust issues like other Tokays. *Oh!*"

Marvin croaked again as another bump sounded beneath them. The whole boat shuddered. Boyd looked to the right. It felt like something had hit them on the side this time.

"I really don't like this, Boyd," Michaela said, clenching his hand. "It doesn't feel right."

Acid churned in his stomach. He put his hand on Marvin's carrier, his mouth going dry. "Easy, boy! We're all okay here. Mickey, focus on a happy place. How about we take off to a private villa in Bali after this trip? Just you and me?"

"I like the villa part," she said through clenched teeth. "I'm still considering the second part."

That sounded promising, but he didn't have an opportunity to question her. Another bump shook the entire boat, causing the warrior in front to reach for his spear. That couldn't be good. "Consider faster, Mickey. By the way, this seems like a good moment to tell you I love you. Always have. Always will."

"Shut up, Boyd." She squeezed his hand so hard the bones seemed to rub together. "Focus on that villa." She lowered her voice. "I'm waiting for you to come out of the water, and I'm not wearing anything."

Shock rolled through him, pulling his mouth into a grin that slipped as the boat shuddered again. "You give me that visual. My brain can't focus on anything right now, Mickey, but—"

The boat shuddered again. The warrior at the helm stood slowly, spear in hand. Boyd looked over his shoulder, and his heart skipped a beat. The warrior at the back was in the same position. Well, at least they hadn't rocked the boat.

A wild part of him wanted to laugh at that thought, but they were slowing down. He turned around to see the boat behind them do the same. Joseph had his knife out. Jesus! Usually he was the soul of peace. Boyd couldn't see Hargreaves, who was sitting directly behind him. One of the warriors shouted something. Sironka stood slowly in the lead boat and spun around, calling out something in response. The other warrior with him stopped rowing. All three boats had come to a rolling stop in the river. Okay, *now* they were sitting ducks. Surely they knew what they were doing.

"I'm just going to remind you, Mickey, that we're in the hands of the tribe's best warriors." Something slithered in the water, and he caught a glimpse of gray-green knotted flesh. A croc!

"I really hate this, Boyd," Mickey said, rocking softly in place. "Tell me again why I love my job so much."

Marvin croaked as the boat shuddered, the wood creaking. "You like helping people—"

The boat lurched in the water as something rammed into it. Hard. Marvin croaked wildly, and Boyd fisted his hand around the carrier's handle out of instinct. The boat jolted again, and he was slammed forward into Michaela. The next time it happened, they were both pitched sideways into the water. The murky water surrounded him, but he kept ahold of Michaela, his jaw clenched hard so he wouldn't accidentally swallow any water. His other hand was still clutched around the handle of Marvin's carrier.

He couldn't see the threat, but he knew something was in the murky water with them.

Then he saw a large, dark shadow moving swiftly beneath the water. Eyes burning, he had to decide who to protect.

He dropped Marvin's carrier, knowing he couldn't hold on to them both, and dragged Michaela to the surface. She was sputtering and coughing as he tugged her closer, protecting her with his body from the behemoth in the water. Wild shouts and cries reached his ears. He squinted through burning eyes. God, he couldn't see squat.

He kicked with all his might and propelled her toward the closest boat. Joseph had his hands out, along with Hargreaves and the other two warriors on their boat. Someone shouted behind him, "Boyd, look out," and he shoved Michaela out of the water to them and swiveled, intending to put himself in the way of whatever was coming toward them.

He saw a hippo surface, its large nostrils spewing water, its eyes a deep brown. Something brushed his leg, and he fought the urge to flail in the water and strike at it. A croc? Another hippo? Jesus, he needed to get out of the water.

"Boyd!" Michaela screamed.

Heart racing, he turned and dove for the boat. Joseph and Hargreaves grabbed ahold of his wet shirt and then his shoulders, hauling him in.

"We've got him!" Hargreaves shouted.

Boyd fell to the bottom of the boat, knocking into the old butler, who promptly handed him a dry handkerchief. The warrior in the helm sliced the air with his spear, and the hippo disappeared. He saw now that the boat they'd been in had completely capsized, and both of the warriors had gone under too. One of them was hoisted aboard by Joseph, and when he scanned the water for the other, he saw him swimming hard for Arthur and Clara's boat. He hauled himself over the side, muscles rippling in the hot sun.

More shouts sounded, and he watched as Sironka returned to his station at the helm of the front boat and began rowing hard. The warrior in the back held his spear over the water. Boyd saw stars for a moment, his heart pounding in his chest, as their boat began to move again too.

"Mickey! Are you okay?" She was still coughing up river water.

"God, Boyd!" She was shaking, he realized, and although he was too, his concern was for her.

"Hand her something to drink," he shouted.

Hargreaves extended a bottle of water. "Here, sir."

"Manners at a time like this, Hargreaves?" Boyd asked, reaching past Joseph to deliver the bottle. "Here, Mickey. Drink it. Slowly."

"Too much water is my problem, Boyd," she said, her voice cracking as she coughed again. "I swallowed a whole bunch of it when something brushed me in the river."

They both knew there could be dozens of waterborne

diseases and microbes in the water. He was not going to freak out. Their medical kit had gone down with the boat, and it was the only one. Clara had brought another one, but he'd sent it back with her overflow luggage, assuming they wouldn't need two.

"You'll be fine, babe." She'd mentioned something brushing against her. Had it really been that close? God, he needed to touch her. Right now. "Joseph, change places with me. I need to be next to Mickey."

With three additional people in the boat, they were right on top of one another. The maneuver wasn't easy, and someone shouted something at them as Joseph awkwardly shifted positions with Boyd, but Boyd didn't care. His anxiety didn't ease up until his arms were around Michaela, her back hugged against his chest.

"You're okay." But Marvin wasn't, and now that he and Michaela were both safely on the boat, the horror of what had happened to his friend spread through him. He hadn't wanted to drop him, but he hadn't seen another way to protect Michaela. Dammit, he should have left him at home.

When Michaela put her hands over his, he burrowed his face into her shoulder, tears filling his eyes.

She seemed to fold into him. "Marvin?"

"I couldn't hold you both," he whispered.

"Oh, Boyd, no!" She started crying. "Not Marvin!"

"Michaela! Boyd!" Her uncle was shouting and waving at them from his position in the lead boat. "Are you two okay?"

"Getting there, Arthur," he called back, lifting his head. Clara was leaning around the big shoulders of a warrior who had his arm around her, her entire face tense with worry. "Sironka, if there's a shortcut, this would be a good time to take it."

The warrior didn't answer, only dug his paddle into the water faster. The other warrior's paddling matched his pace. Another croc emerged from the vegetation ahead, and this one was a fourteen-footer. Boyd thought he was going to get sick. But Mickey's soft crying tugged his attention to her. She needed him. He handed her the handkerchief.

"I don't normally cry," she said. "Sorry."

"Nothing to be sorry about. I have tears in my eyes too."

She shook herself. "Oh, God! We lost everything in that boat, including the sat phone. I won't be able to call Connor."

Her brother would think something was wrong when she didn't check in. "Do you want to go back?" he made himself ask.

If she said yes, he'd find a way to go numb. Right now, he couldn't imagine turning around and traveling in the other direction. It would feel like the loss of Marvin had been for nothing.

She turned her head to gaze up into his eyes. Her hair was plastered to her forehead. He pushed it back as best he could.

"Do you?" she asked softly. "You're the one who lost Marvin. I'm so sorry, Boyd."

He couldn't think about that now. "It's your call. We both know how our spill could have ended. Maybe your aunt and uncle should go back. They'd have a harder time swimming to safety."

"I have to ask them," she said softly. "Aunt! Uncle! Do you want to go back?" The river seemed deathly quiet after the attack, and her voice carried.

"And face that crazy hippo and his friends for round two?" her uncle shouted back. "No way! Clara, honey, what about you?"

"We go forward," she said, steel in her voice. "Did you lose Marvin, Boyd?"

His throat closed right up and he couldn't speak.

Michaela squeezed his hand. "Yes, Aunt," she shouted back.

"I'm sorry, Boyd," he heard her call out. "He was a good friend."

Boyd lowered his head to Michaela's shoulder, looking out across the brown, murky water. Yes, he had been.

But he suspected Marvin would have gladly given his life to protect Michaela.

Somehow, there was comfort in that thought.

CHAPTER 13

Michaela had never been so happy to put her feet on land.

She'd had a few scares in her various treks around the world, but her underwater excursion in a river full of hippos and crocs now topped the list. She knew she was still in shock from the slight shaking in her limbs, and Boyd didn't look much better. His normally golden skin color was gray and his eyes were glassy. He didn't normally cry, but she'd felt the heat of his tears against her shoulder. Poor Marvin.

Poor Boyd.

Her aunt and uncle rushed over and grabbed her into a hug, making her start.

"We were so scared," Aunt Clara said, banding her arms around her.

"We almost lost you," Uncle Arthur said, tears in his voice. "Don't do that to an old man."

Boyd was right. It was for the best that they'd gone into the water, not her aunt and uncle. It horrified her to think what would have happened to them.

"I shouldn't have brought you here," she whispered into Aunt Clara's shoulder. "This was a terrible idea."

"Hush," her aunt said, tightening her hold. "You're still wet and in shock. We'll take care of you now. Sironka says we don't have far to walk to his village. Are you up for it?"

Was there an alternative? "Oh, Aunt, Boyd let go of Marvin to help me."

"Of course he did," her uncle said in his matter-of-fact tone. "I know it's a loss, but losing you would be unthinkable, Michaela."

"Arthur is right," Aunt Clara said. "Boyd's in shock too. The faster we get to the village, the better. Honey, Hargreaves will get you and Boyd some dry clothes. He packed a fresh pair in his suitcase for each of us in case something happened to the luggage. A backup, he said."

Leave it to Hargreaves to be prepared for any contingency. Her clothes were damp and smelled like musky river water. "Some dry clothes would be great. Showing up at the village like this…"

"Who the hell cares," Uncle Arthur spat out. "They're lucky to see you walking after today."

"We won't speak of it anymore," her aunt finished, releasing her. "Hargreaves! Can you bring Michaela and Boyd something dry to change into?"

"Too bad we didn't pack a second sat phone," she said, knowing local phones wouldn't get a signal here. "Connor will be so worried."

"Your uncle already thought of that," Aunt Clara said. "Sironka is going to send back a couple warriors to Simon and Jaali. They both have cell phones, and they can drive around to look for coverage. We just need you to give them Connor's number and your message. I'd send Hargreaves back, but I can't do without him."

Hargreaves approached with a stack of clothes. She recognized some things for her and for Boyd. "Again, I'm terribly relieved you and Boyd survived your ordeal," he said kindly.

"Me too."

"Dr. McClellan seems remarkably upset over the loss of his reptile. He refused to change."

She took both sets of clothes from him. "Thank you, Hargreaves. I'll talk to him."

Boyd was talking to Joseph, but his gaze shifted to her as she approached them.

"I don't need to change, Mickey. We should get going. Joseph says we have about forty minutes of walking, but with your family, we might need a slower pace. God, what a trip! I never should have let Connor talk me into bringing them. Marvin should have stayed home too."

His voice wasn't the normal, steady one she knew. It quavered with tension and guilt.

"Joseph," she said quietly. "Would you excuse us for a moment?"

"Of course. I am so glad you and Dr. Boyd are safe. I am also sorry you learned the truth of one of our proverbs: a hippopotamus can be made invisible in dark water."

Leave it to Joseph to offer them a proverb at a time like this.

"And they kill three thousand people per year," Boyd said, his eyes glassy. "Glad we didn't join those ranks. Right, Joseph?"

She took Boyd's arm and led him toward the edge of the forest. The lush green trees, juniper and other varieties, were a stark contrast to the dry grasses of the savannah. The added dense brush would provide some privacy. "I'm going to change. Will you watch over me?" She needed to talk to him, and she figured her best bet was to appeal to his sense of protectiveness. Besides, she genuinely didn't want to be alone after their ordeal.

"I'm not changing," he said again, positioning himself in front of her as they walked into the glade, his head moving back and forth, scanning the terrain. "Joseph said Sironka was sending two warriors back—"

"I heard. It's better that Connor hears from someone."

"I thought about sending Joseph, but we need him."

He glanced around. "This seems to be a good spot. I don't see anything lurking around."

She didn't see or feel anything either, although monkeys were notorious for being mischievous in forests such as these. So long as it wasn't something predatory like a lion. She couldn't take that right now. "Agreed," she said, lifting her shirt and peering down. "God, I hope I don't have anything 'lurking' under my clothes. I had a moment in the boat when I thought— What is it?"

He was standing in front of a tree, his face leached of color. Staring at her. "I could have lost you."

She charged over to him. "I could have lost *you*!" The reality of it struck her like a physical blow. Losing him would have been agony.

"So you care about me?" He framed her face in his hands, hope now warring with the grief and guilt in his eyes.

"You know I do," she said, putting her free hand on his chest. The other still clutched the stack of clean clothes. "Boyd, this is where I tell you I decided."

"Thank God." He pushed the damp hair back from her face. "Then tell me."

She let out a harsh breath, knowing there was no going back. "I love you, and I want us to be together. I'm willing to work things out."

The hope in his eyes grew brighter, eclipsing those darker emotions, and he pressed his mouth to hers.

The shock, the scare had her opening her mouth to him. She wanted to devour him, and he clearly wanted the same since he thrust his tongue into her mouth and led her in a frenetic dance. He changed the angle of their mouths, clearly needing more. She did as well. The clothes dropped from her hands. She searched for the hem of his shirt and slid her hands under it, needing to touch his bare skin. That was all it took for his control to snap. He pushed her back against the tree, finding her breasts under her shirt and cupping them. Without a bra, his tugs on her nipples had her core burning with need.

Wrenching her mouth free, she gazed into his dark eyes. "*Now.*"

"Are you—"

"Yes!" She kissed him again, hard, as she unfastened his pants and tugged them down. His cock was hot and hard, and the feel of it in her hand made her belly clench. Rucking her panties and pants down to her knees, she leaned back against the tree with her hips tipped forward, a position they'd mastered in situations when a bed wasn't close by and stripping wasn't a wise option. He cupped her bottom in his hands, supporting her.

"I love you," he said as he penetrated her. "It would have killed me if anything had happened to you."

She moaned as she took his entire length, trying to muffle her cries. "Me too. Oh, Boyd, I missed you."

He slid out and then thrust in again. "There's no one but you, Mickey."

Then he started pumping, knowing she needed him. She raised her arms against the tree, biting her lip to control her moans as the heat built. His thrusts turned faster, deeper, harder, and another moan ripped out of her.

She closed her eyes as everything in her tightened, and then she came hard in his arms. He was shaking as he followed her over. He pulled her against his chest, holding her quietly as they came back to themselves. His fingers tangled in her hair as she listened to the beat of his heart. Today had been too close, and somehow that had made everything clear. Yes, they had their problems, but she loved him and he loved her. Surely they could figure the rest of it out.

"You want to know one of the reasons I love you?" she said softly, lifting her face to him like a flower to the sun.

He caressed her cheek. "Why? It's nice to be reminded after all these months in hell."

It had been hell for her too. "Because even after what happened today, you only suggested sending my aunt and uncle and Hargreaves back. Not me."

His mouth tipped up. "I might have aged twenty years today, but the possibility of sending you back didn't dawn on me. Despite how much I want to protect you, being here—doing what we do—it's who you are."

Yes, he had always understood that about her. She thought he was maybe the only person who did. "Let's talk about Marvin. It wasn't your fault."

He bowed his head. "I know that. Might take a while to sink in all the way. I thought about it on the boat afterward. I had a moment where I thought about taking him out of his carrier on the boat, but you know he's like a vampire in the daylight; plus, I knew his croaking upset the warriors. I worried it might escalate things."

"They were nervous when they heard him," she said. "And who knows how a hippo or croc might have reacted to his calls. Boyd, you did the best you could in a horrible situation. I feel guilty too."

He kissed her swiftly. "Don't. I realized Marvin would have gladly taken a dive to protect you, and that helped. I just hate the thought of him drowning like that. He didn't have a chance, and after everything he'd endured to make it this far..."

The tears in his eyes moved her. They'd both always been so tough, but losing Marvin was different. It struck deep. "You gave him more years than he would have had otherwise."

He rubbed the bridge of his nose. "Thanks for saying that. I don't know that I can do another pet after him." He took a deep breath, as if steeling himself, then said, "We should probably get you changed. And yes, I'll change too. Before, I didn't want to settle. I thought if I kept moving—"

"It's shock, Boyd, and it's okay. I'm still shaky too."

He caressed her back. "I'm grateful Sironka and the

others haven't sent a search party for us, although being Maasai, I'm not sure we'd hear them if they were a foot away."

"Not something I want to think about right now after the moment we just had," she muttered, looking around for any telltale flashes of red. She didn't see anything, so she handed his clothes to him.

"Hell of a forethought to pack extras," he said, starting to change as she did the same. "Maybe we need to bring a butler on our future treks."

She thought about those treks. Would they be doing them together? "Boyd," she whispered. "Today really scared me."

He pulled the shirt over his head and then cupped her cheek. "Me too, Mickey. I'm still thinking about that villa in Bali after this. Ready to join me? It won't be any fun without you."

She finished changing. "I'll need a steady supply of girly cocktails."

That prompted a laugh from him. "After today, I might drink them with you."

"Ah...I have to ask. Did you lose your wallet?"

He held it up as he shucked off his pants dramatically. "No, ma'am. Already checked. Your future merchandise is safe."

She'd wondered if her engagement ring was at the bottom of the river with everything else. The loss of it had been an ache in her heart, which had helped her see the truth.

The first easy smile of the day touched her face. "Good."

CHAPTER 14

ICHAELA'S FIRM GRIP ON BOYD'S HAND HELPED HIM
work through his shock and grief. She was back in
his life for good, and if there were an animal heaven—which
Boyd secretly wished were the case—he hoped Marvin
would know.

Sironka had taken it upon himself to usher Clara
through the final ascent to his village, and he still had his
arm around her as they reached the outside fencing. Hargreaves had kept pace with the other warriors, but Boyd and
Michaela had slowed down to keep Arthur company, using
their shock as the reason. He'd been puffing from the elevation, although Boyd had been quick to assure him the Loita
Hills were higher in elevation than his home in Dare Valley.

Of course, Arthur hadn't believed him, calling out for
Hargreaves to confirm it. Apparently the man was as versed
in trivia as he was in everything else. After Hargreaves' confirmation, Arthur had muttered, "A man my age shouldn't
take on elevation bigger than he was used to," but he'd kept
going.

"Arthur!" Clara called out. "You dear man. We made it."

He emitted a grumble, breathing hard. Boyd had
thought to lend him a hand as they walked, but the man's
pride was strong. He had to respect that.

Hundreds of people had gathered to greet them in the village, all dressed in the traditional red Maasai plaid, many of the women wearing beautiful braid-and-beadwork headdresses. But what almost stopped Boyd in his tracks was the smattering of elderly people in the crowd, their thickly shorn white hair stark against their dark skin. His skin broke into goose bumps. Life expectancy for the Maasai was in the low forties, and these folks looked to be in their seventies and eighties, if he were correct.

He leaned close to Michaela's ear. "Have you noticed—"

"The old people?" she whispered, her eyes wide.

"What are you two murmuring about?" Arthur asked.

Boyd shut his mouth. They could investigate this later.

A young woman came forward out of the crowd and placed a baby swaddled in red- and blue-checkered plaid in Clara's arms. She beamed as she touched the sweet face.

"Goodness, they're giving that woman a baby," Arthur said with gusty sigh. "I'm really starting to believe in the visions of these people. It's like they knew…"

Boyd nudged Michaela. "Don't they only do that at marriage ceremonies? Joseph! Can you come here for a moment?"

The man broke off from the warrior he was speaking with and crossed to him. "What's the significance of giving Clara the child?" he asked.

"I've never seen that happen before, Dr. Boyd. We must ask Sironka."

"Arthur!" Clara called over her shoulder. "Come! Sironka wants to introduce you to his parents and their chief."

"Perhaps they are giving my uncle and aunt special respect because they're elders," Michaela said. "They obviously have a number of them."

"Yes, it is unique to their village," Joseph said, nodding with a mysterious smile. "Like Mr. and Mrs. Hale and Master Hargreaves, they have seen many seasons."

Boyd's palms started to sweat, but he reached for

Michaela's hand at the same instant she reached for him. Linking hands, they stared into each other's eyes. The excitement in hers was contagious. Yeah, they were thinking the same thing. The elders' condition suggested the flower was more than simply healing. It was the fountain of youth.

They'd found their Holy Grail at last.

Boyd continued watching as Sironka led Arthur and Clara around, introducing them to a line of villagers. "I imagine Sironka will call us forward when it's time to present us."

When Clara ushered Hargreaves forward, Boyd took his eyes off the elders and looked around the village. There were at least five large traditional loaf-like dwellings in view, constructed with timber poles, mud, and thatch. He wondered what their accommodations looked like. When he and Michaela finally were alone, he planned to celebrate them being alive and finding the flower.

"I plan to tell Sironka you're joining me in the hut tonight," he whispered to Michaela.

"After what happened in the forest," she whispered back, taking his hand, "I hoped you would. We have a lot to celebrate."

"I was just thinking the same thing." Tonight, he'd have her laid out before him naked, and he planned to sup on her skin like a man starved.

"Michaela! Boyd!" Clara gestured with a free hand to beckon them forward. "Come meet everyone."

"Your aunt appears to be in charge," Boyd said softly as they made their way toward the welcoming party.

"She *is* a Merriam, after all," Michaela said, smiling.

"Come see this beautiful child," Clara said, turning around with a radiant smile on her face, the baby tucked snugly against her chest. "Her name is Natanna."

"She's beautiful, Aunt," Michaela said, joining Clara in what Boyd could only call a baby glow.

Sironka gestured to him and Michaela and introduced them, and Boyd smiled at their hosts. They'd be working with these people, and he couldn't wait to get started. But he knew all about introductions and the proper order of things.

"This is Chief Mingati," Sironka said, pointing to the man with the most elaborate headdress.

He bowed, noting that while the chief wasn't the oldest elder, his head was shot with white. "Dr. Merriam and I are honored to be here, Chief Mingati."

"We welcome you to our village," the chief said in English. "You bring us great honor."

Well, Sironka had said a group of them had learned English. That was going to make things a lot easier. Sometimes language was as big an obstacle as culture.

"We look forward to returning many times for your hospitality," Michaela added.

Sironka gestured to the man and woman beside the chief. "These are my parents. They are both aptly named for this meeting. She is Naserian, the one who initiates peace in her community out of love. He is Lemayian, the blessed one."

From their appearance, they looked to be in their late thirties or early forties. In most Maasai cultures, they'd have been at the end of their life, but not here. Boyd wanted to grin but tried to keep cool. "Your names do you great honor. We are pleased to meet you."

The chief raised his hands to the sky. "The couple promised to us has finally come to help us share the flower with the world. We are grateful for this auspicious meeting. Now, let us feast."

Excitement kindled in Boyd's chest. The path here had been brutal, but he was with Michaela again, and they would soon be taken to the Valley of Stars. He squeezed her hand as the drums sounded and people started to dance. Still jumpy from their earlier scare, she jolted. He put his arm around her in comfort, and she leaned in. Part of him wanted to join the party of dancers.

His Mickey was back with him, and they were staying with the fabled protectors of the secret flower! Pinch him.

Sironka led their party through the crowd, and Boyd knew he was grinning at people as they walked by. So much for keeping it cool. They emerged to find wooden stools arranged in a U-shape in front of a large hut. Makeshift firepits surrounded it with people turning roasted meat on spits. From the smell of it, Boyd knew they were going to have some good beef tonight.

Sironka showed them to their seats, and sure enough, there had to be some elders thing going on, because after someone retrieved the baby, Arthur and Clara were seated directly next to the chief, Hargreaves next to them. Boyd and Michaela sat next to Hargreaves, and Joseph sat beside Michaela. A young woman handed Boyd a dried gourd full of milk, and he drank it without wincing. He wasn't a big fan of milk, but it was an insult to turn anything down.

"Oh, this is delicious," Clara announced, holding out her gourd. "What is it?"

Leaning forward around his parents and the chief, Sironka said, "It's mead made from honey—a treat for elders."

"We certainly are that, I suppose, but thankfully we're not the only ones in the village," she said, laughing. "Arthur, how are you faring?"

"Fine, my dear," he said, pushing aside the white hair covering his forehead, damp with sweat. "I can't tell you how happy I am to be sitting down with these fine people."

"You're a trooper, Arthur," Boyd called. "I don't think I've ever met anyone tougher than you three."

"Thank you, Boyd," Clara said. "Oh, are we to have some entertainment?"

A group of people entered the open area between the seats and began to sing and dance, the percussive drums making Boyd tap his feet on the ground. Michaela smiled as another woman brought them new drinks, which smelled like some kind of fermented beer, and plates piled with beef, fried potatoes, and a stew of greens.

His stomach grumbled, and Boyd dug in. "Eat up," he said to Michaela, who was uncharacteristically picking at her food.

"I don't have much of an appetite," she said in an undertone, "but I'm doing my best. I know it's rude not to finish your plate."

"Don't worry, Dr. Michaela," Joseph said, lifting his gourd. "Everyone knows of your ordeal today. It won't be considered bad form."

A lack of appetite was a symptom of shock for some people. He clearly wasn't one of them. "That's nice to hear, Joseph. Still, I'll finish what Michaela can't to save face." He'd done it before.

She put her hand on his back and rubbed it. "Thanks, Boyd."

"I got you," he said, concerned about her color. She looked ashen, and her earlier excitement seemed to be waning, but he told himself it was the close call that had affected her. Hell, he had a feeling they'd both have nightmares for a while, but for now, he was going to focus on the positives.

Clara's laughter boomed out, and he turned his head to watch her gesture to the chief. Arthur's shoulders were shaking as he took another drink of mead.

"Do you think they know the mead is alcoholic?" he asked, noting the red flush on Arthur's cheeks.

"I don't know," she said, sipping her beer, "but you don't need to worry about Aunt Clara. She's like Trevor. They both have that gene where they can drink anything."

Yeah, he'd heard the family stories about Trevor. "How is your brother, by the way?"

"He just got married to a wonderful woman in Ireland,"

she said, a wide smile covering her face. "I've never seen him happier."

"Glad to hear it," he said, wondering if he'd be meeting her family again soon. In the past, he'd been included at family occasions and the like, and he'd mostly enjoyed them despite the difference in their social status, which had made him feel self-conscious. Her family meant everything to her, and because of that, they were important to Boyd.

His family was so different. With his mom working so much, they didn't spend a lot of time together. They loved each other. They just didn't understand each other, but she'd always done everything she could to give him a better life, and he wanted to do the same for her.

"Aunt Clara seems to have everyone hanging on her every word," Michaela said, pressing her hand to her stomach and emitting a slight belch. "Oh, excuse me."

He chuckled. "It's good manners to belch at a Maasai celebration, right, Joseph?"

"Right, Dr. Boyd," the man said with a smile.

He thought about asking Joseph more about the flower and the presence of elders in the village, but the feast didn't seem like the right place. But he was curious about a couple sitting at the end of the head table.

"Joseph, who are the man and woman sitting on the other side of Sironka?" he asked. "They weren't introduced earlier." But he remembered seeing them because Sironka had greeted the woman warmly.

"That's Leshan, Sironka's sister, and her husband," Joseph said. "Like her brother, she was well named. Leshan means one who defends the course of justice. They sent her to Nairobi for schooling to become a lawyer, so the tribe could lawfully own their lands."

"They own it?" Michaela said, brows raised. "And they sent a woman to make the arrangements? I really admire the equality in this clan."

"It's unique to this tribe," Joseph said, gesturing with

his hand. "My wives often joke about wanting to move here to be the wives of a warrior. I tell them they break my heart with such teasing." He let out a laugh.

"I'm assuming the Valley of Stars is included in the land they own," Boyd asked casually. "I'd been wondering about that."

"Yes. The tribe feared the government might take away their lands. Sell them to a timber company. You know how much corruption there is in Kenya, especially with the Ministry of Lands. Maasai land rights mean nothing in this country. Some tribes have gone through the process of acquiring a title only for officials to later use the same law against them to dispossess them of their land. It's atrocious."

Boyd had read up on the Group Representative Land Act and the current status of land rights, wanting to be prepared in case they did find the flower. Working with traditional groups around the world, he'd faced serious land issues before when a superfood or unique plant medicine was found. So had Michaela. This village's flower was going to make those other cases look like a piece of cake in comparison. He'd already looked up the best land rights lawyer in Kenya, wanting to be prepared.

"So the village having the title is no guarantee they'll be able to keep the Valley of Stars," Michaela said, shaking her head. "That's horrible. We'll have to— Perhaps this isn't the time for such talk."

Joseph picked up his drink. "No, but the chief and the leaders are well aware of the situation and think they've found a way to mitigate the problem. But I leave such talk to them."

Boyd's palms were sweating again, but for a different reason this time. The leaders' plan likely involved him and Michaela. He couldn't wait to hear what they had in mind.

"Tell us more about Leshan and how she was chosen,"

Michaela asked as a group of female dancers appeared in front of them, stomping on the ground with their bare feet, their beads tinkling as they danced.

"When Naserian became pregnant, she had a vision of her daughter being the one to secure the land. As you might expect, giving a girl such an honor was rare. It caused much discussion, but in the end, Chief Mingati agreed she would go. When the gods tell you to do something, you do it."

The gods again. But if it worked, it worked, and clearly this tribe had been preparing to share the flower with the world for decades. Not every tribe he worked with had such forethought.

"We all know times are changing, and we must change with them," Joseph said, spearing another piece of meat and raising it to his mouth. "But I pray our beef will never change. We Maasai must always be one with our cattle."

"Michaela and I will do everything possible to help preserve your ways, Joseph." It was part of the mandate of his new company, and very dear to his heart. Plant diversity was as important as people diversity, to his mind.

"We know that, Dr. Boyd, and thank you for it. Everyone needs allies in this world."

"I can't wait to meet Leshan," Michaela said, passing Boyd her mostly full plate.

Boyd couldn't wait to get down to business. "Do you expect we'll go to the Valley of Stars tomorrow, Joseph?"

The man slapped him on the back. "I imagine so, Dr. Boyd. Now, aren't you happy you survived the hippos and the crocs today? The gods favored you."

"I'm just happy that we all made it here safely, Joseph."

"Me too," Michaela echoed, leaning her head briefly against his shoulder.

She was tired. For her sake, he hoped the celebration wouldn't last too much longer.

"It looks like everything is back on track, as your people say," Joseph said.

Putting his arm around Michaela, watching the festivities, he had to agree.

Perhaps the gods did favor them, after all.

***

Clara couldn't help but think she'd somehow found a new home.

The Maasai people were more welcoming than she'd ever imagined for a people known for being wary of strangers. Clearly, they weren't strangers. My God, they'd put the cutest, sweetest baby in her arms. Sironka's beautiful mother had said, "These are all your children now." Tears had popped into her eyes, and for a moment, she'd started to believe Sironka's mother might have seen a vision of her. How else could she have known Clara regretted her lack of children?

Chief Mingati had a surprisingly good sense of humor, and he'd been all too happy to tell her about his first lion kill. According to the chief, it had been an even struggle for survival, the account of which had been so riveting, Clara had perched literally on the edge of her seat. Arthur had listened just as intently, his posture tense, and she'd taken note of his flushed cheeks.

"Arthur, dear," she said when he lifted his gourd again. "You might slow down. I believe the mead has more than honey in it."

"Indeed, Madam," Hargreaves said. His posture was picture-perfect, and he looked almost regal in the fading afternoon light.

"Did you ever think we'd have this kind of adventure, Hargreaves?" she asked, biting into a piece of the succulent beef. Organic and grass fed, of course, and some of the best she'd ever tasted.

"No, Madam, but as I've learned in many years of

service to you, one can never anticipate all eventualities."

"Well, I sure as heck didn't expect this," Arthur said, forking a potato. "Back when I was a boy, I used to pore over the *National Geographic* for glimpses of the greater world. Even knowing the power of photographs and a well-written article, nothing beats a live show. Eh, Clara? I can't wait to write about this trip."

Oh, she knew exactly what kind of "live show" got him hot and bothered. He certainly knew she was open to it later. She should be tired after their trip. Unsettled even, after the horrible events on the river. But she oddly wasn't, and she knew it wasn't the mead. She'd gone through most of her life feeling unwanted, and these people had made her feel so very welcome in such a short time. Sironka had even called her a friend to their tribe—a special honor, he'd said.

A young woman appeared in front of her and bowed, holding out a plate of fresh figs.

Chief Mingati gestured to the plate, his long blue and black furs catching the light. "Figs are a blessing reserved for women in our village. You honor us with your presence, Mrs. Hale."

Even the chief refused to call her by her given name. "How lovely! Figs are one of my favorites." The woman placed them in front of her, bowed again, and departed.

She leaned closer to Arthur. "Remember our last trip, dear? In Provence, you seemed to think you had the upper hand on me. That's when you gave yourself your special nickname."

He snorted. "I got another Merriam engaged, didn't I? You're too competitive, Clara."

Like she hadn't helped J.T. and Trevor and Caitlyn too. "And you're not competitive, Arthur Hale? Hah! I just wanted to point out that I don't see anyone giving *you* anything special. Let's review my list so far: they let me carry the most precious baby, and now I've been given these lovely figs."

He leaned close to her. "Maybe you're just nicer."

"That's not news, Arthur. I'm a downright sweetheart compared to you." She kissed his flushed cheek as he har-rumphed.

"When you're not a pain in my ass," he added, giving her one of his cheeky winks.

"For that, I will not share my figs with you." She popped one in her mouth.

"But we know what you will share later when we're alone, don't we?" he whispered in her ear.

As she chewed the tastiest fig of her life, she returned his wink.

She planned to share every bit of her happiness with him.

CHAPTER 15

ANIMAL FURS AND HIDES COVERED THE FLOORS AND WALLS of the windowless hut Michaela and Boyd had been shown to at the end of the feast. One kerosene lamp lit the space, its smell extra sharp tonight due to her shock. God, what a day. She could still taste the river water in her mouth even though she knew her mind was playing tricks on her.

"Here," Boyd said, carrying over a basin of water. "If you'll let me, I'll help you wash. You look dead on your feet, Mickey."

"I feel ready to fall over, but I'm jumping up and down on the inside, being here with you in the village, so close to the Valley of Stars." Besides, tired or not, she'd never been too exhausted for a sex celebration after a big find, and he knew it. A bath—even one out of a basin—would be a nice prelude. She ran her finger over the bare skin of his arm, enjoying the way she caused goose bumps to rise in her path.

"I love you, you know," he said, the soft light casting half his face in shadow. "I was so afraid I might lose you today."

"You know," she said, "I just wish you and I could be home for the night and then pop back here in the morning.

We'd turn the air conditioner on way low and make a fire. Then we'd make love in front of it."

"Something to look forward to when we get back," he said, his dark eyes fixed on her face. "Personally, I'm just glad we're alone together. When you're more rested tomorrow, we can geek out about all the old people and the whole land rights issue."

"Good idea. It's all so exciting, isn't it?" She tugged off her clothes and shivered as the cool air hit her skin.

"The most exciting trip we've been on, but we knew it would be. And that's the end of this talk. Close your eyes." He dipped the cloth in the basin and raised the hair off her neck.

Heaven.

"I wish I could wash my hair. I lost my dry shampoo and all my toiletries."

"Your aunt still has hers, I'll bet," Boyd said, kissing her neck. "Be right back."

He ducked out of the hut before she could stop him, letting the hide covering the makeshift door drop behind him. Her aunt and uncle might be up to something already, and good for them. They'd both beamed as they bid everyone good night after the festivities. Thank God they were still happy to be along on the journey. Boyd was right. They could have gone down in the river today. She would never have forgiven herself for that.

He reappeared with the bottle in hand and turned her around. "Your aunt was flushed, but all too happy to give you her shampoo—once she finally came to the door."

"I was going to tell you not to bother them," she said, leaning her head back as he dusted her hair and ran a comb through it gently.

"Ouch," she said when he hit a tangle. "I probably look like I have a dozen birds' nests in my hair after today."

"You look beautiful," he said, his hands patient with her tangles. "You'll feel better after this. Then you're going to sleep. Tomorrow, we're going to the Valley of Stars."

"And we both want to be rested for that." The culmination of their dream was within reach. She had to focus on that, not on the terror she'd felt earlier. Not on the grief for Marvin, and for what Boyd had needed to do to help her.

"All right, I did your hair as best I could," he said, picking up the cloth and running it efficiently along her back and bottom. "Who's missing a shower right about now?"

She loved the feel of the cloth running up and down her legs. "Me! Or a hot bath. God, I don't think I could live without hot water from a spout long-term. That's why I ended up not doing Peace Corps. Two years straight would have been too long."

Circling around her in the close space, he slid the cloth between her legs. She let out a quiet moan, closing her eyes. God, she wanted him. Her whole body was tightening with need, every cell straining for his touch. She shivered again, her skin cold from a chill. He needed to work faster, but she couldn't bring herself to hurry him along. She wanted his hands to linger. When he bathed her like this, touched her like this, she felt cherished, a feeling she hadn't known she craved until Boyd had shown her what she'd been missing.

"I didn't do it, because I didn't want to just build bridges and wells," Boyd said, bathing her stomach and breasts. "I told Peace Corps I would suck at that, but they said I'd have learned. Can you imagine the first time someone tried to use something I'd built? It would have collapsed on impact."

She laughed as he tugged on her nipples before washing her neck, shoulders, and arms. "Building isn't your forte. Remember that time you tried to fix that hole in our wall with a little spackle?"

"There is a kind of building I think I'd be really good at, though."

His tender tone had her looking him in the eye. "And what is that?"

"I want to build a life with you, Mickey—one where we work *and* play together. I don't know what it looks like completely, but there's one constant: you and me."

She traced his face. "Just don't ever lie to me or go behind my back again, Boyd."

He ran the cloth over the rest of her face before setting the basin on the floor. "I promise. Just don't ever jump to conclusions and get so mad you won't listen to me. You scared me, Mickey. I couldn't get through to you. For months."

"We have a lot of talking to do," she said, leaning up on her toes and kissing his mouth. "But I want to be with you again. Now, it's your turn to strip. I can still smell the river on you."

"I draw the line at the dry shampoo," he said, following her orders. "It's like putting chalk in my hair."

"You always say that," she said, tugging on the ends of his shaggy hair. "Beats nothing."

"I'm not doing it, Mickey."

She laughed. "Stubborn to the end. All right, let's get you washed."

When she lowered the cloth straight to his package, he growled. "That's the *last* place you're supposed to wash on a guy."

"Like you've ever been a rule follower," she said, giving him a long caress before washing his chest. "The bed looks pretty decent from here. Did you check it out?"

"It's got corn husks under the hide and then a rock-hard board made of juniper. We've had worse."

"Speaking of rock-hard," she said, venturing south again.

"Are you sure? Maybe you should sleep."

She smiled, progressing to his backside and efficiently washing off the grime. "I'm never that—"

"Tired," he finished, turning around and reaching for her hips. "All right. I won't argue with you. I'm pretty clean. Care to make love with me, Dr. Merriam?"

Oh, how she'd missed him calling her that. "I'd love to play doctor with you, Dr. McClellan."

"Then step over here onto my examination table," he said, directing her to the bed. When she sat down, he lowered himself next to her.

"Is the Count Going to Count a Climax?" she asked in the worst imitation of the *Sesame Street* Muppet ever, making him laugh. "One climax, hahaha. Two climaxes, hahaha. Three climaxes—"

"Hahaha," he mimicked, still laughing. "You still can't do the voice right. That's a skit you'll never see. Now, settle down and get serious. You're punchy."

"I've had a rough day," she said, bouncing on the wooden frame. "This is really hard."

He took her hand and placed it on him. "You're darn right it is, and it's getting harder by the minute."

"Oh, Dr. McClellan," she said, batting her eyelashes in the low light like a nurse in a B-movie, "whatever do you mean?"

"I love this punch-drunk side of you. Now, lie back and let me show you how much I love you, Dr. Merriam."

"Yes, sir."

She lay back, and he rose over her as she spread her legs for him. Putting his weight on his elbows, he gave her a wicked smile before taking her mouth in a hot, drugging kiss. Their tongues circled each other, and she put her hand on his cheek to hold him in place, wanting to give him more, take more. He shifted his hand up between her legs, and she moaned, feeling his knowledge of her body in every press of his fingers, light at first and then deeper until she was straining her hips against his hand. She came in a rush, his hot, wet mouth on her neck.

"That's my girl," he said, fitting himself at her entrance.

She lifted to meet him as he thrust into her, going deep—just the way she liked it. Her hands slid to his butt, pulling him in even deeper, never wanting to let him go.

Levering back, he took her hips in his big hands and began to pump, gentle at first and then harder until she wrapped her legs around him. Moaning brokenly now, she threw her arms over her head, needing more, letting him give it to her. Her belly flushed with heat, and then she was tightening up, pulsing in hard, insistent pulls. He filled her, fast and deep, and then he was groaning above her.

He folded over her, still cushioning her from his weight, and she brought her arms around his back. Sweat slicked his spine, and she inhaled the scent of his skin. He smelled so achingly familiar. *My man.*

Coming back to herself, she remembered the nights she'd lain in bed awake missing that special scent in her bed. Other nights, she could smell him, and uncharacteristic tears would fill her eyes at the loss of him. Six months apart, she thought, and here they were again.

After today, she wanted to believe they could make it forever.

Chapter 16

BOYD AWOKE WITH A START, HIS BODY HOT AND FLUSHED with sweat.

The hut was in complete darkness, the lamp having guttered out long ago. He reached out to touch Michaela since she wasn't pressed against him. His fingers encountered her back, and he realized it was no wonder he'd woken up so warm. She was hot to the touch. Had she thrown off the hides because they made her too warm?

He didn't know where the lamp oil was to replenish the lantern, so he climbed out of bed and made his way toward the front of the hut, stopping to pull on his pants. When he eased back the hide, he saw the sky was a bright baby blue, and everyone appeared to be going about their day, the women carrying firewood or jugs of water. Mid-morning. Clearly, he and Michaela had both slept hard.

Making his way back to the bed, he could see that she was lying on her stomach with one leg hanging off the bed, her hair completely covering her face. He sat down and brushed it back gently. Fear coursed through him. He ran his finger lightly down her face and neck, paying greater attention to the variation in temperature. She was boiling. Fever? Please God, no. He tested her temperature again. Without a thermometer, he couldn't be sure—he wasn't

that kind of doctor—but it felt like a high fever. His scientist mind kicked in, listing all the parasites and diseases
lurking in rivers in this area.

Fear covered him like a dark fog. She *never* got sick
on a trek. They used to joke about their cast-iron stomachs
and superhuman constitutions. Then again, she'd never
swallowed this much river water before.

And their catch-all antibiotic for this sort of thing was
at the bottom of the river.

"Mickey." He turned her onto her back. "Babe, wake up."

She didn't grumble or swear like she usually did when
he nudged her. Michaela Merriam was not a morning person by choice, but this was something else. She was sick.
Bad sick. He knew it in his gut.

"Okay, baby." He pulled the hides up to cover her na-
kedness. "I'm going for some help. Be right back."

He pulled on the rest of his clothes quickly and rushed
out of the hut. Outside, he had a moment of panic. Other
people were slowing to look at him, smiles on their faces,
but he didn't recognize any of them. God, he'd left Mickey
alone with a fever in a place of strangers.

Where were the people he knew?

"Boyd!" Clara called out.

He turned sharply to see her walking toward him, her
white hair trailing over her shoulders.

"Good morning!" Clara put her hand on his arm. "Is
Michaela still asleep? Come have some breakfast. You and
Michaela slept like the dead. Arthur, Hargreaves, and I
have been up for hours. We even got Arthur and some of
the other people in the village to do some yoga. I told everyone you both needed to sleep after yesterday. Bad dreams?"

"Mickey is sick, and I don't know who to ask for help.
Clara, it's a fever. She's boiling hot, and I don't—"

"Slow down," Clara said, gripping his arm. "You're having a panic attack, I think, probably because of yesterday's
shock. Breathe, Boyd. Arthur! Hargreaves! I need you."

Her shout had more people turning to watch them. Arthur appeared, coming out from behind a hut. Hargreaves stepped into view, his oil-slick hat in hand.

"Go get Naserian," Clara called. "It's Michaela. She has a fever."

"I'll find her, Madam," Hargreaves called, rushing out of sight.

"Keep breathing, Boyd," Clara said, rubbing his arm. "Arthur, dear, Boyd here is having a moment. Why don't you stay with him while I go check on Michaela? I'm sure she's fine, Boyd."

His heart was suddenly racing too hard for him to argue with her. When he saw stars, he bent at the waist.

"That bad, eh?" Arthur said, patting him on the back. "You're not a man to fall apart, so I'm going to remind you of that. If Michaela is sick, she'll need you to stay strong."

The man was right. He gritted his teeth and stood, still feeling off balance. "She's sick. High fever. The river water is—"

"Riddled with organisms, I imagine. All right, let's not lose it. Here's Hargreaves coming with Naserian and her husband, Lemayian. You didn't get a chance to talk to them at the feast. They're nice people, Boyd."

And they were healers, he reminded himself, trying to grab control of his somersaulting stomach. With the flower...

"I understand Michaela is ill with fever," Naserian said, her demeanor calm. "May we see her?"

"Of course," he said, rushing to the entrance of the hut and pulling the hide back.

Clara stood up from the bed, clenching her hands in front of her. "You're right, Boyd. She's boiling hot. I put a fresh shirt on her for modesty. Naserian, please see to my niece. Oh, Lemayian, I'm so glad you could come too."

The healers walked to where Michaela lay. She still

hadn't moved, and Boyd suddenly remembered the stories Joseph had told him about the men who'd come to seek the flower. They'd fallen ill too. One of them, he remembered, had died, although the man who'd done so had been greedy. Unworthy. Michaela was neither of those things.

"She shouldn't be sick," he said as they both bent over her. "If this is some test by your gods, it needs to stop."

"Boyd!" Clara said sharply. "Enough. Let them examine her." She took his hand, and the trembling told him she was worried too.

"The heat has taken root in her and is strong," Naserian said, touching her cheek before rising. "The two must go to the Valley of Stars and pick the flower."

"But she's sick!" Boyd said, gesturing to Michaela. "She can't travel anywhere. She isn't even moving. Why can't I just go?"

"Because it is not yours to do, Boyd," Naserian said, folding her arms across her red robes. "If you had to choose between having the flower and having your woman, what would you choose?"

"I'd choose Michaela every time," he ground out. "No question. But I shouldn't have to choose. I'm the other half of the couple in your vision. The one who's good with snakes and wild animals. I'd have thought your gods would already have approved of me. There shouldn't be a test."

"There is no test here." Lemayian lifted a regal brow. "You are not the one in our visions, Boyd, only the one who brought the two."

"What in the hell—excuse me—are you talking about? Of course, Michaela and I are the couple. Joseph said so."

"Did he use your names?" Naserian asked, folding her hands. "No, only my husband, the chief, our elders, and our children knew the identity of the couple."

"Are you telling us we came here for nothing?" Boyd rose to his full height. "The woman I love almost died in the river yesterday coming to your village, and now she's lying in here with a fever."

"There's been no mistake," Naserian said, her brown eyes looking straight into his. "The couple is here."

He flinched, done with their riddles. "*Where?*"

"The one who loves snakes and wild animals is standing right beside you, Boyd." Lemayian gestured to Clara.

"Me?" Clara's mouth gaped before snapping shut. "But that's—"

"You and Mr. Hale are the couple in our visions," Naserian said with a soft smile. "Only the pure of heart can take the flower and use it, and the gods have said that is you. Why else do you think we gave you one of our children to hold and honored you both yesterday?"

"Because Clara loves babies," Arthur spat out, wiping his face with a handkerchief. "You can't be serious about Clara and me being the couple you've been waiting for. The fact that we're even on this trip is improbable. What you're suggesting is impossible."

"And yet, you and Mrs. Hale are here," Naserian said in that same calm tone. "According to our tradition, only the female healer knows the location of the valley. If you wish, Sironka and I will take you there to bring back the flower."

"Don't you have any of the flower here?" Boyd asked. "I saw a dozen elders in your tribe yesterday. They must be using it."

"Our stock ran out a week before your arrival to our village," Naserian said. "An auspicious omen. I was waiting for the couple to come with me. It is a two- or three-day journey."

"Two or three days!" Arthur gasped. "You expect me to walk two days?"

"Arthur!" Clara came over and took his hand. "Michaela may need the medicine."

The man growled. "I deal in facts, dear. Fine. Naserian, does this flower really work?"

"It does." Naserian nodded. "As Dr. McClellan said, there are those who have seen many seasons who wouldn't be here without it."

"Why can't you go?" Arthur asked, flicking a hand toward the hide flap leading out of the hut. "I mean, do we really need to come?"

"Yes. Our village has been waiting for the couple with incorruptible souls to help us share the flower with the world. That is you."

"Then we'll go immediately," Clara said, her voice strong and sure.

Naserian folded her hands, her brown eyes direct. "But you must know… Once you take the flower, it is your responsibility to share it. My daughter has the title for the land, and we will make you co-owners."

"Co-owners?" So that was the "solution" Joseph had referenced. He never would have guessed.

"But what would we do with the land and the flower?" Arthur asked. "Boyd and Michaela are the plant people. This is why they came."

"Are you and Mrs. Hale not both searching for a new purpose in your lives?" Naserian asked. "You both are on a new road together, are you not?"

Boyd couldn't believe what he was hearing. Wasn't this supposed to be his find, his and Mickey's? But it didn't matter anymore. All he cared about was getting that flower to her.

"We'll deal with the future later," Clara said, fisting her hands together. "This had better be some flower, Naserian."

"I would not lie to you, Mrs. Hale," the woman said softly.

"I didn't mean to suggest you were," Clara said. "It's only a shock, is all."

"Our gods asked the first chief to keep the flower's location secret from the tribe after he used it to heal a lion on his first hunt," Lemayian said. "This happened many moons ago."

"Sironka told us that story," Clara said, her eyes narrowing. "Remember, Arthur? He's the one who started this tribe after his father exiled him for not killing the lion."

"I don't care what the story is," Boyd said, his jaw ticking. The last thing he wanted to hear was more stories. "Michaela is sick. That's what we need to focus on!"

"We'll be back shortly," Naserian said, bowing shortly. "Then we can depart for the Valley of Stars."

Boyd stalked to her bed, trying to shelve his anger. He felt duped. Worst of all, he was responsible for Michaela being here. She wouldn't be ill if he hadn't been so damn eager to believe he and Michaela were Joseph's so-called couple. If Boyd hadn't been so stupid and gree—

Yes, he'd say it. He'd been greedy, just like those explorers in the old stories about the star-shaped flower. Why else had he been so eager to embark on this trip with Mickey? He'd seen this as their destiny, but he should have asked more questions. He should have...

None of this was going to help Michaela. She needed him. Touching her forehead, he nearly flinched from the scorching heat coming off her skin. The fact that she still hadn't roused worried him more than anything.

"Boyd." Clara came to sit on the other side of the bed, touching Michaela's cheek. "We'll find the flower and bring it back to help her."

"Thank you." He took Michaela's hand.

"I know you're angry and disappointed, but those feelings aren't going to help her, Boyd," Arthur said, emerging from behind Clara and putting his hand on her shoulder. "We all have to focus on getting her well."

Boyd shifted his focus to Michaela's face. Her cheeks were flushed red. "I was just telling myself that."

"I know this sounds crazy, Boyd," Clara said, "but I don't see what other choice we have. Michaela can't travel to a doctor, and the medical kit went into the river. If this medicine can help her, we need to get it."

He looked at Michaela on the bed, swallowing back a surge of emotion. "What if it doesn't work?" he asked, his voice quavering.

"It's going to work, Boyd," Clara said, slapping her hand on her thigh and rising. "You've lost your faith momentarily. Who can blame you? Michaela is sick, and that's enough to make anyone scared. I know I am. But if Michaela believed in this flower, enough to face these odds, then Arthur and I will find it. I don't know about the rest of it. Sharing it with the world and the like. We'll have to see about that."

"No kidding, my dear," Arthur said, shaking his head.

"How could you?" Boyd asked, genuinely interested. "Share it with the world, I mean. It's not your forte."

She crossed her arms and stared at him. "I'm a Merriam, aren't I? My family's company is global. And my husband here is one of the most famous journalists in the world, here to write a story about this find. If we *are* the ones destined to work with this tribe to share this flower with the world, then share it we will. Arthur, let's go."

Clara stormed out of the tent with purpose in her every stride.

"Well, you've lit a fire under her." Arthur tsked. "I suppose it's been a long time coming. Take care of Michaela while we find this infernal flower."

Arthur left the hut with a renewed energy to his stride.

As Boyd turned back to the woman he loved and took her hand, he was overwhelmed by helplessness. What if the journey was too hard for them? His stomach flipped as another thought rocked through him. What if they didn't find it in time?

"Come on, Mickey." Boyd reached for the water basin and cloth, dipping it in the water and smoothing it over her brow. "I need you to fight this fever and wake up."

If Arthur and Clara didn't find the flower soon, he didn't care what the tribe thought the gods supposedly wanted. He'd tear apart this entire countryside with his bare hands until *he* found a cure.

He was not losing her.

CHAPTER 17

ARTHUR KNEW BULLSHIT WHEN HE SMELLED IT. ALWAYS had. Always would.

Following Sironka and his mother up the hill outside the village, he couldn't ignore one fact: the smell of bullshit wasn't anywhere near them. These people believed he and Clara were the couple they'd been waiting for to help them share this flower with the world. Bully for them. But they weren't crazy. He could spot crazy at ten paces.

The fact that they believed it didn't mean *he* believed it, but right now, that flower was his niece's best bet, and he'd be damned if he'd let her suffer. He and Clara had left immediately. Hargreaves had offered to come with them, but Clara had wisely left him behind with Boyd.

Although Arthur had planned on writing about the find all along, it had never occurred to him that he might be part of the story. He was too old to make the news anymore, or so he'd thought before he met Clara.

"Clara, my dear," Arthur said, already puffing, "it's a good thing you've been doing all that walking and yoga stuff. If I can't make it, you'll have to go the rest of the way."

She took his arm. "They said we both must make it, Arthur, and so you shall."

He didn't pull away, telling himself she was flirting

rather than trying to help him up the infernal hill. The ground wasn't rocky, thank God, and after they left this glade, it looked like they'd be heading into dense, shaded forest. Determination had a new friend, it seemed, and her name was Clara Merriam Hale.

God, he loved this stubborn, beautiful woman.

"Fine. I can probably make it to this Valley of Stars, but I can't guarantee a return trip." Two or three days of walking? At his age? Hell, by the end, he'd be like the tired, worn-out antelope they'd seen taken down by a cheetah the other day. In truth, he was more worried about lions. Hadn't Sironka said their first chief had found a lion? That meant lions roamed these hills, a thought that scared the bejesus out of him. He was already worked up enough about Michaela. He didn't need to worry a lion might make a meal out of his beloved before he could kill it, which he would. Nothing was touching Clara. Of course, he'd be happy to leave that task to Sironka. Young men liked to beat their chests. At his age, he was happy to have a pulse.

Naserian looked over her shoulder. "Don't worry, Mr. Hale. Both my husband and I had visions of you and Clara making it to the valley and back. Many times, in fact."

He supposed he should be relieved to hear that.

Maybe he would be if he believed in visions.

His life had been built on facts. He reported facts. But he couldn't deny it was strange that Naserian and Lemayian had seen them in their dreams or whatever. This wasn't the first time he'd had reason to question his world view. He remembered reading an article about a psychic who'd helped the police find both a victim and her murderer.

Perhaps there truly was a gift of sight. He sure as hell couldn't explain it, but he wasn't going to say it wasn't legit.

"Good thing we live at a similar elevation, Arthur," Clara

said, trying to be conversational. "We don't need to worry about altitude sickness or shortness of breath."

Didn't she hear him gasping? "Says you. I'm eighty, woman."

"And in the prime of life," she said, tucking him closer to her side. "We're doing this for Michaela. When you get tired, remember that."

He sucked in more air. "You forget what a stubborn old cuss I can be, Clara. I'll make it. Nothing like family to put steel in a man's bones."

"Well said, Mr. Hale," Sironka said, leading the way, spear in hand.

They walked for a few hours, surrounded by trees. A few times, he heard wild calls from the trees, but Sironka said they were only monkeys. At one point, he caught sight of one of the white-and-black primates. His response was, "I can handle monkeys. It's the lions I'm worried about." He wouldn't ask about other dangers. They had enough to contend with.

Clara laughed, not even breathing hard, God love her. "That's why we have Sironka. How much farther until we reach the valley?"

Naserian said, "Around nightfall, I imagine. We should rest a bit."

Arthur was afraid his feet might not move again. "We should keep going."

"Have some water and take a moment," the healer said, indicating a downed tree. "Sironka, check to make sure it's safe to sit."

"What could be dangerous about a tree?" he asked. None of the trees in the Rocky Mountains where he lived posed a threat.

"It may hold things that bite," Sironka said, walking its length. He used the tip of his spear to lift up the bark.

Clara cried out as hundreds of ants scurried around the bark.

"Fire ants," Sironka said. "Nasty bites."

Arthur swallowed thickly. Couldn't they eat a man alive? "I've changed my mind. I think I'd rather a lion snack on me. Be quicker surely."

"This is not the time to be flip, Arthur," Clara said, her color waning.

Sironka tested another downed tree. "This one is safe."

"That's a relief," Clara said, easing onto the tree and taking a canteen of water Sironka held out to her.

Thank God the man was carrying the pack for everyone. Arthur couldn't have handled the weight. "Anything else you want to tell us about all this, Naserian? I know I speak for Clara when I say we're both shocked by everything that's happened today. Why exactly do you think we're the best people to help you share the flower with the world?"

He was here for Michaela and no other reason, but it wouldn't hurt to ask more questions.

Naserian sat on the forest floor, cushioned by the plants they'd been treading over.

"You both have incorruptible souls. Neither of you will be swayed by bribes or hefty commercial offers. Also, Mrs. Hale is a woman of means and has the power to fight for what she knows is right. Your power, Mr. Hale, comes from your words. Your articles about the flower and our work together will be read by many. People listen to you. It is your gift."

Clara sent him a knowing look. Okay, Naserian had gotten the gift part right. "But we're outsiders."

"Perhaps that's the problem," Naserian said. "It is time to go beyond you as outsiders and us as Maasai and simply look at us all as people sharing this big land with all the oceans. Unfortunately, our people historically haven't been treated well by outsiders, which is why we fear strangers. That time must end. The flower is too important, and people need its medicine."

"If the flower heals as you say, you're right to want help sharing it," Clara said, leaning forward, ever alert. "Your people have been treated abominably if you ask me."

That was an understatement to Arthur's way of thinking.

"What else do we need to know about your visions?" Clara asked.

She was starting to sound like she believed in all this stuff. They'd be talking later for sure.

"Only one aspect I have not shared yet. A man with darkness around him will come and try and take the flower, and you will have to decide what to do."

Arthur and Clara shared a look. This tale was getting wilder by the minute.

Unless... His mind shifted to Iggie. If Customs had finally released him, he'd be able to reach Simon and Jaali. Perhaps he'd insist that the men head upriver, thinking they could find the village. If anyone was going to try and take the flower, it would be him.

Arthur harrumphed. He'd taken one look at the man and known he was a jerk. "What do you see us doing, Naserian?"

She drank some water before responding. "Handling it, but doing so will cause you much sadness. In the end, it will be a good thing for this man, although the truth will not become clear for some time. He does not walk an easy path."

"Happen to know his name?" Arthur asked, making Clara give him a bemused look before she drank more.

"Are you testing me, Mr. Hale?" she asked, laughing. "The gods told me not to share more with you. When the moment comes, you must decide what to do. Any further information will rob the moment of reckoning of its urgency."

Did that mean she didn't have a clear picture of this man of darkness, or was she being sincere?

"Good thing reckoning is my middle name," he blustered.

Clara snorted. "News to me, dear. We should get going. Michaela might be worsening."

"She will worsen before she gets better," Naserian said, her face lined with worry. "Come, you are right. We should continue on. We have a few hours to the next watering hole." She and Sironka started walking again, and Arthur helped Clara off the tree. He wanted to believe Michaela would be all right, but he didn't want to put his trust in such matters. Of course, the woman didn't say whether she improved because of the flower.

"Clara, did you hear—"

"Oh, Arthur, we have enough on our hands. I'm trying not to worry about Michaela. I don't need to start fretting over a 'man with darkness around him.' Good God, it's bad enough."

He reached for her hand. "You're right, my love. Let's go get this damn flower. Hey, Naserian. Does this flower even have a name?"

The woman didn't turn as they walked through another dense copse of trees, the ground dappled with sunlight. "Our first chief instructed us not to name the flower. Easier to keep it secret that way. You and Mrs. Hale can do so if you'd like."

"It must have been hard to keep it a secret so long," Clara mused.

"Before, when there was not much travel in these hills, no one trespassed," she said. "But more people started coming, some with the government or business and some with tourism. Our chief mandated no one could walk our lands without a guide from the tribe. This helped."

"And we had warriors like me to take care of trespassers," Sironka said, flexing his muscles with a smile. "Our tribe has more warriors than other tribes. And our spears are laced with poison and never miss."

He'd have to write about that in his story, assuming they made it back.

"Are those monkeys overhead a threat?" Clara asked.

He looked up to see a group of monkeys above, staring silently down at them.

"They might try and pull you up into the trees, Mrs. Hale," Sironka said, "but they wouldn't be about to swing to and fro if they did."

Arthur increased his pace, ushering Clara away from the little beasts. "Naserian, isn't there a shortcut to the valley?"

She paused and looked at Sironka for a long moment. "I do not like to take it, but perhaps we should, given the urgency."

Clara beat him to asking, "Why don't you like to take it?"

"We must cross a river," Naserian replied. "You have experienced the terrors in our rivers already."

"If it gets us to the flower more quickly, we'll manage," Clara said before he could ask more questions.

Well, if she was up for it, then so was he. Michaela needed them.

They walked through the forest for another hour or so, not a single trail marker in sight. Naserian seemed to know exactly where she was going, which was quite remarkable, if he were being honest. He heard the water before he saw it. Moments later, they were poised atop a large rock, the sun beating down on his head. The shadow of a large bird fell over him and he squinted up at it.

"Looks like an eagle," Clara said, shielding her eyes.

"A black-chested snake eagle," Sironka said, pointing with his spear. "I saw one when we left your campsite. A good omen."

"How are we supposed to get down to the river?" Arthur asked.

Sironka shared a smile with his mother. "You climb, Mr. Hale."

Clara sputtered, God help him, but she started to follow them as they descended from the rock. He did the same.

"I think it's time for you to call us Arthur and Clara," he called, aware the rock face was scratching his hands.

Naserian looked over her shoulder as he made it down to the ground, the beads in her hair bouncing. "You are elders. It is not possible."

And yet they were asking him to stride into these hills and climb down rocks like he was in some Iron Man marathon.

"Beware of the hippos," Naserian said. "They like to nap along the river."

"Nap?" Oh Lord. "Not the kind of nap we like to take, right, Clara?"

"Oh, Arthur, do be quiet." She took a deep breath. "I just saw a crocodile emerge from that brush over there. It showed me its teeth before sliding into the water."

Arthur flashed back to Michaela and Boyd plunging into the water just yesterday, their boat upended. He was starting to hate African rivers. "Please tell me you have a boat stored around here."

Sironka laughed. "No, I was going to strap you both on my back and swim across the river. Mr. Hale, I am a warrior. Not Superman."

So they knew about Superman. He'd have to ask later. "Great, let's get going."

"Stay here while I find the boat," Sironka said, heading toward the water with his spear outstretched.

Just the way Arthur would move if he'd been asked to do the retrieving. No way he'd want to disturb napping hippos. They were bad enough when they were awake.

Something rustled behind him, and he spun around as a crocodile's head emerged from the bush a few yards behind them. Clara hadn't been joking about the teeth. Good god! Its leathery green hide glistened eerily in the sunlight. The thing had to be sixteen feet long.

"Come to me," Naserian called, pulling out a short, wickedly curved club from her robes.

Arthur grabbed Clara and rushed to the woman. She promptly stood in front of him, which didn't make him feel too salty given he didn't know the first thing about stopping crocodiles and she seemed to. Her club was poised to strike.

The crocodile shot toward them suddenly, its short legs moving fast. Sironka appeared in front of them in a protective stance, his spear jabbing through the air. The crocodile received a few stabs to the head before it thrashed away ill-manneredly and disappeared back into the brush.

"He was a big one," Sironka said, lowering his spear to the ground as he turned to face them. "Everyone okay?"

Once he saw no one had been injured—physically, at least—he returned to his task.

"Goodness, that was…" Clara's hand shook as she pushed her hair back behind her ear.

Death-defying? "My heart is beating so hard I might—"

"Deep breaths, Mr. Hale," Naserian said, sheathing her club. She reached into the pouch at her waist and pulled out a pinch of something. "Breathe this for me. It will calm your heart."

"Me too," Clara said, taking her turn after he'd inhaled the herbaceous scent.

He didn't ask what herb it was, but it helped, thank God.

Sironka reappeared, dragging the boat to the water's edge. "Come, let's be off."

Arthur helped Clara onto the boat and positioned her in front of him as Naserian climbed in. Then, as Sironka pushed off and hastened to join them, Arthur turned his gaze to the river. They didn't have far to cross, thank God. When he spied the first hippo in the water not five feet away, he prayed it would leave them in peace. A crocodile surfaced in front of the hippo and the two attacked each other.

"Row faster, my son," Naserian said, poised at the front of the boat.

"Yes, mother," he called, steering them away from all the thrashing in the water.

Clara reached back for his hand, and he clenched her fingers. The sunlight on the water was punishing to the eyes, but he caught the slithers in the water as Sironka maneuvered the boat toward the adjacent shore.

When they reached it, Clara muttered something and then jumped out of the boat behind Naserian, who had her club out again. The brush and trees around them, all perfect hiding places for toothy carnivores, made him feel low on the food chain. He pushed himself out of the boat and watched as Sironka pulled it quickly across the ground to a shady tree.

"That's one hell of a shortcut, Naserian," Arthur said to break the tension.

"Cut down almost a day," she said, releasing a long breath. "I don't think I've prayed that hard for some time."

"Me either," Clara said, meeting his eyes.

He knew what she was thinking. Yes, if they survived it, they'd have one hell of an adventure to share with the grandchildren.

"Let us go," Sironka said when he returned.

"So much for that sign, right, Sironka?"

The warrior's brow rose. "We aren't dead, are we, Mr. Hale?"

A fair point.

Arthur took Clara's hand and followed them into the thicket. They came across more monkeys, who jeered at them from the trees. But an hour later, he got chills at the sight of a small white-brown owl with long ear-tufts, perched in the hollow of a tree a few feet above them. It opened its eyes, and Arthur couldn't believe how golden they were. Then it flew away. Naserian didn't have to say anything about omens. Arthur had felt the woo-woo himself.

They ate sparingly as they walked, the dried meat strips reminding him of beef jerky. Another watering hole provided them with more water to replenish their stock. And they kept walking. Late afternoon gave way to evening, streaks of orange and yellow limning the trees overhead.

When his legs were beginning to turn rubbery, they broke through the forest into a large glade. The sky had turned a deep blue, and a few stars shone in the cloudless sky overhead. Naserian and Sironka stopped, and Arthur and Clara did the same. He watched as the healer leaned down and brushed her fingers across the ground, saying words in her language. A shiver went through him again at the stillness of the place, and he scanned the area, knowing it was special somehow. He'd felt the same way the first time he'd gone into Chartres Cathedral in France.

Hills surrounded them on three sides, lined with trees. Before them, a wide valley spread out, and in the distance, he spotted something white amidst the verdant plant life. The flower... At last!

"Welcome to the Valley of Stars," Naserian said, rising with a smile. "The gods welcome you."

Sironka laid his spear on the ground and said a few words, and then he and his mother began walking forward.

Arthur looked at Clara. "We seem to have arrived, my dear."

She gasped, her gaze straight ahead. "Look, Arthur! Do you see him?"

He squinted in the twilight. "My God, it's a lion. Sironka! There's a—"

It disappeared. What the hell? Where had it gone? The beast had been there one moment and gone the next. There was no way it could have moved that quickly.

Clara grabbed his arm. "It's vanished. Like someone shut off the movie projector or something. Arthur, do you think it was a vision?"

He kept his eyes on the area he'd seen the lion, caution

and curiosity warring inside him. "I don't know, dear. After today, I'd say anything is possible. I only know Sironka seems to have dropped his spear, and I'm tempted to pick it up."

"Well, he'd be the first of us to recognize danger, so I think we're safe. I mean, look at the way he handled that crocodile earlier! Come, let's get this flower. When I was too tired to continue, I'd think about Michaela and her fever. If this flower does what they say it does, I have a name for it."

They came across a plant loaded with flowers, and suddenly Arthur understood why the Valley of Stars had been the name for this land. The flower was tiny, yet the blossoms had a star-shaped pattern with what looked to be a silver center. "What do you want to call it?" he asked, hoping the flower would earn her moniker.

"Life Giver," Clara whispered, plucking off a flower and studying it before tucking it into her pocket. "Let's catch up to Naserian and Sironka. I expect we'll be spending the night here. Picking the flowers in the morning."

He'd imagined the same, but he expected sleep would be elusive in this place. At least there were no hippos or crocs. A mythical lion he could deal with.

"What do you think of the Valley of Stars?" Naserian called as Sironka began to build a fire in a clearing.

"It's beautiful," Clara said, awe shooting through her voice. "Enchanting."

None of her worry for Michaela was evident in her voice now, and he was proud of her forbearance. For once in his life, he didn't have it in him to wax poetic. His niece was ill, and her well-being depended on him crossing that life-threatening river again—after another several hours of hiking.

He wasn't going to let her down.

CHAPTER 18

MICHAELA WAS WORSENING.

Boyd knew it by the way she started moaning in her sleep. Every time she cried out, her body bathed in sweat, he had to force himself not to freak out. Lemayian had given her a tea made from the bark of warburgia, one of their go-to plants for fever. She'd swallowed sips of it without waking up. He knew and believed in the power of plants—hell, he'd made it his life work—but in the face of losing Michaela, his faith was dimming.

"You might take a break, sir," Hargreaves said, wringing out a cloth before returning it to Michaela's forehead again, something they'd taken turns doing since Arthur and Clara had departed for the Valley of Stars that morning.

"I'm not leaving her," he ground out, although the hut had become stuffy and confining. Hargreaves had procured another kerosene lantern, but the darkness still seemed to be closing in on them as night fell.

"You'll be more refreshed to help Ms. Merriam if you take a break."

"You haven't," he spat back. In fact, Hargreaves had showed up unexpectedly this morning, announcing he'd decided to stay behind to help with Michaela, and he hadn't left since.

"I will when you do, sir," Hargreaves said, sitting across from him in a chair he'd brought in. "Perhaps this is a good time to remind you that a fever is the body's natural way of fighting infection. Michaela is also young and in good health."

Which meant squat in this remote part of the country, where the closest hospital was likely a hundred or more miles away.

But lashing out at Hargreaves wouldn't change any of that. He'd been nothing but helpful. "I appreciate you mentioning it right now. I only wish she'd wake up."

"As do I, sir," Hargreaves said, his folded hands signifying only calm. "I'll go for more water. It's a shame we left behind the coolers with the ice. I'd never imagined missing the mere luxury of ice until now."

"Yeah," Boyd said, taking his eyes off Michaela and looking at Hargreaves, who had grooves around his mouth. "Thank you again for helping."

"It's an honor, sir. I only wish I could do more. The first-aid kit I packed doesn't have anything useful for what Ms. Merriam faces. We must trust in Madam and Mr. Hale. I know they will be back as soon as possible."

And yet they were walking God only knew how far, which wouldn't be a picnic at their age. But he nodded and the man left.

Boyd touched Michaela's brow, his fingertips scorching from the heat emanating from her. The fact that he didn't know her exact temperature bothered him. Hargreaves had been right about fevers—they could heal a patient—but they could also kill one. He stopped his mind in its tracks. Best not to think about that.

She moaned again, this time rolling awkwardly onto her side. She vomited in a sudden rush.

He lurched out of his chair and pulled her hair back as much as he could. "Oh, baby!" It wasn't like she had anything in her stomach. She'd barely drunk the tea Lemayian had brewed. The small pot still sat on the table, which they'd moved close to the bed. The empty wooden cup sat beside it.

"Boyd," she whispered, her voice a harsh rasp.

"Yeah, Mickey, it's me." He eased her onto her back, smoothing her hair out, cleaning everything up as best he could with a spare cloth he'd laid out earlier. "I'm right here."

"Where are we?" Her green eyes were glassy and unfocused when she opened them. "My head hurts and my bones ache like crazy. Do I have the flu? I never get sick."

Tears filled his eyes. God, she sounded raspy, so unlike herself. "I remember that about you. Yes, you're sick, but we're taking care of you."

"Where are we? And why is a cow on me?" She pushed the hide off weakly, her cotton T-shirt soaked again.

"We're in Kenya, babe, really close to the Valley of Stars." He traced her cheek softly. "They're bringing the flower to you."

"The flower? Oh, right. We found it. That's good, because I feel wretched."

Hargreaves appeared in the opening of the tent, an earthenware pitcher in hand.

"Don't worry, Mickey, everything is going to be okay. I promise." He knew this wasn't a promise he could guarantee, but he needed to comfort her. It was the one thing he might have the power to do in this situation. "Babe, I'm sorry you're sick."

"Me too." Moaning, she closed her eyes again. "God, I'm so hot. I don't want this on me."

He whisked the hide off her. Her bare legs were slicked with sweat. Water seemed to be pouring out of her. Alarmed, he looked at Hargreaves as the man handed him a wet cloth. "Find Lemayian."

The man rushed out without bowing, a rarity for him.

"Who are you talking to?" she asked. He took her hand,

but it felt limp in his grasp, even though he could tell she was trying to hold on to him too.

"Hargreaves. Who knew he'd come in handy as a nurse on this trip?"

"I can hear the worry in your voice." She was quiet a moment, then said, "Do you know how much I love listening to your voice? I used to close my eyes when we were talking in bed, like that could make me hear it better or something. I missed it when you were gone."

He wiped at the tears in his eyes with his other hand. "Well, I'm back, so there's nothing to miss." He stared down at her. Her long curly hair was sticking to her skin from sweat. He needed to find her a new shirt. But she didn't have any clean clothes after the fall in the river. Now she might die, and it was his fault.

Pain tore through his heart like lightning tearing into a tree. How had he let their fight last for six months? He'd missed all that time. Well, no more. Taking out his wallet from his back pocket, he removed her engagement ring.

"I know you haven't said you'll marry me yet since I haven't officially asked you, but I figure this is as good a time as any to make a vow: I won't ever leave you or let you down ever again, Mickey."

"Good," she whispered, her voice faint. "I'd be so mad at you if you did."

He slid the ring onto her finger and lifted her hand to his mouth so he could kiss it.

"Kiss it and make it better," she whispered. "Mom always did that. I miss her."

"I know you do," he said, his gut roiling at the thought of her family. How would they take it if she worsened? If...

"I suppose if I can't have my mom, you'll do."

Usually a remark like that would have made him laugh. This time it only brought more tears filling his eyes. She was so weak, so feverish, and given the sweat sliding off her, she had to be dehydrated too.

"I love you, Mickey."

"Love you," she breathed out, and then she closed her eyes and went slack again.

He sat there holding her hand, looking at the engagement ring on her finger and telling himself she'd soon be up and well and promised to him for real.

Lemayian appeared, Hargreaves right behind him. The healer held the succulent leaves of the kalanchoe plant. "Hargreaves told me about her change. I brought this medicine. We heat the leaves and lay them on the skin for aches. Since she is so feverish, I will make a fire outside the hut."

"Thank you. What about the vomiting?"

"Give her more tea from the warburgia," Lemayian said, gazing at Michaela in the lantern light. "The vomiting is a good sign."

"A good sign?"

"Yes, the body is not only trying to burn out the sickness but purge it as well. Her body is hard at work, giving us time before Mr. and Mrs. Hale return. I feel it will be tomorrow. I sensed they took the shortcut to the valley earlier. Have faith, Boyd."

Faith was in short supply right now. "How long until the fever breaks with this medicine?"

"As long as it takes," Lemayian said. "The warrior my son sent to take the message to your guides, Simon and Jaali, has returned. He waited until Simon called Michaela's brother and delivered the message. Simon said her brother was very upset."

Of course Connor was upset. He couldn't communicate with Michaela. And her brother didn't even know she was ill. Damn, he missed the sat phone.

"Thank you for sending the warrior," Boyd said. "How far to the closest medical doctor? The vomiting..." Dehydration could kill her quickly.

The man sighed deeply. "Nine hours, I'm afraid. Six walking and the rest driving."

Too long, although he'd guessed that. "What about the closest telephone?" Boyd asked.

Lemayian came forward and touched Michaela's brow. "Also nine hours."

But closer than Jaali and Simon. "Why didn't you tell me that instead of having us send a warrior back down the river?"

"Because that was what you asked of us."

Right. He'd forgotten how literally things could be interpreted sometimes.

"I know you are frightened for your woman, but both Naserian and I have had visions of Mr. and Mrs. Hale returning in time with the flower. A messenger cannot leave until the sun rises, you know. There is no light for walking, and there are many dangerous animals out."

"Of course there are," he said, realizing how far gone he must be to have forgotten.

"Mr. and Mrs. Hale will be back before we can bring a doctor."

He shared a look with Hargreaves before pulling out his wallet. "I can't risk her. When morning comes, can you please send someone to the closest phone and have them call the number on this card? It's a medical evacuation company. They'll send someone from Nairobi." He just didn't know if it would be in time.

"As you wish," Lemayian said, bowing. "I will prepare more medicine."

After he left, Boyd hung his head. "I should have asked earlier," he whispered, his despair and helplessness growing as Michaela muttered senseless words. Each moan or cry was like a lance through his own skin.

"None of us thought to, Boyd," Hargreaves said, wetting the cloth again and placing it on her brow. "Perhaps Lemayian is right, and Madam and Mr. Hale will return before the medevac."

But they were out in the same hills Lemayian had just

reminded him were perilous. What if lions attacked them? They could be delayed—or killed. Anything could happen.

"Do you really think so, Hargreaves?" he asked, fatigue lacing his voice.

The man stood up from his chair and crossed until he was right beside him. Boyd was surprised to feel his hand come to rest on his shoulder. "I *know* they will, Boyd."

Hargreaves' use of his first name only seemed to confirm the situation was dire. He couldn't imagine the butler breaking protocol for any other reason.

Hargreaves resumed his seat beside Michaela on the other side of the bed. "The engagement ring looks good on Ms. Merriam's hand. Let me be the first to offer my congratulations, sir."

They shared a look, and the man's dark eyes held more softness than their usual inscrutability. Boyd knew he was trying to bolster his spirits. "I didn't officially propose yet—I want to do something special for that—but I thought it might..." He couldn't say out loud that he'd hoped a tangible link between them might make her better.

"A good idea, sir," Hargreaves said, dipping the cloth in the pitcher. "If I may ask, sir, what was the real reason you and Ms. Merriam parted ways?"

He poured more tea for Michaela. "Well, in short form, Hargreaves, I'd have to say I felt like Cinderella to her Prince Charming in the relationship."

Boyd lifted her head and pressed the cup of tea to her mouth. She swallowed a little, although she didn't stir.

"An interesting way to frame your relationship," Hargreaves said, bathing Michaela's brow with the cloth.

At one time, he'd thought the analogy clever. Now it only made him sad. "Since we're talking about this, any advice on how to change the story? You've been around wealth your whole life with Clara, but it's not yours. Kinda like Cinderella."

"I'm a butler, sir." Hargreaves set the cloth aside and

rested his hands on his knees. "I know my station. If I may be so bold, I would say you're mistaking prosperity and social status with worth. The problem with your story seems to be that you consider yourself Cinderella in the first place. Isn't the point of the fable that neither wealth nor station is of consequence in matters of the heart?"

"It's different for me then," Boyd said, feeling defensive. "I just wanted to bring something to the table. Be an equal. My own man."

"In your terms, Madam could buy Mr. Hale many times over," Hargreaves said. "Wealth doesn't enter into their relationship. Perhaps it's his advanced years, but Mr. Hale knows he's respected regardless of how much he's worth financially."

His jaw tightened. Hadn't Michaela said much the same thing? But he'd always felt such a powerful need to pay his share of things. He just couldn't afford as much as she could. "And yet their bank accounts still look really different, I imagine. That's never been a problem for them?"

"I wouldn't be privy to such details, but I don't think they would mind me sharing that while Madam still enjoys certain luxuries, she lives in Mr. Hale's more modest home in Colorado because he loves it and because it's close to his family and the life he's made there—one Madam happens to love. They seem to have recognized what is important to each other. Having served the Merriam family for many decades, I can affirm that most of them don't value their wealth over their relationships. You might recall Clara's brother married a woman whom you wouldn't consider wealthy."

A fair point. Assumpta was a proud woman. Had marrying into wealth bothered her? He'd never had the guts to ask. "I've met Michaela's parents, and I can see what you mean."

"Unfortunately, Madam's first husband did value wealth over relationships," the man continued. "The irony is that he was as wealthy as Madam."

"Right now, none of the reasons we fought seem to matter. I only want her to get well, Hargreaves."

"Then we will make it so," the man said, rising from his chair. "I will see if I can help Lemayian. The women would like to bring you something to eat."

He wasn't in touch with his stomach, but he hadn't eaten all day. In the windowless hut, he'd lost all track of time. "I'll step out when you two return and grab something quickly. I don't want to eat around Michaela since she's nauseous."

"A good decision, sir," Hargreaves said, leaving them alone again.

He stared down at Michaela, thinking about what Hargreaves had said. Perhaps he was right. The problem was that he thought of himself as Cinderella, the one from nothing, with nothing. When had he decided he had so little to offer her? And why had money become the measurement of his worthiness?

Some of the kids at the special math and science school he'd won a scholarship to had made fun of the clothes his mother had bought at Goodwill. He'd shrugged it off, but it had bothered him. Then someone had discovered his mother "cleaned up other people's shit," as Freddy Bado had so aptly put it. He'd been embarrassed, no denying it. He'd preferred being seen as "that crazy snake charmer," something he'd overheard someone saying as they passed his house. That boy had commanded respect.

He'd grown up, as people do, and left behind the boy he'd been—until he went to Michaela's parents' house for dinner that first time. That night, he'd seen another world, the kind he'd only previously glimpsed when visiting his mom at work. Old fears of not being good enough had kicked in. When people at work started ribbing him for being Michaela Merriam's boyfriend, the shadow over him had widened until he'd blindly pursued the most lucrative job offer he could find.

Was he over that hump now?

God, he had to be because he couldn't lose her again.

He angled closer to her on the bed, touching her face flushed red from the fever. "I love you. Come back to me."

He and Hargreaves kept a quiet vigil through the night. The vomiting worsened, to the point where Michaela's body was wracked with spasms so great he feared her bones would shatter. The fever continued, her skin as hot as the embers in the fire outside the hut where Lemayian went from time to time to heat the plant leaves before placing them on her body. Boyd braided her hair finally, nearly crying at how weak and lifeless she felt in his arms. At dawn, her fever was still raging, and she began to mumble.

"Fever dreams," Lemayian said from the entrance to the hut, his demeanor grave. "The messenger you asked for is preparing to leave. He is our top runner. Unfortunately, I cannot send one to Mr. and Mrs. Hale since the valley's location is a secret, but I will post a lookout close in the hills to watch for them."

Maasai runners were known worldwide for their speed. "Thank you, Lemayian," he managed, although he wasn't sure how much longer Michaela could go on like this—although he kept plying her with liquid and tea, she was vomiting and sweating something fierce, losing too much liquid. But he had to keep believing—for her sake as much as his own.

"She's strong," he whispered, looking at her laid out on the bed, her body slicked with sweat and so very still—like the fight had gone out of her.

"Of course she is," Hargreaves said, returning to his chair. "She's a Merriam."

Boyd nodded, lowering his head onto the bed beside Michaela, her hand still in his, and did something he hadn't done since his father had left him and his mother.

He prayed for help to whoever would listen.

CHAPTER 19

WALKING FOR TWO CONSECUTIVE DAYS WASN'T FOR SIS-sies, that was for damn sure.

Arthur toddled—yes, toddled—down what Sironka had announced were the final hills to the village. Amen. Hallelujah. The flower would be able to work its magic on Michaela. He'd focused on walking and not worrying, needing every ounce of his strength.

"Clara, my dear, I keep telling myself to be grateful we didn't have another run-in with a mammoth crocodile or hippo, but I fear my body is short on thanks after all this walking."

"After this, I'm considering climbing Kilimanjaro," Clara said, her skin glowing with vigor. "I could make it to base camp. Face down their famed leopards. I'm sure of it now. Hargreaves is game to give it a go."

He didn't have the energy to harrumph. Last night, Clara had conked out, but he hadn't slept a wink. Darn monkeys and other animals had been partying until dawn. Who knew it was cocktail hour in the jungle? And after seeing that lion disappear...

Well, he'd been concerned it was the early sign of a stroke. Except Clara had seen it, and she had all her marbles.

He looked at her. The silver mane of hair trailed down her back, and there was a determined thrust to her delectable chin. In the afternoon light, she was so beautiful she took his breath away, assuming he had any breath left after this journey.

"I've never been prouder of you, my dear," he said, taking her hand.

"Right back at you, Mr. Hale."

"That damn shortcut might have shaved off an extra day, but let's not speak of our perils to Boyd or Michaela. Feel free to regale Hargreaves, of course."

"Agreed," she said with smile. "I'd planned to tell Hargreaves over a strong gin and tonic. You should join us."

"I'll need a double scotch," he said, making her laugh.

As they crested down a hill, a Maasai warrior appeared and waved his spear in the air. Sironka gestured in kind, and the warrior from the village started racing toward them, his arms and legs pumping furiously.

"My heavens," Clara exclaimed. "He could win a marathon at that speed. Sironka, ask him how Michaela is."

Sironka nodded. When the other warrior reached them, the two men communicated in rapid-fire Maa. Arthur grew frustrated listening to the foreign tongue. He wanted news of his niece, but he couldn't make out a word.

"Your niece is still quite ill," Naserian said, turning toward them. "Clara, this man will run and take the flower to my husband, who will make it into a tea."

She eased open the woven shoulder bag Naserian had given her for the flowers they'd harvested together. The woman had taken her own bag for the village. Clara's flowers were to be used for any testing or early production.

And to save Michaela.

"How many flowers does she need?" Clara asked.

Naserian selected a single flower from Clara's outstretched hand. "We will reach the village by the time she needs another. A few hours…" She handed the flower to the warrior. He bowed very formally and spoke in their direction before running off.

"It is a great honor for him," Sironka added. "Let us go. It is not far now."

Still, it felt far on his old legs. To think he'd once used a cane. Then Clara had come into his life, and he hadn't seemed to need it anymore. Of course, she'd put it out of reach to make him walk. And he'd done so...more easily than he remembered. And yet today, he could have used that infernal cane.

"Oh, Arthur," Clara said as they sighted the fence surrounding the village. "We've made it!"

He wanted to kiss her, but there was plenty of time for that. "Yes, and now we must see about Michaela."

People were spilling out of their huts, abandoning cooking fires and other chores, as they entered the village. Chief Mingati approached with other elders and bowed. Arthur had to grind his teeth at the ceremony.

"Welcome back from your journey, Mr. and Mrs. Hale," the chief said. "Our people thank you for the honor you do our ancestors and for your help in sharing the flower with the world. Now, you must see to your niece."

Arthur bowed because he didn't know what the hell else to do. He caught sight of Hargreaves moving toward them in the crowd, his normally composed face lined with worry.

"My God, man, you look a hundred years old," he said when the butler reached them.

"You look little better, but you are a welcome sight." Hargreaves took Clara's outstretched hand, and for a moment Arthur thought the two would embrace. But no, that damn protocol prevented it. He was tired of it.

"Dammit, Hargreaves, if you don't take Clara in hand now, you'll never do it," he barked, "and after what we've been through, she'd find it a comfort."

The butler somehow managed to look down his nose at

him even if it wasn't a full-wattage set down. Nonetheless, he stooped to kiss Clara on both cheeks. "Forgive the impropriety, Madam, but our predicament has been unusual to say the least."

"Thank you, Hargreaves," Clara said, smoothing back her hair. "How is Michaela?"

"Very ill, Madam," Hargreaves responded. "So ill Boyd sent someone to call for medical evaluators from Nairobi. Lemayian administered the flower, and we are waiting for it to take effect."

She was that bad? The news gave him a surge of energy. "Well, good God, man, let's not waste another moment blathering."

When he entered the hut, the shock of seeing her hit him in the chest. He flashed back to those horrible last days with his first wife, Harriet, when she was in the hospital chock full of cancer. "No."

When Boyd turned, his face haggard, Arthur realized he'd said it aloud.

Clara gasped behind him, and then he felt her slide her hand into his. She was trembling. Of course, he was too. Michaela was still as if dead.

"Lemayian gave her the tea," Boyd said, his voice rough as sandpaper. "The medevac people haven't arrived yet, and I don't know when they will. She stopped vomiting, but her fever continues. The flower had better…"

Arthur helped Clara into the chair beside the bed and she immediately took her niece's hand. "Her fever hasn't broken? My God, she's still burning like an inferno."

"I know," Boyd said. "She only woke up once, when I put the engagement ring on her finger. I keep wondering if that's the last time I'll ever talk to her."

Grief dripped from every word.

Arthur shuffled over to Boyd and put a hand on his shoulder. He knew the agony of sitting beside someone he loved, helpless to change her suffering. Of course, Clara had recently sat beside his hospital bed after his heart attack. She'd refused to leave for any reason. It was then he'd realized he was one of the lucky few who'd been blessed with two great loves. When he looked at Clara, she was staring straight at him, her face tense as a wire. He couldn't tell her it would be all right.

"We walked two days for that damn flower," Arthur said, falling back on his old ways. Still, he wouldn't mention their brush with death. Boyd had enough problems without listening to theirs. "If it doesn't work, I'll walk back to that Valley of Stars and stomp on every single one. I don't care if it pisses off that lion."

"There was a lion?" Boyd asked.

"We'll tell you another time, Boyd," Clara said, reaching for a cloth to wipe Michaela's brow.

Actually, Arthur thought it was the best time for this one. "I imagine Michaela might enjoy the story. Right, honey?" He knew sick people could hear things. Even if they didn't understand everything, the voice of a loved one had to be a comfort. He'd certainly felt that way when he'd been sick and scared in the hospital—not that he'd admit it out loud.

Sironka appeared with another chair and gestured to it.

He'd never been so relieved to sit down in his life. "As I was saying…"

He began to tell the story of their trek to the Valley of Stars, leaving out the scary parts. Sironka brought in another chair for Hargreaves, and they formed a half circle around Michaela. Boyd didn't take his eyes off her face, and Arthur wasn't even sure he was listening. But he kept speaking, his voice unwavering. When he reached the part about them finding the flower, Clara reached into her bag and drew one out.

She tucked it into Michaela's hand. "It's shaped like a star, sweetheart. I wasn't sure if you knew that. Of course, the valley was so high up—and it's so dark—you could see a million stars. The flower opens at night, and with the moonlight on them, it's like the stars fell right into the valley."

He let her continue the story, sensing she needed to occupy her mind from worry. When she finished, she took out another flower and extended it to Boyd across Michaela's still form.

"I don't want it. She's all that's important now."

Clara tucked the flower back into her bag. "The ring looks beautiful on her finger, Boyd," she said softly. "I'm sure it was a comfort to her to have it."

His eyes were red-rimmed when he looked up. "I'm going to give her a better proposal. I only wanted..."

When his voice broke, Arthur found himself getting choked up. Time for everyone to steel themselves. "Of course you didn't. A fine woman like Michaela wouldn't want a man to propose to her on bended knee when she was in bed sick as a dog. Come on, now. When was the last time you took a break?"

"He's barely left her side," Hargreaves said gravely. "Perhaps you'll join me for a walk and a bite to eat, Boyd."

Boyd? He'd thought the man had said it earlier, but since Hargreaves never called anyone by their first name, he'd concluded he'd heard wrong. He opened his mouth to comment, but Clara's narrowed eyes had him snapping it shut again.

"No," Boyd said softly. "I won't leave her."

Arthur turned to Clara. "If he's happy to stay here, maybe you and I should go for a bite to eat. We certainly don't need a walk."

She didn't crack a smile, and truth be told, he didn't blame her. "I'll have something later. Hargreaves, will you find Naserian? I want to know what to expect now that Michaela has had the flower tea."

When the regal woman came to the tent, she checked Michaela's temperature. "The fever is lessening."

Boyd shot to his feet, his hand gently touching Michaela's forehead. "I can't tell."

"Wait and see," Naserian said. "Lemayian tells me you have called for help. That is your choice, of course. Until then, we'll keep giving her the tea, and when she wakes, some broth. Arthur and Clara...I will send you the herbal soup we give to warriors. After your journey, surely you have the heart of our great lion too."

When the soup arrived, Hargreaves leaned forward with interest. "How is it, sir?"

"Good," he responded. "Better than your Indian curry."

The corners of the man's mouth lifted into the briefest of smiles, an expression Clara mimicked before she dipped her spoon in for more soup.

"Boyd, you should eat," Arthur said.

"He hadn't wanted to eat around Ms. Merriam, sir, as she was nauseated, but that has passed. Perhaps I could find something for us both, Boyd."

The man just kept staring at Michaela, as if he didn't even hear the suggestion.

"I've done bedside vigils," Arthur said. "You need to keep strong for Michaela, and you can't do that if you don't take care of yourself."

He shook his head. "I can't eat. Nothing matters but her waking up."

Arthur noted the scruff on his jaw and his wrinkled clothes. Well, when someone you loved was sick, the minutiae of daily existence ceased to matter. He didn't fight Boyd about eating and neither did anyone else.

Night fell, and they kept vigil, Naserian and Lemayian visiting in shifts to administer more flower tea. When Clara started to fall asleep in her chair, Arthur decided to leave her be. He knew she wouldn't leave if he suggested it. Boyd continued to hold Michaela's hand, his gaze vigilant on her face.

Arthur felt himself dozing and leaned over to Hargreaves. "Wake me if something changes. I can't keep my eyes open."

"I imagine you'd be exhausted after two days of walking, sir," Hargreaves said. "Naserian was right to call you both warriors."

Wait until he heard the parts they'd left out of their earlier story...

"You look like you've been awake for days too, Hargreaves. Clara and I thank you for your help."

"It's my pleasure, sir."

"Does this mean you're going to start calling me Arthur?" He had to ask.

The man's spine seemed to straighten right up. "No, sir."

He let his eyes close. "Just thought I'd check. Clifton."

A slight scoff was all he heard, and then he let himself succumb to sleep.

A jostling of his arm awoke him. The first streaks of dawn were pouring into the hut.

"She moved!" This from Hargreaves.

Not exactly a pronouncement of clean health. He opened his eyes, fatigue still plaguing him.

"Boyd?"

The soft rasp sounded feminine.

Boyd shoved out of his seat and was leaning over Michaela the next instant. "I'm here, babe. Right here."

"God, I ache..." She looked down. "What's that? On my hand?"

"Clara and Arthur brought the flower, Mickey," Boyd said, enthusiasm lighting his shadowed face. "You drank the tea from it and it's lowered your temperature some."

"I don't feel as hot." She lifted her left hand weakly, moaning. "But that's not what I meant. What's this?"

He took it and kissed her fingers softly. "The ring I got you. When you woke up earlier... I wanted you to remember what I'd told you."

Her eyes closed as she said, "That you love me?"

Tears filled his eyes. "Yes, Mickey. I love you and always will. You rest now."

"Have you been here...the whole time?" she asked.

"Never left you once."

"Stubborn," she said, sounding like she was falling asleep again.

"Like you," he said, standing up beside her bed. "Thank God."

"I think she's going to make it, Boyd." This from Hargreaves.

"Me too," the young man said, pressing his hand to his mouth. "Excuse me."

He strode out of the hut quickly, and Arthur knew why. The relief of a loved one recovering from a frightening illness would cause any man to break down.

Clara stirred in her chair. "Thank God she's going to be all right."

He nodded. "You said it. Now that we know the flower works, my dear, what are we going to do about it?"

She gave him a pointed look as she stretched in her chair. "Exactly what you think."

He'd been afraid of that.

CHAPTER 20

WHEN MICHAELA OPENED HER EYES AGAIN, THE FIRST thing she saw was Boyd sitting beside her.

"You were sleeping so peacefully your family decided to take a break," he said in a voice that sounded funny. Rather like he had a cold. "How are you feeling?"

"I'm still achy, but I don't feel hot," she said, trying to sit up, but her arms shook from the attempt. "All I can remember is the heat. Why am I wearing Aunt Clara's shirt?"

"Because you sweated through the ones Clara and I put on you," he said, nestling her back. "But your fever broke, thank God. The rest of your healing is progressing nicely according to Naserian and Lemayian."

Naserian and Lemayian, the medicine man and woman. The memories flooded back. "I remember now. The flower works, huh?"

"Like a charm, although it's no scientific certainty. But from where I'm standing, so to speak, you're a walking miracle—or will be when you're strong enough."

"Imagine all the good it will do in the world..."

"Yes, but let's focus on getting you better all the way now and leave that for later," he said, pouring her something from a pitcher and reaching for her neck. "You must be thirsty."

"Were you the one forcing me to drink that horrid tea? I was already so hot, it felt like a nightmare. I couldn't push the person away, and they kept insisting."

"Sometimes it was me, and sometimes it was our two friendly healers." He helped her drink, and the cool water tasted fresh.

"You said my aunt and uncle and Hargreaves are taking a break? I want to sit up. Will you help me?" God, she was sticky.

"Well, they're taking care of some business with the tribe," he said, his powerful arms gently raising her up. "There's no bedframe, and you're pretty weak. You're going to have to lean on me."

He positioned himself on the bed behind her and placed her against his chest, the warmth and comfort of his body a welcome balm. "You can be my bedframe any time. When was the last time you slept? Do I look as bad as you?"

"You're always beautiful."

She didn't have the energy to snort. "Bullshit. I'm sticky and my hair seems knotted against my head."

"I braided it."

"You did? I wish I'd been awake for that."

"We can have a repeat performance any time you'd like." He ran his hands up and down her arms, resting his chin on her head. "You scared the hell out of me, Mickey."

"It's not like I meant to," she said, letting herself lean completely against him. "I don't remember much except for the force-feeding of tea, Aunt Clara giving me the flower—where is it, by the way?—and seeing my engagement ring on my hand. Yep, it's still there. Glad you didn't take it off once I was out of the woods."

He let out a harsh sigh. "It was meant to remind you of all the reasons to come back to me. Like your uncle said, you don't propose to woman on her sickbed."

And yet that ring was as strong a symbol of his love as his bedhead. "You haven't slept, have you?"

"I might have dozed here and there once your fever broke, but I tried to keep awake. I wanted to be here when you woke up. During the fever, I..."

His voice broke, and she wished she had the energy to turn and hold him. "What?"

"I was afraid you weren't coming back. Mickey, I need to apologize. If I'd thought you'd get sick, I never would have brought you here."

Guilt? "I swallowed buckets of river water, Boyd. That's it. Now, you'd better tell me everything I've missed."

He kissed the top of her head. "When you're a little better."

"I'm gaining strength in leaps and bounds," she said, turning slightly in his arms to look up at his face. "God, your eyes look like the kind dragons have in those movies you enjoy so much."

"We've redefined red-eye apparently," he said, rubbing the eyes in question.

"I want to know what I missed."

He growled. "Fine, but you have to take a nap afterward. Deal?"

Since turning to look at him made her ache, she shifted to her original position. "You would negotiate with me about this. Fine, I agree. But I've been sleeping for days. How many, by the way?"

"I've kinda lost track of time. Your aunt and uncle got back the day before yesterday, I think."

Had it been that long? No wonder his eyes looked so bad. "You promise to take a nap too? With me?"

Another soft kiss landed in the vicinity of her ear. "I miss a California king bed, let me tell you. The Maasai have a lot of things to recommend them, but bedding isn't one of them."

She gazed down at the cowhide covering her legs and had to agree. But she didn't need to tell him so. "You're stalling."

"Okay, you've got yourself a deal." He blew out a gusty sigh. "Do you want the good news or bad news first?"

"There's good news?" She mustered a pathetic chuckle.

"Yep, here goes. The flower worked on you."

"I already know that, Boyd."

He emitted a rude sound. "The bad news is two-fold. Let's start with this: a medevac team is going to show up for you any time now."

"What?"

"I didn't think to ask how close a doctor or phone was at first. Blame it on the situation. But when you started vomiting, I asked how far it was to the nearest phone—no surprise, it was far—and had them send someone to call the medevac company I engaged for this trip in case of emergencies. I thought they'd be here by now, but maybe it's taking longer to come from Nairobi."

"I can see why you called them in," she said, remembering all the times she'd taken for granted having a medevac company on call. "When they get here, we'll tell them I'm doing so much better."

He worried his lip. "Maybe you should go. Just to be sure."

"But the flower's working." She made herself lean up and grab his shoulders. "I can't leave, Boyd. Not when we've finally found the flower."

"I thought you might say that, which leads us to our second item of bad news. You might change your mind about leaving when you hear it."

She shook her head. "No way."

"Mickey, we're not the couple in the visions."

She felt her mouth part in response. "You're kidding. Someone else has your affinity for snakes? Say it ain't so."

"So," he said, his tone bemused. "Apparently, Peanut, your aunt's old snake, qualifies. Mickey, the tribe believes your aunt and uncle are the couple."

She sputtered out a laugh. "What? Is that why you stayed here?"

"I was told I couldn't go along with Naserian for the flower. It wasn't for me to do. So your aunt and uncle walked for two days straight to go to the Valley of Stars and bring it back to you."

He wasn't kidding. "Holy—"

"Shit, yes, my thoughts exactly."

They fell silent a moment as she took that in. The tribe had been very attentive to her aunt and uncle, now that she thought about it. "So the baby they gave Aunt Clara—"

"Represented all the children in the village, past, present, and future. They believe the gods sent Clara and Arthur to help the tribe share the flower with the world. They're supposedly incorruptible, according to what I've heard, and they're powerful due to their respective stations in life. Your aunt as a wealthy woman and your uncle—"

"As a respected journalist." One of the reasons he'd been included in the trip in the first place. That gave her chills. "My aunt and uncle believe this?"

"Your aunt had Hargreaves learn how to dry the flowers alongside her and Naserian. Right now, they're speaking with the chief and his council. Remember Sironka's sister the lawyer? She was sent to make sure the Maasai officially owned the land so they could share the title with the so-called couple in the visions."

"And they're going to accept?"

"They're discussing the details with the tribe as we speak. Your aunt seems to think there's something to it."

Where did that leave Boyd? And her, for that matter? "What does Uncle Arthur think?"

He ran his hands up her arms again. "He walked for two days at his age to help you, but this next move feels more like Clara to me. She wants to believe in the visions."

"The entire tribe obviously does," she said. "What does Joseph think?"

"He didn't know the full truth of it until now, but he thinks it makes an odd sort of sense. Your aunt says he made a joke about how the gods leave out important details sometimes. You know Joseph."

Yes, he made the best of every situation. "That's why we've always liked him."

She folded her hands over her arms, her gaze resting on the ring on her finger. While it was still a little weird to see it there, somehow it looked and felt right, especially with Boyd's arms around her. "How are they supposed to gather enough flowers to share with the world?"

"Naserian seems to think the three of them will pick the flowers themselves."

"By hand?" This time she had to make the effort to meet his eyes. "At their age? That's insane."

"Why?"

They both turned to the opening in the hut. Aunt Clara stood there alongside Uncle Arthur and Hargreaves.

"I'm overjoyed to see you sitting up and conversing, niece, but am disappointed to hear you're calling our new enterprise crazy."

"But Aunt... Do you really want to come back here a few times a year to hand-pick flowers? You'll have to cross that horrible river filled with all the crocs and hippos." Just thinking about the return trip made her sick to her stomach.

"We've been meeting all day with the chief and the council, and certain things have become clearer to us," she said, coming closer and taking the vacant chair beside the bed. "Haven't they, Arthur?"

Her uncle patted her hand as he sat in Boyd's chair. Hargreaves remained standing until Uncle Arthur pointed to the chair at the foot of her bed. Even the usually spit-and-polished Hargreaves looked like he'd been through the wringer, from the dark circles around his eyes to the spattering of wrinkles on his shirt and pants.

"You don't look ready to conquer the world yet," Uncle

Arthur said, "but you do look better, niece. You aged this old man twenty years."

"Don't speak such nonsense, Arthur." Her aunt's eyes sparkled with new vitality. "This experience didn't age you. It forged you in steel. May I point out that you—a supposedly old man to some people's minds—just walked for two days straight at an altitude that would make many people sick. Other than sore feet and tired muscles, you're fit as a fiddle. Now, we should probably first share the alarming news we heard from the chief."

Boyd seemed to straighten up behind her. "What news?"

"Warriors from three other tribes in these hills and the Sekenani Valley have arrived with great concern about a businessman flying over these hills in a helicopter. He has armed guards, and he's looking for us."

"I didn't think the medevac people came like that," she said slowly.

"They don't," Boyd said harshly. "Also, I would think the person calling them would have told them how to find the village."

"Exactly," Arthur said. "From their description, it sounds like Iggie rented a chopper and some hired muscle. They didn't have uniforms and they were packing AK-47s. My money is on mercenaries."

Oh my God. She'd known he was culturally tone deaf, but this was unacceptable. "Mercenaries are a dime a dozen in Africa," she said softly. The thought of armed men storming through these hills was so wrong, she wanted to jump out of bed and find Iggie just so she could throttle him.

"It's upsetting the surrounding tribes, as you might imagine," Aunt Clara continued. "They aren't used to anyone coming uninvited into these lands, especially with such an aggressive approach. The medevac helicopter is different. I would imagine it would be here soon."

"I'm not going," she said, crossing her arms.

"Somehow I'm not surprised," Arthur said, his mouth tilting into a smile.

Her aunt rose and touched her brow. "She's fit as a fiddle too, and getting fitter every hour. The flower fits its name."

"It has a name?" she asked, eager to hear it.

"Naserian said your aunt could name it." Uncle Arthur was grinning now.

"I called it Life Giver, and so it does. You should both know that Naserian and Lemayian had visions that someone with great darkness would come and try to take the flower."

"Iggie is just the kind of asshole who would do that," Uncle Arthur said.

"He sure is," Boyd said, rubbing her arms.

Did that mean Boyd bought into the visions wholesale, or was he simply suggesting Iggie was indeed capable of this kind of disrespect? She still wasn't sure what she believed. The flower was real and it worked, but she still had questions.

"Looks like things just got a heck of a lot more complicated." Boyd rose, his brow furrowing.

"Exactly," her uncle said. "We're thinking Iggie reached Simon and Jaali after they called Connor, and when the Maasai warrior with them refused to take him to the village and wouldn't tell him our exact whereabouts, he upped the ante, so to speak."

"Iggie doesn't like being told no," she said softly, considering the scenario.

"Who does?" her uncle said. "Or maybe he came from Nairobi with the soldiers and the Maasai warrior got defensive. Right now, we don't know the full story, but the chief has sent some men to check in with Simon and Jaali. Bottom line: Iggie's causing tremendous upheaval in the area. The other tribes feel threatened. Also, he's blabbed his big mouth about the flower. The tribes he's visited have been asking about it."

"Terrific," Boyd muttered.

"How did the tribe explain all their old people before?" Michaela asked.

"The elders kept to their own huts if visitors came around," Clara said. "No one shows up without being announced because no one enters this land without the chief's permission."

"This can't be how the tribe envisioned things going," Boyd said. "It's reinforcing every reason they kept the flower secret in the first place."

"Exactly," Aunt Clara said, "but we're going to do something about it when he arrives. Unless the chief's warriors track them down first."

"We weren't reachable, sure, but it's ridiculous that he'd bring armed men," Michaela said. "And we sent a message. We're clearly not in any danger from the tribe."

"But Iggie wouldn't think like that," Boyd said. "He's paranoid even in a sleek corporate office. The field would worsen that."

"Certainly after being in Customs," she said.

Then the whooshing of a helicopter sounded overhead, and Boyd gently moved her, settling her back on the mattress, and rushed to the entrance. "Don't worry," he called back. "It's just the medevac people."

"I'm still not going," she said, giving him her best smile.

He was shaking his head. "I'll tell them, but let's have them check you out anyway. Maybe I can get a message to your brother on their radio or sat phone, should they have one. Let him know we're okay." Turning to Aunt Clara and Uncle Arthur, he said, "Okay, before I take care of our guests, any other news?"

Her aunt smiled as the commotion outside grew louder and pulled something out of the hand-woven bag on her shoulder. "We now co-own the Maasai's land with them. Notarized by Naserian and Lemayian's daughter."

Michaela squinted. Her gaze caught her aunt and uncle's

names scrawled at the bottom of the deed alongside Chief Mingati's signature. They'd done it, all right.

"Oh. My. God."

CHAPTER 21

BOYD COULDN'T IGNORE THE BAD FEELING IN HIS GUT. Even though he'd left a message with Connor's assistant using the medevac team's sat phone, things still didn't feel right. He hadn't mentioned she'd been ill, however. It hadn't seemed wise to leave an inflammatory message like that. Better for Michaela to tell him in person, so he could see with his own eyes she was okay. Fortunately, the doctors had confirmed she was on the mend, and she had steadily improved over the next two days.

The entire village was still on high alert, but he'd done his best to keep that from Michaela. She was getting well and embracing life in a way that made his heart happy when it wasn't racked with worry about Iggie.

Or the fact that he and Michaela probably would not be ushering the flower into the world after all.

"You're worrying again," Michaela said, rising from the bed. "Come on, it's time for another therapeutic walk around the village and some sun. Where's my family, by the way?"

"They've all taken to village life like eager-beaver new Peace Corps recruits. Your uncle is in the village pub with the men, drinking and sharing news. He's says it's like his Bingo night at home. Funny, but I can't see your uncle playing Bingo. I always thought it was boring."

"Wait! They have a *pub* here?"

"Yep." He wouldn't mention it was for men only. "I can't remember their name for it. Your aunt is teaching some women to knit. Yesterday, they taught her basket weaving."

"And Hargreaves?"

This time he couldn't help but laugh. "He's with the warriors. They're teaching him how to throw a spear and make poisoned arrows. That's some butler your aunt has." He'd never forget the way Hargreaves had stood by Michaela's sickbed with him, let alone the fact that the man had broken protocol to call him by his first name. Man, he might as well admit it. He kinda loved the guy. "Do you think Hargreaves would come and work for me? I think he'd make a great lab assistant."

"Only if you want my aunt to use a spear on you," she said, laughing as well. "Also, no more soups today. I don't care how healthy they are."

"Nothing heals like plant extracts, Mickey, and you know it." So good he was wondering if he could market and sell them—with the village's permission, of course.

"But I feel about ninety percent now. The flower really does work wonders."

"It boosts the immune system faster than anything I've seen," Boyd said, coming over to put his arm around her. "But you're only eighty-five percent, Mickey. Don't push it."

She caressed his jaw. "At least you stopped fussing over me long enough to shave. You were starting to look like a caveman. You need to stop treating me so delicately, Boyd. I mean, you haven't even really kissed me."

"I don't want to drain your energy. Do you realize how sick you were?"

She twined her arms around his neck. "Kisses are healing." Although he didn't want her to push herself, she didn't seem to be straining as she rose on her tiptoes and pressed a kiss to his neck, and man, did it feel good.

She ran her arms down his chest. "Touch is healing. So is sex, by the way."

He snorted. "Are you going to break out your rendition of 'Sexual Healing'?"

"I've always loved that song." Her hands traveled to the hem of his pants. "You're a scientist. Think of all the endorphins you'll release inside me. Oxytocin is as good for the body as it is for the soul. I'll bet the medevac people would have prescribed it along with rest and fluids if it had crossed their minds."

Okay, that had him laughing. "Your clinical attempt to seduce me isn't working."

Taking his face in her hands, she looked him straight in the eye. "Forget the science then. I want to make love with *you*. Don't make me beg you for it, Boyd."

How was he supposed to fight that? He could take care of her and make sure it wasn't too strenuous. He lit a kerosene lamp. "Let me close the door to our lovely hut here. I just hope your family will see the closed door— ahem, hide—and not barge in. If it had a door handle, I could hang my shirt on it or something. Being caught by your aunt and uncle or Hargreaves would rank up there with getting an erection in seventh grade when I first caught sight of Amber Pereguin in a yellow bikini at the pool."

She laughed. "Poor Amber. I remember this story. She asked if something had happened to you and whether you needed a doctor. I'm trying to remember the first time I saw an erection. I think it was—"

"Mickey, we don't have time for erection recollections," he said, shaking his head.

"Then I'll strip. You should do the same. You know,

a hut in a Maasai village works for me. It's not the Ritz, but I've never been that kind of girl."

Stripping off his shirt—the only concession he'd make right now—he joined her on the bed. "This sucker still is hard as a rock, and I miss my pillow. I'm getting soft."

She put her hand on him, and his eyes almost crossed. "Soft? I think not."

Chuckling, he removed her hand. "We're focusing on you. Stop playing around."

Her fingers tickled his chest. "Make me."

"You *are* feeling better," he said, opening her legs. "Now, lie back and shut the hell up." He grinned a little as he lowered his mouth to press a kiss at the apex of her legs.

"Yes, sir," she said with a moan.

His hands came to rest on her hips. "I love you, Mickey."

Leaning up on her elbow, she touched his face. "I know. I love you too. Please, Boyd, make love to me. I know you're trying to be noble here and take care of my needs, but that's not how I want it."

"You were on your deathbed a few days ago," he said, his jaw clenching at the thought. "Don't fight me on this. I want you completely well. I can't..."

She sat up all the way, searching his eyes. "Do you trust me?"

"Yes."

"So trust me when I say I can do this without zapping my energy." She traced his lips. "Be with me. There's no greater healing force on earth."

They kissed, long and slow, and he lowered them to their sides. He caressed her breasts as their tongues continued to dance, and his hand strayed to all the places he'd washed with a wet cloth when she was wracked with fever: the slope of her neck, the curve of her shoulders, the valley between her breasts, and the backs of her knees. His touch was a loving benediction, and he let gratitude wash through him as he felt her skin's cool, smooth perfection under his fingertips. He never wanted to feel it burn like that ever again unless it was in desire. When he reached down to run kisses up her inner thighs, she surprised him by pushing him onto his back and straddling him.

"I need you," she whispered. "Right now."

He helped her lower herself onto him, aware she was already trembling, and groaned at the friction. "Should you be on top?"

"Shut up."

She was always bossy, but then again, so was he. His smile seemed to put one on her face. He raised his knees to support her back since this was how she wanted it, and she moved on top of him, slowly, ever so slowly. *Holy freaking Christ*. The urgency of his body made him want to close his eyes and simply luxuriate in their rhythm, but he didn't allow himself, needing to keep an eye on her. God, she was beautiful. Flushed and sensual in the soft lamplight. His heart cracked wider, love and light spilling out of it. He hoped she now knew how much he loved her.

"Stop watching me like you think I'm going to keel over," she whispered. "You're not with me all the way."

"I can't help being careful after what you've been through." He traced where they were joined, making her moan and cry out. "Come for me."

"Not without you." She ground her hips into him, urging him on.

He sat up with her, arranging her legs around his hips. The position would still be gentle, but it was more connected this way. Deeper. He was fighting the urge to take her harder every second. Threading his hands into her hair, he looked right into those beautiful green eyes of hers.

"Don't hold back on me either," he said, and then he kissed her, pulling her to him. Bringing himself deeper.

She clenched around him, moaning into his mouth as he used tongue and teeth to urge her on. Rocking against her, he swallowed her cries, feeling sweat gather at his spine. Her legs tightened around him, and he knew she was close. He angled back so she'd take him even deeper, and he felt her pulse around him.

"Take more," he whispered, still holding back. "Take everything."

She cried out, going higher for him, and then he pressed his face into her neck and let himself come, biting his lip to keep from crying out himself. God, he'd missed her. That she was healthy enough to be with him like this was a relief, and he felt a huge ball of emotion rise up in his chest. He'd been trying to push it away. Hadn't he cried his guts out in the woods after she finally woke up?

"Hey," she said quietly, rubbing his back. "It's okay. I'm okay."

But she hadn't been, and he couldn't shake the image of the skin he'd just loved and caressed bathed with sweat. "I know. I'm just having a moment. Oh, Mickey... I'm so glad you're better. I was so freaking scared."

She kissed his shoulder. "I'm glad you were with me. I know we think it was the flower that saved me, but having you stay beside me... It kept me going, Boyd. I know it did."

He liked to think that too. "It means...everything that you'd say that after what happened between us... Shit. I'm sorry. I'm pulling it together."

She feathered his hair off his forehead. "You don't need to apologize, Boyd. Heck, I'm probably going to have a complete meltdown in the future about this too. You know how it goes. The body heals first, and then you deal with the emotional side. When I tell my family what happened, I know I'm going to lose it. Caitlyn will start crying or my dad will wrap me up in a bear hug..."

"I'll be right beside you then too," he said, raising his head. "Now you should probably sleep."

He gave her a pointed look, but she only smiled. "Can't. Endorphins and the like. And happiness. I'm so glad we're back together, Boyd."

Tracing her cheek, he grinned back at her. "Me too."

A loud whooshing sounded overhead, and he heard shouts and cries outside the hut. So much for leaving a message with Connor. Clearly, it had been ignored.

"Iggie is here."

CHAPTER 22

CLARA RECOGNIZED THE BLACK HELICOPTER BEFORE IT landed in the middle of the village, causing villagers to cry out and rush for cover.

Well, most of them were rushing away. The warriors had formed a circle around the perceived threat, spears at the ready. Oh, she was going to give Iggie a piece of her mind for not heeding Boyd's message to Connor that they were all fine.

"What a disaster!" Arthur put his arm around her as he reached her. "Is that the same chopper we saw in Ireland?"

"No, Arthur. They have a whole fleet, I imagine." But the Merriam Enterprises logo on the side was as unmistakable now as it had been then. On that occasion, her nephews Connor and Quinn had, quite rudely, landed on Becca O'Neill's land. Their sudden appearance had triggered an episode for Becca, who suffered from acute agoraphobia. Although there'd been reckoning between the Merriam siblings, she knew it had been difficult for Trevor to forgive his brothers for hurting his now-wife. It seemed a bad omen, to say the least, that such a helicopter should be here now. "Iggie must have ignored Boyd's call to headquarters—"

She broke off as the helicopter's door opened, revealing none other than Connor himself, followed by Iggie and four mercenary types in green camo loaded down with an arsenal of weapons. Well, that explained it! If seeing her nephew hadn't boosted her blood pressure, the sight of the warriors brandishing their spears surely did. "My God, who knows what Iggie told Connor."

"The village is readying like there's a war brewing," Arthur shouted over the noise.

"Who can blame them? I need Hargreaves. Immediately." Better to be prepared for any sort of villainy. Iggic wasn't to be trusted. As for why Connor was here like this, they'd see...

Turning, she saw him running toward her, his normally calm demeanor absent at the moment. "Madam—"

"Hide or guard the flowers, Hargreaves, and take Sironka and some warriors with you," she said in a crisp voice. "Just in case."

"A wise move," Arthur said as her butler took off in a mad dash. "Come, my dear. Seems the younger generation has some learning to do regarding the spirit of international cooperation."

"Connor's here?" she heard Boyd say from behind her.

Turning, she saw Michaela doing her best to run after him, breathing hard. "God knows what Iggie told him," Clara responded. "Let me handle this."

"I might share a little blame there," Boyd said, making a face, "which I'll explain later. In the meantime, you might want to make sure the flowers are safe."

"Do I look stupid, Boyd? It's taken care of. Come!"

Connor and Iggie were approaching them, ducking low since the helicopter's pilot hadn't cut the engine. Women were huddling against the huts, their children clutching their red Shúkàs. Oh, this was outrageous. She saw the chief and elders approaching with Naserian and Lemayian, warriors at their sides.

Someone needed to put a stop to this. No, *she* needed to put a stop to this.

Not bothering to see if the others were following, she advanced to the group of warriors circling the helicopter. They wouldn't like her ordering them around, but she was their elder. "Let us pass." No one was close enough to translate, so she made a shooing motion with her hands. They bowed and made an opening in their line. She watched the soldiers with Connor dip their weapons in response. Bunch of testosterone junkies, all of them. It made her sick.

"Connor Albert Merriam!" she called out loud enough to stop the man in his tracks. "What in the hell do you think you're doing? Didn't you get Boyd's message?"

Iggie only glared at her—the odious man!—but Connor yanked on his well-tailored navy suit and strode forward. "Yes, but I decided to make sure for myself that everyone was still alive," he snarled.

"Of course we're alive," Arthur spat out. "We conveyed that in two messages, for God's sake, one to Simon and the one from Boyd."

The chopper noise was deafening. "Turn that damn machine off so we don't have to shout at each other."

Her nephew turned his head and made a slashing motion to his throat, which made the warriors raise their spears again. The engine died finally, and the quiet was a boon to her ears.

"Calm down, everyone," she said, holding up her hand.

Chief Mingati approached with his entourage and called out something in Maa, which made the warriors lower their weapons.

Introductions might be the best way to kick off the détente they clearly needed. "Connor, this is Chief—"

"Not right now, Aunt," he spat, fists at his side. "Now—"

"You have a lot of nerve, coming in here with armed guards, especially after I left you a message," Boyd said, stepping up beside her.

Iggie gave a haughty sniff. "After what Boyd—"

"Not now, Iggie," Connor interrupted. "Your first

message said you'd lost the sat phone, but when Iggie reached your guides, some fearsome warrior refused to tell him where everyone had gone and barred him from finding you."

"I had to have bodyguards after that encounter," Iggie said. "Look at them. Hostile savages."

Michaela inhaled sharply as she joined them. "They're not hostile. They only barred you, Iggie, because you need the chief's permission to enter these lands. Visitors are only welcomed in with an approved guide from the village. Connor, Boyd left your assistant—"

"He called from a phone registered to a medevac company. Yes, I had it back-traced. Why wouldn't I think the worst, Michaela?"

"We lost the sat phone when Boyd and I fell into the river," Michaela responded. "Then I got sick—"

"So you *were* in danger!" Connor lurched forward and grabbed Boyd by the shirt. "Did you hurt her?"

"See here!" Arthur shouted, stepping forward. "Get a hold of yourself. Boyd didn't tell you Michaela had been ill because she was recovering fine, which the doctors had confirmed, and there was no reason to cause alarm."

"Even with this misunderstanding, Connor, why would you show up like this?" Michaela asked. "We've heard about adjacent villages being terrorized—"

"We were *worried* about you, Michaela, and Uncle Arthur and Aunt Clara and Hargreaves," Connor ground out. "I didn't tell anyone in the family you were missing. You were my responsibility. No one in these hills would tell Iggie anything, not even when I joined him. I couldn't trust anything in those messages after what Boyd did to Iggie." He pointed to Boyd. "You and I are going to come to terms at a later date, McClellan, but now that I know everyone is unharmed, all I want to know is whether we have the flower. Michaela?"

Clara had heard from the other Merriam siblings that

Connor had taken his cousin's death hard, but this went beyond that. He'd jumped off the deep end. "What do you think Boyd did to Iggie, my boy?" Clara asked. "Given the appalling way that man treated Hargreaves and Joseph, it wasn't near what he deserved."

"Thanks, Clara," Boyd said with a grimace. "I should probably explain—"

"He bribed someone in Customs to hold me," Iggie shouted, pointing at Boyd. "How can we be sure he didn't poison Michaela or something? He wants the flower all for himself. I mean, it would look like an accident amongst such primitives."

Clara couldn't believe the audacity of Iggie's insult, and the chief and his English-speaking party inhaled sharply at the offense. She was still reeling, but her mind shifted to Iggie's comment about Boyd. Could it be true? He'd alluded to something moments ago, but he hadn't had time to explain. "Iggie, you hold your tongue. Connor, Michaela became ill after falling into the river. Boyd had nothing to do with it. Don't be an idiot. He wouldn't steal the flower or do anything to hurt her. He loves her."

"And yet he made sure to get Iggie out of the way," Connor said in a hard tone. "Boyd, you told Michaela Iggie could catch up when he was released, but you knew he wouldn't be allowed into the village. This was your plan all along, wasn't it?"

"Connor, stop this!" Michaela shouted. "Boyd wouldn't do that."

He made a rude sound. "Mickey, you're in la-la land again. Boyd has been playing you to get what he wants."

"You're the one who made me come along." Michaela turned to Boyd. "Is it true about Iggie?"

His mouth worked before he nodded. "But not because I intended to steal the flower for myself. I've always wanted us to do this together! You and me, Mickey. I don't trust Iggie"—he paused, as if considering how much to say, then added—"and I thought it would be easier to get you back if he were delayed. I'm not proud of it, but I'd do it again. He's a jerk, and the way he showed up here proves I was right."

"You'll never have the flower after this, Boyd," Iggie said, his face red. "This is the end of your pitiful career."

"How dare you—"

Michaela held up a hand. "Enough. Boyd," she said, turning to him, "why didn't you tell me about this? Especially after we got back together?"

"You're back together?" Connor shoved Boyd back two steps before Boyd shoved him back.

Sironka rushed forward and stepped between the two, Clara was pleased to see.

"You stay out of this!" Connor pointed to the warrior and then back to Boyd. "How dare you use my sister like that! You're going to pay for hurting her."

Boyd turned to Michaela and took her hands. "Mickey, please listen. I was going to tell you, but then you got sick. Will you look at me and judge for yourself? You know when I'm telling the truth."

Clara watched her niece study Boyd, her eyes roving over his face. Well, Clara knew the truth. She hoped her niece would come to the same conclusion.

"I believe you, Boyd," she finally said.

"You're acting nonsensical again, Michaela," Connor said, taking her arm. "Your feelings for him have always clouded your judgment. I'm going to have to *make* you see reason. But later. Get the flower and we'll leave."

Clara couldn't believe her ears. Boyd must have felt the same way, because he put Michaela behind him and grabbed Connor by the shirt. The mercenary with the worst buzz-cut stepped forward and yelled, "Step away from Mr. Merriam."

"Stay back," Connor threw over his shoulder to the guard. "You want a piece of me, Boyd? Our deal is more than off. I'm going to bury you, McClellan. In fact, Merriam

Enterprises will never work with you again, and I'll see to it none of our partners do either."

"*Connor!*" Michaela yelled.

Boyd drew him closer until their faces were inches apart. "I should clock you for breaking our deal, but I won't because I got Iggie out of the way, and that's on me. But you should know this, Connor. Michaela and I don't have the flower."

Clara caught the glance he sent Michaela's way asking her to play along.

"You should go and leave these people in peace," Boyd continued, shoving Connor back at last. "God knows you've raised enough of an alarm for a few decades. It's funny, but until now, I was so upset that I forgot the other part of the elders' visions. You know the one, Clara. It's about a man with darkness coming and trying to take the flower. Don't be that guy, Connor."

Clara had to give the boy points for his straightforward manner, and Arthur seemed to think so too by the squeeze he gave her arm. "Listen to him, Connor," she added.

"Boyd's right," Michaela said. "Coming here, especially with armed men, was a mistake."

"Your concern for our safety is appreciated, but this misunderstanding and your aggressive response is unfortunate," Clara said. "You should leave."

"They're trying to get rid of us," Iggie said, his beady eyes narrowing. "I don't like this, Connor. Boyd and Michaela have been here for days getting all chummy with the natives. I don't buy their story."

Clara didn't like the ripple that went through her gut when Connor said, "Neither do I. Where's Hargreaves? He's never far from you, Aunt."

This interrogation was going to stop. "He's doing something for me."

"You don't lie well, Aunt," Connor said with a rude sound. "I hate to do this, but you leave me no choice. We're going to get what we came for. I won't be double-crossed. Least of all by the man who's used my sister so abysmally. Sanders, search the village for my aunt's butler. I want the flower found."

"You're crazy, Connor!" Michaela said.

"Don't be ridiculous," Arthur added. "You're acting like a madman."

He widened his stance, more bruiser than corporate executive. "Frankly, I'm surprised at you, Aunt Clara and Uncle Arthur. I would have expected Michaela to protect Boyd, but not you two."

That did it! Clara stepped in front of him. "We're not protecting Boyd. Let me remind you that you asked us to come along in the first place. As for trying to steal anything from you, frankly, you're the one acting like you want to steal the flower from these people, Connor."

Arthur moved behind her, his hand on her shoulder. "*Clara...*"

She patted his arm. "I love you, Arthur, but I won't tolerate any more of this slander. You're wrong across the board here, Connor, and if Grandpa Emmits were here, he'd tan your hide for insulting these good people and besmirching the Merriam name."

"Is that so?" Connor drawled. "So if your butler doesn't have it, who does, Aunt?"

Arthur muttered under his breath.

She patted his hand again. Bless the man, but she was going to say her piece. "Boyd and Michaela aren't the couple the tribe has chosen to share the flower with the world."

She spotted her dear friend Naserian then and realized she was smiling too. Had the woman foreseen what she was about to do?

He held out his hands. "Well, don't keep us in suspense. Who did they choose?"

She straightened her spine to her full height. "Arthur and me."

"They're colluding with Boyd like you thought, Connor," Iggie shouted. "This is ridiculous."

"I agree," Connor said, his mouth twisting, "but good try, Aunt Clara."

His insouciance wouldn't be borne. "Let me be crystal clear, Connor. We aren't stealing anything from you that isn't yours in the first place. And after this insanity, you're never going to get near the flower. Not as long as I—*we*, sorry, dear—draw breath. Right now, I can tell you that's going to be a long time."

Connor stared her down, his nose flaring. "We'll see about that."

CHAPTER 23

MICHAELA COULDN'T BELIEVE WHAT SHE WAS HEARING from her brother.

Their cousin's death had thrown him for a loop, sure, but this was beyond anything she could have imagined. She'd always looked up to Connor, even when he'd chastised her for the way things had ended with Boyd. Even when he'd insisted she come on this trip. This wasn't the brother she'd admired.

"Are you threatening my wife?" Uncle Arthur asked her brother.

He put his hands on his hips. "No, but I don't like someone standing in my way. Or lying—"

"She's not lying, Connor," Michaela said as her uncle and Boyd both took a menacing step forward.

Connor stood his ground. "Michaela, I want this flower. Let me remind you who you work for: our family's company. Now, who do I need to talk to here? The chief? Usually this kind of thing comes down to a figure."

"They'll be grateful for pennies, given the conditions around here," Iggie said, his narrow nose raised with a clear air of superiority. "All we need is someone to take us to the Valley of Stars. Who wants to make some money?"

Michaela put a hand on Boyd to remain standing when

her legs started to tremble. "Iggie, enough. Connor, this isn't how we do business."

"Stay out of this, Michaela. You're obviously unwell and delusional. We'll deal with that later."

"She's shaking from fatigue, you asshole," Boyd said. "Listen to her, Connor. You and Iggie need to go. Right now."

"We won't until we make a deal for the flower and the land it's grown on," Connor said.

"If you'd listen, boy," Aunt Clara said, lifting her chin. "Arthur and I now co-own this land with these fine people, and we aren't selling."

Connor's eyes narrowed. "More of this ridiculous talk? You're both eighty. All right, say I believe this story. Aunt Clara, you should entrust this find to the family company. How are you going to manufacture the flower and distribute it otherwise?"

Michaela shared a look with Boyd. She'd wondered the same thing, although she trusted her aunt and uncle's discretion more than Connor apparently did. She'd hoped they might choose to honor the agreement Boyd had made with Merriam Enterprises.

Aunt Clara's face tightened with strain, and she and Uncle Arthur exchanged a look. When he nodded, she said, "We've been discussing our options with the elders over the last few days, after we heard about a Merriam representative terrorizing the other villages. Given the approach you've taken, we'll have to select another partner. Someone who has passed the incorruptibility test time and time again."

"But you're a Merriam," Connor said, his mouth twisting.

Aunt Clara paused dramatically, smiled, and then said, "Boyd and his new company will be our new partner."

When Michaela turned to Boyd, his mouth had gaped open. He was as shocked as she was. Then the significance of the news hit her. Merriam Enterprises wouldn't be involved—which meant she wouldn't be involved either. The dream of her and Boyd ushering this flower into the world together? It wasn't going to happen.

"This is what he wanted all along," Iggie shouted.

"We'll make it all legal and discuss the details later," Arthur said. "After these people leave."

Boyd put an arm on Uncle Arthur's shoulder. "That's—"

"I'll take you to court," Connor said, his jaw ticking. "I had a deal—"

"Based on what you just said, your deal means nothing. And you certainly didn't make it with us or this tribe," Aunt Clara said, her tone matching Connor's. "I hate to do this, Connor, but I meant what I said. You're not acting in the best interests of Merriam Enterprises right now."

"My father was right to cut you out of the family all those years ago." Connor ran his hand through his hair. "After this, you'll never see any of us ever again."

Michaela gasped. "Con—"

"You shut your mouth, son," Arthur said, planting his feet now.

"You'd threaten Clara like that?" Boyd asked. "She's your aunt, for heaven's sake, and a total sweetheart despite what you think."

"Thank you, Boyd." Aunt Clara's lip trembled a moment before she lifted her head. "I certainly hope you're wrong, Connor. I'm prepared to speak with our family about my actions. Defend them if I must. Can you say the same?"

"I don't have to," Connor said, laughing harshly. "I'm president of Merriam Enterprises. Michaela, let's go. We're done here."

He gestured to the helicopter like he expected her to follow him like a lapdog, and she stood there, not knowing what to do. Technically speaking, he was her boss. Plus, he was the brother she'd always looked up to and idolized. But he wasn't acting like himself, and the villagers were getting more restless by the minute.

Boyd seemed to sense her confusion because he put his hands on her forearms and looked at her with grim understanding. "Mickey, you should go. If he's threatening to cut Clara out... I know how much your family means to you."

Her gaze fell to the ring on her finger. Since she'd come out of the fever, she'd turned it on her finger in delight, imagining a bright and bold future, starting with a wedding at her parents' house like she'd always dreamed, surrounded by family. But what if her other siblings sided with Connor? What if her mother and father did too?

They'd always treated her as their loveable eccentric. Would that change? Was Boyd right? Would she be the next Merriam to be exiled from the family?

"But what about the flower?" she asked. "We were supposed to work on it together. Then there's us."

He dropped his hands. "Your energy is flagging. Go with your brother."

This wasn't like him. Usually he fought tooth and nail for what he wanted. "You're scaring me, Boyd."

She stared at her aunt and uncle, looking for help, but they didn't offer any wisdom. They were holding hands, noticeably upset.

"He's gotten what he wanted," Connor spat, taking her arm and tugging her away from Boyd. "Let's go. And take that dime-store ring off and give it back to him. It's pathetic."

Boyd punched Connor in the nose before she could blink, and two mercenaries lurched forward to muscle him back.

"If he hadn't clocked you for that comment," Uncle Arthur said, "I would have. Connor, you've lost a part of yourself, son. You need serious help."

"Connor, please!" Michaela shouted.

Her aunt patted her on the back. "Connor, tell your goons to take their hands off Boyd. Right this minute!"

The mercenaries didn't remove their hold on Boyd's arms, and the warriors had sprung to attention again, spears raised. The sound of a young child crying reached Michaela's ears, and she looked over to see a mother on bent knee trying to calm a little girl. The situation was falling apart. Someone was going to get hurt, and if she didn't act soon, those mercenaries might hurt Boyd more. He wasn't one to back down from a fight.

She needed to get Connor out of here. Everything else could be settled later.

"Fine, Connor. Let's go." Michaela turned to Boyd. "We'll talk later."

He shrugged out of the mercenaries' hold and stood there, breathing hard. "I can't risk you being cut off from your family. They mean everything to you. It's bad enough I almost got you killed. Maybe the gods are telling us we're just not meant to be together."

His steady gaze gave her chills. He seemed almost logical about everything. "That's not true." Drums sounded out of the blue, making her start.

"Sounds like Chief Mingati is done with his visitors," Boyd said, his dark eyes intent. "Go!"

"I concur with Boyd," Aunt Clara said, "I think the drums are a war dance. I'm sorry for this, Michaela. Arthur and I will come to Napa to explain to your parents when we return. Take care of yourself. You're shaking like a leaf, dear." She kissed her on the cheek, giving her a squeeze, and then Uncle Arthur stepped in and did the same.

Before retreating to the chopper, Michaela turned to Boyd one last time, taking in his crestfallen face.

"I know you're upset right now," she said as she extended her left hand, "but we'll work this out somehow. And I'm not giving this back."

He touched her hand briefly before saying, "If you want, but it won't mean what we thought."

Her fingers had shrunk from dehydration from her

fever, so the ring was hanging on loosely, much like the bond between them, but she wouldn't let go. "What's wrong with you? I love you, Boyd."

His throat moved. "I love you too. That's why I refuse to be the cause of your unhappiness."

Before she could respond, someone put their hands on her, pulling her back roughly. When she spun around, she realized it was Connor.

"Hey!" Boyd shouted. "She's still sick. Don't treat her like that."

The mercenaries shifted their weight as her brother tugged her forward. The helicopter's engine whined, and then Connor was propelling her toward it, his arm around her waist. He settled her into a chair and buckled her in.

"I could kill Boyd for putting you in a hole like this and making you sick," her brother said, stripping off his jacket and laying it over her. "First, we're going to find you a doctor, and then we'll fly you home."

She didn't have the energy to tell him the medevac people had already checked her out. Her eyes tracked to Boyd standing in the dirt swirling around the helicopter. He'd given up on them. She still couldn't believe it. Then she spotted Aunt Clara, who had her face pressed against Uncle Arthur's shoulder. Connor had threatened to cut her out of the family again. The last estrangement had lasted forty years. Boyd knew the story, and now that he knew Aunt Clara, he understood just how much the separation had harmed her.

Connor laid his hand on her arm for a moment. "Mom will take care of you, Mickey, and everything will be okay, I promise."

He was wrong, and she couldn't believe he was so far gone he couldn't see it. Iggie had a sneer on his face as he sat across from her.

"I always knew Boyd was—"

"Enough, Iggie!" Connor strapped himself in. "Can't

you see she's exhausted? We'll talk about business later. If they think this is the final say, they don't know me."

That's what she was afraid of. None of them knew this new Connor, and she wasn't so sure she wanted to.

The other men filed in, finding their positions, some of them remaining standing by the door, hanging on to a tether suspended from the ceiling. The weapons they were carrying struck her again. They looked like poachers. How had Connor thought this was the appropriate response?

As they lifted off, she peered out the window for one last look at the village. The thatch huts looked like hay bales as they climbed in altitude. Boyd and the rest of her family were only specks on the ground now. She couldn't make them out anymore even when she strained her eyes. The enormity of the situation with her aunt and uncle—and Boyd—hit her with full force, and her entire body shook hard enough to make her teeth chatter.

She was afraid she had lost them and her dream for good.

CHAPTER 24

BOYD LOOKED DOWN AT THE DRIED FLOWERS FROM THE Valley of Stars.

He should be elated, but all he felt was despair. He had the flowers. He didn't have Michaela. That bastard brother of hers didn't deserve her loyalty, but he was family. Connor would make sure he and Michaela never worked together. Sure, she'd said they weren't through with each other, but he could see the writing on the wall. He couldn't be the reason she was exiled from her family.

But his heart hurt, losing her.

Her aunt and uncle had sided with him, though. He still couldn't believe it. If anyone had told them he'd be sitting on wooden stools in Clara and Arthur's hut with Hargreaves after the last few harrowing hours of peacekeeping with the village, he'd have never believed it.

"Boyd, I know this has all been a shock, but you're not the only one reeling here." Clara rose to her feet and put her hand on his shoulder. "Now that we have calmed everyone down in the village, we need a plan for this flower. I appreciated the chief's willingness to trust us after that hullaballoo."

He made himself look up. She was right, and if she could stand tall after what Connor had said to her, he certainly could do the same. "You and Arthur were incredible with the chief and the tribe after that shitshow. I still can't believe anyone could be that culturally insensitive or outright threatening. I mean, I know it was a bad move on my part to keep Iggie tied up with Customs, which led to some additional misunderstandings, but I never would have hired mercenaries. What did they think had happened to us?"

Arthur stretched his legs out. "Maybe Connor has seen that old Stewart Granger and Deborah Kerr movie, *King Solomon's Mines.* Anyway, it's done for the moment, but Clara's right. We need a plan. The Connor and Iggie show could return. Even worried as he was, he acted outrageously."

He hoped for Michaela's sake Connor would be more sensitive to her than he'd been to the villagers. Although she was getting stronger, she'd been white-faced and shaking when she'd left. A relapse after this kind of stress happened to sick people all the time, and she didn't have the flower...

"You're thinking about Michaela," Clara said, resuming her seat. "I'm worried too, but we have to trust she'll be all right. Her brother may be a stubborn fool, but he obviously cares about her. Now, we have some items to discuss. First, I want your promise that you won't bribe an official ever again in our work together...unless you run it by us first."

"My dear—"

"Arthur, I'm not naïve enough to ask for an outright promise from Boyd. Frankly, I think he was right to do it after what I saw of Iggie's character—he has none."

"A scoundrel of the worst sort," Hargreaves echoed, his mouth twisting. "Excuse me, but his sense of superiority even rankled me greatly, and I've been in service for many years."

"No excuse needed, Hargreaves," Arthur said. "None of us would have been upset if a poison-tipped arrow had taken him off to the underworld. All right, Boyd, I'll go along with Clara on this. No bribing officials unless we greenlight it." He coughed out a short laugh, and Boyd almost joined in.

These two...he'd never met their like and knew he never would. "You have it. I'm trying to tell myself the bribe wasn't the reason things got out of hand today."

"It wasn't," Clara said, hitting her fist into her other palm. "Connor is worse off than any of us thought. He needs to face up to his problems and work through them. I only hope Shawn and the others understand what I did. I would hate to lose them when I only just found them again. Oh, dear! Excuse me."

Arthur angled his chair closer and put his arm around her, and Boyd's throat clogged at the sight of her agony. Seeing Clara's pain made him glad he'd encouraged Michaela to go. He never wanted to see such a tormented expression on her face.

"Now, now, let's not go all doom and gloom yet," Arthur said, jostling her. "We'll talk to Shawn and Assumpta and work things out like grown-ups. Clara, I'm glad we'd agreed on our plan with the elders before they got here. I've never been prouder of you than when you told Connor you wouldn't give him the flower simply because he was a Merriam like you."

The shock of that moment had been like a glass door shattering. Boyd had never expected they'd partner with him. He'd made peace with the thought that he wouldn't be able to work with the flower. "Why did you choose me?"

Clara wiped away her tears and gave him a brave smile. "Like I said, you passed the incorruptibility test for both us and the villagers, Boyd. When Michaela fell ill, you didn't go off your rocker like Connor. You stayed by Michaela's side and let us do our duty as the tribe wished."

He rubbed the back of his neck. "I might be a lot of things, but I respect people and their traditions. I'm... Hell,

I'm honored you want to be my partner after everything that's happened. I promise to do a good job with it." Even if Connor tried to blackball him with other companies, plenty of good ones would line up to work with them on a find this big. He wasn't worried.

"We know you will," Arthur said, reaching into his pants pocket. "Damn, I'm out of red hots. Now—"

"I have some right here, sir," Hargreaves said, pulling a carton out of his own pocket and extending it to Arthur.

The older man opened it and made a rude noise. "Leave it to you to have red hots in perfect condition, Hargreaves. I've never been more grateful to you. I think we all could use a treat."

Boyd took one and crunched into it as he held the carton out to the rest of them. They each took one. "Okay, back to the plan. What else needs to happen with the villagers before we can leave?"

Clara leaned forward, chewing her red hot slowly. "I believe we can make preparations to depart tomorrow. Sironka and a group of his warriors will accompany us, the chief said. The sooner we return to the States, the faster we can head off a potential return trip by Connor and Iggie. The elders understand that. I'd like to think Connor wouldn't send back more thugs for the flower, but Iggie might. We need to talk to Shawn immediately."

Arthur nodded, popping another candy into his mouth. "My thoughts exactly."

"Once we get to Nairobi," Clara said, "I'm chartering a plane to take us to San Francisco since the Merriam jet isn't an option anymore. I don't want any arguments, Boyd. I might enjoy sleeping on a hard bed with hides, but I will not fly commercial."

Since her look was directed at him, he opened his hands in surrender, laughing. "I'd offer to split the cost since we're working together, but it's a bit out of my price range. Some of us have to fly coach."

"Not me," Clara said. "Deal with it."

He nodded. "Yes, ma'am. By the way, I'm hoping you and Arthur would do me the honor of being my first board members. I'd like your thoughts on which of the villagers we should invite. Perhaps Leshan since she's a lawyer? Clara, how does chairman strike you? Unless you and Arthur want to flip for it. Hargreaves, I'd be honored to have you on board—ha-ha—as well."

"It's chairwoman, Boyd," Clara said, "and I'd love to take that august position if Arthur doesn't mind."

"Not at all, my dear. *Lead*. You clearly were meant to."

She leaned over and kissed his scruffy cheek. "I have some thoughts on which of the villagers might like to be on the board. But what about you, Hargreaves? Will you join us in our exciting new enterprise?"

His posture ever-perfect in the chair, he simply bowed. "While I am honored, Dr. McClellan, it's not my place. But I thank you for the invitation. I'm most content helping Madam and everyone in the background."

"Are we back to all that mister stuff, Hargreaves?" Boyd asked. "I rather liked Boyd."

"We are, sir," Hargreaves said. "My breach in etiquette was only temporary and due to the extreme nature of the situation."

"Oh, good God, Hargreaves, will you ever lighten up?" Arthur asked.

"Leave him be," Clara said, sending her butler a tender smile. "He's been working with me for decades and only on two occasions has he called me Clara. You don't change the nature of a man, do you, Hargreaves?"

"It's an insult to try, Madam. A man must be who he is. Isn't that right, Dr. McClellan?"

Boyd harkened back to their vigil with Michaela, where Hargreaves had told him his problem was in thinking he was Cinderella to Michaela's Prince Charming. Had he finally discovered who he was on this trip?

Yes, he realized. He'd passed the incorruptibility test and won the trust of these fine people to share a fabled healing flower with the world. His company was going to take off like hot cakes on Sunday morning, giving him everything he'd ever wanted professionally.

If only his personal life wasn't in shambles.

"You couldn't be more right, Hargreaves," Boyd said. "Now, let's have another red hot and discuss what arrangements we need to make before we leave. I have some thoughts on a few scientists I'd like to bring in to do the initial testing."

Of course, he'd hoped one of those scientists would be Michaela. He had to set that aside now.

"What about marketing?" Clara asked him. "You'll have to run me through other big finds like this and how they were launched so we can share our ideas with the village. Chief Mingati and the elders trust us with these matters, but they want to be kept informed as is their right as custodians."

"Of course." He rubbed his hands together, trying to get his internal fire going again. "I can run everyone through a number of successful examples. One thing: you may want to share the flower's location with me at some point, with the elders' approval, of course. I mean, when you think you're *getting up in years*."

Clara chuckled. "I'm glad you've finally realized who you're dealing with, Boyd, after your earlier attempts to make us beg off from this *difficult* journey. Arthur and I are fit as a fiddle, as we've more than proved, and we will be for at least two decades more if I have anything to say about it. I have a feeling this flower will help, but Arthur, you're still going to be doing yoga and tai chi with me every day from now on. We have new responsibilities to uphold."

The older man groaned. "Anything but that pretzel mumbo jumbo."

Boyd patted his back. "After this trip, I have no illusions about who I'm working with."

"Neither do we," Clara said, slapping her thighs and standing. "Now, let's enjoy our last moments with the tribe on this trip. Oh, and Boyd, Naserian said to let the flowers fully dry before we leave. Will you see to it with Hargreaves?"

Before he could respond, she grandly walked out of the tent.

"I already have the proper agreements drafted for Customs," Boyd said. "I was trying to be prepared."

"She trusts you," Arthur said, standing. "Don't mess that up. I'm off to the pub if you want to join me later. More facts and impressions to collect for the series of articles I'm planning about the tribe and the flower. Have fun pressing the flowers, you two."

His amused snort followed him out of the hut.

Boyd looked at Hargreaves.

"Shall we make history, sir?" Hargreaves asked.

"Let's do it."

Hargreaves rolled up his sleeves. "I talked to Naserian about the traditional practices used to dry flowers, and we've been employing a few techniques. Shall I run you through them?"

When he nodded, Hargreaves launched into his dissertation, making Boyd smile. He'd gained three unlikely partners on this trip.

And lost the only one he'd ever wanted.

Sadness engulfed him. Well, regardless of how he wished things had turned out, it was probably time to start over. He'd done it before, after his dad up and abandoned him.

He would do it again.

Chapter 25

A SICKBED WASN'T A GREAT PLACE FOR A FAMILY REUNION. But here Michaela was, drowning in quilts, flowers from the exotic to the pedestrian, and fresh-squeezed juice, while her parents and most of her siblings squeezed in around her. Only Connor was missing. He'd dropped her off at her parents' door three days ago, taken off for the office, and hadn't checked in since. With any of them.

Not that Michaela was surprised. She'd lost her voice trying to reason with Connor the whole way home. Iggie had taken her brother's side, of course, accusing her of siding with the enemy. Which meant Boyd, but also Aunt Clara and Uncle Arthur. Exhausted and unable to speak anymore, she'd finally given up.

Her mother had taken one look at her and insisted she stay in bed for the immediate future. "No arguments, missy," her mom had said.

Now she could at least whisper, but it was still pissing her off not to be heard. She'd shared her story, pausing occasionally to bolster her voice with a healthy sip of juice, and her parents' faces had turned ashen as she'd progressed. None of her siblings had asked her anything. She was sure her mother had insisted they hear her out without asking questions, especially about the ruby ring she was still wearing. Of course, they wouldn't necessarily know it was *that* kind of a ring. She'd decided to wear it on her right hand until she and Boyd made up and he asked her for real. It seemed more honest that way. What Connor had said about her engagement ring still haunted her.

But what haunted her most was how reasonable and resolute he'd seemed about letting her go.

Of course, it was Connor's right to ban anyone at Merriam from working with Boyd. That was one thing, but he didn't speak for the family. He couldn't ban Clara, nor could he ban her. Surrounded as she was with her family, Michaela didn't believe she was in danger of being cast off. But she and Boyd clearly still had serious obstacles to work through.

"Mickey," her mom said, pressing yet another glass of fresh-squeezed orange juice into her hands, "isn't it wonderful Trevor could come visit?" Her brother had arrived this morning from Ireland.

"Yeah, thanks Trev," she rasped. "I know you hate leaving Becca."

His full smile looked just a little forced—everyone clustering around her was wearing the same annoying candy-striper smile. "We all dropped everything the moment Connor told us you'd almost died from some tropical fever. Becca would have come, but she's still working with her therapist on traveling beyond our land. The other day, we walked to the edge of the sea on the cliffs. I was so happy, I offered to share my champagne with Buttercup."

She was glad to hear Becca's therapy was helping. "Can an alpaca drink champagne?"

"Only if it's Dom Perignon," her brother, Flynn, joked from the edge of the bed. "I mean, you shouldn't treat any woman—even a llama—to anything but the best."

They launched into light conversation, everyone pitching in with a joke here or there. She knew what they were doing, but cheering her up could only go so far. The only person not pretending to be a candy striper was her brother, Quinn. He was sitting in the corner of her old room, brooding like he'd swallowed all the fog in London on his airplane ride over. He'd flown in last night and had tried to talk to Connor after other efforts had failed.

The two brothers usually saw eye to eye, even when no one else agreed with them. But she had a feeling Quinn wasn't totally on board this time. Maybe because he was vice president of the company. Maybe because Connor wouldn't talk to him either. He'd held a firm line: *I'm CEO of Merriam Enterprises. I did what I thought was best, and I won't answer to anyone.*

Technically, that wasn't true. He reported to the board, but this was the second time he'd invoked unilateral powers in the months since Corey's death. The first time, he'd attempted to change the company's policy on off-shore drilling without running it by anyone.

"Has anyone heard from Aunt Clara or Uncle Arthur?" she asked in a breathy whisper, cutting into a punchy conversation about nothing. Everyone turned to look at her, their peppy smiles slipping like a tiara on a drunken beauty queen. "J.T., you and Caroline live in the same town. Surely, someone has heard something." They would have had to travel back down that horrible river, a thought that made her sweat bullets. Why hadn't she insisted Connor send back the helicopter for them? Oh, right, because he'd pretty much created an international incident with it.

Her father steepled his hands. "Clara called me the moment they got to a phone to talk about what had transpired, saying she was gravely distressed by everything. I believe her. We all feel that way. She and Arthur are coming here straight away once they reach Nairobi."

Thank God! She put her hand to her throat. "They made it back safely then?"

"Seems so," her dad said, glancing over at her mom, who was giving him a pointed look. "Now, who wants to—"

"No!" She may have lost her voice, but that didn't mean she was going to allow everyone to ignore her. "We are not moving on. We need to talk about this. Is Boyd coming with them?"

Her parents shared that look they'd perfected—the couple-who-reads-each-other's-thoughts one—before her dad answered, "Clara said he would be. Are you upset about Boyd being chosen to work on the flower? We haven't wanted to press you, but you told your mother and me that he'd let you go...yet you have an engagement ring on your finger." She looked down at her right hand as he said it. "Yes, I know it's not on that finger," he continued, "but we weren't born yesterday."

"Oh, for heaven's sake," Caitlyn said, "if she wants us to stop treating her with kid gloves, we will."

"Her health—"

"Mom, I'm almost a hundred percent."

"Your voice is shot, and your clothes are hanging on you like a scarecrow," her mother responded. "We're only trying to look after you. You scared us, Mickey."

Everyone looked on the verge of tears, although some of her tough-guy brothers coughed to cover their emotions. Quinn's jaw even started ticking, reminding her that Connor had said the same thing in his own way. Yes, he'd taken things way too far, but she genuinely believed he'd done it out of worry.

"I know." She pushed aside the rose and cream quilt her Grandma Anna had made when she was a baby. "It scared me too. But we have a huge problem on our hands and that scares me more. I'm afraid of losing Aunt Clara and Uncle Arthur over this." She didn't want to talk about Boyd yet.

Her dad took her hand. "We won't let that happen."

"And Connor is...not himself." She levered herself up higher on the pillows, making everyone lunge to help her. "Stop. I'm not a baby. I might sound like a frog, but...

Listen, the fact that Connor's not talking to anyone is really scary. He hasn't been right since Corey's death. After the to-do he caused in Ireland over Becca's land, I thought this was behind us. But he doesn't seem to be doing any better. In fact, I'd say he's worse. He's not sleeping, and he's making bad decisions." Weren't mercenaries a red flag? Yes, but the red flags had started way before that.

Her dad tapped his knee in an uncharacteristic nervous gesture. "His grief and survivor's guilt are leading him to make some...irrational decisions about how to handle business."

Quinn stood. "I don't like talking about him like this. We haven't heard Connor's side of the story. Now, I'm not saying Michaela is wrong, but I can see why he was worried. After hearing from some stranger that the sat phone had fallen into the river, I would have been deeply concerned too. Especially since some warrior banned Iggie from finding them."

"But Boyd called," Michaela protested. "When did you talk to Iggie?"

"Yesterday," he said, unsmiling. "He presents quite a tale."

"He was horrible, Quinn, to everyone!" Michaela said, her voice straining. "Even Hargreaves."

"Add in Boyd bribing a Customs official to detain a Merriam employee, and I would have feared the worst too," he finished, not acknowledging her comment.

"Boyd didn't mean any harm," Michaela said, extending her hand.

"Bullshit," Quinn shot back. "Your trip was a cluster—. Sorry, Mom. FUBAR."

"That's no excuse to hire a bunch of mercenaries," Trevor said flatly. "J.T. and I worked for Merriam Oil & Gas in countries torn apart by major conflict and we never once resorted to that. Protection, yes, not thugs to terrorize local people."

She appreciated that Trevor hadn't gone out of his way to bash Boyd. She hoped Aunt Clara had also helped Boyd's actions look less scurrilous to her family. Because they needed to embrace him again if he and Michaela were going to make up and get married—she was holding on to that vision despite their current circumstances.

Quinn shook his head. "Trev, we don't know they were mercenaries. They might have been a protection detail. Didn't your guards in Angola or Nigeria carry machine guns?"

J.T. rose and unbuttoned his suit jacket. "They did, but Trev's right. They knew not to threaten locals. That's way beyond the pale."

"A Maasai warrior barred Iggie from searching for you," Quinn said. "Then a bunch of warriors surrounded a Merriam helicopter and pointed spears at our employees, Connor included. That sounds hostile to me."

"Of course the tribe would react like that," Michaela said. "No one enters their land without permission, and they felt threatened, especially after hearing about Connor and Iggie showing up with such force in other villages." She still didn't know how many villages Iggie had visited alone, and at this point, she wasn't sure it mattered. Connor had gone along with it in the end.

"Michaela, you're stressing your voice," her mom said. "Drink your juice."

"But I want to talk about this."

"Well, *I'm* going to suggest we table this discussion for the time being," her dad said, standing up. "Quinn, I don't like talking about these matters without Connor here either, but he's chosen to take that stance. Mickey, here, is rightfully concerned. She *was* there, and I have to say, Iggie doesn't sound very professional. Now, I'm retired, happily so, and I haven't wanted to stick my nose into company affairs. I've wanted to give all of you an opportunity to run things on your own."

"Your father and I agreed that was for the best," her mother said, "but we're not so sure this time. There's no doubt someone needs to reach Connor—both professionally and personally—and right now, your father and I aren't sure we want to put that on you children."

"I'm the VP of Merriam Enterprises," Quinn said, his baritone voice unrelenting. "I know we're family, but this is a business matter. The rules are very clear. If we're concerned about Connor's behavior, the board is obligated to call him in to explain any incident or behavior it deems unbecoming. Anyone on the board can call a meeting with enough votes. Since we're here—"

"Now wait just a moment!" Flynn flew off the bed. "This isn't a conference room—"

"But there are procedures in place for this kind of thing," Quinn interrupted. "I don't want to go behind Connor's back. We do this the right way."

"But he's our *brother*," Caitlyn said, taking her fiancé's hand. "I don't want to handle it like this."

"Do you think I do?" Quinn nearly shouted.

Michaela started shivering, and her mother put another infernal blanket on her.

"How about this then?" their father asked. "Quinn, you email Con and tell him that we'd like to talk about what happened sometime in the next two days. If he remains unavailable, the board will have no choice but to vote on calling him in to explain his actions. This way he fully knows what his options are. He must understand ignoring this situation is unacceptable."

Silence filled the room. Flynn stalked over to the window. J.T. was looking down at his shoes. Trevor's jaw clenched. And Caitlyn had tears pouring down her cheeks. Michaela clutched the blanket as she looked up at all of them. She hated that she'd played a role in all of this, especially since Connor was suffering. She was still mad at him for what he'd done, but she loved him. He was her big brother. She'd always looked up to him.

"I think it's the fairest way," Trevor said finally, "although, Christ Almighty, I hope he chooses the easy way and talks to us privately. Going to the board—"

"Puts us on a track we can't walk away from," Quinn said heavily. "We've always recorded the proceedings, and I'd hate for anything damning to be on record about Con. He can get through this. I know he can."

"I'll go by his office again," Caitlyn said, brushing at her tears. "Did anyone check in with his assistant today? Do we know if he's still there?"

"He hasn't left," Flynn said, kicking the baseboard. "Sorry, but I'm... I pulled the security feed from reception."

"I hate to ask this," Trevor said, "but are we sure he's okay?"

Michaela's gasp had her throat burning. He wasn't that bad, was he? Suicide was something she hadn't even considered.

"He's meeting with his staff regularly," Quinn said. "I checked. Going forward with business like usual."

"Like nothing happened," Michaela rasped, her heart breaking. *Oh, Connor.*

"All right, everyone," her mother said, shooting out of her chair. "Michaela is going to take a nap now. So out. And no talking."

Even her groan was whisper-soft. Pathetic.

Her mom started shooing people out of the room, and no one protested, dammit. A nap! She was a twenty-seven-year-old woman—she didn't need another nap. All she'd do was lie here alone, her mind racing over events, wondering what in the world she should do about everything, with Boyd at the top of the list.

"Daddy," she called since he was the last person leaving the room.

He turned. "Should I close the curtains, Mickey? Usually you love to sleep in the sunlight."

"Will you sit a minute?"

He grimaced. "Your mother will kill me, but maybe she won't notice if we're quick."

She hadn't had a moment alone with him since arriving, what with her mother fussing over her. "Did Boyd really ask your permission to marry me, and if he did, why didn't you tell me when we broke up? I was so mad I couldn't see straight. Maybe it would have helped."

He sat on the bed beside her. "You were madder than I've ever seen you. Even if Boyd hadn't asked me to keep it quiet, I might have decided it was best not to get involved. This was before I turned over my new leaf and decided I *wanted* to get involved in everything that concerned you kids. I'm sorry if you think I let you down."

She worried her lip a moment. "Thanks, Dad. It helps to hear that. I'm scared about Boyd. He just let me go. And Con didn't help matters, decreeing no one at Merriam would ever work with him again. He said he'd *ruin* him."

"We won't let that happen, Mickey," her dad said. "It's not how we do business, even if he weren't important to you."

"Con threatened to exile Aunt Clara, and it scared me. Boyd too, I think." How must her aunt be feeling now?

"Another thing we won't let happen." Her dad's jaw clenched. "Of course, your mother pointed out some of Connor's...ahem...overreaction doesn't fall far from the tree. Didn't I let forty years go without reaching out to my sister? God, I regret that, but I promise you this: Clara is in this family forever."

Tears filled her eyes unexpectedly.

"Don't cry, honey," her dad said, reaching for her hand and giving it a squeeze. "I know it seems bad, but we'll fix things."

Honey? He'd never called her that.

"Boyd's pride got hurt too." Just thinking about it made her heart ache. "Connor even made fun of the ring he gave me. He called it a dime-store ring."

"But it's perfect for you," her dad said, lifting her hand and gazing at it. "I told Boyd the same thing when I asked to see it. You wouldn't want anything flashy, but that ruby has fire, just like you. He said he hoped you'd feel that way but he also hoped to buy you a more expensive one later on. I told him you didn't care about such things, but I couldn't blame him for wanting to give you and those he loves more. Did he tell you he plans to buy his mom a house? I have to admit, I admire the boy and understand where he's coming from. I feel the same way about taking care of your mother and all of you kids."

"Oh, Daddy, I miss him so much," she said, more tears leaking out.

He squeezed her hand a moment, his gaze steady. "Of course you do, Mickey. You love him."

Yes, she did, but her confusion was overwhelming right now. "I don't know how to make this right for everyone," she said, turning the ring on her finger. "There's my job and Connor and Aunt Clara and Uncle Arthur to consider."

"You don't have to make this right for everyone, Mickey. Only you and Boyd." He tucked the cover over her. "You're still exhausted from your ordeal. Once you're better and rested, you'll figure out what to do. I have faith in you. In the meantime, how about you let your dad do some thinking himself? Would you trust me to be your partner in getting Boyd back?"

Emotion clogged her strained throat. "I'd love your help, Dad. I'm also hoping Aunt Clara and Uncle Arthur will be able to help too. I wish you could have seen her in the village. She looked like she'd found something she'd been searching for her entire life."

Her dad pressed her softly back into the pillow. "I'm glad for her. She hasn't had a very fulfilling or happy life until now. Sounds like she's making up for lost time. Now, you go to sleep. We'll be around when you wake."

She was feeling tired. Didn't mean she liked it. "Fine. I'm going to sleep."

He kissed her sweetly on the hair, a gesture so rare she had to close her eyes to prevent her tears from falling. "I love you, Mickey. Trust me, we'll make this right."

As he left the room, she promised herself she would remember this moment forever. It was the first time her father had ever told her he'd take care of things for her, and even at her age, somehow it was a comfort.

Wasn't that love for you?

CHAPTER 26

A RTHUR HAD HIS MATCHMAKING HAT ON AGAIN.
He and Clara and had agreed Boyd and Michaela
needed to reconcile. No ifs, ands, or buts about it.

Right now, it felt like someone had stomped his hat in
the dust on the savannah, sure, but it still fit.

The flower was a marvel, and he had no doubt Boyd
was the perfect person to help introduce it to the world, but
Life Giver still wasn't worth losing the love of a lifetime. He
and Clara had arranged for a get-together with Shawn and
Assumpta to fix anything Connor's foolhardiness might
have broken. But Arthur had gotten to thinking it would be
good to include Boyd, and Clara had agreed.

Only their new partner didn't know that. They'd only
told him to meet them in their hotel room. Was it a setup?
Yep, and the Merriam contingent didn't know about it either. He'd convinced Clara to keep it quiet, unsure how Michaela's parents were feeling about Boyd.

The poor man had barely cracked a smile since they'd
left the village. Desperate times and all that, as Hargreaves
would say...

Speaking of which, he turned to Clara. "Is everything
ready?"

"Hargreaves is going to position himself by the door in

case Boyd or anyone else tries to leave," Clara said, fussing with the lunch tray on the coffee table for the umpteenth time.

"Clara, dear, I know you're nervous about this meeting, but give the poor sandwiches a rest. If you rearrange them in one more pattern, they may go on strike." Did she realize the last pattern looked like their star-shaped flower?

Hargreaves came forward with a vase stuffed with white roses and put them beside the tray. "Everything looks perfect, Madam."

"Glad you took those roses out of our room, Hargreaves," Arthur said. "They were making me sneeze."

"Just don't sneeze in here, dear." She worried the diamond bracelet on her wrist, the one she'd insisted on buying this morning from the jewelry store in their luxury hotel, informing him she needed some extra sparkle after their ordeal. Since she was still shaken up, he hadn't made a joke about diamonds being a girl's best friend. She would have socked him.

A knock on their door sounded, and Hargreaves crossed to open it. "Dr. McClellan, it's good to see you. I hope you had a restful night in your own bed."

"Didn't sleep a wink," Boyd said, his tone dry. "Thanks for asking, Hargreaves. I thought I'd missed a soft bed and pillow, but it didn't help my insomnia any."

That would explain his bad mood. Well, the poor boy was heartbroken. Couldn't expect him to have pep in his step.

"Perhaps warm milk would do the trick, sir," Hargreaves responded, always helpful.

Arthur harrumphed. "Oh, for heaven's sake. Boyd has heartbreak, not insomnia. Warm milk won't help. Now that we're back, Boyd, what do you plan to do about your condition?" He pulled out the red hots he'd bought at the small grocery around the way. Clara liked her diamonds. He liked his red hots.

"I'm going to work with you and Clara on the flower," he responded, sitting down on the gold silk couch in their sitting room.

"Keeping focused sounds like a good idea right now," Clara responded, sitting beside Boyd. "Truthfully, there's something Arthur and I thought needed our immediate attention. We want to make sure Connor and Iggie don't do anything else to hurt the village. I hope you will excuse the liberty we took to address that, Boyd."

His eyes grew wary. "What do you mean?"

Arthur patted him on the back before sitting beside him. "This is where you need to trust us, Boyd. As partners..."

"Why is my skin starting to break out into hives?" he asked.

"Hargreaves, find some calamine lotion for Boyd right away." Clara pressed a hand to her forehead. "Is it too early for gin and tonics?"

"Now my skin is really crawling," Boyd said, looking around the room like he expected someone to jump out. "What did you do? Invite Connor here to bury the hatchet? I told you he won't be able to blackball my company, although he can try."

"It's not Connor," Arthur said, grabbing his arm when he started to rise. "Funny how that didn't strike either of us as a good idea. It's Shawn and Assumpta. We think it's important for them to hear your account of things as well as ours. You'll recall we weren't in the village the entire time. You were."

His eyes grew wary. "I don't think this is a good idea. I can't be too high on their favorites list right now. Hargreaves was there. Let him fill in any blanks."

"It's not my purview, sir," Hargreaves responded, standing in his butler posture across from them.

A knock sounded, and Clara said, "Now I'm feeling sick."

Arthur waved Hargreaves off and stood. "Don't worry, dear. We're going to make this all right." Even if he had to use some choice words. He was not going to allow the woman he loved to lose the family she'd just gotten back after decades of estrangement.

Still, he understood Boyd not wanting to come between Michaela and her family. Clara's estrangement from the Merriams had wrecked her life.

When he opened the door, he was surprised to see Shawn and Assumpta weren't alone. They'd brought a surprise guest, and it wasn't Michaela. He wanted to groan. They'd brought Quinn, who was nearly as hard a nut as his brother.

"Thank you for coming," he said, extending his hand to both men and kissing Assumpta on the cheek. "Come in. We also invited an additional guest."

"Did they bring Michaela?" Clara asked, rushing to greet them. "Oh, it's you, Quinn. What a…lovely surprise. You're visiting from London then. Hello, Shawn and Assumpta. Thank you for coming."

Arthur gestured to his wife, who was wringing her hands. "In case you haven't picked up on it already, Clara's sick to the stomach at what transpired."

"*Arthur*."

"Well, you are, and I see no reason for us to languish in small talk for half an hour before we get down to brass tacks. How is Michaela?"

"Yes, how is she?" Boyd asked, rising from the sofa.

Quinn's jaw seemed to harden like cement, but thankfully Shawn crossed the room and extended his hand to Boyd.

"She's getting stronger every day," Shawn said. "It's good to see you, Boyd. I'm glad you're here. I was going to call you after we met with Arthur and Clara and ask to meet."

Boyd's eyes narrowed, but he shook Shawn's hand. "I'd

have been curious about your invitation, Shawn, and out of respect, I would have gone."

"Does that mean you'd take a meeting with me, Boyd?" Quinn asked, setting his weight. "There's a boxing club in Sonoma I'd love to invite you to."

"Quinn, I know you have your perspective, but remember what we asked of you when we invited you to come along," Assumpta said, crossing to Boyd and kissing his cheek with a knowing glance at her son. "Good to see you, Boyd. Thank you for taking care of Michaela. Now, shall we all sit? It seems you have lunch for us. Clara, it looks delicious. Hargreaves, I'm sure your touch is all over things. Thank you for going to the extra trouble."

So they were going to do the bullshit dance, after all. Arthur wanted to bang his head against the wall.

"It was nothing," Clara said, gesturing dismissively. "I was just asking Arthur and Hargreaves if was too early for gin and tonics." She gave an agonized chuckle, the poor thing.

"Oh, get her a drink, Hargreaves," Arthur said, motioning for their guests to take a seat in the common room, which was frankly over the top, what with its two sofas, separated by an overstuffed armchair. "Anyone else? I'll have a whiskey."

"White wine for me, Hargreaves," Assumpta said, sitting and arranging her skirt over her knees.

"A drink sounds like a capital idea," Shawn said, taking a seat beside her. "Whiskey neat."

"Bourbon neat," Quinn said, snagging the chair.

"Crow for me, Hargreaves," Boyd said, resuming his seat between Arthur and Clara. "Straight up."

Now that's what Arthur called a good start. *Way to go, Boyd.*

"I'll do what I can with the recipe I'm familiar with, Dr. McClellan," Hargreaves said, his mouth noticeably twitching. He bowed and left the room. Arthur hoped he was calling room service for the drinks, but it wouldn't shock him if Hargreaves had a bar rigged up somewhere in this crazy suite, which had as much square footage as their house in Dare Valley.

"I'm not sure what you've heard about the trip, but there's no denying I bribed a Customs official to delay Iggie for a few days, which seems to have contributed to other misunderstandings," Boyd said, putting his hands on his knees and meeting their eyes. "All I can do is explain why I did it and hope you might understand."

"Let's hear it, then," Quinn said, resting his ankle over his other leg.

"You might recall I worked with Iggie for six months at Merriam," Boyd said. "When Connor insisted on Iggie joining us, I was concerned for a number of reasons. First, Iggie isn't a field guy; second, he's not known for his cultural sensitivity."

"But isn't he Indian?" Assumpta asked. "That seems odd."

"Just because someone is from another culture doesn't mean they're culturally sensitive," Boyd said. "Third, I was concerned about his inclusion. Connor never sent someone to supervise Michaela before, and I didn't trust Iggie not to interfere with what we were doing. Also, like I told Shawn before we left for Africa, I planned on winning Michaela back. I worried about doing so in front of her boss, especially since Connor had demoted Michaela in the first place for her romantic feelings for me."

"My two cents," Arthur said. "Boyd's actions weren't the best, but he was right to get Iggie out of the way. The moment the man stepped back onto the plane, he treated Hargreaves like crap, and you can always tell a man's character by how he treats people. His superiority complex was never more apparent than at the village, where he openly insulted the villagers. Connor should never have sent Iggie in the first place."

"It's not my place," Clara said, "but after seeing Iggie in action, if I were his boss, I'd fire him without a second thought."

"But like you said, it's not your—"

"Quinn," Shawn interrupted. "Let them continue. I believe we're on a constructive track here. Thank you for sharing your thoughts on Iggie. Now, what else can we do to fix things? Clara, it bothered me terribly when Michaela said you were worried this could cause a rift between us."

Clara swallowed thickly, and Arthur wished he'd sat beside his wife. They'd put Boyd in the middle to show solidarity, but right now, he wished he could take her hand.

"After Connor and Iggie's actions, Arthur and I couldn't in good conscience entrust the flower to them, and as such, our family company. I wasn't sure how everyone would take that decision. Connor made his opinion rather clear. I mean, I lost all of you over a business matter before."

"This isn't the same situation," Shawn said, leaning forward. "Come on, Clara. After our reconciliation in Provence, have a little more faith in me. You and Arthur brought back the flower that saved our daughter, alongside Boyd and Hargreaves' care of her."

"I didn't do anything much but sit beside her, Shawn," Boyd said, clearing his throat. "Arthur and Clara and the flower deserve all the credit, along with the villagers who trusted them."

The boy's heartbreak was turning him into an idiot, and Arthur wasn't having any of it. "Boyd, you put an engagement ring on her hand to keep her strong and give her hope. You didn't sleep for days. I'd say that's plenty."

"Hargreaves didn't rest either," Boyd said, making Arthur want to kick him. Oh, this younger generation! When would they learn to listen?

"We owe Hargreaves a debt as well," Assumpta said.

"Now, let's talk about Connor's actions," Shawn said, his mouth flattening. "As you might expect, this is hard for all of us. We love him. But from what Michaela told us, he didn't act like himself."

"Haven't you spoken to him?" Clara asked.

Shawn took Assumpta's hand. "No, he dropped Michaela off at the house and has refused to speak to any of us. Without going into everything, all the kids came home to see Michaela, and we're all deeply concerned. When Connor refused to discuss the event, Quinn rightly pointed out that we need to handle this as a business matter. We gave Connor the chance to talk to us privately. He hasn't. Now, the board has called for a vote to make him appear and account for his actions."

Clara gasped while Arthur's mouth went slack. The board? Damn it all to hell. That meant Connor's actions would be on record. That stubborn, thick-headed…

"I'm sorry to hear that," Boyd said gravely. "You all must be incredibly upset."

"The meeting is tomorrow," Shawn said. "We felt the matter urgent enough to call it on such short notice."

"I don't know what to say," Clara said, "except that I'm sorry. I wish things had gone differently in the village."

"Can you tell us more about what happened?" Shawn asked. "I brought Quinn along since he's the vice president of the company. Depending on how the meeting goes tomorrow, Quinn might need to bring notes from this meeting."

"I hope to heaven it doesn't come to that," Arthur said, shaking his head, "but let's get this over with. I'll share my impressions of what happened to kick things off. Please, Clara, Boyd, jump in when you have something to add. Best get this over with as efficiently and factually as possible."

He fell into his journalistic shoes easily and began telling the story, using some details from the draft articles he'd been kicking around and others from memory. Hargreaves appeared with the drinks and doled them out as

Arthur continued to speak. Clara only offered a few other details, mostly about how upset the chief and the villagers had been, something he would have let the reader discern for themselves from the events as they were told. Boyd remained silent to the end.

Assumpta's face was ashen, Arthur noted as he finished, and Shawn was looking out the window, his face a profile in desolation. Only Quinn was staring at them with complete focus, no emotion evident.

"Do you have anything to add, Boyd?" Quinn asked.

***

Boyd shook his head. He didn't think he should say anything. The situation had gone nuclear from what it sounded like. If Connor was refusing to speak to anyone, he was worse off than anyone had thought.

Shawn turned back to look at him, resting his elbows on his knees like a tired man. "Michaela mentioned to me that Connor made some ugly comments about the future of your new company, Boyd. While I know it would be better coming from him, I still want to apologize. You have my word and Quinn's that no one at Merriam Enterprises will slander you."

"As for working with your company," Quinn said. "Bribing a Customs official is not the sort of behavior we tolerate, especially since you did it to detain one of our employees. That detail will be shared with the board in my overall accounting. I can't say how the members might respond."

Meaning Boyd might still be on the no-work list for Merriam Enterprises. "I understand that." Boyd inclined his chin. "Hearing there will be no disparagement is more than I expected, frankly, but I'd appreciate it if you'd keep the bribe out of the official minutes for the board meeting."

Quinn was quiet for a moment and then said, "I'll talk to Legal. Without any solid evidence of the bribe other than your confession, I wouldn't want to open us up to a lawsuit later."

"I concur, so let's move on." Shawn clasped his hands. "Michaela also told me what Connor said about the ring you bought her. Obviously, he overstepped in other ways too, but that comment was below the belt. Like I told you before, it's the perfect ring for her."

He had to fight the urge to pinch the bridge of his nose as his throat closed up. All he could think of was the stubborn set of Michaela's jaw as she told him she was keeping the ring, that they'd work things out. He just couldn't see how. Tomorrow, his actions would be shared with the board. No one at Merriam would be eager to work with him after this. Given what Michaela had told him about her family—how she'd always felt like the odd one out, able to contribute only through the company—he didn't like the idea of putting her in the middle.

Boyd tried to smile. "I appreciate you saying that, Shawn, but you have nothing to be sorry for."

"It sounds like things got out of hand and very personal," Quinn said, his poker face worthy of admiration. "As vice president of Merriam Enterprises, I also want to apologize. Aunt Clara and Uncle Arthur, you have my word that nothing further will happen to the village. Please convey my apologies to the chief and everyone else. Iggie should have understood that you can't just walk onto Maasai land without an invitation, and he was wrong to become aggressive when denied. I'd like to think that the head of our division would have possessed enough judgment to understand the village was merely being protective to keep the flower a secret."

Boyd had to give Quinn credit for the way he was handling things. It couldn't be easy for him to acknowledge that his own brother and division head had made poor decisions.

"While Connor is still acting president," Quinn said,

pausing finally to pick up his drink and take a healthy sip, "my hands are a bit tied on dealing with Iggie, but I promise you that I'm going to push to have him fired immediately. His actions aren't in keeping with Merriam Enterprises."

Was that a tremor in his hand? Boyd knew the two brothers had always been especially close, and it wouldn't be easy for Quinn to take a stand against his brother.

"Thank you for all that, Quinn," Clara said softly. "We'll convey your message to the village. I have to admit it's a huge load off our minds."

"You're doing what's right, Quinn," Arthur said, "but we both know it can't be easy."

"It's business," Quinn said, taking another fortifying drink. "All right. Unless you have anything else to share, I'm going to leave now."

Clara rose and crossed to him, putting her hand on his arm. When he got to his feet, he towered over her.

"I hope our decision to work with Boyd on the flower won't preclude you from issuing us an invitation to come visit you in London sometime," Clara said. "I know you might not wish to hear this right now, but Grandpa Emmits would be proud of you for how you're handling this."

"You're right. It gives me no pleasure to hear it, but it's my job. If there's nothing else... Uncle Arthur. Boyd."

Striding out of the room, he nodded to Hargreaves and disappeared. Assumpta stood and faced Clara.

"I didn't know how I was going to feel once I heard your side of things," she said, "but I can tell you this. I would have done the exact same thing in your place—after trying to knock some sense into Connor. This doesn't change anything, Clara. I know how much you value our family. What you've done for J.T. and Trevor and Caitlyn and now Michaela..."

Clara sniffed, making Arthur reach for a handkerchief

and pass it to her. "I love them to pieces. I wish none of this had happened. Oh, Assumpta, I'm so sorry about all of this. What do you think will happen tomorrow?"

Boyd wondered the same thing. Would Connor refuse to show up? Would he arrive and refute their account? God, what a nightmare. Michaela must be tangled in knots. Would she blame him if things went badly?

"I don't know what will transpire tomorrow," she said, pressing her hand briefly to her mouth. "Boyd, I want to say...I don't know what happened completely between you and Michaela, but she loves you. We have enough trage-dy on our hands right now. Don't let this come between you two. I don't know what Connor said about the ring, but Shawn's right. It's perfect for her. You've always known what she needs, and that's what makes a strong partner-ship."

Arthur elbowed him. "Listen to Assumpta, Boyd."

"Boyd has a good head on his shoulders," Shawn said, inclining his chin at him. "He knows who he is and what he wants. I'd say this trip only crystalized that for him. I'm going to step outside a moment with Boyd if that's all right with all of you. Be right back."

Seeing no choice but to follow him, Boyd rose and walked out of the suite with him.

After the door closed, he faced the man. "How is Mi-chaela really?"

Shawn rubbed the back of his neck. "Hoarse as a frog. Stubborn as an ox about resting. Upset about Connor and this whole situation, of course. Heartbroken to be at odds with you."

He shifted on his feet at that. Well, he was in the same boat.

"You know, Boyd, I told Michaela to let me help her find a way to win you back. There isn't another fabled flow-er you want, is there?"

The man's wry smile didn't crack him. "I appreciate the

goodwill, Shawn, but I can't see any way around this. Being a Merriam means everything to her, and she said working at the company is how she does her part. How she belongs. I'd never be happy if I caused any bad feelings between her and her family. This situation with Connor might very well do that. You didn't see how he acted toward me. And I him."

"So you had some heated words—"

"I threw a punch at him, Shawn, for manhandling Michaela, and he had his thugs— Never mind. Do you really think there won't be tension when I show up with Michaela for a family function? Quinn's gotta be more pissed than he's letting on, and surely others have strong feelings about what happened. I won't do that to her."

Shawn shook his head. "Leave the others out of this. You and Con will work it out then, as men do. Despite my son's current state, he loves his sister. He wouldn't want her heart broken."

Boyd wasn't so sure of that. "I'm the last guy Connor would want for his sister. He's made that abundantly clear."

"His opinion doesn't matter. Michaela's does, and she wants you. You wanted her badly enough to try and win her back. Now you have. She's still wearing your ring, for heaven's sake."

Okay that crushed him. But then he thought, if that were true, why hadn't she even called him? She was stubborn. Maybe her dad was wrong, and she had given up on them too once she'd gotten home and had time to think. "I appreciate your concern, Shawn, but the only thing that matters is Michaela getting better, and me being around won't help that. It will only cause more stress."

Shawn's mouth twisted, and Boyd sensed he was weighing whether Boyd was right on that point.

"I hate all of this, but I don't know how to fix it. Not right now, anyway. I think I'll follow Quinn's lead and take off too." He couldn't handle talking about this anymore.

"Tell Arthur and Clara I'll give them a call later. Please give Assumpta my regards."

He started to walk down the hall, focusing on making it to the elevator. Once he got there, he could close his eyes and rest his hand on the wall in despair.

"In a perfect world, family aside," Shawn called, loud enough for the cleaning crew in the hallway to look up, "what would it take to make you want to marry Michaela, Boyd?"

For a private man, Boyd knew Shawn's question was totally out of character. He called over his shoulder, "I've always wanted to marry Mickey, and I always will, but this isn't a perfect world, Shawn," and increased the length of his strides.

When he reached the elevator, he punched the button eight times, the wait intolerable. All he wanted was to escape. Shawn was still standing in the hallway, as if contemplating going after him. The door opened, and he rushed in, relieved the car was empty. Lowering his head, he thought about Shawn's question.

What *would* it take?

A miracle, and Boyd McClellan's life had never run in that direction.

CHAPTER 27

MICHAELA HAD TO BEG HER MOTHER TO BE LET OUT OF her sickbed.

She wasn't going to miss the board meeting about Connor or give anyone her proxy. He was her brother, and the incident in question had happened on *her* business trip.

When she arrived at Merriam Enterprises' headquarters with Caitlyn and Flynn, they took the elevator to the top floor and greeted the five nonfamily board members alongside Trevor, who'd gone ahead with Quinn in a last-ditch effort to convince Connor to handle this outside of a meeting room. From their haggard faces, they'd clearly made no progress. J.T., who no longer served on the board, had tried to approach Connor last night with Flynn and Caitlyn, but he'd refused to speak with them. Their parents' beseeching hadn't worked either.

Quinn finally went to the head of the table, taking Connor's normal chair. Michaela had to wonder if he'd done it intentionally to make Connor's absence feel less conspicuous. But that was ridiculous. Her brother wasn't there! How could he make a more conspicuous statement than that?

As everyone sat down, Quinn said, "I've asked our chairman for the floor today to kick off a meeting none of us wanted to happen. Connor Merriam is my brother, and as the vice president of Merriam Enterprises, I felt it my duty to walk you through recent events. Although he was summoned for this meeting, he's neglected to appear before us today."

Caitlyn took Michaela's hand under the table, and Michaela reached for Flynn's. She still couldn't believe Connor had chosen not to speak for himself. He had never shied away from anything in his life.

"If you'll let me," Quinn said, letting his gaze crest over the people at the table, "I'll give an account from my interviews with the main parties on the recent scouting trip to Kenya. Michaela, if you'd like to add anything at the end of my summation, you're welcome to. I'd hoped to spare you the effort since you've been ill."

Everyone turned to look at her, so she said, hoping her voice didn't sound too scratchy, "I'm much better, Quinn, thank you."

"Now..." Her brother laid out the facts leading to the trip, the people involved, and the various accounts he'd heard, including Hargreaves' and Iggie's stories. The non-family board members all frowned in tandem, like a thunder cloud had passed over them, at the mention of Iggie being detained by Customs due to a bribe from Boyd to an official. They didn't know Boyd like her family did, and she could understand how damning such an action sounded. She wanted to defend him, but Quinn's crisp summation didn't allow for any interruption.

She listened as he laid out Aunt Clara and Uncle Arthur's thoughts on events, fairly told from her perspective. Regarding Boyd...

Her heart felt like it had a stomachache as her brother relayed that Boyd's account was in concert with her aunt and uncle's. Quinn also noted that Boyd had both cared for her while she was ill and apologized for the bribe.

"Before I ask Michaela for any additions," her brother said, laying his hands flat on the table like he was trying to steel himself for what he was about to do, "I'd like to conduct our first order of business. In the absence of a CEO, a board member can ask for the power to initiate the firing of a Merriam employee. I hereby call a vote for such a power to fire Dr. Ignatius Vajra. His actions are unbecoming of a representative of this company. Who will second?"

"I will," Trevor called out immediately.

"All in favor?" Quinn asked.

Everyone raised their hands, Michaela noted, without hesitation. She was happy to have the motion pass. Iggie might have a brilliant mind, but he didn't deserve to work at Merriam. She was glad to see him go.

"Motion carries," Quinn said, tapping his hand on the table. "Now, Michaela, is there anything you'd like to add to events? I'm sure I'm not the only person in the room who is relieved your health is returning."

Murmurs of assent carried to her from the members around the table. She found it challenging to smile in response. "As Quinn said, I had good caretakers in Dr. Boyd McClellan and Clifton Hargreaves. Of course, I'm not sure what might have happened if my aunt and uncle, Clara Merriam Hale and Arthur Hale, hadn't undertaken a difficult journey to the Valley of Stars with the tribe's medicine woman to bring back the medicinal flower."

"Thank goodness this so-called mythical flower is everything you thought it was," a board member, Emeline Harris, said across from her. "It's a shame Merriam Enterprises' agreement with Dr. McClellan is void. Such a find would have big market implications. Do we know who Dr. McClellan has chosen to use for manufacturing and distribution now that Merriam is no longer his partner? I don't assume there's any way to bridge the relationship, Michaela?"

"I'm not sure I want to bridge it," said Jason Anderson, a longtime board member. "I mean, this man had one of our employees detained."

"I understand your feelings, Jason," Quinn said before Michaela could defend Boyd. "Connor agrees with you, but after hearing everyone's accounts, I believe it's an extreme stance and bad for business. Dr. McClellan apologized and I truly believe he regrets what he did. Both my father and I have assured him there will be no slander from any Merriam employee about either him or his company, and given the legality of the situation, our legal department counseled me to strike any mention of the bribe from our record of today's meeting."

Michaela's throat thickened, and she sunk back into her chair in relief. She hadn't dared hope Quinn would handle the situation with Boyd so fairly.

"Given that, shouldn't we push to be considered for our former role?" Emeline pressed. "I would think Dr. McClellan would be eager for an olive branch from a company like Merriam Enterprises given he's just starting out."

If only an olive branch were possible, but the decision wasn't up to Boyd and Uncle Arthur and Aunt Clara. "No, Emeline, I don't see any way to do so professionally. Clara and Arthur co-own the land with the tribe and are joint custodians of the flower. After the way Merriam Enterprises represented itself, they chose Dr. McClellan's company. I doubt the Maasai tribe would want us involved."

"Still, it's a shame," Emeline said. "We're going to be cut out of huge profits." She'd been invited to join the board because of her strategic market insights, but right now, Michaela didn't really care about their bottom line.

"I'm sure everyone finds it a shame," Quinn said, flicking her a glance, "but Michaela is right. We had a shot, and frankly, we blew it. Now, let's discuss the topic we'd all rather avoid: the behavior of Connor Merriam."

"Don't bother."

She looked over her shoulder and gasped. Connor

stood in the double doorway with a piece of paper in his hands.

"I'm tendering my resignation, effective today, given recent events and this meeting."

He was *what*?

"No!" Trevor yelled.

"You can't, Connor!" Caitlyn called.

"Connor," Quinn said heavily, rising to his feet. "Sit down so we can talk about this."

He looked around the entire room, pausing on each person. "I don't see why. You don't believe I'm fit to serve as CEO of Merriam Enterprises."

"We won't accept your resignation," Flynn said, surging to his feet and coming around his chair. "This meeting was to discuss—"

"A rap on my knuckles?" Connor's voice was harsh. "Spare me. I told you when I returned that I won't account for my actions, and that remains true. I acted in the best way I saw fit to protect two Merriam employees and safeguard a business agreement."

"Then tell us your side, Connor," said Paul, another non-Merriam board member. He rose to his feet. "I've known you for a decade, and I want to hear your account. You can have my seat."

"No," Connor said crisply. "This is the second time members of this board have questioned my judgment. Clearly, the board is not behind me."

"If you mean the oil and gas decision," Trevor said, fisting his hands at his sides, "we're past that."

"Are we?" Connor asked with a scoff. "If you could vote today, Trevor, would you reinstate all future off-shore oil exploration and projects?"

Trevor's mouth twitched before he said, "I would reinstate them, yes, but that's my opinion. We have a board here—"

"So we do. As the current CEO of Merriam Enterprises, I

kindly ask the chairman to call for a vote on this matter, per our company's bylaws," Connor said, coming closer to the table. "Trevor's feelings on the off-shore project in Ireland brought this to a head, but it's been boiling under the surface ever since. I changed our business plan to protect other Merriam employees from the kind of explosion that led to the deaths of Corey Weatherby and his colleagues. Many of you questioned my unilateral decision on that matter, so today we vote on it. Mr. Chairman."

Lloyd Mathers, an old pal of their father's, turned to where Connor was standing beside him. "Very well, Connor. On the matter of reinstating Merriam Oil & Gas' original policy on future off-shore exploration and projects, how say you?"

Michaela bit her lip, but she didn't hesitate. She raised her hand and watched as the rest of the table did the same.

"Good," Connor said, "one show of no confidence. Now, if you're not willing to accept my resignation... Regarding my actions in the recent business agreement with Dr. Boyd McClellan and the trip to Kenya, Mr. Chairman, again, I ask for a vote. Were my actions unbecoming of the CEO of Merriam Enterprises?"

"Connor," Lloyd said, pushing back his chair and taking her brother's arm. "Come sit down. Quinn has shared accounts from various parties who were present for these events. Let's hear yours."

"I've said what I plan to say on the matter," Connor said, shrugging him off and glaring at the room. "Call the vote, Lloyd."

His demanding tone had the chairman sighing heavily. "You're dead set on making this difficult, aren't you, Connor? All right, I'm calling for a vote. Who among you believes Connor acted unbecoming of a chief executive of Merriam Enterprises?"

Michaela couldn't stand it anymore. She rose on shaky legs. "Connor, don't do this! Please. You need counseling, maybe, because of Corey, but—"

"Counseling?" He chuckled darkly. "When it snows in hell. Now vote!"

Sinking back down, she looked at Caitlyn, who was swiping at tears. He was really going to force them to do this. Fighting tears herself now, Michaela started to raise her hand. "I'm sorry, Connor."

Other hands rose slowly, and Michaela's heart broke with each of them. Quinn's was the last to rise.

"Damn you, Connor," Quinn said, glaring at him. "Why did you have to choose this?"

Her brother only shook his head. "No, damn all of you. Now, make it official. Two strikes against a CEO means termination."

"Probation for six months," Quinn said, his voice harsh.

This time Connor laughed outright. "The press will eat you alive once the minutes of this meeting get out. You have no choice. Fire me. Then I can get the hell out of here." He tore his resignation letter in half and let it fall to the floor.

Lloyd presided over the vote to fire Connor. Her brother didn't bother to wait for the last hand, which made it unanimous. He left in a flurry through the double doors.

"Mickey, you're shaking," Caitlyn said, touching her softly on the arm. "Do you need to lie down?"

She shook her head mutely. The stress and shock of the situation were making her tremble.

Standing, Lloyd unbuttoned his jacket. "I've known this family since your father and I went to graduate school together in Chicago, and today's events gave me no pleasure. But we have a duty, and right now, we have a vacancy at the helm. I'd like to call for the promotion of Quinn Merriam to the position of CEO. All for?"

Her brother glanced down, his face shadowed, as everyone voted him in. Once Lloyd announced it, he stood to address them.

"I'm finding it hard to be grateful for the promotion given how it came about, but I love this company and will continue my duty in serving it. I do thank you for your confidence in my leadership, and I promise I won't let you down. Now, I'd like to suggest this meeting be adjourned."

"Seconded," Lloyd called.

Caitlyn wrapped her arm around Michaela, helping her to rise. "Flynn, Mickey needs to go home. Will you help me get her to the car?"

"Oh, Caitlyn," she whispered, and her sister hugged her briefly.

"Come on," Caitlyn said, leading her out of the boardroom, "you're tired and we need to take care of you before we fall apart."

"I can't believe he pushed it," Flynn said, putting his other arm around her. "What was Con thinking?"

"He wasn't," Trevor said in a savage voice. "He's all torn up inside. I have half a mind to go after him and punch him. He twisted our arms. No one else wanted this."

"Violence won't solve anything," Caitlyn said. "Lose the tough-guy routine for a moment. Michaela is—"

"Fine," she said, but she wasn't.

Her brother had just been fired, and it was partly her fault.

Was he lost to them for good?

CHAPTER 28

CONNOR WAS *OUT*?

Boyd couldn't wrap his mind around Clara's announcement.

"How is that possible?" He'd known it was in the realm of possibility, but rather like living on Mars. Way out there.

"He pushed for a vote," Clara said, twisting her diamond bracelet. "Shawn's voice cracked when he told me. Oh, this is horrible. I feel responsible in some ways."

Boyd did too, but he knew people made their own choices, and Connor had made a few bad ones. But Michaela and the rest of the Merriams must feel horrible. Surely this would make all of them, even Shawn, hate his guts. He'd been right to let her go, but God, it still hurt like hell.

"Clara, if my opinion counts at all," he said, "you did the right thing. Standing against your nephew and the family company on behalf of the village made you one of the most admirable women in the world."

"Hear, hear," Arthur said, crossing from where he'd been looking out the French doors of their suite. He put an arm around her. "It's a shock. No one argues that, but Connor could have addressed this in a different manner. My God, I hope he finds the help he needs."

"Shawn said no one knows where he is," Clara said, worrying her diamond bracelet. "Not even Flynn, and you know he's got every tech gadget at his fingertips."

"Maybe some time off will help him," Boyd said. "Connor's probably been working twenty-hour days since he started working for the company at sixteen." A man could snap under that kind of continued pressure.

"All right, I'm pushing that aside for now," Clara said with a firm shake of her head. "How are we coming along with partners, Boyd?"

He almost hated that word now. How long would it take for his brain not to immediately flash to Michaela when he heard it? "I have three solid companies preparing proposals to share with the tribe. I didn't tell them about the find per se, but I asked them for their best offers as the president of a new company that plans to discover the next big plant medicine." Luckily, they'd believed he was capable of that, something that had boosted his corporate confidence.

"Good thinking," Arthur said, tossing him a red hot.

"It's good to hear such encouraging news," Clara said. "Now, when are you going to visit Michaela and make up with her?"

He fell back into a chair as Hargreaves came in with a tea service. "Clara, how can you ask that after what just happened to Connor? No Merriam would welcome me with open arms, least of all Michaela." Again, the thought about her not calling him burrowed under his skin. Maybe everyone was pushing for something Michaela didn't want anymore.

"You're wrong about Michaela, and you're wrong about the Merriams, Connor excluded perhaps," Clara said, coming over and sitting on the adjacent couch as Hargreaves poured three cups of tea. "Thank you, Hargreaves."

The butler nodded, but not before sending Boyd a significant look as well.

"Boyd, you love Michaela and she loves you," Arthur

said, sitting beside him. "Like I tell all the young people, love is a choice, and when you hit a bump in the road, you fix it. So fix it. We're here to help."

"I don't see how you can," Boyd said, holding up his hands. "Like I told Shawn, love isn't enough in our case. With the Connor situation, the Merriams are going to band together more than ever, and they should. I like all of them. Well, mostly. Connor and Quinn were always hard-ass mysteries to me. But seriously, I'm a reminder of their unhappiness, and I won't do that to Michaela."

Arthur rolled the red hot around his teeth. "What if Clara and I got all of the Merriams—except Connor—to sign a petition saying they'd support you and Michaela getting back together and not take a sock at you at the holidays?"

Boyd shook his head. "Be serious."

"He is being serious in his own fuddy-duddy way, Boyd," Clara said heavily. "So, you don't want to be the cause of any unhappiness. It's laudable. But I think you're selling the Merriams short."

How could she think that after her own exile years ago? They might have mended fences now, but Shawn clearly had tempered. He didn't believe the same could be said about Quinn and Connor, and who knew what the rest of them thought? "Did you see the way Quinn looked at me at your impromptu soiree the other day? Big Bad Wolf number two is still around, and it sounds like he's Michaela's boss now. Do you really think he's going to pat me on the shoulder and joke with me over the Merriam punch bowl?"

Clara huffed more than she sighed. "So it won't be easy. It's still no reason not to try."

"Too much is stacked against us," Boyd said, ignoring his tea. "And I've had time to think about something else. Michaela's always wanted to work on the flower. It's been her dream. It's bound to come between us if I'm working on it and she's not. I wouldn't even be able to tell her about my finds."

"I hate thinking you might be right there, Boyd, as much as I hate drinking this infernal tea," Arthur said, pushing it back when Clara pushed it toward him.

"Green tea is good for you," she said, her Merriam green eyes narrowing. "Michaela not working on the flower is a problem. It's been bothering me as well."

"Connor really screwed that up." He popped in another red hot.

"Yeah, he did," Boyd said, rising to his feet. "I'm going to take off. I have some other matters to see to. When are you two heading back to Dare Valley?"

"In a few days," she said, "but we'll see you before we go, of course. How about dinner here in our suite tomorrow night? I'd like you to walk us through how many flowers you expect you'll need in the next six months so Arthur and I can plan our return trip to work with the tribe."

Arthur groaned. "It's not that I don't love the village, but I hate that damn river. When I get home, I'm making Jill and Brian remove Hungry Hungry Hippos from the twins' playroom. And I'm confiscating any copies of *Fantasia*. I do not want any of my relations thinking hippos are nice animals. I'll tell them to run if they ever see a live one."

"Oh, Arthur, you'll only scare the children," Clara said, waving her hand at him. "Come on, Boyd. I'll see you out."

She walked with him to the front door and gave him a hug, something she'd started to do every time she saw him. He had to admit he rather liked it. She was a dear woman.

"Don't give up hope, Boyd," she said, poking him in the stomach like she sometimes did her husband. "Arthur gave himself the moniker of the Matchmaking Jedi on our last trip, and I'll confess, it ticked me off some. But if I can pull something off to bring you and Michaela back together, I figure I'll be ahead of him, and I do so love the sound of that."

He kissed her cheek. "You're wasting your time, but I wouldn't dare say that to a woman who trekked up and back to the Valley of Stars."

"Smart boy," she said, patting him on the back. "Now, get out of here. I have some thinking to do."

He wouldn't let himself hope—it was too painful—but she'd surprised him before.

Perhaps Clara Merriam would be his miracle.

CHAPTER 29

CLARA WAS AS READY AS SHE'D EVER BE. The sight of the double doors leading to the CEO's office still gave her heartburn, but she bore down and let herself inside. She knew she looked her best, clad in an elegant black suit with cream heels, her hair coiffed like a corporate executive. Arthur had insisted this was her show, the silly man, but at least he'd promised he'd be waiting for her back at the suite with Hargreaves, gin and tonic fixings ready.

"Aunt Clara," Quinn said, typing hard enough on the keys to remind Clara of an angsty drummer, "if my father hadn't told me that you wanted to talk about Michaela's happiness—something we're all worried about—I wouldn't have been able to give you my time. With Connor leaving, you might imagine I'm more than swamped. I'm under siege."

And she was about to propel a business cannonball at him from her hastily prepared trebuchet. "Then let me come to the point. May I sit?"

"Please," he said, gesturing to the seat in front of his massive paper-covered desk.

"Indulge me a moment. Is it fair to say some in the pharmaceutical world might notice you fired your department head around the same time Connor was replaced as CEO?"

"Not just in that world, Aunt, something I'm preparing a plan for now."

"Daunting, no doubt. If they dig, they may discover the trip to Kenya and other events. While the tribe Arthur and I are dealing with aren't open to outsiders, other tribes visited by your brother—in a Merriam helicopter, no less—may well choose to share events with interested parties."

His mouth twisted into something like a snarl. "How does this involve Michaela and how do you plan to help? By telling all the Maasai to keep things under wraps?"

"I can't make that promise," she said, pressing her hands on her thighs. "But I did look at the company's profits in the pharmaceutical area over the last five years. They've been strong, but recent events could change that."

"I know that," Quinn said like a cross bear. "I plan on fixing it. I need to hire someone to replace Iggie and finalize a damage control plan. You aren't suggesting I replace Iggie with Michaela?"

She fought back an unladylike snort. "Of course not. That still wouldn't address the main components of Michaela's happiness. Boyd and the flower."

"We can't work with you on the flower."

"No, but your sister can if she's no longer working for Merriam Enterprises."

His brow rose. "You want me to fire my own sister?"

"No. I think you should spin off the natural health science part of the pharmaceuticals subsidiary and sell it to Evan Michaels. As you know, he's a billionaire who legitimately wants to make the world a better place, and he's just created a new company backed by your brother J.T. called GreenSolutions, so it has family ties, which are important to Michaela."

"You want me to sell off a profitable Merriam subsidiary to improve my sister's love life?" Quinn asked, putting his elbows on the desk and studying her like she was mold on top of his leftover takeout.

She wouldn't back down. "Evan has the kind of vision your Grandpa Emmits had about the future, and your current subsidiary is in big trouble after Kenya. I think your health science department would be the perfect addition to what he's doing. It's run by Chase Parker—"

"I know Chase and think he's one of the best CEOs out there, but—"

"If this new flower really is the miracle cure Boyd and Michaela believe it to be, wouldn't it make sense for it to be distributed by a company whose entire mission statement is about improving the world?"

"And Michaela and Boyd could work together on the flower like they wanted all along." He sat back in his chair and smoothed his silk tie. "Boyd's on board with this?"

"I ran my idea by your father first to see if it would fly. I haven't talked to Boyd about it yet."

Quinn rose and came around his desk, resting his backside on the edge. "I want my sister to be happy—I could give a flying flip about Boyd—but this is—"

"A practical solution," she said, withdrawing the folder she'd prepared from her handbag and handing it to him. "You're going to look like you have egg on your face in the market once news of the...incident in Kenya gets around to other competitors' water cooler talk. I mean other companies and local groups may never want to work with another Merriam employee after hearing how your brother and department head hired mercenaries to threaten the Maasai. You remember how badly World Wildlife Fund's contributions fell when people heard they'd hired mercenaries to kill poachers?" She tsked, and Quinn's jaw started to tick. Good, she was getting through to him.

She went on: "Arthur isn't planning on including these

disparaging events in the articles he's working on, but he and I are going to be called for interviews once Boyd issues a press release about the flower. I won't lie if we're asked directly about the mercenaries, and neither will Arthur."

His green eyes were hot as they stared her down.

"Boyd doesn't have a manufacturing and distribution partner yet," she said, matching his regard. "I figure you can save yourself an uphill battle in the health science world—"

"What about Michaela?" Quinn asked, cutting her off. "She's a Merriam. Do you really think she'll want to work for another company?"

And Clara wasn't a Merriam? Oh, she could box his ears. But she knew a person got more flies with honey than vinegar. "J.T. is on Evan's board and is an investor in GreenSolutions. It already has Merriam ties. And yes, she'd do it to have Boyd and to work on the flower. With your blessing...I'd say it's a certainty."

"And Boyd?" Quinn asked. "Is he to have everything then? He detained one of our employees."

Clara narrowed her eyes at him. "He'd be selling his company to GreenSolutions as well. That's what we call compromise, my boy. Besides, he loves your sister and he saved her life. I'm telling you right now, Quinn Merriam... Arthur and I might have brought back the flower, but Boyd kept her going by sitting at her bedside for two days and nights without a care for himself. When you consider my proposal, you might consider that along with your sister's happiness." She stood, yanking on her suit jacket. "Good day."

Striding out of his office with dignity, she punched the elevator button hard enough to break a nail. Well, she'd done her part. If Quinn wanted to be hardheaded, there was nothing she could do about it.

No one had ever said matchmaking was easy.

***

Michaela threw the new set of magazines aside after her mother left the room.

She'd banned all academic journals and Michaela's phone, saying she wouldn't listen to any back talk given the state Michaela had come home in after the board meeting. Her mother had sworn up and down she was running a low-grade fever, but would she show the thermometer to her? Nope. Assumpta Merriam was going to have her way. End of story.

A knock sounded, and she breathed a sigh of relief. Her mother wouldn't knock. "Come in."

Quinn entered and closed the door, decked out in one of his Big Bad Wolf suits. He looked haggard though, as if Little Red Riding Hood kept evading his teeth.

Oh, she shouldn't joke about it. This week had been horrible for everyone.

"What are you doing here?" she asked, sitting up higher on the pillows. "It's two o'clock on a Wednesday. Flynn told me you turned down everyone's offer to go out for a beer last night. Of course, Mom wouldn't let me go. She's got me in lockup."

"For good reason," he said, sitting on the bed after unbuttoning his jacket. "She's worried about a relapse after the other day. Work with her. She told Dad she's this close to calling the doctor back in." He held up two fingers an inch apart for emphasis.

"I'm sick of this," she said, huffing back into the pillows. "You need me back at work—"

"I need you to get well," he said, shaking his head and looking down at his lap. "That's why we have sick leave. Now, as for the reason I came..."

She wanted to reach out to him. He looked so vulnerable suddenly, and it struck her that his life had been upended as surely as hers had been.

"Aunt Clara came to my office yesterday with a business idea after talking it over with Dad. I wasn't very receptive at first, but I looked over the folder she prepared, and I have to say I'm starting to think she might have some Merriam business sense after all. I can see why Dad told her to talk to me."

Michaela rolled her eyes. "She has a B.A. in business, Quinn, and you should have seen her with the Maasai."

"She thinks we might be smart to sell off the health science arm of Merriam Pharmaceuticals," he said, playing with the edge of her quilt. "After what happened with Connor and Iggie, we're going to have an uphill battle in that market for a while, especially if word gets out. Iggie has been making some threats since he's unhappy with our decision to let him go, something I didn't mention to Aunt Clara."

Oh, dear. "So he's being a jerk to the end, huh?"

"Yeah, and he's not our only problem." He paused. "I reviewed the file on your so-called demotion, and I disagree with the findings. You shouldn't have been the one to broach a nondisclosure with your boyfriend. That's ridiculous. You weren't his manager. Iggie and Human Resources didn't do their job. His lack of management has been causing problems for some time from what I've seen. I don't know how Connor missed it." His face darkened.

Her own heart clutched. "Iggie was good at kissing... ah..."

"Ass?" He harshly laughed. "God, hearing you say that in your froggy voice is pretty damn funny. I must be tired."

"And stressed. You have a lot on your shoulders. Thank you for reviewing my demotion. It felt...wrong at the time."

"Iggie also didn't treat Boyd well. I had it in confidence he led the charge on calling him a scurrilous nickname."

"Michaela's Boy Toy? I didn't know until this trip. He'd wanted to handle it on his own."

Quinn rubbed his jaw. "I'd have wanted to punch Iggie in Boyd's place. Still do for how the nickname shines on you."

She pulled a pillow onto her chest. "Working at Merriam brings talk like that, I suppose."

"No one's ever said a bad word to my face, but you're right. We have to earn our spots in the company even more than the next guy. Or girl. Now, what would you think if I told you I was thinking it would take too much effort to turn our Plant Sciences division around and that we'd do better to sell it off to someone we trust? I have enough on my hands right now."

"Where would that leave me?" she asked, shock reeling through her.

"Working with Boyd on the flower at this new company if Aunt Clara has anything to do with it," he said, a half smile on his mouth. "That's what you want, right?"

His face was never far from her mind: that ever-present smile just for her, the cheeky look in his eyes when he teased her about everything from the way she pronounced some Latin genus families to her tendency to clip the curb when she parallel parked.

"It's everything. But with Connor... I feel like I need to help. I can't walk away from you guys."

"Yes, you can," Quinn said. "Don't make me fire you. I've had a belly full of that this week."

Tears filled her eyes. "You're serious?"

Quinn took her right hand and studied it. "Before I came up here, I asked Dad why he gave Boyd his blessing to marry you in the first place. He said Boyd sees you for who you are and loves you for it."

"I'm his baby elephant," she said, tired enough to give in to tears.

"His what?" Quinn asked. "Jesus, don't cry. You never cry."

Her face flushed, but she told him the story about their encounter with the baby elephant on the trip. "You must think I'm crazy."

"No, I think you really love him," Quinn said, squeezing

her hand before resting it back on the pillow she was holding, "which makes the brother in me happy."

It was like a switch had been flipped, and her brother was suddenly sitting beside her bed, not one of the Big Bad Wolves.

"I for one am pretty grateful for that."

She reached her hand out to him and he clasped it, smiling softly.

"Me too."

"Now, let's brainstorm how you're going to convince him that Aunt Clara's idea is for the best—it'll require him to make some changes too—and that we Merriams aren't going to nail him when you're not looking." He flashed her the first easy smile she'd seen from him in a long time.

"Yes, let's brainstorm," she said, feeling hope bloom in her heart. "You might call Dad too. Oh, and Aunt Clara and Uncle Arthur." They were matchmakers, after all.

She was going to need everything in her arsenal to get Boyd back.

Chapter 30

THERE WAS A *BABY ELEPHANT* STANDING IN HIS FRONT YARD. The hairs on the back of Boyd's neck rose as the cute beast seemed to smile at him, raising its trunk like a greeting. He stood openmouthed in the doorway as he tried to process everything. This couldn't be a coincidence. It was tethered to the tree in the middle of his lawn!

"I'm not taking this little fella back to the rental place until we talk," a familiar voice said.

He turned his head and saw Michaela sitting in one of the folding chairs he'd brought out to the front porch when he couldn't sleep. He gauged her features for cues about her health. Her skin had returned to its normal golden hue, but she was still rail-skinny. And her beautiful green eyes were shadowed. The ring he'd given her was on her right hand, shining like fire in the morning sunlight. Oh, and she wasn't wearing a bra, dammit. She knew that drove him nuts. Was it a message about being free or going back to the field with him?

"I didn't know the zoo was in the rental business now," he said, nodding to the baby elephant.

"Hargreaves helped me find her."

"I'll have to send him a thank you card." What was his friend thinking? Then he thought about Clara and Arthur.

They were in on this as surely as the sun set over the savannah. Terrific.

"That's Apricot, and she's here to remind you of what I mean to you."

You're my baby elephant. God, why had he ever said that? "Your voice sounds better, at least, but my neighbors aren't going to be thrilled to have an elephant in my yard. Okay, the kids might. But who's going to shovel the poop—"

"I like your new place," she said, staying seated and kicking her legs out like she planned to stay a while. "You always wanted a house."

"I'm renting it." And he couldn't exactly kick her out. She'd brought a bloody elephant. "Are you drinking enough water? Let me get you some."

"My mother has me drinking so much water and juice that I slosh when I walk," she said. "Sit down and hear me out, Boyd. I'm not taking Apricot with me until you do."

He'd expected as much. "Apricot is a horrible name for an elephant. Who thought this one up?"

"The elephant part?" she asked with a smile.

He nodded.

"Hargreaves. The man is wickedly ingenious. Even Quinn had to bow to his strategic mind. Dad said you told him there was no new flower we could use to lure you back, so we improvised. I had a full team help me since I can't do without you. Ready for my proposal?"

He wanted to clap his hands over his ears. Wasn't his heart aching enough? "Fine, get it over with, but I don't see things changing."

Why hadn't she brought up Connor yet?

"So you said," she said, twisting her ring. "I'll cut to the chase. Aunt Clara had this idea."

He shuddered. "And then Hargreaves helped with the elephant. I'm afraid to ask what's next. A parade down my street with a band singing a love song dedicated to me?"

"I might arrange that if you remain stubborn," she

continued. "Nothing has been done with this proposal yet, so don't go off half-cocked when I tell you."

"Me?" He pointed to himself. "You rented a baby elephant."

She smiled. "Apricot is cute. Okay, back to what I was saying... Connor and Iggie's actions will reflect badly on the Merriam Pharmaceuticals Plant Sciences department even though their employment has been terminated."

Her voice was the same one she used to recite the various genus names in the nightshade family: monotone. "I was afraid to mention it. I'm sorry about Connor, Mickey. Clara told me what happened. I know you may not believe it, but I never wanted anything like this to happen. I can't be as benevolent about Iggie, though."

"Me either on the Iggie side. Let's not talk about Connor right now. I might get emotional. It's all pretty raw and fresh still."

He clenched his hand into a fist so he wouldn't reach for her hand. "I imagine."

"Anyway, Aunt Clara talked to Quinn and convinced him that it might be better to sell off the Plant Sciences department to another company, one still friendly to the Merriams. J.T. might have given it a billion as a start-up investment—"

"Why don't little money fairies like that ever visit me?" he asked dryly. "Never mind. What company are we talking about?"

"GreenSolutions."

He blinked. "Billionaire inventor Evan Michaels, right?"

"Yes, his company's mission is to foster more alternate energy, but Aunt Clara thought plant science might be interesting to him as a subsidiary. We'd all be a lot better off as humans if we used more natural supplements and cures when they're appropriate. Evan is a game changer, and perhaps he'll take on the medical community to both

educate them on plant science—like the flower, for example—and convince health companies to provide coverage
for natural supplements and cures. You know they usually don't cover things like vitamins, supplements, or even
acupuncture. But I digress." She looked him in the eye. "I
would be working for GreenSolutions if Evan buys us."

And not for her family business? That would be huge.

She stood. "I know you want to have your own company, but what if you came under GreenSolutions as a subsidiary and merged with the department I'm bringing with
me? Boyd, then we could both work together."

"A merger?" Sure, he'd wanted his own company, but
he wanted Michaela more. They wouldn't just collaborate
on the flower. They'd work together on everything. If this
was what it took...

Oh, he was going to kiss Clara when he saw her.

"You can dictate any terms you want. Boyd, it's like
you've created Facebook or the iPhone in the plant science
world. But why not let someone help you take it to the next
level quickly and easily, someone Aunt Clara and Uncle Arthur know and trust? You asked why the little money fairies couldn't visit you. They just did."

The elephant trumpeted at that moment like it was
punctuating Michaela's remark. He thought about the baby elephant who'd come up to their Rover and stared at
them, its eyes full of wisdom.

She poked him in the stomach, and he grunted. "This
is a win-win, Boyd, but Aunt Clara and Uncle Arthur won't
run with it unless you consent, and you'll get no pressure
from their side whatsoever about it."

His mind was spinning. "I'm supposed to believe that
with Apricot munching on my tree here? What about working for your family? That's what you've always wanted."

"Yes, but here's what you don't seem to get. I won't be
happy without you either." She put her hand on his chest,
which he didn't remove. "This way I'd still feel like I'm

working on something for my family, something we all believe in, which would save me from guilt at family functions or any professional weirdness, and you'd still stand on your own two feet, which I understand better and promise to support better."

He took her shoulders because she was blowing him away. "You'd do that for me?"

"Of course I would! This would be *our* company to run. Yes, we'd have a parent company in GreenSolutions, but we'd mostly be independent. Like the...oh, what did Quinn tell me in our brainstorming? Like the Claussen Pickle company under Kraft Foods or Gerber baby food under Nestlé."

He had to take a breath. "Your brother used a *pickle* company as an example for us?" Was there a joke there? The revelation that Quinn was apparently on board was mind-blowing enough.

"My dad, Quinn, and Aunt Clara gave me all these facts and figures to ingest before they thought I was ready to talk to you." She drilled her finger into his chest. "They ran me through my presentation to you like four times."

Four times? "I've always wanted to work with you, Mickey."

"The last reason is the most important, so listen closely." She looked straight into his eyes, and his heart started to beat again for the first time since they'd parted. "I love you, and I don't want to be without you. Not now or ever for the rest of my life."

"Oh, babe."

"You wanted to marry me before," she said, smoothing the area over his heart. "I know I hurt you, and I'm sorry. You forgave me after you got over our fight six months ago. I got over it too and forgave you in Kenya. Can't we do that again today?"

He covered her hand with his own. "I want that more than anything, but I have to ask. How is your family going to feel about me being with you? Clara clearly worked some magic on Quinn."

"Yes, she did, and thanks for keeping me on track." She walked back to her purse and pulled out a folder and a present with a big lime green bow. "Exhibits A and B for the presentation."

He took them from her, shaking the gift. "Any reason I should be scared?"

"Open the folder first," she told him.

His eyes scanned the professionally typed memo on Merriam stationery.

Petition of Support for Boyd McClellan and Michaela Merriam

Her entire family had signed it, with one notable absence: Connor. Well, he wasn't surprised.

His throat thickened. "Arthur's work, no doubt."

"Yep," she said, patting his back. "You can read the rest later. Some of my siblings got creative. They listed specific things you might be worried about."

"Like?"

"Like...poisoning you," she said, her smile bright, but her eyes kept searching his. "That was from Trevor, although he had a few more creative additions. Caitlyn said she promised not to drown you in a vat of lavender water."

He started laughing. "You're kidding."

"They want me to be happy, and they're also glad you helped save my life. Now, open the present. I had to give Flynn credit on this one."

When he tore it open, he shook his head. "A *Dora the Explorer* DVD box set. He shouldn't have."

"This was his way of assuring you he wouldn't mess with your cable again—unless you didn't marry me, of course."

That got his attention, and when he met her eyes, he found himself smiling back at her.

"Remember this ring you brought with you on our

safari adventure?" She held it up and it glinted in the light. "I'd really like you to put it on my finger for real now that my presentation is over. So, what's it going to be, Boyd?"

***

He tucked a lock of her long goddess hair behind her ear, making sure to remember this moment for the rest of his life: the day he got all his wishes at once.

"Since we can't keep the baby elephant, how do you feel about picking out a new reptile to live with us?"

Her face transformed into a wide smile. "I'd love one!"

He pulled her to him. "You can name it, assuming you don't want to call it Dora."

She threw her arms around his neck. "I suppose I should be glad you don't want a snake. I could do it, but our kids..."

Kids? "One thing at a time, Mickey." He took her face in his hands, gazing into her watery eyes. "You're tired, babe. You rarely cry."

"I even cried in front of Quinn and freaked him out." She socked him. "Of course I'm crying. I thought I'd lost you for good, you moron."

Moron. He loved hearing her call him that. "So did I," he said, letting any final walls around his hurting heart fall.

"I'm sorry," she whispered.

"Me too, Mickey, me too." He'd always believed in the power of a good apology between two people who loved each other. "I have to ask, though. Are you mad at me about Connor?"

She shook her head, wiping away her tears. "No. And neither is anyone in my family. He's angry at everyone in the family right now and isn't talking to us. We're hurting, yes, but even though the petition is funny, it's from the heart. Aunt Clara worked her magic again."

"I'll have to find her a rare snake as a present."

"Uncle Arthur will kill you," she said. "Not sure about Hargreaves. Oh, I've missed you, Boyd."

He kissed her lightly on the lips. "I've missed you too, Doc."

She socked him again, and he made a good show of it hurting just to make her smile wider. "I'm going to remind you that it took a baby elephant—"

"Our children will love this story." He took her right hand and removed the ring. "I believe we have the perfect witness for this proposal. My dear, if you'd follow me into the yard. I think Apricot wants to hear what I'm about to say."

"*I* certainly do," she said as he put his arm around her to make sure she made it safely down the stairs. "You're coddling me. Don't. My mother has doled out enough for everyone. You should have seen what she made me drink to bring my voice back the whole way. Slippery elm tea."

He grimaced. "Vile but effective. I'll have to thank your mom for taking care of you when I see her again. It was hard to see you leave like you did. I worried about you relapsing."

"I'm fine now," she said, patting Apricot when she extended her trunk. "You'd better move fast. She thinks you have food in your pockets."

Sure enough, the damn elephant was rooting its trunk around his waist. "Red hots! Of course. Arthur gave me some and I pocketed the extras when he wasn't looking. He's a candy pusher."

She laughed when Apricot nudged him in the nuts, making him push her trunk away. "That's rather forward of you, Apricot. Now, see here. No touching, please. This is for my lady here."

The elephant gave a rude noise in response. Michaela was biting her lip, trying to muffle her laughter. "Maybe we should go inside—" he started.

"No way!" Michaela cried out. "This is perfect. I'm your baby elephant, after all."

Her smirk made him grimace. "I'm never going to hear

the end of that, am I? A guy tries to be romantic. Fine. Michaela Merriam?"

"Yes, Boyd McClellan?" She was smiling for real now.

He sank to one knee. "I've loved you from the moment I watched you split open those—"

"Can't you be a *little* more romantic?" she asked with a pointed glance. "I don't want frogs in my proposal."

"An elephant is all right, but frogs... God, I need a manual." He cleared his throat. "Let me try again. How's this? Michaela Merriam. I love you more than anything and want to share my life and career with you."

"Oh, I like that part," she said, pushing the hair back on his forehead.

"Will you marry me?"

"Yes!"

Apricot roared and shoved Boyd onto his butt with her trunk before he could kiss Michaela. "You spooked her, Mickey. Please, kiss me before she decides to trample me for my red hots."

"I think you're safe," she said, flowing back into his arms and planting one right on his mouth. "Now, put the ring on my left hand."

"You're so bossy. And you didn't wear a bra today to make me crazy, right?"

"Yep, and that's not all I have planned. Just think how much you're going to love me when I boss you around at our new workplace." Her wink was downright conspiratorial.

"And where do you think that might be?" he asked, bringing her hand to his lips and kissing it. "The world is our oyster."

A mischievous glint entered her eyes, and he tilted his head to the side in response. This was going to be good.

"I have the perfect place for us. Small-town life with really great restaurants and fun shops. Miles away from some of the best ski slopes around. Good housing prices.

Excellent schools. Wonderful people from all accounts, including my brother J.T. and his wife. GreenSolutions is based there, and so are your newest business partners."

He was already eager to be there. "Sounds awesome. Where is this mecca of paradise?"

"It's this magical place called Dare Valley."

CHAPTER 31

CLARA HAD A NEW NICKNAME FOR HERSELF.
She'd decided on it this very afternoon, looking at Boyd and Michaela beaming in the middle of the Merriam celebration of their engagement.

She pulled Arthur over to the portico to gloat. The view would allow them to catch all the action. "Arthur, my dear, you might be the Matchmaking Jedi, but you will kindly refer to me going forward as the Matchmaking Closer." She wouldn't mention she'd run it by Hargreaves earlier. "I'm having cards made. Would you like some? Gold-embossed, excellent linen stock, and such?"

He barked out a laugh. "Clara, I'm happy to help this next generation of Merriams find love since my work is done with the Hales, but if you think I'm going to offer my services outside of our respective families, then you've got a screw loose."

Her mind was perfectly sound and he well knew it. "I deserve extra points for Boyd and Michaela announcing their imminent relocation to Dare Valley." Oh, she was tickled pink. First, J.T. and Caroline and now their new business partners with the flower. Who knew what other Merriams might be lured back to Dare Valley? Caitlyn and Beau still hadn't settled on a home base. She'd have to get right on that and use her new allies to seal the deal.

"Here, you get an extra red hot. Not that you made that happen. From what Michaela said, moving to Dare Valley was her idea."

Being a Merriam woman, Clara understood her niece's need for independence. In Michaela's shoes, she wouldn't have admitted Clara had planted the idea either.

"You're still beaming from the news at home," Clara said, feeling aglow from it herself. "More babies on the way."

"You've gotta love Jill," Arthur said, shaking his head in a way that drew her attention to its need for a trim. "From the moment they put my granddaughter in my arms, I knew she was a talker. She just couldn't keep a lid on her pregnancy. Then she had to spill the beans about Lucy and Andy being pregnant too."

Clara was delighted for both couples. "Who needs newspaper reporters when you have Jill?"

"She could source information for our entire Local section." He sipped his single malt. "I used her a time or two as a source before I retired. After checking with another source for confirmation, of course."

"Of course." He was a thorough man, something he proved to her every day in their marital bed, bless him.

"Aunt!" Quinn called, striding away from the bar with a whiskey in his hand. "I talked to Boyd and Michaela, and we'd appreciate it if you'd meet with us tomorrow morning to help prepare our proposal for Evan Michaels. We're getting right on it. J.T. can't be involved since he's a board member, but Dad volunteered to provide an extra set of eyes. He was the king of mergers back in his day."

Quinn might have been a hard case when she'd first entered his new office, but he'd more than come around.

"Your father made the best merger of his life with your mother," she said, waving when her brother looked over. "I'd love to join you all. Thank you for including me, Quinn."

He nodded crisply. "Thank you for the idea. We Merriams owe you." Something flashed in his eyes, and he added, "I've never seen Michaela so happy, and Boyd and I had a good talk earlier. I wanted him to know I hold no bad feelings about the trip or what happened afterward. The petition didn't seem enough."

His face darkened then, and Clara put her hand on his arm. "Any word from Connor?"

Shaking his head, he said, "No, and he's making it difficult for Flynn to find him. Trevor's come up empty as well. We're all worried."

The poor man had cleaned out his office and hadn't gone back home. In fact, he seemed to have skipped town altogether. "Hopefully this time away will help..." She broke off and shared a look with Arthur. Time didn't always help people in need and they both knew it. It very much depended on how he spent it.

"Yes." He cleared his throat. "Can I get you another gin and tonic, Aunt? Uncle Arthur, how about another whiskey?"

"Why the heck not?" Arthur finished his drink and thrust out his highball. "This is a celebration, after all."

"Thank you, Quinn," she said, giving him her glass as well. "Hargreaves can make mine. I know you have a lot on your plate. You don't need to be our bartender."

"I never mind tending bar," he said, smiling more easily now. "There's something relaxing about it. But I'll talk to Hargreaves. J.T. and Caroline told me no one makes a better gin and tonic."

"It's because Hargreaves was around when the first gin and tonic was made," Arthur quipped, earning him a gentle nudge in the ribs from his wife. "He's ancient, you know."

"The gin and tonic was invented in India by British

officers in the 1800s, Arthur. For a newspaperman, you sometimes get your facts wrong. You'd better not do that in your articles on the flower and our Maasai friends."

Quinn laughed. "Perhaps you should grab that pith helmet Aunt Clara had you take on safari, Uncle. It might help set the mood."

Arthur was blustering as Quinn walked away. "I'll never live down that infernal pith helmet. Next time we go to Kenya, I'm bringing my own hat and packing my own things. You and Hargreaves take way too many liberties, my dear."

They would be going to Kenya again, and she couldn't wait. For a woman who'd spent so many years alone, she now had connections across the world. She felt like she finally had the makings of a legacy, much like the man next to her. But she wasn't through yet...

Not by a long shot.

She linked their arms together, gazing into his blue eyes. "Tell me truly," she said, hoping to rile him. "Are you sore I was the one who fixed things up between Boyd and Michaela?"

"I came up with the damn petition, didn't I?"

"It's not in the same class as a merger, my dear."

He arched a brow like he knew what she was about. "Very well. I need to up my game. But Hargreaves might have us both beat. I mean, the baby elephant was genius. Even I wouldn't have thought that up, least of all finding a way to rent one."

"He's ever resourceful." And he loved this family as much as she did, she thought, watching him instruct Quinn on how to make the perfect gin and tonic, stirring it slowly but thoroughly with unmatched proficiency.

"Of course, I'm not sure I'll be up to matchmaking next," Arthur said, making her pull her gaze away from the bartending lesson.

"Whatever do you mean?" she asked, eager to hear about their next adventure.

"I might be putting on my old investigative journalist hat if Connor doesn't surface soon," Arthur said heavily. "He's a troubled man, Clara, and he needs his family now more than ever."

She felt the same way, but if a man didn't want to be found… "You think you can find him when Flynn and Trevor can't? They're more tech savvy than you are, I'm afraid to say."

"My dear," he said, caressing her cheek. "Clearly, you've never seen the legendary Arthur Hale at work. Tech savvy. My God, woman, what do you think we did before technology? We relied on our guts. We researched leads. We talked to people. Narrowed down possibilities. Dammit, we got shit done. Excuse my French."

He clearly was on a roll, and she wasn't going to be a naysayer. Connor was a serious subject, after all, and if Arthur thought he could find him, all the better. "I look forward to seeing you in action, my love."

Of course, she was going to do her part to help him, especially after their last trip. Part of her still felt responsible for what had befallen her nephew. "Got any ideas on where to start looking?"

He rubbed his jaw and took his time answering. "If I know anything about human nature, I'd say a grieving man who thinks he's lost everything goes to visit the person he lost."

Her mouth parted. Oh, he *was* good. It's no wonder he'd won numerous Pulitzers. Not that he needed a bigger ego. "Chicago."

"Exactly, my dear."

***

He was lost.

Staring at the shiny new gravestone marking the final remains of his best friend, cousin, and college roommate, Connor couldn't ignore the truth.

Nothing was working anymore, and he couldn't see a way out.

He studied the grave dotted with fresh white lilies, likely from Olivia. The only details on the plain marker were his best friend's birth and death. Corey Weatherby, age forty—the same age as Connor. No mention of him being a terrific father of two or the longtime husband to sweet Olivia, whom he'd married a year after college. Back then, Connor had done things like decorate their honeymoon car with the requisite shaving cream or crank call them on their anniversary, pretending to be a sex therapist asking them to join a couples' study.

That playful side of him was as gone as his friend.

God, he wanted to kick the marker down and howl at fate. Life was so fucking unfair. He'd completely lost his faith in his ability to make it conform to his wishes.

Michaela's near death on that damn safari trek had driven the final nail in the coffin. He knew his family wanted to talk to him, but he couldn't take it right now. He also didn't have a clue what to say. They wanted him to go to counseling or some other bullshit. No way. He might be lost, but he wasn't crazy.

Part of him hated to worry them, but the other part—the one filled with white-hot rage—thought they rather deserved it for betraying him. Of course, he couldn't blame them for what they'd done when it came down to it. They'd almost lost Michaela, and that was on him.

Corey's death was his fault too.

In the end, that's why he'd demanded they remove him as CEO. He couldn't be trusted anymore. He knew it. They knew it.

"I'm sorry, Corey," he whispered aloud, words he hadn't been able to say out loud after the funeral four months ago. "I let you down. It's my fault you're not here, dammit! I can't change that, but I will make good on the promise I made you on the day you married Olivia. Remember? We were waiting for the priest to give us a signal and suddenly you up and asked me while I was fixing my cummerbund."

He'd been horsing around, and Corey had grabbed his arm.

"Con, I want you to promise me something."

"Anything, man."

"Maybe I'm being weird, but it's like I can see my whole life before me. Someday, I might not be here anymore. We work in the oil and gas industry and some pretty dicey places. I'm not tempting fate. I'm only being smart. You're my best friend and there's no one I trust more. I want you to promise to look out for Olivia and any kids we have. God, kids! I can't wait for that."

Connor had given his word without a thought. Corey was young. He was just being emotional on his wedding day. The moment passed, and neither of them talked about it again, but when Max was born, Corey made Connor his godfather. Then again when they had Joseph. Both boys looked so much like Corey that Connor had often teased Olivia by asking if she really had any part in making them, earning him a soft punch in the gut.

Then the unimaginable had happened, and she'd wept uncontrollably in his arms at the gravesite on that horrible sunny day. Oh, the fates had seemed to be jeering even then. A tragedy like Corey's death deserved bleak, stormy weather, not the kind that had everyone in Chicagoland out in droves with smiles he couldn't take seeing on their faces.

He'd called Olivia a couple times when his mother had gone to help her with the boys, something she'd done for him, he knew, as much as the family. Their brief conversations had been so painful he'd been drenched with sweat afterward.

But it was time to face her and the kids and help them in whatever way he could.

He was a man who kept his promises.

DEAR READER,

I hope you loved my homage to a witty romantic adventure like *Romancing the Stone*. Please give it a review for Arthur and me!

You know it's funny: my first few weeks in my new home of New York, I met Michael Douglas at a local watering hole while working on one of my book releases. Suddenly he was asking me what I was working on and what I did, and I had this odd compulsion to say I was like Joan Wilder, that movie's writer heroine, but without the heaving bosoms. I thought better of that answer, and we had a nice chat—the first actually since I've run into him since. Anyway, that's all to say I'm hoping I'll run into Harrison Ford as well and say, "Have you ever thought about Dr. Jones going after a magical healing flower?"

You'll be happy to know I'm already working on the next few Merriam books. I've shared on social media how I'm deep into aromatherapy research—Ibrahim opened up the world of essential oils to me—and I'm so excited about this heroine. Everyone is loving the new concoctions I'm coming up with as I test things out, and I anticipate a companion book with wonderful recipes to go along with the fiction novel, much like I've done in the past with COUNTRY HEAVEN and its cookbook. I'm also sharing some initial #livewell tips on social media, so I hope you come check them out if we aren't already connected to my public front porch, so to speak.

Connor's story is up next, and it's a doozy. As you might expect, he's turning into my most difficult hero, perhaps since Clayton Chandler in FIREFLIES and MAGNOLIAS. Is his heroine going to be strong enough to match him? You bet she is, and with a heart of gold too. SUNFLOWER

ALLEY will be a special journey for everyone, the Merriams included.

Thanks again for continuing to embrace this beautiful family and for supporting me as I write and share the treasures of my heart.

Wishing you every joy and happiness,

Lots of love,

Ava

About the Author

International Bestselling Author Ava Miles joined the ranks of beloved storytellers with her powerful messages of healing, mystery, and magic. Millions of readers have discovered her fiction and nonfiction books, praised by *USA TODAY* and *Publisher's Weekly*. *Women's World Magazine* has selected a few of her novels for their book clubs while Southwest Airlines featured the #1 National Bestseller NORA ROBERTS LAND (the name used with Ms. Roberts' blessing) in its in-flight entertainment. Ava's books have been chosen as Best Books of the Year and Top Editor's Picks and are translated into multiple languages.

71440476R00205